New Irish Short Stories

Edited by
JOSEPH O'CONNOR

D0307641

faber and faber

First published in 2011
by Faber and Faber Limited
Bloomsbury House
74–77 Great Russell Street
London WC1B 3DA

Typeset by Faber and Faber Limited
Printed in England by CPI Bookmarque, Croydon

A CIP record for this book is available from the British Library

ISBN 978–0–571–25527–6

In affectionate memory of
David Marcus, 1924–2009

Contents

Introduction

DAVID MARCUS, TO WHOSE MEMORY this collection is
dedicated, was a poet, a memoirist, a publisher, an anthol-
ogist. He promoted the work of so many Irish writers
that it would be impossible to list them all here. Those
who knew him well – as I did not, alas – remember a
man of immense warmth and wit. He was courteous,
wry and avuncular in his dealings. He wrote elegant,
grammatically impeccable, rather lawyerly letters, on his
old-fashioned portable typewriter. In company he was
a person of mischief and charm. Nobody will ever do
more for Irish literature.

When David Marcus liked your work you were
happy, for his standards were high. He ran the New
Irish Writing page at the now-defunct *Irish Press* newspaper for many years, encouraged by others including
Anthony Glavin and the heroic Dermot Bolger and a
sometimes-unacknowledged champion, Sean McCann.
It is fitting that the present collection includes fiction
from Glavin and Bolger and from Sean McCann's son,
Colum.

This book offers new short stories from internationally celebrated masters of the form and from writers at the start of promising careers. We have a winner of the American National Book Award, a winner of the Dublin Impac Literary Award, a multiple winner of the Whitbread and a winner of the Booker. We have nominees for other major awards, including the Orange Prize and the Costa, and a couple of Guggenheim Fellows. It was David's quietly insistent way as an editor to publish the work of talented newer writers among the established. In that sense, and perhaps in others, I have borrowed from the wise inheritance he bequeathed. He might, or might not, have approved of my selections – he could be a tough critic as well as a kindly one, and he had his tastes, as all editors have. But I believe he would have liked the idea of the mix.

I have tried to reflect something of the variety of contemporary Irish writing. The collection offers stories set in Ireland written by authors born in that country and from writers born and raised elsewhere but living here now. I have not been overly focused on passport requirements. If you're Irish enough to qualify for the Republic of Ireland football team under the one-grandparent rule, or to cheer for it, even ironically, when it's playing against our friends in England, you're eligible for a seat on the squad bus. That said, I had to persuade the great Richard Ford, a Mississippian with Cavan blood, that his professorship at Trinity College Dublin and the respect in which his work is held by so many Irish writers of my generation make him one of us and always will. Literature opens citizenships of affection, as every reader knows, and Ireland is in need of them these days. New York film-maker and best-selling novelist Rebecca Miller lives and writes in Wicklow. I thank her for allowing herself to be coaxed on board. Emma Donoghue sent a story from Canada, Philip O'Ceallaigh from Bucharest, Joseph O'Neill and Belinda McKeon from Manhattan and Brooklyn, and Peter Murphy from another country perhaps called The Future. (As Colm Tóibín says, 'They do things differently there.') Glenn Patterson, Kevin Power, Gerard Donovan, Eoin McNamee and Mary Morrissy show the punch and extraordinary capaciousness short fiction can have. Viv McDade, Elaine Walsh, Órfhlaith Foyle and Angela Power are impressive talents; it is a pleasure to introduce their work to a wider audience.

The shortest piece is very short; the longest is long. Some stories engage with life outside Ireland, in the traditional outposts of Irish emigration and in newer ones; others engage with the realities of an Ireland convulsed by change in recent years. Several are set in an older, more secretive place that still casts its shadows across our fantasies. A handful of the stories do not allude to Ireland in any way. Indeed, some of the authors whose work appears here would be reluctant to define their work as 'Irish fiction' at all and would question what each of those words means. I have tried, if not to destroy categories, to elasticise them a bit. Purists will see much to complain about. But as my Francis Street grandmother was fond of saying, some people are never happy unless they're slightly miserable. I have tried to bear this in mind.

The short story seems to be experiencing something of a renaissance in post-Celtic Tiger Ireland. Journals such as *The Stinging Fly*, edited by Declan Meade, have provided a home for dozens of new writers whose exhilarating work, sceptically aware of the pantheon of the past in Irish fiction, has often pushed at boundaries. Brendan Barrington's fine journal *The Dublin Review* has published beautiful short stories and essays. Cooperatives of writers have formed themselves up and down the country; the Internet has proved important as a means of getting work out. Self-publishing is no longer always seen as a poor relation. There are more writers' groups and workshops than ever before. Great credit is due to Ciaran Carty at the *Sunday Tribune* in Dublin, where the New Irish Writing page now appears monthly, offering short stories and poetry. Indeed, Ciaran Carty has been to my own generation of Irish writers what David Marcus was to several earlier generations: an advocate, a friend and a hero. The Hennessy family, of Cognac fame, should be thanked for sponsoring the literary awards that bear their name, a set of prizes that offer recognition to Irish writers starting out on a road that can be challenging and lonesome. And the publishers of this book must be acknowledged and warmly thanked too. It is hard to think of any London publishing house that has done more to support the Irish short story. Irish publishers might take a leaf from Faber's book.

Several of the authors whose work is included here have long been among my own touchstones, my Easter Island figures, as a writer, but first as a reader. Others, younger voices, have made it wonderfully evident that Ireland is still a country, for all its innumerable shames, where the empathies involved in the sharing of a story are valued for their possibilities of hope and healing. To make neighbours of William Trevor and Órfhlaith Foyle, of Colm Tóibín and Kevin Barry, of Roddy Doyle, Christine Dwyer Hickey, Julia Kelly and Aifric Campbell, is to raise at least the possibility that we can walk from the tomb of sordor that several of these stories rage against. Some of the testimonies are dark. Others are strange. And while some are bleakly funny, or funnily bleak, I hope there is a refreshing lack of the easily attained laughter that is only grief on a good Irish day. That so many of them manage to find such unearthly beauty in their refusal to flinch is a testament to the mercies of language. We are surrounded by advertisers, propagandists of the slick, chancers, salesmen, illusionists, liars. In Ireland we have banks with no money, apartment blocks nobody wanted, politicians we don't trust, an economy in ruins, a church so disgraced by child abuse and cover-up corruption that it must alter itself profoundly or die. We are witnessing the return of the mass emigration that haunts the work of John McGahern, while our leaders encourage us to bleat about how upbeat we are feeling. The Republic is approaching the centenary of its foundation, yet there has never been a time when so many of us weren't quite sure what Ireland is for. Old certainties are shattered. We got fooled, and we know it. But sometimes, in the Irish sentence, the greatest thing we have ever invented, we glimpse what we yet might be. The arts have brought the consolation of dignity to Ireland at a time when we sorely needed it.

In many of the stories presented here, absence is a presence. And the omissions from any anthology are as interesting as its selections. There are indeed several writers whose work I would have liked to include but on this occasion that wasn't to be. Some hadn't a story they felt was ready to face the reader; others were in the middle of a project, wrestling with its demands. Some, unfortunately, don't write short stories any more, and that tells its own story too. It's a particular regret that these pages don't include a story by an immigrant to Ireland from the developing world; hopefully, future such collections will do so. And the work being done in what is sometimes dismissively called 'genre fiction' – in crime writing, for example, and in the popular novel and in children's literature – is often as reflective of the contemporary realities of Ireland as is any Irish novel likely to be reviewed on the London literary pages. But I believe that the writing offered here has something of the clamorous music of Ireland now, the strangeness and yet the beauty of a country that is passing through adolescence, one glance on its painful childhood, another on the horizon, poised somewhere between denial and hope.

David Marcus told me once: 'Choosing my writers isn't hard for me. If they have something to say, I love them. The work chooses itself. Then, what it needs is luck. And readers. Always readers.'

Here is a collection of writers with something to say. This reader was convinced and enthralled.

Joseph O'Connor
Dublin, 2010

Beer Trip to Llandudno

Kevin Barry

IT WAS A PIG OF A DAY, AS HOT as we'd had, and we were down to our T-shirts taking off from Lime Street. This was a sight to behold – we were all of us biggish lads. It was Real Ale Club's July outing, a Saturday, and we'd had word of several good houses to be found in Llandudno. I was double-jobbing for Ale Club that year. I was in charge of publications and outings both. Which was controversial.

'Rhyl . . . We'll pass Rhyl, won't we?'

This was Mo.

'We'd have come over to Rhyl as kids,' said Mo. 'Ferry and coach. I remember the rollercoasters.'

'Never past Prestatyn, me,' said Tom Neresford.

Tom N. – so-called, there were three Toms in Ale Club – rubbed at his belly in a worried way. There was sympathy for that. We all knew stomach trouble for a bugger.

'Down on its luck'd be my guess,' said Everett Bell. 'All these old North Wales resorts have suffered dreadfully, haven't they? Whole mob's gone off to bloody Laos on packages. Bloody Cambodia, bucket and spade.'

Everett wasn't inclined to take the happy view of things. Billy Stroud, the ex-Marxist, had nothing to offer about Llandudno. Billy was involved with his timetables.

'Two minutes and fifty seconds late taking off,' he said, as the train skirted the Toxteth estates. 'This thing hits Llandudno for 1.55 p.m., I'm an exotic dancer.'

Aigburth station offered a clutch of young girls in their summer skimpies. Oiled flesh, unscarred tummies, and it wasn't yet noon. We groaned under our breaths. We'd taken on a crate of Marston's Old Familiar for the journey, 3.9 per cent to volume. Outside, the estuary sulked away in terrific heat and Birkenhead shimmered across the water. Which wasn't like Birkenhead. I opened my *AA Illustrated Guide To Britain's Coast* and read from its entry on Llandudno:

'A major resort of the North Wales coastline, it owes its well-planned streets and promenade to one Edward Mostyn, who, in the mid-19th century . . .'

'Victorian effort,' said John Mosely. 'Thought as much.'

If there was a dad figure among us, it was Big John, with his know-it-all interruptions.

'Who in the mid-19th century,' I repeated, 'laid out a new town on former marshland below . . .'

'They've built it on a marsh, have they?' said Everett Bell.

'TB,' said Billy Stroud. 'Marshy environment was considered healthful.'

'Says here there's water skiing available from Llandudno jetty.'

'That'll be me,' said Mo, and we all laughed.

Hot as pigs, but companionable, and the train was in Cheshire quick enough. We had dark feelings about Cheshire that summer. At the North West Beer Festival, in the spring, the Cheshire crew had come over a shade cocky. Just because they were chocka with half-beam pubs in pretty villages. Warrington lads were fine. We could take the Salford lot even. But the Cheshire boys were arrogant, and we sniffed as we passed through their country.

'A bloody suburb, essentially,' said Everett.

'Chester's a regular shithole,' said Mo.

'But you'd have to allow Delamere Forest is a nice walk?' said Tom N.

Eyebrows raised at this, Tom N. not being an obvious forest walker.

'You been lately, Tom? Nice walk?'

Tom nodded, all sombre.

'Was out for a Christmas tree actually,' he said.

This brought gales of laughter. It is strange what comes over as hilarious when hangovers are general. We had the windows open to circulate what breeze there was. Billy Stroud had an earpiece in for the radio news. He winced:

'They're saying it'll hit 36.5,' he said. 'Celsius.'

We sighed. We sipped. We made Wales quick enough, and we raised our Marston's to it. Better this than to be stuck in a garden listening to a missus. We meet as many as five nights of the week, more often six. There are those who'd call us a bunch of sots but we don't see ourselves like that. We see ourselves as hobbyists. The train pulled into Flint, and Tom N. went on the platform to fetch in some beef 'n' gravies from the Pie-O-Matic.

'Just the thing,' said Billy Stroud, as we sweated over our dripping punnets. 'Cold stuff causes the body too much work, you feel worse. But a nice hot pie goes down a treat. Perverse, I know. But they're on the curries in Bombay, aren't they?'

'Mumbai,' said Everett.

The train scooted along the hot coast. We made solid headway into the Marston's. Mo was down a testicle since the spring. We'd called in at the Royal the night of his operation. We'd stopped at the Ship and Mitre on the way – they'd a handsome bitter from Clitheroe on guest tap. We needed the fortification: when Real Ale Club boys parade down hospital wards, we tend to draw worried glances from the whitecoats. We are shaped like those chaps in the warning illustrations on cardiac charts. We gathered around Mo and breathed a nice fog of bitter over the lad, and we joshed him, but gently.

'Sounding a little high-pitched, Mo?'

'Other lad's going to be worked overtime.'

'Diseased bugger you'll want in a glass jar, Mo. One for the mantelpiece.'

Love is a strong word, but. We were family to Mo when he was up the Royal having the bollock out. We passed Flint Castle, and Everett Bell piped up.

'Richard the Second,' he said.

We raised eyebrows. We were no philistines at Ale

Club, Merseyside branch. Everett nodded, pleased.

'This is where he was backed into a corner,' he said. 'By Bolingbroke.'

'Bolingwho?'

'Bolingbroke, the usurper. Old Dick surrendered for a finish. At Flint Castle. Or that's how Shakespeare had it.'

'There's a contrary view, Ev?'

'Some say it was more likely Conwy but I'd be happy with the Bard's read,' he said, narrowing his eyes, the matter closed.

'We'll pass Conwy Castle in a bit, won't we?'

I consulted my *AA Illustrated*.

'We'll not,' I said. 'But we may well catch a glimpse across the estuary from Llandudno Junction.'

There was a holiday air at the stations. Families piled on, the dads with papers, the mams with lotion, the kids with phones. The beer ran out by Abergele and this was frowned upon: poor planning. We were reduced to buying train beer, Worthington's. Sourly we sipped, and Everett came and had a go.

'Maybe if one man wasn't in charge of outings *and* publications,' he said, 'we wouldn't be running dry halfways to Llandudno.'

'True, Everett,' I said, calmly, though I could feel the colour rising in my cheeks. 'So if anyone cares to step up, I'll happily step aside. From either or.'

'We need you on publications, kid,' said John Mosely. 'You're the man for the computers.'

Publications lately was indeed largely web-based.

I maintained our site on a regular basis, posting beer-related news and links. I was also looking into online initiatives to attract the younger drinker.

'I'm happy on publications, John,' I said. 'The debacle with the newsletter aside.'

Newsletter had been a disaster, I accepted that. The report on the Macclesfield outing had been printed upside down. Off-colour remarks had been made about a landlady in Everton, which should never have got past an editor's eye, as the lady in question kept very fine pumps. It hadn't been for want of editorial meetings. We'd had several, mostly down the Grapes of Wrath.

'So how's about outings then?' I said, as the train swept by Colwyn Bay. 'Where's our volunteer there? Who's for the step-up?'

Everett showed a palm.

'Nothin' personal in this, lad,' he said.

'I know that, Ev.'

Ale Club outings were civilised events. They never got aggressive. Maudlin, yes, but never aggressive. Rhos-on-Sea, the Penrhyn sands. We knew Everett had been through a hard time. His old dad passed on, and there'd been sticky business with the will. Ev would turn a mournful eye on us, at the bar of the Lion, in the snug of the Ship, and he'd say:

'My brother got the house, my sister got the money, I got the manic depression.'

Black as his moods could be, as sharp as his tongue, Everett was tender. Train came around Little Ormes

Head, and Billy Stroud went off on one about Ceaușescu.

'Longer it recedes in the mind's eye,' he said, 'the more like Romania seems the critical moment.'

'Apropos of, Bill?'

'Apropos my arse. As for Liverpool? Myth was piled upon myth, wasn't it? They said Labour sent out termination notices to council workers by taxi. Never bloody happened! It was an anti-red smear!'

'Thatcher's sick and old, Billy,' said John Mosely.

'Aye an' her spawn's all around us yet,' said Billy, and he broke into a broad smile, his humours mysteriously righted, his fun returned.

Looming, then, the shadow of Great Ormes Head, and, beneath it, a crescent swathe of bay, a beach, a prom, and terraces: here lay Llandudno.

'1.55 p.m.,' said Everett. 'On the nose.'

'Where's our exotic dancer?' teased Mo.

Billy Stroud sadly raised his T-shirt above his man boobs. He put his arms above his head and gyrated slowly his vast belly and danced his way off the train. We lost weight in tears as we tumbled onto the platform.

'How much for a private session, miss?' called Tom N.

'Tenner for twenty minutes,' said Billy. 'Fiver, I'll stay the full half hour.'

We walked out of Llandudno station and plumb into a headbutt of heat.

'Blood and tar!' I cried. 'We'll be hittin' the lagers!'

'Wash your mouth out with soap and water,' said John Mosely.

Big John rubbed his hands together and led the way – Big John was first over the top. He reminded us there was business to hand.

'We're going to need a decision,' he said, 'about the National Beer Scoring System.'

Here was kerfuffle. The NBSS, by long tradition, ranked a beer from nought to five. Nought was take-backable, a crime against the name of ale. One was barely drinkable, two so-so, three an eyebrow raised in mild appreciation. A four was an ale on top form, a good beer in proud nick. A five was angel's tears but a seasoned drinker would rarely dish out a five, would over the course of a lifetime's quaffing call no more than a handful of fives. Such was the NBSS, as was. However, Real Ale Club, Merseyside branch, had for some time felt that the system lacked subtlety. And one famous night, down Rigby's, we came up with our own system: we marked from nought to ten. Finer gradations of purity were thus allowed for. The nuances of a beer were more properly considered. A certain hoppy tang, redolent of summer hedgerows, might elevate a brew from a seven to an eight. The mellow back note born of a good oak casking might lift an ale again, and to the rare peaks of the nines. Billy Stroud had argued for decimal breakdown, for seven-point-fives and eight-point-fives – Billy would – but we had to draw a line somewhere. The national organisation responded badly. They sent stiff word down the email but we continued to forward our beer reports with markings on a nought-to-ten scale. There was talk now of us losing the charter. These were heady days.

'Stuff them is my view,' said Everett Bell.

'We'd lose a lot if we lost the charter,' said Mo. 'Think about the festival invites. Think about the history of the branch.'

'Think about the bloody future!' cried Tom N. 'We haven't come up with a new system to be awkward. We've done it for the ale drinkers. We've done it for the ale makers!'

I felt a lump in my throat, and I daresay I wasn't alone.

'Ours is the better system,' said Everett. 'This much we know.'

'You're right,' said John Mosely, and this was the clincher – Big John's call. 'I say we score nought to ten.'

'If you lot are in, that's good enough for me,' I said.

Six stout men linked arms on a hot Llandudno pavement. We rounded the turn onto the prom and our first port of call: the Heron Inn.

Which turned out to be an anticlimax. A nice house, lately refurbished, but mostly keg rubbish on the taps. The Heron did, however, do a Phoenix Tram Driver on cask, 3.8 per cent, and we sat with six of same.

'I've had better Tram Drivers,' opened Mo.

'I've had worse,' countered Tom N.

'She has a nice delivery but I'd worry about her legs,' said Billy Stroud, shrewdly.

'You wouldn't be having more than a couple,' said John Mosely.

'*Not* a skinful beer,' I concurred.

9

All eyes turned to Everett Bell. He held a hand aloft, wavered it.

'A five would be generous, a six insane,' he said.

'Give her the five,' said Big John, dismissively.

I made the note. This was as smoothly as a beer was ever scored. There had been some world-historical ructions in our day. There was the time Billy Stroud and Mo hadn't talked for a month over an eight handed out to a Belhaven Bombardier.

Alewards we followed our noses. We walked by the throng of the beach and made towards the Prom View Hotel. We'd had word of a new landlord there, an ale fancier. The shrieks of the sun-crazed kids made our stomachs loop. It was dogs-dying-in-parked-cars weather. The Prom View's ample lounge was a blessed reprieve. We had the place to ourselves, the rest of Llandudno apparently being content with summer, sea and life. John Mosely nodded towards a smashing row of hand pumps for the casks. Low whistles sounded. The landlord, hot-faced and jovial, came through from the hotel's reception.

'Another tactic,' he said, 'would be stay home and have a nice sauna.'

'Same difference,' sighed John Mosely.

'They're saying 37.2 now,' said the landlord, taking a flop of sweat from his brow.

Billy Stroud sensed a kindred spirit: 'Gone up again, has it?'

'And up,' said the landlord. 'My money's on a 38 before we're out.'

'Record won't go,' said Billy.

'Nobody's said record,' said the landlord. 'We're not going to see a 38.5, that's for sure.'

'Brogdale in Kent,' said Billy. 'August 10th, 2003.'

'2.05 p.m.,' said the landlord. 'I wasn't five miles distant that same day.'

Billy was beaten.

'Loading a van for a divorced sister,' said the landlord, ramming home his advantage. 'Lugging sofas in the piggin' heat. And wardrobes!'

We bowed our heads to the man.

'What'll I fetch you, gents?'

A round of Cornish Lightning was requested.

'Taking the sun?' enquired the landlord.

'Taking the ale.'

'After me own heart,' he said. 'Course round here, it's lagers they're after mostly. Bloody Welsh.'

'Can't beat sense into them,' said John Mosely.

'If I could, I would,' said the landlord, and he danced as a young featherweight might, raising his clammy dukes. Then he skipped and turned.

'I'll pop along on my errands, boys,' he said. 'There are rows to hoe and socks for the wash. You'd go through pair after pair this weather.'

He pinched his nostrils closed: what-a-pong.

'Soon as you're ready for more, ring that bell, and my good wife will oblige. So adieu, adieu . . .'

He skipped away. We raised eyes. The shade of the lounge was pleasant, the Cornish Lightning in decent nick.

'Call it a six?' said Tom N.

Nervelessly we agreed. Talk was limited. We swallowed hungrily, quickly, and peered again towards the pumps.

'The Lancaster Bomber?'

'The Whitstable Mule?'

'How's about that Mangan's Organic?'

'I'd say the Lancaster all told.'

'Ring the bell, Everett.'

He did so, and a lively blonde, familiar with her forties but nicely preserved, bounced through from reception. Our eyes went shyly down. She took a glass to shine as she waited our call. Type of lass who needs her hands occupied.

'Do you for, gents?'

Irish, her accent.

'Round of the Lancaster, wasn't it?' said Everett.

She squinted towards our table, counted the heads.

'Times six,' confirmed Everett.

The landlady squinted harder. She dropped the glass. It smashed to pieces on the floor.

'Maurice?' she said.

It was Mo that froze, stared, softened.

'B–B–Barbara?' he said.

We watched as he rose and crossed to the bar. A man in a dream was Mo. We held our breaths as Mo and Barbara took each other's hands over the counter. They were wordless for some moments, and then felt ten eyes on them, for they giggled, and Barbara set blushing to the Lancasters. She must have spilled half again down the slops gully as she poured. I joined Everett to carry the ales to our table. Mo and Barbara went into a huddle down the far end of the counter. They were rapt.

Real Ale Club would not have marked Mo for a romancer.

'The quiet ones you watch,' said Tom N. 'Maur*ice*?'

'Mo? With a piece?' whispered Everett Bell.

'Could be they're old family friends?' tried innocent Billy. 'Or relations?'

Barbara was now slowly stroking Mo's wrist.

'Four buggerin' fishwives I'm sat with,' said John Mosely. 'What are we to make of these Lancasters?'

We talked ale but were distracted. Our glances cut down the length of the bar. Mo and Barbara talked lowly, quickly, excitedly there. She was moved by Mo, we could see that plain enough. Again and again she ran her fingers through her hair. Mo was gazing at her, all dreamy, and suddenly he'd got a thumb hooked in the belt loop of his denims – Mr Suave. He didn't so much as touch his ale.

Next, of course, the jaunty landlord arrived back on the scene.

'Oh Alvie!' she cried. 'You'll never guess!'

'Oh?' said the landlord, all the jauntiness instantly gone from him.

'This is *Maurice*!'

'Maurice?' he said. 'You're joking . . .'

It was polite handshakes then, and feigned interest in Mo on the landlord's part, and a wee fat hand he slipped around the small of his wife's back.

'We'll be suppin' up,' said John Mosely, sternly.

Mo had a last, whispered word with Barbara but her smile was fixed now, and the landlord remained in close attendance. As we left, Mo looked back and raised his voice a note too loud. Desperate, he was.

'Barbara?'

We dragged him along. We'd had word of notable pork scratchings up the Mangy Otter.

'Do tell, Maur*ice*,' said Tom N.

'Leave him be,' said John Mosely.

'An ex, that's all,' said Mo.

And Llandudno was infernal. Families raged in the heat. All of the kids wept. The Otter was busyish when we sludged in. We settled on a round of St Austell Tributes from a meagre selection. Word had not been wrong on the quality of the scratchings. And the St Austell turned out to be in top form.

'I'd be thinking in terms of a seven,' said Everett Bell.

'Or a shade past that?' said John Mosely.

'You could be right on higher than sevens,' said Billy Stroud. 'But surely we're not calling it an eight?'

'Here we go,' I said.

'Now this,' said Billy Stroud, 'is where your seven-point-five would come in.'

'We've heard this song, Billy,' said John Mosely.

'He may not be wrong, John,' said Everett.

'Give him a seven-point-five,' said John Mosely, 'and he'll be wanting his six-point-threes, his eight-point-sixes. There'd be no bloody end to it!'

'Tell you what,' said Mo. 'How about I catch up with you all a bit later? Where's next on list?'

We stared at the carpet. It had diamonds on and crisps ground into it.

'Next up is the Crippled Ox on Burton Square,' I read from my print-out. 'Then it's Henderson's on Old Parade.'

'See you at one or the other,' said Mo.

He threw back the dregs of his St Austell and was gone.

We decided on another at the Otter. There was a Whitstable Silver Star, 6.2 per cent to volume, a regular stingo to settle our nerves.

'What's the best you've ever had?' asked Tom N.

It's a conversation that comes up again and again but it was a lifesaver just then: it took our minds off Mo.

'Put a gun to my head,' said Big John, 'and I don't think I could look past the draught Bass I had with me dad in Peter Kavanagh's. Sixteen years of age, Friday tea-time, first wage slip in my arse pocket.'

'But was it the beer or the occasion, John?'

'How can you separate the two?' he said, and we all sighed.

'For depth? Legs? Back note?' said Everett Bell. 'I'd do well to ever best the Swain's Anthem I downed a November Tuesday in Stockton-on-Tees, 19 and 87. 4.2 per cent to volume. I was still in haulage at that time.'

'I've had an Anthem,' said Billy Stroud of this famously hard-to-find brew, 'and I'd have to say I found it an unex-ceptional ale.'

Everett made a face.

'So what'd be your all-time, Billy?'

The ex-Marxist knit his fingers atop the happy mound of his belly.

'Ridiculous question,' he said. 'There is so much wonderful ale on this island. How is a sane man to separate a Pelham High Anglican from a Warburton's Saxon Fiend? And we haven't even mentioned the great Belgian tradition. Your Duvel's hardly a dishwater. Then there's the Czechs, the Poles, the Germans . . .'

'Gassy pop!' cried Big John, no fan of a German brew, of a German anything.

'Nonsense,' said Billy. 'A Paulaner Weissbier is a sensational sup on its day.'

'Where'd you think Mo's headed?' Tom N. cut in.

Everett groaned, 'He'll be away down the Prom View, won't he? Big ape.'

'Mo a ladykiller?' said Tom. 'There's one for breaking news.'

'No harm if it meant he smartened himself up a bit,' said John.

'He has let himself go,' said Billy. 'Since the testicle.'

'You'd plant spuds in those ears,' I said.

The Whitstables had us in fighting form. We were away up the Crippled Ox. We found there a Miner's Slattern on cask. TV news showed sardine beaches and motorway chaos. There was an internet machine on the wall, a pound for ten minutes, and Billy Stroud went to consult the meteorological satellites. The Slattern set me pensive.

Strange, I thought, how I myself had wound up a Real Ale Club stalwart. October 1995, I'd found myself in motorway services outside Ormskirk having a screaming barny with the missus. We were moving back to her folks' place in Northern Ireland. From dratted Leicester. We were heading for the ferry at Stranraer. At services, missus told me I was an idle lardarse who had made her life hell and she never wanted to see me again. We'd only stopped off to fill the tyres. She gets in, slams the door, puts her foot down. Give her ten minutes, I thought, she'll calm down and turn back for me. Two hours later, I'm sat in an empty Chinese in services, weeping and eating Szechuan beef. I call a taxi. Taxi comes. I says, where are we, exactly? Bloke looks at me. He says, Ormskirk direction. I says, what's nearest city of any size? Drop you in Liverpool for twenty quid, he says. He leaves me off downtown, and I look for a pub. Spot the Ship and Mitre, and in I go. I find a stunning row of pumps. I call a Beaver Mild out of Devon.

'I wouldn't,' says a bloke with a beard down the bar.

'Oh?'

'Try a Marston's Old Familiar,' he says, and it turns out he's Billy Stroud.

The same Billy turned from the internet machine at the Ox in Llandudno.

'37.9,' he said. 'Bristol Airport, a shade after three. Flights delayed, tarmac melting.'

'Pig heat,' said Tom N.

'We won't suffer much longer,' said Billy. 'There's a change due.'

'Might get a night's sleep,' said Everett.

The hot nights were certainly a torment. Lying there with a sheet stuck to your belly. Thoughts coming loose, beer fumes rising, a manky arse. The city beyond the flat throbbing with summer. Usually I'd get up and have a cup of tea, watch some telly. Astrophysics on Beeb Two at four in the morning, news from the galaxies, and light already in the eastern sky. I'd dial the number in Northern Ireland and then hang up before they could answer.

Mo arrived into the Ox like the ghost of Banquo. There were terrible scratch marks down his left cheek.

'A Slattern will set you right, kid,' said John Mosely, discreetly, and he manoeuvred his big bones barwards.

Poor Mo was wordless as he stared into the ale that was put before him. Billy Stroud sneaked a time-out signal to Big John.

'We'd nearly give Henderson's a miss,' agreed John.

'As well get back to known terrain,' said Everett.

We climbed the hot streets towards the station. We stocked up with some Cumberland Pedigrees, 3.4 per cent to volume, always an easeful drop. The train was busy with daytrippers heading back. We sipped quietly. Mo looked half-dead as he slumped there but now and then he'd come up for a mouthful of his Pedigree.

'How's it tasting, kiddo?' chanced Everett.

'Like a ten,' said Mo, and we all laughed.

The flicker of his old humour reassured us. The sun

descended on Colwyn Bay, and there was young life everywhere. I'd only spoken to her once since Ormskirk. We had details to finalise, and she was happy to let it slip about her new bloke. Some twat called Stan.

'He's emotionally spectacular,' she said.

'I'm sorry to hear it, love,' I said. 'Given you've been through the wringer with me.'

'I mean in a good way!' she barked. 'I mean in a *calm* way!'

We'd a bit of fun coming up the Dee Estuary with the Welsh place names.

'Fy. . . feen . . . no. Fiiiif . . . non . . . fyff . . . non . . . growy?'

This was Tom N.

'Foy. Nonn. Grewey?'

This was Everett's approximation.

'Ffynnongroyw,' said Billy Stroud, lilting it perfectly. 'Simple. And this one coming up? Llannerch-y-mor.'

Pedigree came down my nose I laughed that hard.

'Young girl, beautiful,' said Mo. 'Turn around and she's forty bloody three.'

'Leave it, Mo,' said Big John.

But he could not.

'She comes over early in '86. She's living up top of the Central Line, Theydon Bois. She's working in a pub there, live-in, and ringing me from a phone box. In Galway, I'm in a phone box too. We have to arrange the times, eight o'clock on Tuesday, ten o'clock on Friday. It's physical fucking pain she's not in town anymore. I'll follow in the summer is the plan, and I get there, Victoria Coach Station, six in the morning, eighty quid in my pocket. And she's waiting for me there. We have an absolute dream of a month. We're lying in the park. There's a song out, and we make it our song. "Oh to be in England, in the summertime, with my love, close to the edge."'

'Art of Noise,' said Billy Stroud.

'Shut up, Billy!'

'Of course, the next thing the summer's over, and I've a start with BT in Liverpool, and she's to follow on – October is the plan. We're ringing from phone boxes again, Tuesdays and Fridays but the second Friday the phone doesn't ring. Next time I see her she's forty bloody three.'

Flint station we passed through, and then Connah's Quay.

'Built up, this,' said Tom N. 'There's an Aldi, look? And that's a new school, is it?'

'Which means you want to be keeping a good two hundred yards back,' said Big John.

We were horrified. Through a miscarriage of justice, plain as, Tom N. had earlier in the year been placed on a sex register. Oh the world is mad! Tom N. is a placid, placid man. We were all six of us quiet as the grave on the evening train then. It grew and built, it was horrible, the silence. It was Everett at last that broke it; we were coming in for Helsby. Fair dues to Everett.

'Not like you, John,' he said.

Big John nodded.

'I don't know where that came from, Tom,' he said. 'A bloody stupid thing to say.'

Tom N. raised a palm in peace but there was no disguising the hurt that had gone in. I pulled away into myself. The turns the world takes – Tom dragged through the courts, Everett half mad, Mo all scratched up and one-balled, Big John jobless for eighteen months. Billy Stroud was content, I suppose, in Billy's own way. And there was me, shipwrecked in Liverpool. Funny, for a while, to see 'Penny Lane' flagged up on the buses, but it wears off.

And then it was before us in a haze. Terrace rows we passed, out Speke way, with cook-outs on the patios. Tiny pockets of glassy laughter we heard through the open windows of the carriage. Families and what-have-you. We had the black hole of the night before us – it wanted filling. My grimmest duty as publications officer was the obits page of the newsletter. Too many had passed on at forty-four, at forty-six.

'I'm off outings,' I announced. 'And I'm off bloody publications as well.'

'You did volunteer on both counts,' reminded Big John.

'It would leave us in an unfortunate position,' said Tom N.

'For my money, it's been a very pleasant outing,' said Billy Stroud.

'We've supped some quality ale,' concurred Big John.

'We've had some cracking weather,' said Tom N.

'Llandudno is quite nice, really,' said Mo.

Around his scratch marks an angry bruising had seeped. We all looked at him with tremendous fondness.

''Tis nice,' said Everett Bell. 'If you don't run into a she-wolf.'

'If you haven't gone ten rounds with Edward bloody Scissorhands,' said John Mosely.

We came along the shabby grandeurs of the town. The look on Mo's face then couldn't be read as anything but happiness.

'Maur*ice*,' teased Big John, 'is thinking of the rather interesting day he's had.'

Mo shook his head.

'Thinking of days I had years back,' he said.

It has this effect, Liverpool. You're not back in the place five minutes and you go sentimental as a famine ship. We piled off at Lime Street. There we go: six big blokes in the evening sun.

'There's the Lion Tavern?' suggested Tom N.

'There's always the Lion,' I agreed.

'They've a couple of Manx ales guesting at Rigby's,' said Everett Bell.

'Let's hope they're an improvement on previous Manx efforts,' said Billy Stroud.

'There's the Grapes?' tried Big John.

'There's always the Grapes,' I agreed.

And alewards we went about the familiar streets. The town was in carnival: Tropic of Lancashire in a July swelter. It would not last. There was rain due in off the Irish Sea, and not for the first time.

Winter

Dermot Bolger

THE DRIVER OF THE TOW TRUCK was unsure if he would make it up the overgrown woodland avenue to the old woman's former home. Luckily the day was so cold that last night's frost had never fully thawed. It was setting in hard again with the approach of dusk. So although the wheels were churning ugly tyre marks from the grassy avenue they had not yet become stuck. A branch broke off an overhanging tree, leaving yet another long scratch mark along the side of the mobile home the truck was towing. Walking behind it, in her seventy-second year, Eva threw the branch into the undergrowth. This second-hand mobile home and these few acres of Mayo wood-land were the last two things she still owned. The wood had become neglected during the three decades since anyone last lived here. Fences were broken, with damage caused by cattle wandering through the trees and farmers freely helping themselves to fencing stakes. The trees – many of the new ones planted by her son, Francis, where he was an idealistic horticulture student – were silent in this November twilight. The quietude, unbroken even by

23

the cry of a solitary bird, made the engine sound loud as the driver switched gear, preparing for a particularly steep bend ahead.

This was the third time in fifty years that Eva had come to make her home here in Glanmire Wood. On the first occasion in 1927 she had been a young bride from Donegal, unwisely marrying into the haughty Fitzgerald family who then still owned half the local village and had once owned half of Castlebar – a family who had still expected locals to lift their caps and step off the road whenever a Fitzgerald motor passed.

The woods had rarely been silent in 1927 because her husband was happiest when stalking through them with his Holland ejector twelve-bore gun and a dog at his heels. At dusk Freddie would bring his daily bag of slaughtered woodcock and pigeon for display on the front step before she was expected to pluck the carcasses and cook them for the few guests they managed to entice here. He had used whatever money she brought to the marriage to convert the house into a shooting lodge in the unshakeable but mistaken belief that Glanmire Wood would be thronged with like-minded hunters from what he termed 'the mainland'. He had not factored in a depression, an economic war and how drink would take possession of him in almost equal proportion to how loneliness took possession of her, with no money, few guests and two small children; with the county bailiffs drinking in a local bar for Dutch courage before venturing cautiously up this avenue to serve writs on them.

Their hesitancy was partly related to the four hundred years' residency of the Fitzgeralds and partly to do with the twelve-bore gauge of his Holland ejector.

Poor Freddie, who had longed for a son who was a replica of himself. He hadn't needed Francis to be a genius or a statesman once the boy was someone who understood the best cover for shooting woodcock, the merits of retrievers over red setters, the measure of good whiskey and how to deal firmly but fairly with an ever-decreasing number of servants. Eva remembered Freddie buying Francis his first gun when the boy was barely nine years old and helping him to wedge it into his shoulder. It was one of the rare occasions when Freddie had not seemed awkward in physical contact with his son. Francis's first lucky shot had killed a rabbit on this avenue, causing Freddie to rush off to the guests, boasting about his son, while she held Francis in her arms, letting him cry for the dead rabbit as they hid in the woods like hunted creatures whose slightest movement might betray them.

Freddie's exasperated expression for his young wife in those years was that she 'lived in the ether'. Before her marriage Eva had tried to paint and write poetry. During her marriage she had tried to simply survive. Survival had meant emigration for Freddie and her to find work in England in 1936, with all the furniture in Glanmire House being sold to appease the bailiffs but its crumbling mil-dewed rooms being retained in her husband's tight grasp.

Those high-ceilinged rooms had been freezing on the winter night in 1939 when Eve came home here for the second time. She had been bringing her two young children to safety three weeks after Freddie enlisted in the British Army. Despite her apprehension that Hitler's war could spread to Ireland or that they might starve here in Mayo, she had shared her children's sense of excitement on that night. Coming home had felt like an adventure. They were not just running away from blacked-out streets and the threat of bombing raids: Francis and Hazel had been escaping the rules and strictures of English boarding schools, and Eva had been fleeing from having to confront a floundering marriage. The war years had allowed her to hide away in this closeted wood, with just her children and Maureen, a young maid from the village who became a best friend to each of them in turn.

But tonight, as she returned here for the third time, Eva was running away from nothing. She was returning simply because this wood was the last place left from which nobody could evict her. Freddie had disinherited her in his will; just like he had disinherited Francis after discovering that his son was homosexual. He had left these few remaining acres to their daughter, who had married a rich coffee planter in Kenya, the sort of vigorous outdoor man whom Freddie had admired. Freddie could never have expected that his nomadic wife would eventually inherit this wood; the estranged wife in the ether who talked rot about people's yearns to be fulfilled; the woman who – after years of separation – tracked him down to the hospital where he was dying and insisted on nursing him, even though his dying words were to remind Eva that he would leave her penniless.

Glanmire Wood finally now belonged to her, but at what a price. Eva doubted if she would ever feel warm again or know hunger or any other sensation except numbness. Since hearing the news from Kenya two months ago she had rarely bothered to light the small stove in her mobile home. Whenever she remembered to do so it was only for the sake of the three cats who had found their way to her as strays. This malaise perturbed the two younger cats who incessantly rubbed against her legs, wanting Eva to stroke them. But Eva had spent most of the past two months sitting motionless indoors in the small caravan park where she had been living in Wexford, only venturing forth to get cat food. When her news emerged, local people had started to bring her beef stews. They possessed no understanding of what a vegan ate and imagined that she only abstained from meat because of her poverty which was obvious to everyone since she moved back to Ireland two years ago.

Old married couples had kept shyly appearing in the muddy field when nobody else was around, pleading with her to take some nourishment. They had talked about how isolated she must feel with the makeshift caravan park empty where her berth was the only one still occupied in winter. These neighbours meant well, and, after they left, her cats had feasted on the hot food, while she broke up the proffered biscuits and cakes to scatter as crumbs for the small birds who flocked around her home.

A caravan park was an odd place to call home, but she had lost track of the places she had called home since leaving this wood at the end of the Second World War, when there were no more uniforms and military postings to provide a buffer zone in her marriage, when Freddie arrived back with his MBE and diseased liver and hastily arranged discharge for drunkenness in the officers' mess, when Maureen had emigrated to America and Eva had left Mayo and left Freddie.

Home briefly became a house in Dublin where she taught joyful art classes in her kitchen to children who seemed too cowed at first to understand that they did not need permission to express themselves. It was fulfilling, but, after giving up her happiness for so long to make other people happy, and with her children grown, she had needed to know if she could fulfil her dream of being a writer. Home had become a succession of cheap *pensions* in Tangier in Morocco and rented rooms in mountain villages in Spain where she had nurtured her dream until it was extinguished, taking encouragement from any faint words of praise in the neatly typed rejection letters that took weeks to reach her.

By the mid-1960s, home had become the small attic of a lodging house in London so that she could be near her son whom she loved with a protective passion. She had been intoxicated by his radiance when he was happy and felt a desperate foreboding when forced to witness his despair. Being written out of Freddie's will hurt him, though many things hurt him because Francis had felt everything in life intensely, leaving himself so open to love in the clandestine underworld in which he was forced to live that the final rejection by his older lover had proven too much. It was eight years since Eva found him with blue blotches on his skin and his limbs arrayed as if he had tried to rise from the floor one last time to get more pills from the bathroom in case the first over-dose was not enough. It was Eva who had cradled his body and said, 'My precious darling, I'm just so glad they can't hurt you any more.'

She thought that she had known the true depth of despair amid the grief that followed his death. She had survived only by finding herself a bolthole as the care-taker in a Quaker hostel in Portobello populated by anx-ious young Americans whose families disowned them as draft-dodgers. Her duties involved rising at 6 a.m. to wash down the long hostel tables and tiled floors. She had loved this back-breaking work, although her arthritic joints had ached in the cold, because it had allowed her no time to grieve. Her grieving had been done alone in the evenings and walking alone through London at night, unable to let go of the consuming anger she felt at this death.

Eva still felt guilty that her daughter's death in Kenya four years later did not cause her the same anguish. Her love for Hazel was always different because Hazel never needed her in the same way. At times, Hazel's exasper-ated affection for her carried an echo of Freddie's impa-tience. Hazel had definitely been a Fitzgerald. She was the practical one in the family and such a headstrong fighter that Eva had never believed the police reports from Kenya that Hazel had also killed herself. Eva had only caught glimpses into Hazel's life in Kenya: a world of servants and heavy drinking in the club. Eva knew that she would not have liked that life, and she had not liked what it did to Hazel. Hazel must have been drinking heavily the night that she decided to race the night train, determined to reach the level crossing first. Hazel the daredevil, the blonde beauty whose photograph always featured in the *Irish Times* when she rode at the Dublin Horse Show. What level of despair causes a woman to race along a red dirt road in Kenya, determined not to be beaten by a train or by anyone. She had never sent her mother a photograph of the map of scars that lined her face after the train tipped her back wheel and the car spun as out of control as her life. Yet a fighter like Hazel would never have left behind a daughter just ten years old, would never have fed a pipe from a car exhaust into the back seat of her car and – in such a hot climate – would never have wrapped herself up tightly in a blanket, like the police report detailed, in a way that replicated the way that she loved to lie in her bed as a girl in this wood during the freezing winters in the war years.

Eva would never know if anyone had placed Hazel's body, already dead, in that car. All she had known was that she had a granddaughter on the far side of the world who needed her. She had put aside her grief and suspicions to make it clear that if Alex was sent to a good Protestant boarding school in Dublin, like Hazel had talked about, Eva would return to Ireland. It was for Alex's sake that Eva bought this mobile home two years ago so that the child would have somewhere to go when her classmates went home at midterm, so that there could be somebody close by who made her feel loved.

The only person who had not called to her in Wexford in recent weeks was the farmer who owned the field where the caravans were parked, the man who wanted her gone so that he could rent her berth for more money to some rich Dublin family who would only disturb him on sunny weekends. Eva had resisted his subtle innuendos to leave because it was important to be somewhere within reach of Alex's school, but that Wexford field held too many memories now. She had been surprised at the most unlikely neighbours who called in Wexford when news spread that she had hired this tow truck to transport her to Mayo: people with whom she had only exchanged a few words when proudly wandering with Alex along the beach at Curracloe or last year when she walked for days in search of her old tomcat, Martin Buber, after he ventured out on a night hunt and never returned.

The tow truck slowed to a halt now, blocking the avenue. Eva picked her way carefully around to the cab door, which opened.

'There's a chestnut tree overhanging the path,' the driver explained. 'I just might be able to swing around it.'

Eva walked past the truck and onto the daffodil lawn where she had scattered her Francis's ashes eight years ago. The boarded-up house looked in the same condition as when she had come here last spring on a day trip with Alex to show the child where her mother had been born. However, the sun had been shining on that day, with the wild flowers into bloom. Eva sat on the front step to watch the man manoeuvre past the chestnut tree and park her mobile home in front of the ivy-covered main door. He switched off his engine, climbed down and looked around, concerned.

'Is this really where you want it, Mrs Fitzgerald?'

'Yes.'

'I can swing it around to the side if that would make it easier for you to run a water pipe from the kitchen.' He paused. 'I mean, you have a water supply here, don't you?'

'There used to be one decades ago.'

'How will you survive without water?'

This man thinks that I'm demented, Eva thought, *a lost old bird who should be kept in a cage.* 'Survival is the one thing I am good at. The poor cats will be terrified. You might lift down their baskets.'

The driver went to say something and then changed his mind. He released the three cats who ran around the lawn in great circles after their confinement. The oldest of them, Queensly, glared reproachfully at Eva and refused to let the old woman come near. The driver put concrete blocks in place to stabilise the mobile home, and Eva climbed inside. Her books had been packed into boxes for the move, with the crockery carefully wrapped up. The cats would be starving, and she needed to feed them. The responsibility for their care was the only thing that kept her going. She called their names at the door, but they refused to respond, still having not forgiven her. The noise of the spoon against their bowl brought them scurrying in, however, ill-tempered after their long confinement. They pushed each other greedily aside as they ate. Dusk had settled in. She went out to the driver who was putting down additional concrete blocks to serve as steps up to her door. He would be anxious to get his truck back down the avenue before all daylight was gone.

'You've a long journey ahead,' she said.

'Sure haven't I the radio for company.' He looked around him at the darkening trees. 'This is a lonely spot. Is there anything more I can do for you, Ma'am?'

'No. You've been really kind.'

'Does anyone know you're here? You're very isolated in this wood. In Wexford they said that you were some class of artist, or was it a writer? Nobody seemed quite sure.'

'I was never quite sure myself.'

The man opened the cab door and climbed up. 'Whatever you are, Ma'am, I wish you happiness.'

'Thank you.'

He switched on his headlights, slammed the door and drove off. The gathering dusk seemed more pronounced after he was gone. Eva re-entered the freezing mobile home, suddenly nervous on her own. It felt ridiculous to feel anxious in this place that had once been home. But she had always slept in the house, with candles and log fires lighting up familiar rooms. It was too dangerous to enter any part of the old house now except the basement. Eva had lost count of the number of fallen trees that had smashed onto the roof over the years. Last spring she had explored the basement with her granddaughter, climbing up the back stairs to peer towards the rooms where Hazel and Francis had run as children, unsure if the floor would still take their weight. On that trip she had discovered that intruders had torn out the last Georgian fireplace with its black marble surround. When dragging it across the front hall the floorboards had collapsed, plunging the heavy fireplace down into the wine cellar below, which was haunted by the ghost of a former butler. Traces of blood had suggested that at least one intruder had been injured, though since the Troubles broke out again in the North you were never sure what traces of blood in a remote location signified.

Staring now at the dark ruin, Eva questioned the wisdom of returning to a place with so many ghosts. An anonymous *pension* back in Morocco or Spain might have been better, somewhere warm for her arthritis and her soul. But she lacked the will to start travelling again. Finding some candles in a packing case she struck a match. It spluttered out, and she had to close the caravan door before a match would stay aflame long enough to light two candles. Placing them on the low table, she sat back on the window seat, which she still thought of as Alex's bed. It was Alex who had looked around the mobile home in delight on her first visit and christened it 'The Ark'. It didn't feel like an ark now, but the walls would look better when Eva's pictures were re-hung, the shelves less bare when the old books were unpacked. Eva understood the routine of moving better than anyone, because she had spent so much of her life doing so.

It would be time enough to start unpacking tomorrow. The clock had not been wound for days, but she knew it was only around half five. There seemed nothing else to do except get into her bed fully dressed and hope not to wake until morning. Eva ate some carob chocolate, because she felt that she ought to. Then she opened the skylight to allow the cats to come and go. They would be disorientated but would enjoy exploring the crumbling house to the consternation of mice who had found refuge there. The caravan felt even icier with the skylight open, but – apart from her concern about what might happen to the cats – Eva hardly cared whether she was found frozen to death here in the morning.

This thought sounded self-pitying and was therefore wrong. As a young woman she remembered reading a D. H. Lawrence poem about how a bird could fall dead from hunger without having ever felt one moment of self-pity. But such stoicism was easy in print. In the past two months Eva had found that the solace of books had failed her. Even Martin Buber's great theological study, *I and Thou*, brought none of the comfort that one touch from his namesake, the missing tomcat, would have provided. But where philosophy failed, her body's instinct for survival took over. Tomorrow she would try to uncover the pipes from the ancient water tank mounted on masonry piers behind the house and use the rainwater collected there for boiling.

The two kittens scrambled up the empty bookshelves and jumped expertly through the gap in the skylight. But Queensly stayed behind, watching Eva with wise, compassionate eyes. The old cat climbed slowly up onto Eva's lap and settled down, seeking not to be patted but to offer whatever warmth she could.

'Good mother puss,' Eva said softly. 'Wise old mother puss.'

Queensly lifted her head to listen, then sprang off Eva's lap to approach the door. Somebody was out there. Eva heard solitary footsteps crunch the frozen grass. She remembered how Freddie had often returned alone to Glanmire during the last years of his life. Perhaps this was his ghost outside about to enter the dark ruin with a bottle of Skylark whiskey in his pocket. But these footsteps lacked the peculiar sound which Freddie's crippled foot used to make. They stopped outside the caravan. The voice that called out belonged to another time. It had aged greatly but was still unmistakable.

'Mrs Fitzgerald? Are you in there?'

'Yes,' Eva replied, unsure if the voice was real.

The door opened, and a figure stooped her head to enter, stamping her wellington boots to inject some warmth into her feet. 'Mother of God, Mrs Fitzgerald, you can't be sitting here getting your death of cold. Have you not even got a stove?'

'I have,' Eva said. 'I just haven't lit it.'

'Well it's high time you did.' The young woman drew closer, only she wasn't a young woman anymore. Maureen's figure had become thickset, with glasses and permed hair tinted slightly blue. But her essence had not changed since the morning in 1939 when she stood before Eva as a girl in old clothes ready to scrub down the flagstones on her first day as a maid.

'Is that really you, Maureen?' Eva asked in wonder. 'I thought you went away years ago to America. I often think of you enjoying every mod con over there.'

'And amn't I the dumbest woman in Christendom not to be over there still enjoying them. Instead I'm back living in my sister's bungalow. My weekly highlight is bingo in Castlebar every Tuesday night. You remember my sister Cait, don't you, Mrs Fitzgerald? She married Jack Dowling from out Carrowkeel way.'

Eva nodded, recalling a barefoot child standing up proudly on her father's ass and cart when Maureen's father would arrive with turf for them during the war. Freddie might have always referred to Maureen as 'the maid' in his letters, but during the war years she had been like a younger sister to Eva and an older sister to Hazel.

'Now let's get a fire going before we turn into icicles.' Maureen opened the cast iron stove to peer inside. 'Mother of God, but you're an awful woman, Mrs Fitzgerald. The fire is set and all if you'd only toss a match in its direction.'

'I wasn't cold.'

'Are you codding me? A polar bear would need an electric blanket tonight. Will you not come up to Cait and Jack's bungalow and stay with us?'

'No.' Since she received the news from Kenya nothing had been able to touch Eva. If she had cut her own wrists she would not have been surprised to find her blood too frozen inside to seep out. But now in Maureen's presence she felt an infinitesimal stir inside her, a foretaste of human warmth, like a hairline fissure in a sheet of ice.

'Well, pass me the box of matches and we'll make do here so. We knew colder nights together in that old house during the war.'

Maureen closed the skylight despite Eva's protests, saying that if the cats wanted to come back in they could knock at the door like Christians. She rigged up a cylinder of gas and soon had a kettle boiling under a blue flame as she opened the stove again, and added in larger sticks and some turf. Finding a fork among the cardboard boxes, Maureen knelt before the stove to toast a thick slice of stale bread.

'I had every mod con in the States true enough,' she said. 'A dish washer, air conditioning and more television stations than you could shake a stick at. But there were nights when I'd have swapped them all for the chance to make toast on a fork by an open fire.'

'When did you come back?'

'Six months after my Frankie died from cancer. They introduced protective masks in the chemical factory where he worked twenty years too late.'

'I'm sorry,' Eva replied.

'You would have liked Frankie. He was a laugh. Even with a name like Bergsson he claimed to be half Irish. Bald as a coot by the age of forty and always smiling. He had a black man's big teeth and a Cavan man's laugh.'

'You're still hurting over him,' Eva said softly.

'To tell you the truth, Mrs Fitzgerald, every week the loneliness hurts more. When I was a girl here in Mayo the nuns made it sound as if I had only to hold a boy's hand and I'd fall pregnant on the spot. Frankie and I were thirty years sharing a bed without one sign of a child stirring, and it wasn't for lack of trying. Oh, I had the best of neighbours in Boston, but neighbours are no substitute for kin when you find yourself alone. This toast is ready now. Where did you pack your butter?'

'I'm a vegan now. I don't eat butter.'

Maureen raised her eyes. 'Mother of God, all the cows will be thrilled. They can enjoy a lie-in on Sundays. What do you eat so?'

'A soya spread, when I can get it.'

Maureen brought over the toast and two cups of black tea. The caravan was starting to feel warm. Queensly deserted Eva to settle on Maureen's lap.

'This is the high life,' Maureen remarked. 'Here I am, dining with the gentry.'

Eva smiled. 'I'm hardly gentry anymore. I doubt if there's a soul in the village poorer. Name anyone else living in a caravan.'

'Where you live doesn't change who you are. Folks

around here still see you as a lady. The big truck pulling this yoke was spied coming through the village. The
whole parish is wondering how you think you can survive up here. Now eat up your toast.'

Eva put down the cup she had been holding between
her hands mainly for its warmth. 'I'm not hungry.'

'I know,' Maureen said. 'Food has lost any taste since
my Frankie died. But I make myself eat. I can't believe
that poor Master Francis and Miss Hazel are dead. I can
see them still as children roaming about through the
woods here. After Frankie died I found myself talking
about him to strangers on the subway in Boston, to anyone who would listen. I couldn't seem to stop blathering
away. But a real lady like you wouldn't do that. She'd
suffer in silence, bothering nobody, stuck away in the
back end of a wood. Cait and I cried our eyes out for
you when news reached Mayo about your granddaughter. You and I never had any secrets during the war, Mrs
Fitzgerald. If you'd like you could talk to me.'

Maureen's fingers stopped stroking the cat and slowly
entwined themselves with Eva's gnarled fingers. Both
widows sat in a silence that was broken only by the cat's
peaceful breathing. Then Eva spoke.

'She was two months away from her fifteenth birthday
and so beautiful. You never saw a child like her, Maureen,
interested in everything, longing to embrace life. All the
girls in the boarding school in Dublin loved her. They
envied her going back to spend the summer with her
father in Kenya. It was such a simple thing to happen,

to get an insect bite. But they had no antibiotics and she caught a virus out there in the bush, too far away from any hospital. Everyone did everything they could, nobody was to blame. Everyone was heartbroken. I keep trying to be positive, Maureen. Alex will never face the problems that you and I have, she'll never grow old and lonely, she'll never lose her radiance. She was perfect and died perfect. I tell myself her death was quick and she didn't suffer much. But my heart is broken beyond repair. Ten years ago I had a son, a daughter and a grandchild. I would have endured any torment and given my life gladly to save any of them. It just makes no sense that I'm still here while all three are dead. Life is simply not fair.'

Eva's voice was quiet but she was crying. A kitten began to scratch at the door and Queensly stirred and stretched. Eva kept a tight hold of Maureen's fingers.

'But life isn't fair, is it?' Maureen said. 'It's not fair on those it takes and not fair on those of us who get left behind. What can we do?'

Eva relinquished her grip and rose to open the door and let in the kitten. The faintest trace of blood stained his paws. Out in the darkness he had been on a killing mission. Eva gazed out at the darkness.

'We can live our lives,' Eva said. 'What other choice do we have? These mornings when I wake up – no longer even caring if I wake up – I feel oddly free. It's a terrible freedom, but it's the freedom that comes from knowing there is nothing more that life can do to you, that fate can have no more tricks up its sleeve. I'm numb with grief, Maureen, I don't know if I'll ever feel warm again. But I'm afraid of nothing now. My sleepless nights are over because there is nothing left for life to snatch away from me.'

'Close over that door and keep out the cold,' Maureen replied. 'Remember the long nights during the war when we used to sit up talking, leaving the house only to fetch firewood? This time we can do the other way around. We'll sit out here on the lawn and only go into the house for firewood. There's enough wood there to get the stove going for ever.'

Eva laughed: a sound she had forgotten. 'Won't Cait be worried?'

'She'll think I'm off in Castlebar chasing after some bingo announcer with sideburns.' Maureen's smile could not prevent a glimpse into her own loneliness. 'Jack will have the telly blaring full blast at home. They can have a good bicker like married folk do and I'll not be missed. You can tell me your story, Mrs Fitzgerald, and I'll tell you mine. We're two old ladies going nowhere fast. We've all the time in the world now.'

Larry, Lay Down

Aifric Campbell

LARRY FOUND A HOBBY WITH EQUIPMENT, a counterpoint to the screens and the phones that yelled at him all day long. He bought a Canon Rebel second hand from B&H with a standard zoom, so he wouldn't have to get too close. But walking down Canal Street to his first evening class he felt conspicuous, the carry case banging against his hip.

Cool, said a voice by the noticeboard. It was a boy with crystal eyes, airbrushed skin and a tumble of golden curls. 'Languid' was the word that came to mind, the way the boy teased a slow finger along the protruding lens. The kind of word Larry's mother would use, the kind of way she would trace the spine of a book. The boy was modelling for 'Life, Advanced,' which was just next door to 'Photography 1' so Larry followed him down the corridor stealing glimpses at the cut of his jaw, the tender earlobe, all the parts of a magnificent whole.

Clicklick, said the boy at breaktime and framed his hands into an air camera. Larry fiddled with the lens cap. Come on, said the boy, arranging himself against the wall.

What, here? Larry gestured at the corridor, the passing students, but he could see already where he would crop, right there at the breastbone. Practice on friends and family, the teacher had just told them, take close-ups of your cat. But what if no one is available, what if you don't have a cat? Larry had wanted to say. Was this going to turn out like everything else where you're the only one who doesn't have what is needed?

Pardon me, a woman's hair appeared in the viewfinder. We're starting everybody, the teacher's voice called out through the open door. My number's on the board, said the boy, backing away.

The next morning in the office Larry found he could already see things more clearly. He was alert to the arresting visuals in the everyday: a spreadsheet slashed with red pen, a jacketed swivel chair, Janine balanced on the spike of one pump. Financial Controls was teeming with artistic possibility. He positioned the Rebel on the corner of his desk and studied its form, a squat polycarbonate Cyclops with rubber grip. This is the one for you my friend, Avram had pointed to the wall where Agassi smirked beneath his mullet. Image is everything, he jabbed Larry rather hard in the chest and threw in a polarising filter, introduced him to the world of accessories that he would one day need.

Larry trawled the city for hours on Saturday until he found a benched couple in Union Square. His heart fluttered over a bump, his mouth dry but oh, how they glowed on his cinescreen that night: the girl with neon flip-flops leaning back against the boy, the boy's lips grazing her hair. A scarf with thick beige bobbles covered her jeans like a fungus. So elated was Larry the next morning that he called unannounced to his mother's apartment with a fistful of lilies which she batted away, shielding her nose from the stink. He sat at the marble counter and placed the camera case centre stage while she poured green tea, but his mother did not seem to notice so he took out the Rebel, trapped her in the viewfinder. Put that away this instant, she shrieked, scrunching the satin robe to her neck and stared aghast as if Larry had dropped his pants.

It was a look he remembered from childhood examinations when he stood in shorts and singlet while she catalogued every feature that was not-hers. It was as if there had been a download failure that had robbed her son of the physical advantage that should have been his: the elegant frame of the ectomorph, the fine high cheekbone, the strong straight canines. Larry was a mean trick played by spiteful elves in the womb. And the plainest of babies, even Larry himself could see beyond the chubby smile.

At fourteen he was besieged by a plague of pimples so ferocious they resisted all medication. Dermatologists peered down at his face while his mother fretted in a Chesterfield. She insisted he max out on Accutane but the spots mutated into pustules that advanced down his neck where they would burst at the slightest touch, leaking gobs of green pus. She took him to a tanning salon and Larry muttered about skin cancer. Oh for Chrissake, she snapped, what would you rather be? Which was a question that seemed vast and unanswerable. That night Larry attacked himself in the bathroom mirror, squeezed and scratched until his face was pocked with blood. From then on it was mostly his mother's side profile he addressed, she shielded her eyes at the dinner table and then one morning he saw Gloria scuttle past with a breakfast tray.

Larry boarded a train to Schenectady, the Rebel snug by his side. Birch trees lined the track like spindles, a sunflashed storm raged behind his lids. But back home his daytrip was a paltry thing. The Hudson on screen was wide, brown and empty. A huddle of ducks looked staged, the pampas chaffed with gold was weedy and cheap. Nothing remained of the glory he had witnessed, his homage to nature was in tatters. There are things that happen in your life that feel scripted, a movie that might be made. Larry decided to stick with the human form.

He found the boy's number on the noticeboard, a page with feathered strips unevenly cut. His name was Harrison and he knew how to strike a pose. How to handle Larry's gasp when he slipped off his T-shirt to reveal 'Necrophilia' tattooed in blue across his hairless chest. Harrison was vague about why, and it wasn't clear if he even understood the word, it had been some other, older guy's idea when he was just fifteen. Which was three years ago in Buffalo where he had an uncle who'd lived there his whole life without ever seeing Niagara Falls. There was some kind of problem with sibilants, so Falls was Fallth and Harrison was Harrithon. But Larry liked the way this plumped his lower lip and he copied it himself later in front of the mirror, whispering 'lithp, lithp.'

At that first session Harrison had stood in front of him, fingers toying with the belt of his jeans. But Larry spoke sternly, so there would be no misunderstandings.

I just need a subject.

You going to thell the phototh?

No, said Larry astonished, for why would he sell what he had just found?

Harrison frowned, sucked on a beer. Larry said he would pay him for modelling, and Harrison seemed comforted by the idea of a transaction.

The flashgun startled them both. Harrison giggled, cracked another beer and fell asleep on the sofa. Larry stayed up arranging the photos on screen. Gave each jpeg the kind of caption he'd seen on wall tags. *Boy, reclining.* He lingered over the data, the time of capture, zooming in and out, but all the faults were compositional, the subject himself was blemish-free. Larry built a slideshow, made Harrison float and dissolve, ripple and fade across the screen. He added music, Coleman Hawkins, the kind of stuff his mother used to play at dinner parties where couples gathered round the long table in the state room, as she called it, underneath the chandelier.

When he woke the sofa was empty and Larry thought fifty bucks was missing from his wallet, but perhaps he was mistaken since the Rebel was still there along with Harrison's digital self. But it was exhilarating: to be robbed, to be rubbing shoulders with street characters, to have something that Harrison wanted. Really, it occurred to Larry, as he doodled through the month-end presentation, people's eyes had always seemed to slither over him as if they failed to find any feature worth settling for.

He braved the exhibition advertised on the notice-board, black-and-white shots of abandoned workshops in Arkansas, lathes and circular saws, old girlie calendars pinned to the wall. The photographer wore skinny black jeans, caressed a scrawny arm. Boniness was a feature of the arty crowd as if all this creation was burning them up. Harrison had some sort of supporting role, arranging a fan of leaflets on a table, serving drinks on a tray. Larry didn't usually like to linger but this time he did and eventually Harrison appeared by his side. Walking uptown Larry saw how people just couldn't stop staring. Harrison sat in a cowhide throne in the Royalton, and there was a parade of people he knew, a woman in red velvet, a man with a grey ponytail.

Doors slid open for Larry with Harrison by his side – tables materialised in overbooked restaurants, barmen begged for his order, the service industry was transformed. Everyone looks at you, said Larry, surprising himself with the sting of utterance. Harrison grinned, reached for the pretzels. How can you eat that stuff? said Larry. I mean just think. All those hands dipping in, where they have been. And anyway why *did* you cut loose from Buffalo? Harrison shrugged. It was hard to explain, longer sentences fatigued him so he relied on a repertoire of gestures. Larry saw a girl mutter something behind her hand to a friend who caught his eye, looked quickly away. The barman smirked knowingly. Larry would like to tell them all that there had been a girl once and that it was not unpleasant but it was not repeated. Melinda had slender wrists and a Labrador who got kicked out of blind-school training for underachievement. The framed certificate of release hung on the wall of her walk-in, and Larry was staring at it when Melinda told him there wasn't, like, *time*, you know. But what did that even mean? All these people speaking in unfinished sentences, like the whole world was contained in the gaps.

Two weeks went by, and Harrison missed 'Life'. Larry searched but Canal Street was full of transience and Harrison was not there. And then he reappeared outside Larry's building in the Tuesday dusk, nonchalant, as if this had been previously arranged. Larry showed him the new reflector. A huge white weightless moon that would illuminate his face, the gold on the other side to honey the skin. Hold still, he said, but Harrison kept on playing with the disc, twisting it into a mini circle and letting it spring back like a magic trick.

Harrison said he was going to Florida in December. Some guy who invited him and maybe a few others –

Harrison wasn't totally sure – to his pad in Key West. A pool with big plants tumbling into it.

You should theee the phototh!

And you're going?

Dude, I'm *there*.

Dude? Larry mouthed while Harrison sprawled on the sofa. And Larry recalled a raucous night in the Keys from his freshman year. A restaurant called Bagatelle and no one to be romantic with, the waitress swaying to the music with the smeared dishes stacked on her arm. An argument about manatees, how they were so impossible – those things, those flippers like stumps. It turned nasty somewhere near the Six Mile Bridge, a gas station where they stopped to piss and someone got left behind who might have been Larry. He can't remember if what he saw was the disappearing tail lights or the abandoned person receding. Time blurs history and memory spits up treasures and nasties that cannot always be recognised.

Do you even know this man? he wanted to say. Instead he gave Harrison a house key. A spontaneous offer that took him unawares but it was just a temporary arrangement to help him out between moves from one friend to another. And maybe to show him that Florida was not the only option. It turned out that Harrison could cook the most incredible stir-fry, and Larry adored that fresh feeling of welcome when he turned the key and the door swung open onto music and food. But often it was quiet with signs that he had been – a towel bunched on the floor, a dripping faucet, a shower of crumbs on the countertop. Not on Tuesdays, Larry had said, because Mariella came to clean – Cool, Harrison raised his palm. Larry wished that Harrison would stick to a schedule, this randomness was unnerving but he knew it was all good experience – his last 360 review had highlighted Larry's problems with empowerment and flexibility. Trust issues, his boss said. Just try to be more accommodating.

And Larry liked the way Harrison had just giggled about the wallet. Like he understood there was something special between them that could not be undone by a misdemeanour. He had a tripod now, it made him feel they were on safari filming wildlife as Harrison moued and played on the bed, the chair, while Larry documented the history unfolding in front of him.

The week before he left, Harrison lay on the rug with a sketch pad while Larry circled him with the Rebel. He said he'd always liked drawing, and maybe Larry could see something in the shading of a column.

Larry ambushed himself with a tattoo while Harrison was gone. He fussed over word size and position. The woman – underfed with tarry hair – yawned and pointed to his hip. He wrote down the word in careful capitals so there would be no misspellings. Her needle bit, like a determined insect or maybe a scorpion. It was almost more than he could bear, and Larry wondered if he needed to become accustomed to pain. You want it or no? The woman held out a little white pill. Normally Larry would never take anything from hands that could have been anywhere – but these were uncertain times, so he swallowed. You know, she paused to stretch, I did this guy yesterday, he told me in Bangladesh the kids don't get named till they reach their first birthday because the parents don't think they're going to survive.

Sad, he murmured, clenching against the pain.

She sighed, picked at a cuticle.

Harrison lost his curls in Florida, came back with a buzz cut that clung to his skull like a pelt. And there was something different in his performance. He pouted so close to the lens you could see pores. Larry did not like this, he did not like the way that Harrison touched the tripod with lewd suggestion, dry humping and mincing – yes mincing – around the room with his shirt off. There were purple bruises glowering beneath the golden skin but Larry was making the big leap from auto to manual and this took all his concentration. He muttered about f-stops. He wanted to do a long exposure using the dying light so Harrison had to remain absolutely still. He explained the problem with aperture and shutter speed but something kept Harrison in perpetual motion. The images on screen revealed a restlessness that suggested someone on his way somewhere. Larry thought of the souls in the dark wood, the crayoned picture he drew for his mother of the Seventh Circle of Hell when he was eight and still believed in the possibility of being adored. But Harrison was not a suicide, he was a beautiful boy with a speech impediment.

Since the Florida assignment Larry has been feeling brittle, the sound of twigs snapping. He keeps a noise simulator by his bedside so he can be soothed by a heart-beat or waves crashing on the shore. He drifts, remembers Nantucket summers, pootling mopeds and a hermit crab sinking into the sand, his mother stalking off towards the marina, the teetering marriage and a divorce narrowly averted when his father obliged with a heart attack. And suddenly, miraculously, Larry's acne beat a hasty retreat, leaving behind a minefield of scars and the hunched posture of the afflicted. As he trailed the casket out onto the street Larry wondered if this was his father's gift from the grave. But there was a trade-off: growth ceased and Larry stalled for ever at five foot seven, which rendered him invisible in the world of men. *Excuse me*, battling forward at bars and concerts and nightclubs. Girls looking over his head into the eyes of another.

Larry trudges through January slush to an exhibition on Washington Street.

Hey, check out the stripes. A girl with a silver wig points from Larry's sweater to a long rectangular canvas and then back again.

Wow, says another. An almost perfect match.

My God, where did you even get that? A twitter of girl laughter, like wind chimes.

If you lay down, says Silvergirl to Larry, you could be like part of the painting.

Cool, Harrison grabs Larry's elbow. A cluster gathers with a craning of heads and the artist himself turns to look.

Can he? Silvergirl spins round and pouts at the artist who nods grandly.

Lay down, Larry, Harrison nudges him.

Yeah Larry, lay down.

Larry takes a step backwards. Oh come on, it'll be fun, Silvergirl tugs his sleeve. A guy with a yellow bandana holds up a video camera and Harrison shoves Larry forward.

You need to be right *here*, says Silvergirl-choreographer, yep, yeh, right – okay now bend down, she prods him expertly the way the swimming teacher used to line them up for the high dive. There you go now.

And Larry is flat on his back on the floor blinking at the spotlights that twinkle high overhead and everyone peering down at him like the dermatologist chair again.

Shuffle up, *up*, right to the baseboard. Hands by your side, Silvergirl barks and the camera whirrs and people press closer, flip open their cells.

Oh it's so *funny*, and they're laughing, the faces looming over him, hair flopping forwards. Everyone knows him *now*, all these strangers calling Larry's name and taking his picture because he is part of it *now*. Harrison like a ringmaster corralling the crowd. Larry turns his head sideways and sees Silvergirl is wearing silver platforms and her toenails are navy velvet with little stars. There is a frigid rush of air down here and he closes his eyes.

But why exactly are they laughing, is it the sweater or maybe it is him, maybe they are laughing at Larry's cratered face? And then Harrison crouches down and straddles him and a rapturous roar goes up from the crowd. With one hand flung above his head like a cowboy Harrison grabs Larry's belt with the other and the girls are screeching Oooh and the shutters are clicking and the guy with the yellow bandana is circling like a buzzard.

Harrison's thighs lock Larry in a vice grip. Silvergirl tucks in snug behind Harrison, wraps her long white arms around him and the crowd urges them on. Harrison is bucking and thrusting now, Yippee-yie-yay, his shirt is open, the crowd is whooping and Larry is straining against all this friction, and he tries, he really does try to join in the fun of being ridden but his spine is banging against the floorboards, and he hisses, Harrison no, baring his teeth. But this is the bucking bronco performance of Harrison's life. Silvergirl pulls off his shirt from behind so he is bare-chested and gleaming when Larry screams GET OFF and jerks his hips upwards with a force he does not know he possesses. Harrison's head whips backwards, cracks into Silvergirl's face. The crowd gasps, then rushes forwards. Omygod, she is moaning behind covered hands, and Larry can see blood streaming from her mouth or her nose, he can't tell which. Harrison helps her up, her long legs splayed like a foal, then other arms encircle her and shepherd her away.

And all those who remain turn to stare down at Larry, crinkle their disgusted lips as if he was a turd on the floor.

ATH-HOLE, says Harrison and kicks Larry's thigh, hard enough to hurt.

Fucking creep, spits a girl with a red mouth and kicks him in the arm.

Larry groans, rolls onto his side, bends his knees and closes his eyes, tries to zoom out and away, wills his spirit to exit his body but it clings on, his Larryness, and he can see the photo, how it would be, *Man on floor*, as the footsteps recede and clatter away down the stairs.

Visiting Hours

Emma Donoghue

SHE SAYS SHE CAN'T, BUT that's what they all say. It's not that they're lying, they just don't know their own strength. It's a sort of humility, they bow down before the hugeness of the pain, they all say it at some point: 'I caaaaaan't.'

'You're doing great,' I tell her. 'You're marvellous. Big breath now.'

It's the visiting hours I find most interesting, actually. Not as exciting as the birth, of course, but they give me more to think about afterwards. The mum and the baby, well, that doesn't vary much (thank God, or nature I suppose). In nearly every case I've had – seventeen and freaked out, or forty-five and worn out – she stares down as if she's been looking all her life for this one face. As if she's scared by how much she loves these miniature fingernails, this chamois-soft skin, these purple heels already.

But the rest of them, you never know how it's going to go. Grannies who get proprietorial before the cord's been cut; I had one who wanted to catch the baby herself, but I told her that was my job. Other grannies who just ring in from the golf course. Aunts tight with jealousy, or dragging in five of their own (noses running). An uncle with the reek of whiskey off him, and lots of hearty granddads trying not to hear the gory details, and one who couldn't stop crying. ('It makes me feel so fecking old,' he said in my ear.) A toddler in an 'I'M A BIG BROTHER' T-shirt who had no idea what was going on; a twelve-year-old who looked like she would put a pillow over the newborn's head the minute they got home. And the dads – don't get me started. The tight-jawed and the high-as-a-kite, and some who check in with the office while waiting for the epidural to kick in. In my experience they don't faint like in films, but they bang into IV lines and knock the monitor belt off and yelp at the sight of blood. Or a trace of meconium, even more so; one of them ran to the nurse's station, roaring, 'She's shat all over the birthing ball!' I had one fella doubled up with what he swore were 'sympathetic contractions'. Most of them aren't in physical pain but would gladly lie down in front of a train rather than watch her go through any more of this. They make protests as if they're at some customer-service desk: 'Surely you can do something' or 'This is ridiculous.' Some of them are convinced that 'midwife' is a euphemism for 'student nurse', and they keep demanding to see the doctor. A couple of times I've had to send them out in the corridor, just to give the woman a breathing space.

So this morning goes great, she stays very calm, very quiet in herself. Some first-timers seem to know what they're doing as if it's their eighth. The dad keeps up the counter-pressure on her hips I showed him; he's speechless, wet round the hairline. Coming up to the second hour of pushing, she says something in a little-girl's voice.

'What's that, Marie?'

'She said she can't,' he tells me, almost growling.

'You're doing great,' I say to her, 'you're marvellous. Take a breath. I think you're crowning. Will I check again?'

'No time –' Her voice spirals up and up and up.

'Chin down,' I remind her, but I don't even get to say 'Push' before it's out in my hands. A girl, a shock of black hair on her.

Kisses and tears, the usual. She's lying on Marie's chest; he adjusts the little blanket over her foot. He – Joe, his name is – says in my ear, 'Shouldn't she be crying?'

'No hurry, sure there's enough of that in life.'

Afterwards is when it gets interesting. Joe stays for the afterbirth and the stitches and all, then he goes out. When I go to the nurse's station for some juice for Marie, I pass him talking on his phone: '. . . ten ounces, man, you should have been here! She was astonishing, jaysus, I'm in awe. Listen, Mick, come in the minute you get this –'

'No mobiles in here,' I mouth at him, and I'm thinking I've never heard anyone call his father, or father-in-law, 'man'. But then he does have a tattoo – a bird of some sort, under his left ear.

I'm helping Marie with the first latch-on, a while later, with Joe a foot away, his lips moving slightly as he memorises what I'm saying: 'Brush the middle of the upper lip with the nipple, that's it, till her mouth opens really wide . . .'

That's when I hear the ruckus outside the door. An English voice, loud and husky. ' . . . what I keep telling you!'

Joe straightens up – guiltily, I'd have said. 'Sorry, I'll just –'

He goes out, shutting the door behind him. I carry on helping Marie – 'move the baby, not the breast' – but her neck has stiffened; she knows what the altercation in the corridor is about.

'Course I'm immediate family, I'm the dad ain't I, technically?' That's not Joe, it's the other voice.

I pretend not to hear a thing. 'Brush her lip again, that's right . . .' The baby's falling back to sleep anyway, so I'm about to suggest we try again later when the door swings open and in comes the Englishman.

Leathers, piercings, the whole deal. 'Darlin'!' He presses a kiss on Marie's mouth.

'Howarya, Mick,' says Marie tiredly.

'Didn't our old groupie do well?' he asks Joe. He bends again towards the newborn, though without lifting his shades I don't know what he can see. 'Wow, so teeny, I nearly missed her. 'Allo, redface!'

'They're all that colour,' she snaps.

'No, but seriously, what a stunner! Welcome to the world, baby. Oi, she's got my hair.'

In the silence, I grab the bouquet (birds of paradise) off

the bed before it can spear the baby.

Joe's hovering like an uninvited guest. 'I can't believe you missed it, man. I know you wanted to be there, I left you a message as soon as she went into labour –'

'Didn't hear it till I got off the phone with Sherry,' Mick assures him. 'Seems to think I pay her fifteen per cent to sit around on her arse and tell me times are hard. And traffic was dire as per fucking usual.'

'Sure he's never been on time for anything,' says Marie. 'Remember all those soundchecks you and Niall and Dieter had to do on your own, Joe?'

Joe laughs and so does Mick. 'Crazy days, crazy days,' says Mick.

Marie's not laughing. 'I did think maybe you'd make an effort, this one time, for your own –'

None of them say anything for a second. 'Are you hurting at all, Marie?' I murmur.

'A bit. Cramps.'

'I'll bring you some ibuprofen. And a vase for these.' I just want to get out of that room, actually.

The Englishman has produced a small bottle of Veuve Clicquot from his trench coat and is scraping at the foil with one long nail. 'No alcohol on the ward,' I mutter in his direction as I brush by.

'Ah, just a toast to these two beautiful girls.'

'I'll wait for my painkillers,' says Marie.

'Which in my experience only double the kick!'

Her voice gets harder. 'You don't change, do you?'

'He's only having a laugh,' says Joe anxiously.

'It's hard to laugh when you've got six stitches in your perineum.'

'Spare me!' moans Mick.

Joe passes me at the nurses' station a minute later. 'Just going out for a smoke,' he says, raising two fingers to his lips as if I need the term explained.

'South Exit's the quickest,' I tell him. And then, wanting to set him a little more at ease, I add 'Smokers recover faster.'

'What's that?'

'They're back on their feet the day after the operation. Motivation!'

He doesn't just laugh, he lets out a jagged whoop.

It wasn't that funny. 'How're you doing, a bit shaky? Birth takes a lot out of –' I stop myself before 'fathers'. 'Big day,' is all I can think to say.

'That's putting it mildly. Never the same again!'

'Very true.'

'We won't know what's hit us when we take her home,' he says, as if answering the question I didn't ask.

'Ah, you'd be surprised; after a week you'll have the hang of it,' I tell him. Then, 'Go on, have your cigarette. I'll bring Marie her tablets.'

'She gave up the day she did the test,' Joe volunteers.

Painkillers? I think, horrified. And then, 'Smoking?'

'Yeah. Will of iron!'

'More power to her.'

He's still hovering. 'Gave up Mick the week after.'

'Ah, right,' I say, rearranging the flowers.

'He's cool with it,' says Joe, staring at the signs that say OBSTETRICS, DELIVERY, NICU. 'I mean, with me. You know, muscling in.'

It's a funny term for such a mild-mannered guy. 'Great,' I murmur, still fiddling with the flowers.

Then he wanders off in the wrong direction, towards the West Exit, and I head for the medication cupboard.

Marie is on her own when I go in. Well, apart from the baby, of course. I suppose I think of a mother and newborn as one person still, except on those rare, awful occasions when a woman puts her face in her pillow and says, 'Take it away.'

I have no intention of being nosy, but as I hand her the tablets and a paper cup of water I find myself asking, 'Your visitor left already?'

'A "lunch date",' she quotes, with a slight curl of the lip.

Does that mean she wants to talk about it? 'So is he planning to be . . . involved?'

'That's the idea.' She swallows her second tablet. 'Joe's idea, actually.'

My eyebrows go up.

'Mick had been off touring Germany. He's got a band called The Layabouts,' she explains. 'Joe was on keyboards, used to be. Now he's teaching.'

'Good lad,' I say under my breath.

She blinks at me.

'I have a soft spot for men who knuckle down to breadwinning when there's a baby on the way.'

Marie grins through her fatigue. 'Well, Joe said it was only fair to get back in touch, invite Mick to be . . . "part of all this".'

'Like, an actual . . .'

'Well, we still have to sort out the details.'

I nod, and stroke the baby's arm with my fingertip. Newborns always look oddly muscular in the shoulder.

'She'll live with me and Joe, of course. But he kept insisting it wasn't fair to leave Mick out. That if it was him, if it was the other way round, he – Joe – couldn't bear not to know his own child.'

But it never would be the other way round, I'm thinking.

'We haven't decided about the birth cert,' she adds uneasily. 'But Mick's keen. The way he freaked out, when I first told him – well, I've never regretted giving him the push. But just because he was a lousy boyfriend doesn't mean he'll make a lousy father, does it?'

'I suppose not,' I say, as neutrally as I can.

'The more the merrier, I suppose. I mean, the more people to love her.' And a tear drops on the swaddled baby, turning pale pink to red for a minute. 'Sorry to spill my guts like this,' says Marie unevenly.

'No bother.'

'You probably think we're all mad.'

'Oh, I've heard stranger stories, trust me. All shapes and sizes,' I add rather incoherently.

'It'll just take a bit of imagination, I reckon. A bit of goodwill all round.'

Good luck, I think grimly, tucking in the sheet, but I keep my mouth shut.

Marie sleeps a bit; whenever I put my head in, Joe – in the armchair – is holding the baby very still on his knees like a holy chalice of oil.

The Englishman shows up again later, heading into Delivery, and I guide him to Marie's room.

'Visiting hours are over in five minutes,' Sister reminds me.

'He's the . . . they're both the dads.'

Her thin eyebrows tilt. 'God help the child.'

For a second I think she's quoting Billie Holiday.

'Tattooed by its first birthday,' she adds nastily as she turns away.

I don't listen at Marie's door, but as I'm going past a few minutes later I hear a raised voice: 'No way!'

I let myself in quietly. Mick is holding the baby up like an award statuette. I want to tell him to mind the studs on his jacket.

'Not Jane, man!'

'I like it,' Joe is saying. 'We both do.'

'Ah c'mon, no child of mine is going to be a plain Jane! She needs something to make her stand out from the crowd in kindergarten. Garbo, I don't know.'

'Garbo?' Marie repeats incredulously.

'Charmian? Chaka Khan? What did Geldof call his – Fifi Trixibelle?'

'You're just taking the piss.'

'Jane's a family name,' Joe puts in.

'Which family?' Mick demands.

'Marie's.'

All at once the energy's gone out of the argument. I take Marie's pulse – which is high, but no wonder.

The Englishman bounces on his heels, whistles softly to the sleeping baby. He transfers her to the crook of his arm, strokes the back of one furled hand with his thumb. 'Whatever happened to Baby Jane?' he murmurs.

'Drop it, man,' says Joe. It's the first time I've heard him angry.

'C'mon, darlin,' grip it. Grip my thumb.'

'The grip thing doesn't kick in for a while, it says in the book.'

'Listen to Doctor Spock,' Mick sneers.

At which point I announce, 'Time's up, gentlemen. The ladies need their sleep.'

I expect Mick to object, or ignore me, but he purses his lips and puts a kiss on Jane's dark hairline. Handing her back to her mother, he says, 'It's been a trip.'

'I've sketched out a sort of schedule,' says Joe suddenly, holding up a pamphlet titled 'Bowel Function after Birth'. It's got a chart in pencil in the margin.

The other two stare at him.

'Just a few ideas,' he tells Marie. 'Mick could come in, like, once a week, and as she gets to know him he could take her off on walks, maybe. Or we'd go out on our own while he minds her. Then once she's, whenever she's weaned, there's no reason why he couldn't have her one night a week, maybe.'

'Right, see how it goes,' says Marie stiffly. 'Assuming he turns up on time and doesn't mess her around.'

Joe ploughs on. 'She could call you, I don't know, maybe me Daddy and you Dadda. Or should we be Joe and Mick?'

The air is thick with good intentions. I am cringing even before Mick gives a long, theatrical sigh.

'God, I love you, man. Both of you. You're family, you know? Always.'

Uh-oh.

'Thing is, I'm not sure how the actual hands-on stuff is going to fit with my plans right at the minute. Which bites, obviously. Sherry says if we want the corporate gigs, which is where the bucks are these days, then we really have to base ourselves on the West Coast for a while.'

'Like, Galway?' asks Joe.

I don't think he's being stupid, he's just doing his best.

'Like, LA.'

'I knew it,' says Marie under her breath.

I should be gone by now, but I can't move. I pretend to be adding something to Marie's chart.

'You knew he was moving to the States?' Joe asks her in bewilderment.

'I knew he'd fuck us over again, one way or another!' Marie's voice is shrill, but that's all right, she gave birth today. She's my patient, she can take a bedpan to this gobshite's head if she needs to.

Mick slips his shades back on and puts his hands up in one smooth pacifying gesture. 'When you guys got in touch, I was moved, you know? I thought I'd put the move off for a couple years. But I don't think that's going to be doable.'

'Do you not give a damn about her?' demands Joe.

'Marie? Sure I do.'

'Jane!'

'Yeah, yeah, Jane. She's a gem, she's the real deal,' says Mick with a regretful nod. 'But this whole daddy thing, it's not me. It just struck me today. I wouldn't want to get into it and then . . .'

'Not be able to get out of it?' suggests Marie icily.

' . . . arse it up. Ultimately, you know, you've got to do your thing.'

'What does that even mean?' Joe's speaking through his teeth.

'Stick to what you're good at, you know? Which for me is, like –' Mick strums the phrase on the air – 'rock 'n' roll!'

They are both staring at him.

'But hey, I'm gutted it's not going to work out. But you guys will do great on your own. No hard feelings, eh?'

'No harder than they ever were,' says Marie.

After he's gone, I say, 'Everyone all right?'

Both of them nod, like children.

'He's right. You're going to do just great.'

'The thing is, he's not even that good at rock 'n' roll,' Joe remarks, and our laughter wakes the baby.

Festus

Gerard Donovan

NOT LONG AFTERWARDS WHEN IT WAS all done, Festus
Burke understood that he went to the top of the hill
because he must have known what was going to happen
to him and the people in the town below, that peaceful
saucer of streets and bricks laid out below on the plateau
between the mountains and the coast. It was early morning and an ocean fog curled up to the first houses and
wrapped around the church spire. There hadn't been a
wind in days, but in the faint first light the white mist
scuttled on a breath coming up from the water, silent
and free over the empty streets. He sat and watched
quietly. Something was going to happen. It was the same
feeling that drew him directly to the hillside from his
house down below, his narrow bed in the top room
where the light rarely reached. But from here he could
see everything.

Around the mountain a river flowed under a stone
bridge, scratched in different seasons by hanging bram-
bles and strawberries: he followed along the silver string
where it flowed through the town before spending itself

into the waves. On the sea side of the town, the moor air mixed with salt along the strips of sand in small bays that sheltered idle boats, some tethered to the stone pier in the harbour. Like the river, a single road coiled down the slopes out of the wilderness and ran until it met the bridge and then the line of houses that led to the square.

He'd come up this morning, grabbing grass and roots until he met the trail that raised him in awkward steps to the sky in high mountain fields that sometimes rolled upward with bales of hay stuck in yellow pins to the stubble under a purple sky, in different seasons sometimes lines of green grass in ridges under calm weather. On the far side of the mountains, a flat plain of scrub and stones and sand stretched east, eight hours by car to the cities.

The bridge road was the only way in and out through the mountain. Another less-travelled road, flooded often in bad weather, went south to north through the town to swampy ground and the valleys. From the heights he saw laid bare the cross of both roads where they met in the town, and above fast clouds raced shadows under them, changing in seconds anything that might be recognised again.

Being up this high made Festus feel he could see into the past and the once prosperous town under that shifting mist, the throng of busy shops that used to be. In better times the town population swelled during the tourist season, when the good mountain road brought busloads of visitors into the desolate paradise across the barren miles. From a population of a thousand people, the town had dwindled to four hundred, and with Easter here, some of those were gone to relatives. The good times would come once more, he was sure, and only waiting would bring them again. Those buses would arrive once more out of the sky along that road and unload the gold of cameras and room reservations.

For two years a wild silence crept like vines across the fading fabric of that once famous place: the sinister hand that once kept this place remote had found it again. The fish were gone from the sea, the boats tied up. In those summers neither sun nor tourists had visited for any length of time. For those few who did arrive along that road, the town was a stop on the way to someplace else. One of the two hotels had shut, and the wide footpaths studded with sycamore trees and flowerbeds and benches were grown over with grass and weeds. Businesses were for sale or shuttered, and in empty houses curtains replaced the people who could not sell their properties and left to wait in other places for things to change. In their gardens 'For Sale' signs rode out the seasons like hardy flowers.

Festus sat quietly in the morning chill. The place had a deserted feel, not a soul that he could see. Because of the mist flowing up from the water and draping the buildings, he thought the town could be wearing a veil. Not many important moments ever came to him in life, and though better people might see that strange moving stillness as an accidental beauty of nature, Festus Burke saw it as a sign. This was a town that should never be allowed to change, it was perfect the way it was with the ocean on one side and a mountain on the other, safe from what lay beyond. A wind in his ear blew the scent of a yellow flower. Then he lay on his side on a crush of leaves and red berries that fell from a starving tree. In the stillness he watched the spreading roots of the mist and tried to understand what it meant before heading down the slope and changing into his working clothes.

He drove his small yellow Fiat with the practice of years along the road north to the fishing village on the coast, ten miles of tight bends and waving briars from stone walls, every gear change, every touch of the brake deep enough in him that he could daydream on the way. He passed the solitary police building with the blue lamp out front; once the town had its own police station, but it was shut down and moved north among scattered villages. Once a day a lone policeman drove through town vainly in search of crime before returning to the countryside and the building with the blue lamp.

The fishing village was grey and silent as Festus approached. He parked the Fiat near a tangle of nets and barrels beside a red trawler with rows of wooden seats in the hull that ferried tourists and goods out to the island, an hour's sail. He worked as a deckhand. It wasn't a job people wanted, but it was all he could get. You don't need a degree to fling or catch a mooring rope, to carry crates and bicycles and feed on and off board, to steer a hull to and from the same place sixty times a month.

Before he could hoist the gangplank to the trawler, someone shouted his name from the end of the pier. He followed the sound to the dark pub, where Ned Madigan the trawler owner sat at the counter in front of two glasses of whiskey and two beers already poured. The fireplace burned and the smell of a toasted cheese sandwich lingered.

'Listen,' Madigan said, 'there's no sailing this morning with the weather. We'll try this afternoon. Come, take off your coat and sit down.'

To Festus the weather was no worse than other days they had sailed, but Madigan was already drinking, and he saw no one on the pier, no groceries set in boxes or building materials stacked ready for loading. What Festus saw out the pub window was an empty concrete enclosure with an opening to the sea on one side, not the busy place it used to be on a weekday morning. The red trawler was tied up and still, bobbing in slow water, no workers hovering around it like gulls to ready it for sea. He felt the flames at his back and relaxed.

Fifteen years ago he got the job because Madigan was a friend of his father's. At that time Festus had just finished with school and wanted to save up and then do what was next, whatever that was. He did not have the marks to get into the college, he was slow with numbers and reading and thinking in general, and didn't want to do any more of it. The teacher took Festus aside and said that clever and intelligent were two different things and then told him his grades, Ds and Cs. He could learn a trade and travel the world. Remember that many famous people couldn't spell, the teacher said, and slapped him on the back and took the next fellow into the corner of the yard. Festus remembered seeing the other fellow's face fall at his results too, it was a bad day.

So all that time ago he began what was meant to be a summer job in this little village out the road north of the town, hauling crates and bicycles and groceries aboard at the pier and off again on the island. The money was good when he had none before. But somehow it became a winter job, and before Festus knew it, the first Christmas passed and he was still sailing the rolling seas out of the mouth of the bay. No trade learned, no travels, still living with his parents. More Christmases came, more springs, more long summer days. He postponed his future until it made itself clear to him. Every day he went to sea; every day his former schoolmates went to college and good jobs. They ran into each other less and less, and with less and less to talk about there was no glue, and the friendships of the classroom fell away. The country was suddenly doing well, everyone was busy and had more money and somewhere else to be, but he had the same money as before. Sometimes a life creeps up on you and it isn't the one you planned.

When the money dried up, his friends lost their jobs. Two years ago Madigan put him on a three-day week because there weren't enough tourists to even account for the fuel. The shorter week meant a little less money, since Festus owned the car he drove to work in and lived with his mother and did not have to pay rent. But then a two-day week tipped the scales: he had more time off work than on.

And today he'd turned up for work and there wasn't any, not one day.

The television hummed above the counter, a news item about deep-sea fishermen reporting something in the deep outwaters. A reporter said they had not seen ocean currents like this, they could not describe what they'd been seeing, but that something was wrong with the ocean. The camera turned to a fisherman beside his boat: 'The truth is I don't want to go so far out now, even if the fish was still all there, and they're not, and I don't trust that water.'

Festus and Madigan sat at the counter. Madigan said what a good man Festus's father was, always a hard worker and a quiet man. He ordered another round before rustling a newspaper for the news while Festus stared suspiciously at his drink. Something was wrong. In all the years at this job, Madigan never had him in for drinks, he liked to drink on his own. The man behind the counter polished the rim of a glass. The flames were the loudest thing in the room.

Madigan coughed and tilted the newspaper until half his face appeared, a lampshade of white hair circling the pink bulb of his bald head.

'By the way, Festus, I have to let you go. I'm sorry, but the work isn't there any more.'

Festus thought it was some joke for the morning. But no one was laughing, and the man cleaning the glass fit it carefully with a clink into a line of other glasses. Madigan had swung his axe, and the basket received a head. Briefly laid again on his shoulders, Festus heard that head speak:

'But I've worked here all my life so far.'

'I'm sorry, Festus, but that's it now.'

'You knew my father.'

'I'm very sorry.'

The newspaper covered Madigan's face again, the man behind the counter picked up another glass and held it to the light, twisting it in his fingers. Festus took the whiskey and finished it in one tilt, then walked down the pier and drove back home, swerving to avoid the drops that filled the hollows of the road under the bandage of low cloud. As the mountain took up more of his windscreen he refused to look at it. The mechanical action he'd performed countless times took over, every twist and turn of a familiar journey, and all for nothing, all for the last time.

Outside his house in town he parked the yellow Fiat and walked to the pub in the hotel and sat at the table nearest the fire.

He swung ropes at his thoughts to grapple them together, to fit them into his small panic. A drink appeared in a waitress's hand and he placed money into that hand. He stared out the window at the street, emptying his glass and getting another, drinking to a freedom he did not want. The rich sour taste that made a fish of his tongue did not remove the taste of his loss. Madigan could have let Festus work a single day a week, even for appearances, at least he'd still have the job when the tourists came back and the work was there again, he'd have kept something if not the job. Even if it meant no money. Something should be done. Festus raised the glass to his lips and did not know what should be done, but someone should do something.

Animals

Roddy Doyle

HE REMEMBERS CARRYING THE WATER tank into the house, trying to make sure he didn't trip over a step or a child. The boys were tiny. And the girls – the twins – must have been so small he can't even imagine them anymore. He can't remember filling the tank or dumping the fish into the water, but he sat cross-legged in front of it while the boys gave each fish a name and the eldest, Ben, wrote them in a list with a fat red marker. There were seven fish, seven names – Goldy, Speckly, Big Eyes, and four others. They taped the list to the side of the tank and by the end of the day there were black lines through three of the names and four fish still alive in the tank. The tank stayed in the room – in fact, George left it there when they moved house two years later – long after the last of the fish had been buried.

The animals always had decent, elaborate burials. Christian, Hindu, Humanist – whatever bits of know-ledge and shite the kids brought home from school went into the funerals. George changed mobile phones, not because he really wanted to but because he knew the boxes would come in handy – it was always wise to have a coffin ready for the next dead bird or fish.

He came home one Saturday morning. He'd been away, in England. The house was empty. Sandra, his wife, had taken the kids to visit her mother in Wexford. George put his bag down, went across to the kettle, and saw the brand new cage – and the canary. And the note, red marker again: 'Feed it.' And he would have, happily, if the canary hadn't been dead. He had a shower, phoned for a taxi, waited an hour for it to arrive and told the driver to bring him to Wacker's pet shop in Donaghmede.

– Are yeh serious? said the driver.

– Yeah, said George.

– What's in Wacker's that's so special?

George waited till the driver had started the taxi.

– Pets, he said.

He was pleased with his answer.

– All right, said the driver.

He went through the gears like he was pulling the heads off orphans.

Wacker – or whoever he was – had no canaries. Neither did the guy beside Woodie's. Or the shop on Parnell Street. When the kids got home the next day they found that the canary had turned into two finches. George explained it to them, although they weren't that curious; two of anything was better than one.

– A fella on the plane told me that finches were much better than canaries. So I swapped the canary for these lads here. A boy and a girl.

– Cool.

He'd no idea at the time if that was true – the male and the female – but it must have been, because they made themselves a nest, and an egg was laid. But nothing hatched. Sandra bought a book and a bigger cage and better nesting material, and the two finches became three, then five, then back to four, three and two. More funerals, more dead bodies in the garden. They got an even bigger cage, a huge thing on wheels. The finches, Pete and Amy – he knows the names, as solidly as his kids' names – built a nest in the top corner, a beehive of a thing. Amy stayed in there while Pete came out, hung on the bars of the cage and looked intelligent.

George went to his mother's house one day, to change a few light bulbs and put some old crap up into the attic for her. He made a morning of it, smuggled the book he was reading out of the house, bought a takeaway coffee, drove to the seafront and stayed there for an hour after he'd finished at his mother's, parked facing Europe, reading, until he got to the end of a chapter – *The Mambo Kings Play Songs of Love* – and needed to go for a piss. He drove home and walked into the end of the world. Sandra had decided that the morning needed a project, so herself and the kids had wheeled the cage outside and had started to go at it with soapy brushes and cloths. A child opened the hatch, Pete flew out, and George found four hysterical children in the kitchen, long past tears and snot, and a woman outside in the back garden, talking to the hedge.

– I can hear him, she said.

– Where?

– In there, she said.

She was pointing into the hedge, which stretched from the house to the end wall. It was a long garden, a grand hedge.

– I can hear him.

George could hear the kids in the house. He could hear lawnmowers and a couple of dogs and the gobshite three doors up who thought he was Barry White. He couldn't hear Pete. But he did hear – he definitely heard it – the big whoop of a great idea going off in his head.

– Listen, he said. I'm going to bring the kids to Wacker's, to see if Pete flew back there. Are you with me?

Sandra looked at him. And he knew: she was falling in love with him, all over again. Or maybe for the first time – he didn't care. There was a woman in her dressing gown, looking attractively distraught, and she was staring at George like he was your man from *ER*.

– While I'm doing that, said George, – you phone Wacker's and tell him the story. You with me?

– Brilliant.

– It might work.

– It's genius.

– Ah well.

It did work, and it was George's greatest achievement. The happiness he delivered, the legend he planted – his proudest moment.

All of the gang in Wacker's were waiting, pretending to

be busy. George carried the girls up to the counter; the boys held onto him.

– Dylan here's finch flew away, said George. And he was thinking that maybe he flew back here.

The lad behind the counter looked up from the pile of receipts he was wrapping with an elastic band.

– Zebra finch?

Dylan nodded.

– He flew in twenty minutes ago.

– Flaked, he was, said an older man who was piling little bales of straw and hay. Knackered. Come on over and pick him out, Dylan.

There were thirty finches charging around a cage the size of a bedroom. Dylan was pointing before he got to the cage.

– Him.

– Him?

–Yeah.

The older man opened a small side door and put his hand in. He was holding a net and had the finch out and in his fist with a speed and grace that seemed rehearsed and brilliant.

–This him?

–Yeah.

–What's his name again?

– Pete.

The new Pete wasn't a patch on the old Pete – he was a bit drugged looking. George liked the finches but they were a pain in the neck – the shit, the sandpaper, food,

82

water. He was halfway to Galway one day when they had to turn back because they'd forgotten about the birds and who was going to look after them; they couldn't come home – they were going for two weeks – to a stinking kitchen and a cage full of tiny, perfect skeletons. They found a neighbour willing to do the job and started off again, a day late. Sandra told George to stop gnashing his teeth; he hadn't been aware that he'd been doing it. The fuckin' birds. But then, another time, he was up earlier than usual – this was back home. He went into the kitchen and saw Dylan sitting in the dawn light, watching the cage, watching Pete and Amy. George stood there and watched Dylan. Another of those great moments. *This is why I live.*

George is walking the new dog. A cavalier spaniel. A rescue dog. He looks down at it trotting beside him and wonders again what *rescue* means. The dog is perfect, but it had to be rescued from its previous owners. He's walking the dog because he likes walking the dog and he has nothing else to do. His kids are reared and he's unemployed. He's getting used to that – to both those facts. The election posters are on every pole, buckled by rain and heat – it's early June and the weather's great.

The guinea pigs stayed a day and a half and introduced the house to asthma. George came home from work – he remembers that feeling – and the boys showed him the Trousers Trick.

– Look, they said, and brought him over to the new cage – another new cage. There were two guinea pigs inside, in under shredded pages of the *Evening Herald*. Ben, the eldest, opened the cage and grabbed one of the guinea pigs, and George's objections – unsaid, unexplored – immediately broke up and became nothing. The confidence, the sureness of the movement, the hand, the arm into the cage – the kid was going to be a surgeon. He held the guinea pig in both hands.

– What's his name?

– Guinea Pig, said Ben.

He got down on the kitchen floor. Dylan had grabbed the other pig and was down beside his brother.

– Look.

They sat, legs out and apart. It was summer and they were wearing shorts, and that was where the guinea pigs were sent – up one leg of each pair. George watched the guinea pigs struggling up the boys' legs, heard the boys' laughter and screams as they tried to keep their legs straight. Dylan sat up and pulled a leg down, to make room for his guinea pig to bridge the divide and travel down the other leg. It was a joy to watch – and Ben actually became a barman. That night, he started coughing and wheezing, and scratching his legs till they bled. His eyes went red and much too big for his face. They suddenly had a child with allergies and asthma and the guinea pigs were gone – replaced by the rabbits.

The first dog ate one of the rabbits. George wasn't sure anymore if it had been one of the first, original rabbits. He could go now, he could turn and walk to Ben's place of work, the next pub after George's local – a fifteen-minute walk – and ask him. It's early afternoon, and the place will be quiet. He can leave the dog tied to the bike rack outside, have a quick pint or just a coffee – the coffee in a pub with a bike rack is bound to be drinkable. He could do that – he has the time. But he doesn't want to seem desperate, because that's how he feels.

The Lost Decade – that was what the American economist called it, Paul Krugman, the fella who'd won the Nobel Prize, on the telly – a few weeks before. He hadn't been talking about the last decade; it was the next one. It already had a name, and George knew he was fucked.

The quick decision to get rid of the guinea pigs – George hadn't a clue now what had happened to them; something else he could check with Ben – had brought biblical grief down on the house. Ben had actually torn his T-shirt off his own back.

– It's my fault! It's my fault!

– Ah, it's not.

– It is!

They filled the car and headed straight to Wacker's. Did George ever go to work back then? His memory is clogged with cars, years, full of happy and unhappy children. Shouting at traffic lights, trying to distract the kids, getting them to sing along to the Pretenders' Greatest Hits, the Eurythmics' Greatest Hits, the Pogues' Greatest Hits. *We had five million hogs and six million dogs, and seven million barrels of porr-horter.* Sandra held Ben's hand and walked him around the pet shop, looking at his eyes. She kept him well away from the guinea pigs. She bent his head over a bucket of rabbits.

   — Breathe.

   — Mammy, I am breathing. I have to.

   — Let's see you.

George watched Sandra examining Ben's eyes, face. He was keeping the others outside, at the door, so they couldn't gang up on Ben if he failed the test and they had to go home empty-handed. But he could tell, Ben was grand. They'd be bringing home a rabbit.

They brought home three, and the dog ate one of them. He didn't *eat* the rabbit, exactly. He perforated the spleen and left it on the back step. The rabbit looked perfect, and even more dead because of that.

Suffer, your man Krugman said, when he was asked how Ireland should deal with the next ten years. Well, this is George, suffering.

Those years, when the mortgage was new and money was scarce, when the country seemed to be taking off, waking up or something, when the future was a long, simple thing, a beach. When he could hold Sandra and tell her they'd be fine, she'd be fine. The first miscarriage, her father's death, his own scare — he'd never doubted that they'd be grand.

He stands outside the pub, away from the windows — he doesn't want Ben looking out and seeing him there. He isn't even sure if Ben is on today, or on the early shift.

Gone. That certainty. It wasn't arrogance. Maybe it was — he doesn't know. It doesn't feel like a sin or a crime. He exploited no one; he invested in nothing. He has one mortgage, one credit card. One mortgage, no job. Seven years left on the mortgage and no prospect of a fuckin' job. He'll be near retirement age by the time they . . . *he* gets through the lost decade. He'll have nothing to retire from and the dog he's tying to the bike rack will be dead. And there won't be another dog. This one here is the last animal.

The girls found the rabbit on the back step and they went hysterical — everyone went hysterical. No one blamed the dog. It was his instinct, his nature. So George couldn't get rid of him. But then he bit Ben's best friend, and fuck nature; he was gone, down to the vet, put out of George's misery.

— It's for the best.

Goofy was the dog's name. Simon was the friend's. Simon was fine but the dog was a bastard. Refused to be trained. Stared back at George as it cocked its leg against the fridge and pissed on it. A bastard. And George hid it, the fact that their dog was a bad-minded fucker, the fact that maybe his family had created this monster. He got up before the rest of them every morning and mopped the shit and piss off the kitchen floor before they woke, had the place clean and smelling of pine when they came in for their Coco Pops and Alpen. When Goofy took a chunk out of Simon — when George heard about it, when Sandra phoned him at work, as he ran out to the car — he actually felt so relieved that guilt never got a look in. Two stitches for Simon, death to Goofy. A good bottle of Rioja for Simon's parents.

He didn't have to bury Goofy, or the unfortunate twit that came after him, Simba. George reversed over Simba – heard the yelp, felt the bump – jumped out of the car and, again, felt relief when he saw that it wasn't a child that had gone under the wheel. He looked around; he was on his own. He grabbed Simba's collar and hauled him to the front gate. He looked onto the road, thanked God that he lived in a cul-de-sac, and dragged Simba out to the road. Then he went in and told them the bad news; some bollix had run over Simba. And felt proud of himself as he wiped tears and promised ice cream and prawn crackers. He never told anyone what had actually happened and had never felt a bit of guilt about the cover-up. Although the oul' one across the road looked at him like he was a war criminal and he wondered if she'd been looking out her window when he'd dragged Exhibit A down the drive. But he didn't care that much, and, anyway, she was dead now too. There's a gang of Poles renting that house now – or, there was. It's been quiet over there for a while, and he wonders if they've left, moved on. There are stories of cars abandoned in the airport car park; the place is supposed to be stuffed with them.

He pats the dog. She's a tiny little thing, smaller still on a windy day when her fur is beaten back against her.

– Twenty minutes, he says.

He's actually talking to the dog, out on the street. He's losing it.

He straightens up. He looks down at the dog. He can't leave it here. It'll be stolen, the leash will loosen – she'll run out on the street. He can't do it.

He pushes open the pub door. He was right – it's quiet. It's empty. There's no one behind the bar. He waits – he doesn't step in. He wants to keep an eye on the dog. Then there's a white shirt in the gloom, and he can make out the face. It's Ben, his son.

– Da?

– Ben.

– Are you all right?

– I'm grand. I've the dog outside –

– Bring her in.

– I don't want to get you in trouble.

He shouldn't have said that – it sounds wrong. Like he's trivialising Ben – his job.

– It's cool, says Ben. I can say it's your guide dog.

He's come out from behind the bar. He's twenty-two but he's still the lanky lad he suddenly became six years ago.

– I'll get her, he says.

He passes George, and comes back quickly holding the dog like a baby.

– She had a crap earlier, George tells him.

– That's good, says Ben. So did I.

He puts the dog down, ties the leash to one of the tall stool legs.

– You sit there, he says. So she can't pull it down on herself.

– Grand.

George sits. Then he stands, takes off his jacket – it's

too hot for a jacket; he shouldn't have brought it. He sits
again.

– Quiet, he says.

–Yeah.

– Is that the recession?

– Not really, says Ben. It's always quiet this time. What'll
yeh have?

–What's the coffee like?

– Don't do it.

– No coffee?

– No. Nothing that needs a kettle.

– I'll chance a pint.

He watches Ben putting the glass under the tap, holding the glass at the right angle. He's never seen him at
work before and knows that he'd be just as relaxed if the
place was packed, the air full of shouts for drink.

– Everything okay, Da?

– Grand, yeah. Not a bother.

– How's Ma?

– Grand, says George. Great. Remember the rabbits?

–The rabbits?

–The hutch. Goofy killed one of them. Remember?

–Yeah.

He puts the glass back under the tap. He tops up the
pint. He pushes a beer mat in front of George. He puts
the pint on top of it.

– Lovely.

George gets a tenner out of his pocket, hands it out
to Ben.

– There you go.

Ben takes it. He turns round to the till, opens it, puts in the tenner, takes out George's change. He puts it beside George's pint.

– Thanks, says George. There were three rabbits, am I right?

– Yeah, says Ben. Not for long, but.

– What were they called?

– Liza, Breezy and Doughnut.

– And Goofy ate Breezy.

– Liza, says Ben. Why?

– Nothing, really, says George. Nothing important. It just came into my head.

The pint's ready. He hasn't had a pint in a good while. He tastes it.

– Grand.

– Good.

– Good pint.

– Thanks.

– Do you like the work?

– It's all right, says Ben. Yeah. Yeah, I like it.

– Good, says George. That's good.

He hears the door open behind him. He looks down at the dog. She stays still.

– Good dog.

Ben goes down the bar, to meet whoever's just come in.

George loves the dog. Absolutely loves it. She's a cavalier. A King Charles spaniel, white and brown. George loves picking her up, putting her on his shoulder. He knows what he's at, making her one of the kids. But she's only a dog, and she's doomed. George watched a documentary on Sky: *Bred to Die*. About pedigree dogs. And there was one of his, a cavalier, sitting on the lap of a good-looking woman in a white coat, a vet or a scientist. And she starts explaining that the dog's brain is too big – *It's like a size 10 foot shoved into a size 6 shoe*. The breeders have been playing God, mating fathers and mothers to their sons and daughters, siblings to siblings, just so they'll look good – *consistent* – in the shows. Pugs' eyes fall out of their heads, bulldogs can no longer mate, Pekingese have lungs that wouldn't keep a fly in the air. And his dog has a brain that's being shoved out of her head, down onto her spine.

He leans down, picks up the dog. He can do it one-handed; she's close to weightless.

Ben is back at the taps. Pulling a pint of Heineken for the chap at the other end of the bar.

The dog on George's lap is a time bomb.

She's going to start squealing, whimpering, some day. And that'll be that.

He won't get another one.

– Remember Simba?

Ben looks up from the glass.

– I do, yeah. Why?

– I hit him, says George.

–You never hit the dogs, Da.

Ben looks worried.

– No, says George. With the car.

– With the car?

– I reversed over him.

– Why?

– Not on purpose, says George. I was just parking.

Fair play to Ben, he fills the glass, brings it down to the punter, takes the money, does the lot without rushing or staring at George.

He's back.

– Why didn't you tell us?

– Well, says George. I don't really know. Once I saw it wasn't one of you I'd hit, I didn't give much of a shite. And the chance was there, to drag him out to the road. And once I'd done that, I couldn't drag him back – you know.

– Why now?

– Why tell you?

– Yeah.

– I don't know. I was just thinking about it – I don't know.

– It doesn't matter.

– I know, says George. But it would have, then. When you were all small.

– No, says Ben. It would've been all right.

– Do you reckon?

Ben looks down the bar.

– Listen, he says. We all knew we had a great da.

George can't say anything.

His heart is too big for him, like the dog's brain. The

blood's rushing up to his eyes and his mouth. Him and the dog, they'll both explode together.

Absence

Christine Dwyer Hickey

THE FIRST THING HE NOTICES is the silence. He's in the back of a cab, a few minutes out of Dublin Airport, on a motorway he doesn't recall; cars to the left and right of him, drivers stiff as dummies inside. And he thinks of the Mumbai expressway; day after day, people hanging out of windows, exchanging complaints or pleading with the sky. The outrage of honking horns. And the way, for all the complaining and head-cracking noise, there is a sense of something being celebrated.

Frank had known not to expect an Indian highway – youngfellas piled on motorbikes and leathery-faced old men wobbling along with the luggage on top of buses – but what he hadn't expected was this. This emptiness.

He has the feeling they may be going in the wrong direction and, when a sign comes up for Ballymun, wonders if the driver could have misheard him. Frank thinks about asking, but doesn't want to be the first one to break their silence. At the airport there had been a moment while lifting the luggage in, when a word might have been enough to start up a conversation. But a look had passed between them for a few tired seconds, and somewhere inside that look they'd agreed to leave each other alone.

He'd been expecting the descent through Drumcondra anyhow. Had it all in his head how it would be. The escort of trees on both sides, the black spill of shadow on the road between. There would be the ribbed underbelly of the railway bridge and then, where the light took a sudden lift, a farrago of shop and pub signs running down into Dorset Street. He'd been half looking forward to playing a game of Spot the Changes with himself.

A memory comes into his head then: a day from his childhood, upstairs on the bus with Ma. They were on the way to the airport, not flying anywhere of course, just one of those outings she used to devise as a way to keep them 'off the road' during school holidays. They'd spend the day out there, hanging around, gawking. At the slant of planes through the big observation lounge windows. Or the big destination board blinking out names of places that vaguely recalled half-heeded geography lessons. Or outside the café drooling over the menu where one day when Susan had demanded to know why they couldn't just go in, Miriam had primly explained, 'because it's only for fancy people.'

Miriam loved the fancy people – passengers with hair-dos and matching clothes. Johnny had no time for them; too showy off, he said, flapping their airline tickets all over the place, like they thought they were it. And because Johnny had felt that way, Susan and Frank had too. In any case, they preferred to look at the pilots and air hostesses who really were it, striding through the terminal, mysterious bags slung over their shoulders, urgent matters on their minds. Not a hair out of place as Ma always felt the need to say.

Upstairs on the bus – three kids kneeling up looking out the long back window. Ma sitting on the small seat behind. In the reflection of the glass her head sort of see-through like a ghost's. He'd kept turning around to check she was still there, with a solid head and real brown hair on top of it. Her hands were in their usual position – right one for smoking, left one for her kids: to stop a fall or wipe a nose or give a slap, depending. He'd been holding onto the picnic, the handles of two plastic bags double-looped around his wrist. Minding it, and making a big deal out of minding it too, because the last time when Susan had been in charge she'd left the bag at the bus stop. A low throb in his wrist, he'd the handles wound that tight and the farty smell of egg sandwiches along with the fumes of the bus making him feel sick and hungry all at once.

In the memory he doesn't see Susan, and this bothers Frank now as it bothered him then. That was the thing about his big sister; it was a relief when she wasn't with them, riling Ma up and agitating the atmosphere with her general carry-on. Yet he still always felt the lack of her. She was being punished most likely, left behind with one of the tougher aunties or locked into the boxroom for the day. Punished by exclusion. Because, as Ma would often say, 'slapping Susan was a complete waste of time.' Not that it ever stopped her.

And that's it – the memory. No beginning, no end, meaning little or nothing. Yet it still manages to catch him by the throat.

Frank leans forward, 'Actually, that was Ballyfermot I wanted, not Ballymun,' he says.

'Yeah, I know.' The taximan grunts.

The first Dublin accent he's heard, apart from his own, in nearly twenty years – and that's about all he is getting of it.

The roadsign for Ballyfermot gives him a start, like spotting the name of someone he once knew well in a newspaper headline. A few minutes later they are passing through the suburb of Palmerstown, and Frank is struck by the overall beigeness; houses, walls, people, their faces.

At Cherry Orchard Hospital, the traffic tapers to a crawl. The hospital to the right, solid and bleak as ever, and, still firmly in place, the laundry chimney that had been his view and constant companion during his three months there when he was a kid. He can feel Da now. Trying to get into his head, shoulder up against it, pushing.

They draw up alongside the hospital gate, walls curving into the entrance, and it comes back to Frank, the lurch of the ambulance that night, the pause and stutter of the siren as if it had forgotten the words to its song. And him coming out of his delirium just long enough to see snowflakes turning against the black glass of the ambulance window and wondering how come he was sweating so much when outside it was cold enough for snow. He had asked where they were and when the ambulance man said Cherry Orchard he'd thought it the loveliest name he'd ever heard.

The taximan tuts at the traffic then switches on the radio. A voice comes out talking about money. Another voice over a phone line, shaking with nerves or possibly rage. The taximan reaches out and switches the silence back on.

Frank remembers now the sound of the ambulance doors whacking back and the sensation of being hoisted up and lifted out into the darkness and the cooling air. And looking up into the muddle of snow he had got it into his head it was cherry blossom falling down on him.

He must have been ranting about it all during the illness anyhow, because after he got better Da bought him a book of the Chekhov play. He was a fourteen-year-old youngfella who fancied himself as a bit of a brain, mainly because that's what everyone kept telling him. Yet he couldn't get beyond the first few pages of what seemed to him a boring old story about moany-arsed people with oddly spelt names. He'd kept turning back to Da's inscription – *To Francis, my namesake, who, unlike the author, got out alive. With fondness, Frank Senior* – and trying to understand at the time, what the hell did it mean or why – why would his Da write to him like that? Like he was a grown-up, like they were strangers?

The taxi begins to move again; the cars break away from each other, and Ballyfermot comes into view. Frank looks out the window. As far as he can see, nothing much has changed, apart from one modern-looking lump of a building further down the road. It looks like the same old, bland, old, Ballyer that it always was. Rows of concrete grey shops under a dirty dishcloth sky. Even the weather is utterly familiar: stagnant and damp. The threat of rain that might or might not bother to fall.

He can't remember the address. Not the name of the road, not even the number of the door – it just seems to have fallen out of his head.

He can remember everything else though, that the road is long and formed into a loop and that the house is on the far end of the loop. And that the turn for the road is coming up soon. He begins to feel queasy; in his gut, the Aer Lingus breakfast shifts. And he wonders again, as he wondered while eating it, what had possessed him to order it, because it certainly hadn't been hunger. Nostalgia then? For what? Sunday mornings, bunched up together in the little kitchen, steam running down the walls? Or Saturday nights when Ma and Da would come rolling home from the pub. Ma slapping rashers onto the pan. Da voicing the opinions he hadn't had the nerve to express in the pub, hammering them out on the formica table. Ma agreeing with each revision, laughing at just the right moment. The waft crawling upstairs into Frank's half-sleep: black pudding, burnt rashers. Shite talk.

He presses his fingertips into his forehead, rotating the loose flesh against the bone of his skull. The skin on his face feels greasy and thick for the want of a shave, and even though his nose is stuffed from the flight he can tell he doesn't smell the sweetest. He should really go to the house first, clean himself up a bit. A quick shave, a change of shirt. But he isn't ready for the family, the neighbours – all that.

'What time is it there?' Frank asks the driver, whose finger even manages to look sardonic when it points to the clock on the dashboard. Frank looks down at his own watch, sees that it agrees.

Three minutes to eleven. All he has to do is say, 'if you wouldn't mind taking the next right – just up along here.'

He holds the sentence in his head for a moment. But the car skims past the turn and the moment has gone.

The taximan speaks, startling Frank with the sudden rasp of his voice

'Where to?'

'Oh. Let's see, you know the church just up the road there? If you could just – .'

'Right.'

'Actually, maybe if you could, you know, pull in around the corner down the road a bit and – .'

'Right.'

'Or?'

He sees the eyebrows go up in the rear-view mirror.

'No, that'll be fine. Down that road there, near the school, grand, that's grand.'

The car takes the broad corner, passing the slate-grey church. Frank looks down at his feet.

The shock of the taxi fare – he feels like saying, Christ you could travel from one end of India to the other for that. He hands over a note and says nothing. The taximan picks up a pouch and begins pecking at coins. He opens it wider and peers down into it. 'You home for good or a holiday?' he mutters as if he's talking to some little creature in the bottom of it.

'A fortnight,' Frank says, holding out his hand for the change.

'Listen – I do the airport run, so when you're headin' back – give us a shout – right? I'm only down the road. And I'll do you a good deal,' he pokes a business card at Frank, 'off the meter like.'

'Oh thanks,' Frank says, 'that's good of you.'

The taximan shrugs – 'Yeah, well, business is crap, is all.'

Frank slips the card into his pocket.

He pushes the haversack back into the seat, opens the front zip and edges his hand in. The haversack is bloated; the space is tight. He can feel the taximan watch as he rummages around. He pulls out a black tie, bit by bit, holding it up for a moment like a dead eel between his fingers. Through the mirror their eyes meet. The taximan nods. Frank nods back

On the kerbside he goes to work on his tie, slipping it under his collar, sliding the ends into place, planning the next little tie-making step in his head. He considers his entourage; one large suitcase bandaged in plastic – courtesy of Mumbai airport security – and one bulky brown haversack plonked down beside it. His most recent mistakes scurry like mice through his head. Why hadn't he replied to Miriam's email, told her he had decided to come? Okay, if he couldn't face the house, but why hadn't he had a shave in the airport? Or, at the very least, why hadn't he thought to get out at one of the pubs down the road – had a wash, a quick drink to steady the nerves, maybe even asked the barman to hold onto the luggage for a while? Why? Why? *Why?*

Frank stops. From the school across the road comes the flat chant of children's voices. Choir practice. A phrase is repeated three, then four times. In between a woman's voice calls out – 'Again. *And* again. Now and *gooood.*' He imagines her lifting her hands, holding the blend of voices and notes on her palms for one perfect second before letting them slip through her fingers. Frank thinks of his first job in India when, as a young teacher, he was railroaded into taking choir practice even though he hadn't a note in his head. His hands shaking as he tried to remember the hurried instructions the headmaster had given him. Dozens of keen brown eyes following his every move. Until suddenly he'd just got the hang of it. The pleasure then, in the power of his least little gesture. The music passing back and forwards between himself and the children. Waves of sound on a small ocean. Every child bursting to please. One boy, an awkward child, had frightened him with the intensity of his emotion. His name gone now, but the face still there. The boy had his arm in a sling – he was a child who always had something bruised or broken.

Frank stands listening to the end of the song. His mind settles. He completes the knot in his tie, patting it into place.

A few minutes later, he is struggling through the doors of the church; suitcase before him, big brown haversack like a chimpanzee up on his back. Frank keeps the boy in the choir in his head – the gapped front teeth, the flap-away ears, the sling on his broken arm stiff with dirt. He pushes the luggage into a back corner under the balcony floor and then steps into a nearby pew. Dilip – that was the name of the child. One day he just stopped coming to school – vanished. Nobody seemed to know where or why.

The interior of the church settles around him. There's a chill, musty odour on the air: old incense and decades of sweat. He glances up – the coffin catches his eye. Too small. It seems way too small for Da. Da had been a big bloke, tall with plenty of meat to go with it. Unless he had shrunk?

Frank sits down and begins sidling along the empty pew, moving in fits and starts, as if making room for people behind him. He takes Miriam's email from his pocket and reads it again.

Frankie, I'm sorry to tell you Da passed away yesterday – a sudden death. He was gone before he hit the
ground so at least there was no suffering. I hope this
message gets to you Frankie. I got the address through
the embassy who got it from the old school where you
used to work and they've agreed to send it to try to
locate you. It's the only way I have of contacting you.
Anyhow I'll hope for the best. Frankie, Ma is not well
at all and it would mean a lot to her if you were here.
She's an old woman now and what happened, well it
was a long time ago Frankie. Anyway, I'll leave it there.
It's been such a time, I really hope you can make it. But
try to let me know, Miriam.

Frank folds the email back into his pocket and moves
up another space. Maybe all men feel this way in the end,
he decides, that the coffin built for their father is built for
a lesser man.

Beneath his line of vision he can make out the front-
row mourners; banked together, solid and dark. Yet he
can't bring himself to look directly at them, knowing
full well that if he does he won't be able to stop himself
from guessing who owns which head on whose shoulders, these people he would have grown up with, these,
now, strangers.

He can't find anywhere to put his hands. He tries
clasping them in front, then shoving them into the fold
of his arms, then down into his jacket pockets. Finally, he
grips them onto the bar of the pew in front.

The priest's voice drifts into the echo. 'If I speak in the tongues of men and of angels . . .' And suddenly he thinks he sees Susan. It comes into his head that she's over there, on the far side of the church and that if he were to turn and look he would find her: hair tied back in a long black ponytail, dark-green coat on her straight Irish dancer's back. He feels a bit shook – disabled, almost. As if his legs don't belong to him. His stomach is bouncing. The breakfast churns. Air. He needs air.

Outside in the grey light he loses his bearings – morning or evening? But if it were evening it would have to be dark by now.

In the middle of the churchyard, the hearse is waiting, big square jaw open at the back, ready to suck the coffin in. A long Mercedes car for mourners is parked a little way behind it. Two funeral attendants stand nearby, heads close together, under-breath laughter and a night-before story. They see him and break apart; soft sprung steps taking them off in opposite directions. They remind him of FBI agents: the height, the long black coats, the haircuts, the inscrutable faces. And the broad shoulders of course: coffin ledges. The Mercedes has three rows of seats and Frank wonders why they should need so many. It comes to him then, the whole shape of the family will have changed by now: a husband, a wife maybe; sons, daughter, nieces, nephews; grandchildren.

It begins to rain, sharp little pins on the skin: not heavy but spiteful, he'd forgotten Irish rain could be like that.

One of the attendants opens the boot of the car and begins easing out large black umbrellas. The bell tolls; a slow funeral toll. Frank presses the collar of his jacket into his neck and moves around to the side of the church, staying close to the churchyard's boundary wall. He notices long marks scrolled on the concrete; piss stains or rain stains, he can't decide which.

In a few minutes' time Da will be carried out, and he wonders whose shoulders will bear him; Johnny, the uncles, the cousins? Maybe they'll leave it up to the funeral attendants. Not that it really matters, who takes him out, who sinks him into the clay. In a short time he'll be gone anyway. Worm meat, as Advi once said.

Out of sight now, Frank steps into the alcove of the porch on this side of the church. A favourite spot when he was a kid; the door always locked – a place to see without being seen, to smoke and slag anyone who passed through the gate. He misses the smokes now, the company of them, the distraction.

He needs to think. But his mind is already blocked up with too many thoughts: his first monsoon in Bombay; Advi's father's funeral; the girl in the church with the dark-green coat; Da's coffin; the worms wiggling in the ground in a knot of greedy anticipation; the green coat again.

He comes back to his first monsoon:

Up on the flat roof with Advi and Gopal. Stoned, of course, which had lit up the details and made everything seem oh so profound. Advi's father not long dead. Frank not that long in India. The sky one minute a hearth of orange and red, the next splitting like skin on an overripe fruit. In a matter of moments, people on the streets below were wading through water; schoolbags and briefcases over their heads. It was high tide, and across the rooftops they could see the Gateway of India bashed by sea waves. It had looked like a ship out at sea. Youngfellas making a run at the waves, spindly legs and arms frantically waggling. After a while, all visibility was lost to a thick dirty curtain of rain. They squeezed under the shelter, a sort of makeshift construction on the east side of the roof, Frank rolling another joint, the other two telling funeral stories. At first he hadn't been sure if they were having him on – Advi with his vultures, Gopal with his burning widows – although by then, even just a few short weeks into his first year, nothing would have surprised him about India. Advi told them that when his father died he was laid out on a slab at the top of a tower, under an open sky. Vultures looping overhead. The Tower of Silence, this place was called. The name alone had chimed in Frank's head. 'You mean you don't put him in a coffin?'

'Oh no, no. Just lay him out naked.'

'Not a shroud or a blanket or something?'

'Nope. Total birthday suit, man. Go out as you've come in.'

'And the vultures actually, you know, actually?'

'Eat him?' Advi said, 'they pick the bones clean – yum, they love it. It's the Parsi way.'

The idea had horrified Frank and he said so.

'Oh come now really – what difference does it make?' Advi asked, 'coffin or not? Above the horizon or below? Worm meat or vulture feed? We're all fucked by then anyhow.'

It was the funniest thing they'd ever heard – or at least the dope had made it seem so. The three of them fell on the ground laughing. Advi and Gopal had rolled out from under the shelter. Frank had very nearly pissed himself, could hardly move, or even see. Except for the odd glimpse through the beating rain – of a coffee-coloured face, a crescent of gleaming teeth, clothes plastered on two slender bodies, a hand reaching out to touch a blue-black head of glistening hair. And, of course, the first brief crossing of his mind that there may have been something more than friendship between his two new Indian friends.

Frank sees a man walking towards him, coming around from the front of the church, huddled into himself, smoking a cigarette. He can feel the man watching him. The step slows, and now he's standing right in front of him, uttering a cautious 'Frank?'

A small bloke, legs like two sticks in denim; could be any age from forty to sixty.

'Frankie, is that you? Jaysus it is.' The man smiles, showing a bar of brown teeth. 'Ah it's great to see you it is, great you could come man, you look bleedin' great you do, like a – I don't know – banker or a politician or some big bleedin' shot inanyway. How've you been? *Where've* you been even? Like everyone thought you were – you know – *dead*.'

The man's handshake is weak, his voice has a woman-ish whine to it. Frank tries to find a place for him in his memory. A neighbour? A friend of Johnny's? A relative then? Whoever he is, he stinks of last night's beer.

'Sorry, to hear about the Da, Frankie, and that. I know now, we had our differences but, like, he wasn't the worst.'

'Thanks,' Frank says.

'I wouldn't mind but I only seen him the other day. Ah yeah. We passed each other on the road like. I didn't speak to him or nothin' but he looked great, he did Frankie.'

Over the man's shoulder Frank sees the churchyard filling: legs, elbows, a bloom of black umbrellas. There's a smell of cigarettes, little hums of reverent chatter. He is struck by how big everything is: the cars, the people – especially the people.

The man squints up at the rain then edges in under the lip of the roof. He starts talking again. 'Here, Miriam was only sayin' about you last night at the removal and that the way she didn't know what to do about finding you and all and she'd sent a whatyoucallit email and was –.

'I've only just arrived, haven't had a chance yet to – how is she anyway?'

'Well, like I wasn't actually talkin' to her meself, I sort of more overheard her like. She was a bit upset about poor old Susan and that. Brings it all back doesn't it – a funeral?'

'Yes, yes, it does.'

'Ah, she was a lovely girl Susan. A bit wild, but sure so fuckin' wha'? Here, where is it you are now inanyway – Australia or somewhere is it?'

'India.'

'India! Jaysus, what the fuck are you doin' there? India! Ah, don't tell me Frank – smoker's paradise, eh? I mighta bleedin' known. Ghanji on the Ganges and all that – wha'?'

'Ah, I gave that up a long time ago. I live there now.'

'Oh. And what do you do there, like, how do you spend your time?'

'I work.'

'Oh right, yeah.'

'I'm in education.'

'Ah, you always had it up there Frankie,' he tips the side of his head, 'so what are you, like a teacher and that?'

'I used to be a teacher. It's more administration now. For a charity.'

'What like, you work for nothin'?'

'No. It's, it's difficult to explain.'

'Oh,' the man looks away, disappointed or embarrassed, Frank can't tell which.

He can't find the hearse – the crowd, the brollies, have blotted it out. He's beginning to think he's missed Da's exit when the murmuring voices suddenly stop, and, although he can't see the church door from here, he can tell the coffin is coming out. The crowd parts; a space is made around the hearse, and he sees the high-gloss finish of coffin wood. There's a funeral attendant at each side;

shoulders of experience keeping everything steady. The rest of the pallbearers are of uneven height. Something familiar about one man: the shape of the profile, the dip of the head. The coffin is hoisted then lowered towards the opened back of the hearse. It still looks too small.

The funeral attendants stand aside, and he can see now the man who had looked familiar is Johnny. He watches his brother pass through the crowd to the far side of the churchyard joining two men by the railings. He looks old – older than he should do anyhow. Hands in the trouser pockets of a suit that is way too big for him. He doesn't seem to notice the rain. He reminds Frank of a chicken, the way he stands, half talking to his mates, half looking around with a hungry, twitchy eye.

'For how long were you there inanyway, Frankie?' the man says then.

'In India? About twelve years.'

'I thought you went, you know, after Susan?'

'Well, yeah, I went to London first, then India.'

'And you never went back to the old house after – you don't mind me askin'?'

'No, and no I didn't.'

'Ah they done it up lovely after, Frankie. Brand new. Not a mark on it. Your Ma does keep it like a little palace, she does. Ah look – there's Miriam now. Looks great, doesn't she Frankie?'

He sees her then, a middle-aged woman, well preserved, well dressed. A tall man beside her, obviously the husband, two tall sons who are almost men.

'She done well for herself. Married a solicitor, she did. That's him. Kids go to college and all. Are you married yourself Frankie?

'No.'

'Kids?'

'No.'

'Not that you know of inanyway – wha?' the man nudges the air and gives a little laugh.

'No.' Frank says, 'I've none.'

The man lights another cigarette then takes a step closer to Frank. There's something needy in the gesture like he's desperate to hold onto his company. Frank looks away. He sees Ma now. He sees her standing close to the hearse surrounded by aunties who are buckled with age. Miriam's husband is holding an umbrella high over her head. Her face. Her face, when he sees it. Not as old as he'd expected but just as hard. A man comes up to pay his respects, she rests a hand on his arm. Her slapping hand. He can't look at her face anymore, only the hand. He thinks of it now, as a separate entity, cleaning and polishing windows, doors, brasses, removing stains only she can see. He thinks of the sound of it slapping a leg, a face, folding into a fist to punch the back of a head. Or half drunk and slightly off kilter, flipping rashers onto the pan and later all floppy on the edge of the sofa, trying to smoke a cigarette. He thinks of it turning the key in the lock of the boxroom door.

'Susan wasn't wild,' Frank says.

'No?'

'She was different.'

'Oh yeah, well I didn't mean like –'

Frank listens to the man beside him sucking on his cigarette, hawing it out in sharp short breaths. After a minute he turns back to him, 'were you thinking of going up to the graveyard yourself?'

'Ah you know me Frankie, I wouldn't like to intrude and that. I'll probably just go to the fuckin' pub after. Pay me respects then, you know?'

Frank looks at his thin face, cold sores around his lips, skin on his hand, mauvish and blotched, his lip struggling with the tip of the cigarette. 'Look, could I ask you to do me a favour?' he says.

'Sure man, of course you can. Just name it.'

Frank reaches into his pocket and pulls out a fifty euro note. He holds it towards the man. 'Could you keep it to yourself that, well, you know, that you saw me here.'

'Ah, you don't have to give me that, Frank, honest you don't.'

He can see the man's hand is trembling to take the note. Frank presses it into his fingers. 'No, go on, really. Take it. Have a drink on me, I want you to. Just don't say anything about seeing me.'

'Sure Frankie, if that's what you really want?'

'It's just. I mean, I just –.'

'All right Frankie, yeah, I know. I know. All right.'

The man scratches his face, then his hair. 'You haven't a fuckin' clue who I am, do you?'

'I'm sorry,' Frank says.

He shrugs and lifts his hand as if to shake Frank's then seems to change his mind and settles on a half-salute. Frank watches him go, head down, shoulders hunched, scuttling close to the churchyard wall.

He looks over the geometry of the churchyard, the arrangement of angles and shapes: each in his own little section. The funeral attendants, who look like FBI agents again, are sending out silent instructions. Everything shifts, everyone moves. There's a sound of car doors slamming, the spark-up of individual engines. A black-haired girl in a green coat hurries across the churchyard, dashes the butt of a cigarette to the ground and hops into the back of a car. The green coat he saw from the corner of his eye in the church. Not really like Susan, after all. Nothing like her, in fact.

The hearse budging towards the gate now, the coffin inside it snug between glass and chrome – a perfect fit. The long Mercedes, filled with shadows, following behind. They pass out onto the road, skim the far side of the railings, then disappear.

He imagines the hearse, the cortège behind it, skirting the roundabout, gliding past the school, the shops, the pub on the corner before taking the turn into the road where Da lived all the days of his married life.

He can picture the hearse nosing along the slow endless curve past the squeeze of houses he'd counted every day on his way home from school and the railings he'd sat on and the gates he'd swung out of and all the kerbs he'd battered with footballs, and later then, much later, the hundreds of windows behind their veils of net that had followed him like eyes behind burkhas, during the black weeks and days, after Susan.

Frank takes the taximan's card out of his pocket. He waits a few minutes for the churchyard to drain – of people, cars, sound.

Leaving for Kenosha

Richard Ford

IT WAS THE ANNIVERSARY. WALTER HOBBES WAS DRIVING uptown to pick up Louise at Trinity. She had the dentist at four – a cleaning, and her night guard adjusted – then the two of them were slipping off for a ridiculously early dinner at the place she liked. Cyril's, out the Chef Highway, a higgle-dee-piggle roadhouse on stilts that the hurricane had comically missed. Later on they'd go back to his condo for Louise's homework and a Bill Murray movie. This was New Orleans.

It was his day for Louise. Betsy, Louise's mother, was driving out to appraise subdivision plats in Mississippi, then was sleeping over at Mitch Daigle's across the lake. Which meant Ultimate Mojitos and maybe a joint and some boiled shrimp. Hobbes had been divorced a year. Betsy'd 'fallen in love' with Mitch while showing him a house – an anniversary present he planned for his wife. An anniversary that hadn't quite come off. Now and then Walter saw Mitch's ex-wife Hasty, at the Whole Food. Once a great, auburn-haired, husky-voiced Alabama stunner, a former Miss Something at UAB,

117

she'd grown now sturdy in her young middle age. In the Whole Food she'd looked at Walter resentfully, as if he'd sent his wife to commit espionage on her less-than-perfect marriage. Once, he'd turned unexpectedly, and there she was in front of the lettuce, artichoke and celery bins. He'd instantly smiled while a silly, dauntless smile had begun on her face, too. But then her shoulders sagged. She pursed her lips, shook her head in frustration, her chin turned down. She put a ringless palm out in front of her like a traffic cop – keep away – then she pushed her green basket along, leaving him where he stood, as the sprinklers all came on at once.

'We observed a moment of relative silence today for the poor flood victims,' Louise said. They were driving up famous Prytania Street, past the French Consul's gated residence, with the drooping tricolor out front and the big black Citroen in the circular drive. Outside the air was ninety-eight, but with the a/c going it was pleasant enough. Kids with their uniform shirt-tails pulled out were pranking along the steamy sidewalk, gesticulating and laughing raucously. The privileged from another private school nearby. The dentist was close.

'Did any of your classmates lose someone?' her father asked.

'I suppose so,' Louise said. Louise was in the sixth and knew everything about everything. 'Ginny Baxter – who's black. She and I both opened our eyes at the same time and almost laughed. It was like everybody was praying, but they weren't of course. It was weird.'

'Did you remember your device?' Louise's 'device' was her night guard, which she was having adjusted by Dr Finerty. She'd begun grinding at night and in the daytime, too – when night guards weren't socially plausible. Finerty believed this to be a result of her parents suddenly divorcing when Louise was exactly ten years and two months old. Louise had shared her belief it was a result of the hurricane. Though any child grinding her teeth seemed a small, unrecoverable tragedy.

Louise sighed a profound sigh, placing her two small hands in her lap and twiddling all her fingers like a librarian. She ignored her father's question about her device as if it was a subject too delicate to discuss. 'I have two requests,' she said, riding along.

'The court will entertain two requests.' Hobbes was a lawyer, of course. 'As long as one of them isn't skipping the dentist.'

Louise liked the dentist, who was a jowly round-belly Irish jokemeister who went on Catholic retreats in the woods where he read Kierkegaard and Yeats, sat alone, and thought long about Thomas Merton. Louise thought this was bizarre but interesting. Finerty was divorced, too, from a pleasantly round Presbyterian woman who'd years ago returned to County Down without directly explaining herself. He always complimented Louise on her beautiful white teeth, which she enjoyed hearing.

'Ginny's family is taking her out of school after today. They're moving away. I want to take her a sympathy card or whatever, and say goodbye. She'll be gone tomorrow.'

'That's very considerate of you,' Walter said. School had been going less than a week, and already this was happening. Louise allowed nothing about his commenting that her consideration was a nice feature. She had her hands deep in her knapsack now, digging out the green plastic case that held her night guard. They were on the dentist's street. Amelia, off St Charles. A big apartment block. A Chinese take-out. A Circle-K. 'Why're they leaving now?' He was angling the big Rover in at the curb. He intended to sit in the waiting room, read *Time* magazine, then chat up Finerty about red-fish fishing off Pointe La Hache (which they never did together), discuss the euro and the Catholic Church – all, once Louise was finished.

Louise had her green case clutched in both hands. 'Her father works for UPS' – she said it like a word: 'ups', versus 'downs'. 'He got this transfer. To Kenosha. Where's that?'

'Kenosha's in Wisconsin. If it's the same one.'

'Ginny said that. It is.'

'It's up on Lake Michigan.' He'd gone there once with some fellow students when he was in law school in Chicago. A million years ago, though only fifteen. 'It gets cold up there.'

'Do you think there're a lot of black people who live there?'

'There're a lot of black people who live everywhere. Up there, too.'

She was silent. This was enough to know from him.

Louise was getting out of the car, or starting to. She

said, 'Would you go buy a nice card for me? Please? While I'm in here suffering? Then can we go out to her house and I can give it to her?'

'Where would Ginny live?' Their afternoon routine was being diverted – which could spell trouble. Kids liked routines and said they hated them.

'I have the address. It was on her knapsack just like mine is.' Louise said the name of the street, which was way east out St Claude, almost to the parish line, in the part where most houses had been destroyed two years ago today. A wasteland was out there. 'They're leaving tomorrow,' Louise said. His daughter had long straight honey-brown but rather mousy hair and wore brown tortoise glasses that made her look business-like, older than twelve. Older than twenty. She was wearing her blue plaid school kilt and her standard wrinkled white blouse and white knee socks. She looked perfect. Was perfect.

'We can certainly do that,' Hobbes said.

'They have gobs of cards at Wal-Mart,' Louise said. 'I bought one for you there this year.' Her mother took her to Wal-Mart for durable play wear. Or used to.

'What would you like any card to say?'

Louise looked in at him gravely from outside the door. She'd been thinking about this all day. '"Have fun in Kenosha",' she said. '"We'd love to have you come back. Love, Louise Hobbes."'

'I doubt if I'll find one that says exactly that,' Hobbes said. 'You'll have to write in a message. I'll get you a plain one.'

'But get a very pretty one. No flowers. No birds.' Gasping late-afternoon heat swarmed the cavity of the car. Louise was outside the door, holding it open, looking in at her father as if he needed better instructions. 'Maybe get one with a New Orleans theme. So she'll remember everything and be miserable and miss me.' Her green night-guard container bulked in her small hand. Her nails were painted a similar green and were chipping. Green was her color for now. Nothing frightened her or seemed impossible yet.

Often at night that summer Walter lay awake in his metal and glass bachelor apartment high above the swank, curved sweep of the Mississippi – container ships and tanker ships hung at anchor, white running lights smudging the dense airless darkness – and wondered what had caused Betsy suddenly to need to divorce. It hadn't seemed at all necessary. Mitch Daigle wasn't a bad fellow, but not someone to leave life over. He'd known Mitch on the Young Barristers Round Table, been friendly doubles opponents for at least one summer at the River Bend. Mitch came from Mamou, a suavely handsome, nervous-eyed coon-ass boy, who'd come into the city from across the Atchafalaya the way Walter had come down from Mississippi – for a big lick in the oil and gas fascination, now long gone. Life left bestilled. There'd been a slew of them: young men – boys, really – who'd arrived out of law school ready to make their stand and get well. There hadn't been a need for long establishment. New Orleans didn't require that. You needed seed money and nerve, and everybody had that for a while. He and Mitch had each gone into an old, good white-shoe firm, then drifted away to smaller outfits with the money tide. Betsy had helped him find a suitable Greek Revival house on Palmer Street and on the 'come-back' showing, fucked him on the client's teaster bed. It all went south then. Betsy 'explained' she'd read a book in college in South Carolina, something about lost children caught in a cyclone on a South Sea island. All the animals on the island – bird, lizards, fuzzy creatures – went crazy out ahead of the storm. It had become fashionable to blame as many bad things as possible on the hurricane – things that would've happened anyway, shortfalls in character the hurricane could never have begotten. As if life weren't its own personalized storm. He knew you needn't think about why things happened. Lawyers made up those reasons. It was widely known to be nearly impossible to admit that things, in fact, *did* happen.

Still. Life was lived in your head – even for Louise. You tracked back toward the cause of things out of habit, but got little for it. Betsy had 'thrown herself' into her work, was living alone in a condo like he was, being a part-time mom, and was spending this evening on a hot screened porch, drinking rum and staring out toward the distant lights of the city, becoming bored with life all over again, just in some entirely new way. A shame you couldn't go back the other way. Re-leash the storm.

★

The Wal-Mart lot felt hotter than any place he'd been so far that day, the mostly empty, paper-strewn parking expanse buttery with petroleum fumes from the river. It of course had been damaged then looted, then looted again for good measure and not been reopened long. Ants on the cupcake. A few souls – a large Negro women in skin-tight, fuchsia shorts trailing her tiny kids and a muscular young man in a Saints jersey and baggy jeans – were strolling out the entrance-exit, navigating full shopping carts.

Inside was instant relief from the cooking heat. Walter was dressed for the office – a suit and tie no one else in Wal-Mart was wearing. No one looked at all like him, which made him prompt to get his business over with. The general human feeling in the vast, merchandise-clotted space, dimensionlessly farther than you could see under severe fluorescence, was of people – families, shoppers, grannies in wheelchairs, abandoned kids, slack-jawed young-marrieds in from the country – all making a late afternoon of it, taking their spoiled leisure, letting Wal-Mart be what their day offered. Only the size of the biosphere made it feel strangely empty within.

He asked of the friendly/elderly merchandise checker where greeting cards might be found and went straight there – a long, tiered and racked section between school supplies and the discount wines – and where no one was there to help. The chlorinated air was freezing, and he'd sweated his hairline and his shirt collar. There was no reason, though, to make a complex assignment of this. What he'd choose wouldn't please Louise anyway. Left to herself, hours would be expended determining the perfect card, which would then have been repudiated later.

Most of the tired offerings were for conventional observances – graduation, birthday, anniversary, confirmation, birth, sympathy over a mother's death, illness, events requiring good humor. There were a lot of these. But no message-less cards, except two with sex themes – one, some wit had already written on and drawn in a picture of a large smiling penis with a moustache. 'Hey-o!' Not so easy to fit your private need for expression into a category some soul in Kansas City has already found words for. You ended up finally buying one, signing it, sealing it up and sending it off, then letting thoughts voyage elsewhere. Compromise was all.

Lots of cards depicted black people, although they were mostly tan, clean-cut black people wearing chinos and oxford shirts and women smiling out at fields of colorful cornflowers, wearing gold wedding bands, with children who looked like they'd done well on their science projects and were ready for Harvard. They weren't much like the people in Wal-Mart. Ginny Baxter might also not appreciate a card semi-personalized to her race. It was because of her race that she'd soon be moving. It was tempting to seek out one of the red-smocked sales associates who was a person of color and ask if she or he might be offended if a well-meaning white child gave their black child a friendship card in which the human beings depicted were more or less 'black'. Or would it be insensitive? Possibly a hoot? Or just one more thing white people didn't get – of which there was a growing cavalcade. Such feelings were enervating.

Here was one that said, 'Have a Wonderful Trip!' A bright red mini-van full of waving, smiling tan children was portrayed pulling out the wide driveway of a big blue suburban home with a great leafy oak tree in the healthy, grassy green yard. Lots of festive colored balloons rose into a clean blue sky, which must've been California. A message pledged, 'We won't be happy 'til you're back!' Louise would loathe the Negro characters and think it was all queer and 'inappropriate'. She'd hate the mini-van and the house and the tree and the smiles and the balloons. These black people were also obviously headed to Orlando, not Kenosha. There was nothing he could do right, here. A task past his capabilities. Louise could've made a perfect card out of red construction paper and affixed her own clever, tender wording. Only she'd have been embarrassed, unsure, mortified. Too painful. A father's job, this was. Louise never really asked for much.

When he first knew Betsy Montjoy, when he was new in New Orleans and a fresh lawyer, he gave her cards he'd customized. 'Walter specials.' 'Sorry to hear you've been in the hospital.' To which he'd magic-marker in 'mental'. 'It's your birthday.' He'd added '100th!' Betsy loved 'funny', would already be smiling in the car seat or across the table in Gautreaux's – awaiting. It usually prompted her to say 'You're a nut', or that he was 'pretty wild and most likely dangerous', or he was 'probably the clever-est man in the world'. None of which was true. He was, instead, Walter B. Hobbes from Minter City, Mississippi, a skinny, good-natured oil and gas guy who read the *WSJ*, the *FT* and *Petroleum Times*, voted Democratic, wore tan suits with penny loafers and sometimes loud bow ties and argyle socks from Brooks, and hoped that all this meant she would marry him. Which for a while it did.

He plucked a card that featured a big cartoon goose with its orangey beak taped shut and its big riddling goose eyes bulging in sweaty, exasperated excitement. It read, 'It goose without saying. . .' Opened, little red hearts were floating around the inside atmosphere, where the goose was again pictured, this time smiling, its beak untaped and '. . . I miss you' splashed in big electric-yellow lettering. Louise could customize it. In her knapsack she maintained a plastic bag of colored Sharpies. Something clever would occur to her on the drive to Ginny's house – once she got over not liking it. Ginny would forget all about it in two days, anyway. A card wouldn't make it to Kenosha, which Louise instinctually understood. There were no ready words for Ginny's adventure or Louise's loss. Possibly no words for anyone's.

Francis Finerty was standing outside his little dentist's office – the comfortable Mediterranean-looking former family home he'd bought when he and his wife Mary Jane came in the seventies. A honeymoon that lasted on, a fresh go, away from bombs and soldiers in the Antrim Road.

He'd converted the house to a one-chair office, where he was standing out front in his frosted pink dentist's smock and talking animatedly to Louise on the steps. Louise was the day's last patient. He wouldn't want her waiting out by herself. Finerty was Walter's dentist, and he was Betsy's dentist. He might've been Mitch Daigle's dentist. He was a not-so-tall, round, jowly exuberant Irishman with sadly drooping blue eyes and bushy hair and a predilection for laughter that made New Orleanians like him, if not quite warm to him. He enjoyed telling mildly disgraceful stories from his youth when your mouth was propped open, full of metal. He didn't tell these stories to Louise, of course.

'I was on to explaining the concept of the phantom limb to your young medical scholar here.' Finerty came down to the car with Louise, his lilt all ramped up for her sake. Louise wouldn't have noticed. She had no conception of what was Irish. Louise, however, had clearly explained to him she intended to be a doctor, something she'd just made up. Finerty was holding open the car door for her to climb in with her night-guard container and plastic bag of free dental supplies. He smiled down upon her, a smile meant to indicate something was secret and collusive between them – which Louise wouldn't have allowed either. Finerty had two grown daughters his wife had left him with, and who were now Americans. They both frustrated him and lived in New England. He liked to aver connections between dental practice and the clichéd priestly vocation he rumored he'd chosen against – conceivably unwisely. He had a fleshy flat nose, a rucked reddish forehead and thick Groucho eyebrows he could make cavort in pursuit of humorous effects in off-color Paddy stories related behind his dental mask. Sometimes he closed his eyes when he spoke – to discourage a reply.

'Are phantom limbs part of your general discussion of night guards and teeth grinding today?' Walter ducked to see Finerty through the open car-door space. More blasted desert air crowded in to where he was.

'Along in a general discussion of loss,' Finerty said. His eyebrows did indeed jink up as his black eyes widened. Finerty had a gargly voice and stiff, curly priestly hairs on the backs of his dense and subtle hands. Loss, possibly divorce, possibly disaster had been the unmentioned subtext of all treatment today. Appropriate to the anniversary of the hurricane, but not exclusive to it.

In her seat, Louise frowned at Hobbes from behind her tortoise shells, in case he was about to say something disallowed – about her. Louise had constructed her own 'look': studious, often stern, implicitly loyal and – in a way that only she understood – sexy. She abruptly smiled to exhibit her new shiny-clean teeth. Her smell was faintly medicinal.

Finerty also liked resorting to mock philosophical palaver at the conclusion of appointments, as if a spiritual dimension also haunted tooth extractions and partial bridgework and needed to be developed, yet couldn't properly be using regular dental–patient lingo. Francis

Finerty, Walter felt, was a fully engaged spiritual man, and the loneliest man he knew. Better to stay with fishing.

'Apropos of the season,' Walter said to the salient issue of loss.

'Apropos of the season precisely.' Eyes closed. Finerty laved his soft hands together like an understanding undertaker. 'A loss becomes its own elemental presence, which is the essence of Beckett, if you don't mind a dentist saying so.'

'How're her teeth?'

Finerty smiled. He had small, blunt teeth of his own, carelessly spaced. 'Entirely lovely. And she knows it, as well.'

'And I know how to take care of myself,' Louise said rudely. She smiled garishly at her father and revealed now the yellowish, translucent Lucite night guard she'd just snapped in place over her perfect incisors. 'I have to wear this all my life,' she said.

'At least until the tension in that life subsides.' Finerty smiled, too, then pulled a face of mock dismay.

'Like I said,' Louise said.

'We're working away on that,' Hobbes said.

'If we knew what went on between women and men we likely wouldn't need dentists a-tall, would we?' Finerty pushed the car door to and stepped back onto the curb in a dainty, little hefty man's hop.

'He's a creep,' Louise said instantly. Finerty was twelve inches away behind the cool window glass, still talking away about women and men. She didn't mean it. She was only impatient.

'No, he's not,' Walter said. 'He's a smart man, and likes you.'

'Everybody's smart,' Louise said, her night guard still bulging inside her lips, as Walter eased them away from the curb. Finerty was left waving.

'This is *SO QUEER!*' Louise had the goose card open and was appraising it menacingly, furiously. 'Why's this bird got tape on its stupid mouth? *What* goes without saying? Didn't I say no birds? "I miss you"? It's disgusting.' It was true he hadn't considered the goose a bird.

They were driving out St Claude, a wide, rubbish-cluttered boulevard through the once-thriving all-black section of (now) shut-down schools, caved-in and looted appliance stores with wrecked white goods scattered on the sidewalk, a closed and boarded-up Hardy's. A closed gas station. A closed ramshackle bar with a rough, red front and a tilted, inert neon roof sign. Mars Bar. Ruined houses were still 'designated' by the cruciform code the soldiers used two years before. People were on the streets – mostly black, unobservant, vaguely mission-less. Standing. Only every fourth traffic light seemed to be working. The city had yet to 'come back'.

Louise was officially mortified by the faulty card selection. It made Walter feel disheartened since Louise would now be resentful and wrongly misunderstood into the evening. *Their* evening, now casually adrift.

'I thought you could use Sharpies and customize it into something funny. Or sweet.'

'Like what? It's stupid.' She promptly tore the goose card in half and then in fourths and then in eighths and spitefully threw the pieces on the car floor. 'Now I don't have anything to give. Thank God.'

'You still have your winning personality,' Walter said. 'That'll make Ginny change her mind about leaving. Plus, I risked my life at Wal-Mart.'

'Fuck Wal-Mart. And you didn't risk your life. That's racist.' Louise turned away to the spent cityscape and crossed her legs tightly. Did Finerty's Irish daughters deport themselves thusly in times of turmoil? After the mother'd hied off? Finerty would've had novel approaches. He, himself, lacked even one.

'How old are you?' Steering cautiously through a signal-less intersection. Here was no place for a wreck. People were in a bad mood here. No police around to save you.

'Old enough to say "Fuck Wal-Mart",' Louise said. 'And a lot more.'

'Well, try to save back something nice to say to Ginny.' Louise had pronounced an address on Delery Street before she went ballistic on the offending card.

'I'm not going without a gift. *That* goes without saying.' Louise had righteous anger always at her disposal now. A relatively recent asset.

'Well, you'd better concoct something fast. It wasn't about a card, anyway. It was the gesture that counted. Or would've been.'

'What am I supposed to say?' Louise sniffed, as if

possibly she might cry a little, or at least try. This was *not* one of her assets. Or her mother's. Dry eyes were their redoubt.

'Okay,' Walter said. 'Let's see. How about "Dear Ginny, I'll miss you when you're gone." Or, "Dear Ginny, I hope your new life in Kenosha is wonderful." Or, "I hope I see you again." Those seem serviceable.'

'They're pathetic.'

Louise was working her teeth hard and did *not* now have her device in.

'No, they're not pathetic. They're things that shouldn't go without saying. This is a part of your education.' It was pompous, but he meant it – though she would ignore it.

'Why did you get divorced?' Louise said blazingly. It had been her default accusation for some time. Always brandished from ambush. A rabbit out of a mean hat.

'I don't know,' Walter said, seeing a Delery Street sign ahead – a paper placard someone had stapled on a telephone pole in place of the regular sign, hurricaned away. All around the sign were other handwritten notices, many in Spanish, advertising 'DEMOLICION DE SU CASA.' 'REPAROS.' 'NO SE SIENTE SOLA.'

'Yes, you do,' Louise said angrily. 'Was it your fault?'

'I'm sure it was,' Walter said.

'Why did you even do it, then? You were bad.'

'Nature doesn't like to be observed,' Walter said. Again, he felt profoundly fatigued. 'It'd be better if nature did. At least a little. Sometimes.'

Louise looked at him contemptuously, blinking her small, intense brown eyes behind her glasses, fists clenched, her sack of dental supplies still in her lap. Louise had gained weight in the last months. She had an adolescent pimple on the side of her forehead near her hairline, which she was leaving unattended out of malice. The torn-apart goose-card pieces were scattered on her black school shoes.

'I don't understand you,' Louise said. She was now twenty-five, he was her poor-communicator boyfriend, they'd just broken up, possibly for the last time.

'I know,' Walter said, slowing for the turn on Delery by a great empty-windowed, weather-beaten high school. 'It'll have to do for now, though. It'll be an interesting subject for later life.'

'What *later*?' Louise said victoriously. 'There won't be any later.'

Delery – long, straight, pot-holed, refuse-strewn – was a street of wreckages. Where the flood had churned through, homes had been flattened, floated off foundations, had their roofs removed and spirited away. Others – the compact brick ones – had been scoured out and ruined, too, but in a way that left the outside walls sturdily standing. Weeds thrived in lots where concrete slabs had held houses. A sleek, fiberglass sporting craft had been miraculously hoisted then deposited on top of a white frame bungalow, and at another domicile an ancient green Studebaker had been shoved through the front door into a living room. All achievements of the water. Most of the houses bore the familiar dark stain of high water above the casements and the same hash marks left by rescuers. One house proclaimed 'No Pig Found/9-10' beside its door. Another simply said, 'One Dead Here.'

Farther down and out toward the lake, beneath the baking white sky, a crew of young, shirtless and aspiring black boys was busily gutting a house and loading usable timbers and shingles onto a sagging pickup bed. Almost no one was living out here or in the surrounding blocks of battered streets. All was becoming fields again. A few surviving trees. The long view. It was the lower 9, the submersible land that had always been poor and black, but had been a place to live. Louise's school had made a field trip to here, and afterwards gone back and committed moving poems all about it, painted gawdy, desolate landscapes, written letters to kids in faraway cities, predicting everything would be restored soon and become even better. Come back.

Louise had sunk into silence, possibly interviewing complimentary phrases she would address to Ginny when they got to where Ginny lived. Possibly, too, the dead weight of destruction – mute, grammar-less, attractively foreign – had struck her dumb. Ahead, some white men – electric utility workers in yellow plastic helmets and white jumpsuits – were gathered around a light pole, connecting or disconnecting power. Two wrecked houses behind them had temporary trailers parked in their front yards. Though no one was in sight there. A brown-and-white spotted dog stood in the grass beside the littered street and stared at Walter's car but didn't move as it eased past.

'This is horrible,' Louise said, as if she'd never seen any of it before. She pressed her nose to the window glass, her glasses frames ticking the pane. They had a reason to be here. Everything went without saying.

The address numbers on the few standing houses were leading them to the place they were going, which was not much farther. 'Ginny lives with her grandmother,' Louise said gloomily. She sighed softly, apparently bored, emitting a small cloud onto the window glass. She had found her way to resolute again.

Ahead, in the next emptied-out block, waited a collection of vehicles none of the other houses or lots had out in front of them. A man was in the street, hefting household articles – a chair, a small table, a lamp – into the open back of a shiny red and white U-Haul that was promoting the state of Idaho on its side. 'It's not just potatoes!' Slightly different from the happy-family card at Wal-Mart.

'There's Ginny,' Louise said, buoyant, no longer bored. She knew everything she would say now.

A child dressed in exactly Louise's uniform stood on the opposite side of the street from the man loading articles. Two cars were parked, there, in the weeds where a house had been but where now was a white concrete slab. She was just watching. A relic chain-link fence recollected a backyard where an old-fashioned mangle iron-ing contraption sat marooned. Everything else around Ginny was open ground with different concrete squares dotting where houses had been down Delery. A single, steepled white church rose in the distance. Gulls soared above everything, singing out soundlessly. A low husk of another tan school building sat off in the humid mid-dle ground surrounded by nothing. It was striking – the character of destruction – always diverse.

Louise was out of the car before Hobbes could get properly stopped. From where she stood in the weeds, Ginny saw Louise, knew her, but didn't move or signal surprise. Louise marched straight to her and started talk-ing, as if this was an official visit. She took Ginny's hand and waggled her arm until Ginny said something and smiled. Louise and Ginny looked alike in their school uniforms and tortoise-shell glasses and long straight hair.

Across from where the girls were talking stood a remarkably new house, raised to a man's height on new blond-wood pillars, everything freshly painted bright blue with white trim. A new smooth, white concrete driveway was laid, new azalea plantings set in against the base of the pillars, bright plastic geraniums in window boxes, a thick green carpet of St Augustine fresh off the truck. On the elevated front porch, a tiny, desiccated, eld-erly black woman in a long skirt stood watching the man load boxes and suitcases into the red-and-white square trailer – all things he'd brought from inside the house.

For a moment the man didn't acknowledge anyone

had arrived. Then he stopped loading and looked first at the two girls and at the Rover and at Walter Hobbes getting out. He was a moderate-sized, beige-skinned man with short, well-tended hair, wearing a tank top he'd sweated through completely, plaid Bermudas he'd also sweated through and black basketball sneakers with knee-high white socks. His skin was wrong – far too light – to be Ginny's father. But he stood a moment, then came across the street, wiping hands on his shirt.

'Louise wanted to come say goodbye,' Walter said. Everything was knowable here.

'All right. That's good,' the man said. He was thirty-two, smooth-muscled, compact. He might've been a UPS man. Mannerly, observant, implacable.

'They're in the same class,' Walter said.

'Okay.' The man regarded the girls again. Ginny and Louise were now locked in a fast privacy. 'Ginny,' he said, interrupting them. 'This is Louise's daddy.' Louise and Ginny stopped talking and both looked at Walter. Walter waved. Ginny waved back. Louise turned away.

A second woman appeared onto the high porch of the blue house, beside the small, elderly desiccated woman. She was very dark-skinned, and tall and statuesque, her hair in corn rows. Her face even from the street appeared reproachful.

'I'm Walter Hobbes.' Walter extended his hand to be shaken.

'Jerry,' the black man said and shook Walter's hand with a not-at-all-firm grip. He was almost featurelessly, smoothly handsome, his tan face shiny in sweat. He had a small gold stud in his left earlobe, something he possibly wouldn't wear to work. On his left bicep was a faded tattoo that said 'Sheri' in ornate cursive script. He wore a gold wedding ring.

They both stood then in the unmoving heat and looked down the street of a few remaining ruined houses and emptied lots in the direction of the lake and the soaring opalescent sky. This was the girls' visit now, and they were conducting it. Nothing need be said by the adults about what it was to be a UPS man, or to be a practitioner of the law, or to leave for Kenosha in the white heat of August.

'What do you do?' Jerry said, as if in any case he needed to find this out.

'Oil and gas law,' Walter said. It sounded quaint to say that out here, to be that.

'I get that,' Jerry said. 'I'm UPS.' It told its story. The 'best' company there was. Best benefits. Best working conditions. Best customers. Not like working at all.

'Is that your house?' Walter admired the bright-blue shotgun with the two women on the raised porch watching him as if he might be posing as someone he wasn't. Louise suddenly laughed and said, 'Oh *you*. You're so funny.' The skinny spotted dog that had been up the street now trotted past and turned out into what had become empty fields.

Jerry waved at the women and smiled. 'It's my mother-in-law's.'

'It's pretty,' Walter said.

'It's where her old house was 'til the storm came in. Some people showed up from a church, some volunteers. Told her they were going to build it back. And they did. She didn't even ask why. She just moved right in like nothing had happened. She's from the country. Nothing really surprises her.'

It was odd to live in a new house where everything had been blown away and scattered, Hobbes thought. It could be insulting to say that, of course, since it might not be true.

Jerry regarded the house as if his thinking was along those same lines but found it acceptable. 'We moved in with her when our house got ruint. But I took a transfer up north. I ain't turning that down. My wife wants to stay on here. But . . .' He didn't finish.

'How does Ginny feel?'

Jerry ran a hand down his bare arm – the one with the 'Sheri' tattoo – to wipe off sweat. The sun was burning straight on them from behind clouds. Walter's suit jacket was wetted through. 'It's just a game to them. A big adventure.'

Walter looked at the girls together. It might be true.

'Tell me something good about Wisconsin,' Jerry said. His brows raveled as if he would take whatever was said seriously.

'It's on a lake,' Walter said. 'It gets cold. The Packers play there.'

Jerry said, 'I'm starting to be worried about that cold.'

'They have seasons,' Walter said. 'That's a plus. We don't have those down here. You might learn to like it.'

'Okay,' Jerry said and paused to let this dimensionless idea cycle past. 'I went through Chicago in the Navy,' he said. 'But. That was in the summer.'

Then they were silent and motionless while their little girls conferred and walked a few yards farther down the street, arms gripping each other's waist. They had their last little girl things to impart, more private than earlier.

'So, how're *you* doin'?' Jerry said amiably. The two women on the scorching porch turned and passed back through the sliding door that closed with a sucking sound. One of them was laughing, saying, 'You know how *he* goes . . .' An air-conditioning unit behind the blue house hummed incessantly, a comforting noise Walter hadn't heard until now. Jerry's question meant, '. . . since the hurricane that happened . . . What's been doing?' But more generally, too.

'How am I doing about what?'

'Well.' Jerry kept smiling. 'Whatever you're all about. Whatever's up. You know? You hangin' in there?'

Walter looked down the street at Louise Hobbes, her kilt, her knee socks, her glasses. She was caressing a lock of Ginny's black hair – just the spidery tips. Just touching.

'I'm hangin' in,' Walter said. 'I guess that's what I'm doing. Isn't that right?'

'There you go,' Jerry said, still smiling. He also looked down toward the girls – lost now in each other's past and present.

Walter watched Jerry's hand extend, ready to be shaken again with the same not-quite-firm grip.

'Good to meet you,' Walter said. Almost suddenly.

'Okay, then. You be careful.'

'Absolutely,' Walter said, taking the large, soft, unmeaning hand in his own. Behind him his other hand found the over-warm door handle of the Rover. He smiled at Jerry, whose last name he didn't even know. Baxter might be another man. Someone no longer in evidence.

'We're leavin', quick as I'm loadin',' Jerry said, walking back to his trailer, carrying on talking. 'Make it to Memphis tonight. Be to Wisconsin tomorrow. Work the next day. You know how it is.'

'Great,' Walter said. 'Have a safe trip.'

'If it ain't already snowin'.'

'It won't be.' Walter said. This had been enough.

'There it is,' Jerry said, going leisurely on up the concrete drive toward the house.

He merely needed something new to capture his attention now, to occupy him for the time he'd be here. Far down Delery, where the workers in yellow helmets were collected around the light pole, a police cruiser turned into the street and began slowly toward him. Get in the car now, he thought, turn up the air, wait for the children to finish their goodbyes. He had reasons to be here.

Louise sat in her seat with her legs crossed again, hands in her lap, very pleased with herself. She'd come away with the victory – 'She's lucky to be moving away' – watching the hopeless demolished neighborhood glide past in the other direction. They were back to St Claude, where it was possible again to view the city center, far away, as if from a desert floor or an ocean – tall bank buildings in the gritty haze, new hotels, office towers that had not been ruined by the hurricane. The city – the middle, where Walter worked – always seemed to be where it shouldn't be when seen from a distance. Once, flying in, from somewhere, the plane had banked to the west so he'd gazed straight down the river's course to the old section – the Vieux Carré – the part all tourists knew about. What a laughable mistake to put a city down here, he'd thought. A man from Des Moines would tell you that. Nothing promised good from it.

'Did you do okay without a card?' Walter said. They were finally bound for their hilarious early dinner at Cyril's. The Baxters were sorted out, sent on their hopeful, toilsome way. Bill Murray would come later. Louise's mother was now inexplicably though comfortably across the lake on Mitch Daigle's porch. He would, indeed, be at work tomorrow, himself.

'I definitely did,' Louise said. Vivid sunlight sparkled in through the windshield, the kind that could give you a headache.

'It's good to know you can put things best in your own words. It's harder, but it's better.'

'Whatever,' Louise said. 'Or buy a better card, maybe. Or not go to Wal-Mart, which was my idea, which I'm sorry about. Or not have any friends at all.'

'One at a time,' Walter said. Her jaw was working, grinding.

'Do you think possibly *I* could move?' Louise said. 'Before very long?' The torn goose-card clutter lay under her shoes.

'Well. *You* could move to Wisconsin, maybe live on a glacial lake surrounded by stately conifers, go to a country school and learn to canoe and memorize the legends of the Chippewa and have your classmates say "golly" and "Jeez Louise".' He looked at his daughter proprietarily, reached across and touched her shoulder to indicate he wasn't making fun of her, though he was. Many things would be possible for her in time. Not even much time. Some of them would surely be good.

'No,' Louise said. 'I was thinking about going to Italy or maybe to China. Or Ireland. Alone. And never seeing anybody I know today ever again.'

'Would you include me?' Hobbes said.

'And mother, too,' Louise said, and gave him a look of sudden anguish. A look that saw another future.

For that instant, then, Walter experienced the sensation of something being just about to happen. All around. A sensation of impendment – not necessarily bad or good, but something there in the offing. Though if he paused in his thinking at that very moment, as he'd recently learned to do, didn't follow thoughts all the way to where they led – or even came from – then this sensation could develop into something not so bad. In a day he'd forget it so that when it offered itself again it would again surprise him. This was a smart child – Louise – though not smart beyond her years. She would be allowed to forget many things, too.

He went on then with his dutiful driving, the center of the city still a remarkable feature in the evening's steamy distance. He needn't make the effort to answer a childish question about Italy and China. In her life she would definitely go to these places. It was best, he felt, to let things just pass away from the moment.

Somewhere in Minnesota

Órfhlaith Foyle

I WAS SITTING IN A DINER in God knows where in Duluth, Minnesota, during wintertime and the waitress was concerned for me. She liked my accent and noticed my bruised face.

She said, 'Who's been hurting you, sweetheart?'

I don't like it when people use sweet language on strangers. Sweet language belongs to lovers. But she was kind. A little bit old with worn blonde hair, the sort that was dying before she was, and the fat had fallen in her face. I wanted to draw her so I ripped a napkin from the dispenser and took my pencil from my pocket. My phone buzzed against my hip twice then switched to message mode.

The diner door opened, and the waitress called out, 'Hey John.'

John raised a salute. 'How are you these days, Hetty? The kids?'

Hetty laughed. She said her husband had come over with the kids yesterday. She said they were all grown up now and one of them wanted to be an archaeologist. He always did like finding dead useless things, she said.

I tried to ignore her voice but it had a good rhythm to it and it helped me move my pencil.

Hetty called over, 'You okay there girl?'

I don't know if she wanted John to see me or maybe she just didn't want to talk about her kids and husband anymore, but she made John look.

Now some men you just know they like to see hurt women. John stared right at me, and the muscles jumped across his jaw and his eyes lit before his head went back down over the menu.

I glanced to where Hetty was pouring coffee for some other customer. Her arms bulged from beneath her little-girl waitress uniform. Her earrings chimed, and she was singing along to the radio. A few minutes later, she served John his coffee and his 'usual'.

The diner was big and bright and the voices were loud. My phone buzzed again. I had lost the count by now. I finished drawing and watched an old man talk into his chicken dinner. Bits of chicken fell from his beard and his knee was jiggling hard under his table.

'How are you getting on?' Hetty called over to me. I curled my hand over my napkin and on she came, high heels clicking fast, and I saw John raise his expression from his coffee to my face.

I gave him a smile. He fit a potato from his fork to his mouth.

When I was a little girl, my mother said that I watched people too much. I made them scared and angry, she said. But it was just the way my mind turned when it saw something it liked.

Hetty was humming 'You Are My Sunshine' as she reached me. She stopped humming as soon as she saw what I had done.

I had made her younger with darker hair similar to what I had seen growing from her roots, and I had fluffed it about her head because it made her neck longer that way. I had corralled the fat from under her chin and replanted it in her cheeks. I had widened her eyes so that she looked as innocent as she might have been once.

'Do you like it?' I asked.

Hetty snatched it and held it aloft. 'Hey John, we've an artist here.'

John stuck his head out from his neck and focused on the napkin.

'Looks just like you did this morning, Hetty.'

Hetty laughed and folded the napkin into her apron pocket. Then she tried to touch my face, and my insides crept to my backbone. I stood up fast and nearly fell into her.

She took hold of me. 'Take it easy, sweetheart.' She clucked her tongue. 'Who did this to you?'

I said, 'The Ladies, please?'

Hetty started to bring me towards the back of the diner but I stopped her.

'Just show me please.'

Hetty dropped her arms from me. Her voice went sharp. 'What's your name?'

'Frankie,' I told her.

She held her hands just beneath my chin but not touching me. 'You go in there and take as long as you please, Frankie. Food is on me.'

The ladies room smelled of synthetic cherries. It had pale green walls, and there were false blue and pink flowers stuck in a yellow vase on a shelf beside the sink's mirror. I locked the door and stripped to my slip. I filled the sink with cold, cold water. I just wanted to freeze the pain inside me. I dampened the corner of my blouse and patted at the blood on my forehead.

The diner music piped into the air above me. I stared at my face. My phone buzzed. Peter's name was flashing so I answered.

'Hey,' I said.

'Whereabouts are you?' he said.

'Somewhere in Minnesota,' I answered.

'Christ Frankie, just tell me you are still in Duluth.'

I stared at my reflection as I dabbed at my face with one hand while I held my phone in the other. Peter's voice babbled on. He mentioned 'crisis' more than once. He mentioned money a little bit more. He took a breath, and I waited. I put my left hand into the freezing water and felt the cold wet on my wrist.

'Frankie, just come back.'

I heard the background noise of music and glasses and people's voices. I almost saw the tall white walls holding my paintings and the shiny clean skin of everyone there.

'Frankie, just come back now.'

I said nothing and waited. Peter breathed in and out.

'Fuck your father Frankie,' he said.

I waited some more seconds then I switched off the phone.

The piped music stopped then sputtered on. My face was beginning to swell. I ran my tongue over my lips to feel the sting. I knew I'd have to go outside, finish whatever had been cooked for me and make some kind of conversation that Minnesota Americans would appreciate. I'd ease on into their lineage, find an Irish link and marvel it big. They liked it big here.

'Hey Frankie . . . you still in there . . . ?'

A man's voice came through the wall.

So I answered, 'Yes?'

'You okay?' said his voice.

'I'm fine, yes.'

'I'm going to piss,' he continued. 'And the acoustics in here are astronomical.'

I rested against the sink as the sound of piss rivered through the wall.

Hetty knocked on the door. 'You okay in there, honey?'

I heard her giggle and say, 'Hey John, watch where you put your hands.'

I looked at the mirror and whispered, 'Hey John, watch where you put your hands.'

I smoothed down my hair then went back out into the diner. John watched me sit and Hetty came over with the food.

The chicken on the plate seemed alive. It glistened up

from under slow-moving brown gravy. Boiled greens hung on its thighs, and there was some potato, mashed into the shape of a deflated ball, burnt on the edges, smeared in yellow cheese. I willed the chicken to stop moving. I counted to ten with my eyes closed and felt something move in front of me. When I opened them, John was seated opposite. He had his coffee and apricot pie.

He said, 'Eat the chicken. It's good.'

I peeled off some thigh meat with my knife then covered it in mash.

'Hetty does the best gravy,' John said.

He cut a chunk from his pie and stuck it in his mouth. He had a nice mouth. Thin but well curved. I decided not to talk just yet, and maybe he appreciated the tension because he smiled and hummed a little then glanced over to Hetty who winked at us both.

'She's been married five times,' John mentioned. 'Only one of her husbands gave her kids. She loves those kids but she can't stand having them for more than three days.'

I nodded and continued to peel meat and mash together.

'That's the thing about Hetty,' John said. 'She can act the love just as long as she's not near it too often.'

He smiled and pointed his fork at my face. 'So you coming in here looking like that gets her mother instincts all in a tizzy.'

'You and Hetty,' I stated.

He shrugged. 'We're friends.' He smiled. 'We like meeting people.'

I nodded and chewed on chicken. John smiled at my bruises and cut an apricot in two with the side of his spoon.

'Hetty likes to help people.' He smiled. 'So do I.'

I said nothing while I scraped a square of cheese from my mash.

'I'm just here to eat,' I told him.

John smiled and shook his head. 'With a face like yours you should be in hospital but you're not. Makes me and Hetty wonder.'

I glanced around the perimeter of the café. I noted how far I was from the main entrance, and a thin delight of fear ran from my throat to my guts. I breathed in and kept smiling. The old man caught my smile and raised his hand in greeting. A group of silent kids were reading comics in another booth. I had picked the café because I had thought it seemed the sort of place people got lost in for a while.

'I've just left my boyfriend,' I said.

John nodded. 'He do that?'

'No.'

'Then who did?'

The chicken and mash turned sour in my throat as I swallowed it down.

'I did this to myself,' I admitted out loud.

John's eyebrows rose. He looked across at Hetty, and her smile slid from him to me.

I glanced at my phone. I told myself five more minutes, or maybe dessert and coffee, then I'll ring back.

After Peter first saw my paintings, he wanted to know where my father was.

'Dead,' I told him.

Peter had dark hair and green eyes. I had watched him move about the gallery like a long cat on longer legs. I presumed him gay but what he really was was a boy who just wanted to love somebody like me.

'I kidnap men on a regular basis,' I half-warned.

'I don't mind,' he half-promised and smiled like a boy from a fairy tale. He stood under a painting of mine – a backbone with arrowed sinews – and said it was as if I was drawing the birth of a ghost.

John kept digging pieces from his pie but looked at me from under his eyes. Hetty smiled over. Her earrings jangled, and she gave me the thumbs up. She reached behind the counter then held up the *Duluth Tribune*, open to the arts section. My normal face was there.

'You're famous,' she stage whispered at me.

I smiled at her. She was nothing like my mother. My mother told me I looked like my father as I slept. She said I had more of his genes in me than any of her other children. She said once he had finished with me I was like something poisonous. She said what he put in me I'd keep in me for ever.

Hetty came over to our table with more coffee.

'How come you're not where you're supposed to be?' she asked.

I didn't answer.

'You like the chicken?'

153

'It's good,' I lied to her.

I glanced at her blue eye shadow and her white–flour soft face. Her lipstick was cracking. John pushed his hand towards mine, waited a second, then finger-tipped my knuckles.

I didn't like that. I didn't like the way he played on my fingers, where rings should be, where things that twinkle with good love should be.

'It's my father's anniversary,' I blurted.

'For what?' John asked.

'He died three years ago,' I said.

Hetty coughed. She tapped her fingers on the table then on her mouth.

'Hey, let's get wine after I finish up here,' she suggested.

John smiled. 'Tash will be worried if I'm too late.'

Hetty glanced at me. 'His fiancée,' she explained.

She sat in beside me, slipped off her shoes and reached down to rub her nylon toes. A smell rose from them, and I helped myself to more coffee.

'I can be late for a bit,' John said.

He had dry skin, and his fingers were ragged. He saw me looking.

'I work with wood,' he said. 'Sometimes the resin reacts with my skin.'

'Need to hand it over to someone,' Hetty picked a string of chicken from my plate and laid it on her tongue. 'Fifty means you're not so young.' She elbowed me. But don't he look good for fifty? Like a really old thirty-year-old.'

154

She giggled, and the chicken string spat out of her mouth and onto the table. She picked it up, rolled it into a ball between her fingers then dropped it to the floor.

'Hey,' she remembered and pulled out the napkin from her apron pocket. 'You've got to sign this.' She handed me her waitress pen, and I signed my name under the sketch. She tried to touch my cheek.

'So, who did that?' she said and settled her fingers into a small claw over the napkin.

I gave her back her pen. 'It doesn't matter.'

Hetty smiled large at John.

'She looks like your Tasha, don't she John? Just like you want to bundle her up in your arms and take her home.'

'Tasha wouldn't like that,' John guessed.

'We can go to my place,' Hetty decided.

'What would we do there?' I asked.

Hetty stroked her finger along my left hand. 'You're cold,' she said. 'We could warm you up.'

'It *is* too late,' I said. I hunched my shoulders in, then I said:

'The last time I did this, I was in Florence.'

'Oh yeah,' Hetty said with her big, bright smile, and her teeth flashed with clean saliva.

'His name was Matthias. He was Swiss-German. He was very polite.'

John and Hetty didn't say anything.

I took out my phone and switched it on.

Hetty took it from me and ran through its call list. 'Who's Peter?'

'Turn it off,' John told Hetty and held his hand out for it.

'I don't do threesomes,' I said.

Hetty went back to stroking my hand. John smiled.

'Doesn't matter,' Hetty said. 'We can just talk.' She touched the side of my face. 'Maybe we could give you a bath, we could clean you up.'

I kept on eating. Hetty got impatient. She sucked her tongue against her teeth and hummed. John was waiting for me to say something. I stared at his face. This close he looked old and too soft, the sort of softness that I didn't want to touch. I thought of my father and the skin beneath his eyes.

So I said, 'I paid a ten-year-old boy to beat me up today.'

My jaw clicked on a tiny chicken bone. John stared at my bruises and the faint colour of blood over my face. I stared right into his eyes.

'A ten-year-old,' I insisted.

Hetty growled at me. 'What kind of game are you playing?' She kicked John underneath the table. He coughed and sloshed his coffee. I was tired. The pain was fading except for the headache at the back of my skull, and I pressed the top of my spine hard against the back of my seat.

'Hey,' John barked.

I looked at him. I saw him trying to screw some kind of threat into his eyes but I didn't want to play after all. I yawned and stretched my jaw, and the pain rose like nails into the back of my skull.

'He liked my colouring pencils,' I explained.

Hetty's face went slack under her make-up. 'What the . . . ?'

John warned her: 'I don't have time for this.'

He put my phone back down on the table. Hetty shifted to the edge of her seat, fluffed out her hair over her forehead then took away my knife and fork.

I glanced from John's face to hers. 'And I paid him ten dollars,' I told them.

John rubbed his watch against his chin. He was too old to react the way Peter had done. He didn't admire the perverse romance of it all.

Peter had stayed. Peter had promised to make me new again but failed. Peter who sat at a table in Florence and said he didn't want this game anymore.

Peter looked at me. 'I don't think you want love, Frankie. I don't think you're built for it.' He poured some wine. 'Maybe you should just leave me one day. Maybe I could take it.'

John slapped his hand on the table top. He stood up.

'No psychos,' he said. 'Not anymore.'

'But she's pretty,' Hetty started to negotiate yet she was half-standing and her toes were crawling for her shoes.

John gave her a look so she stood up, cracked her towel against the edge of the table and lowered her face close to mine.

'I never liked bitches like you.'

I looked up at her. I could see holes in her skin where the make-up had dripped off from the heat of her grill.

'All waiting to be patched up like dogs,' she spat. She sucked up the dribble on her lips, and I put my hand over my coffee cup when she grabbed my plate.

John was talking to the old man. Hetty went back behind the diner bar and began wiping it. I watched everyone's movements in slow motion.

John walked out of the diner.

Hetty turned up the radio.

The old man winked at me. I glanced at his hands inside his fly. The old man laughed, and Hetty flicked out the newspaper into the air before shaping it edge to edge on the diner counter. The comic-book kids got up and walked out.

I rang Peter. Then I remained in place, watching the dark night outside the diner's windows and the car lights looping backwards and forwards like mad eyes with nothing to hold them.

The last time my father hit me I was twenty-one years old. He stood back and waited a few seconds before he fixed my hair behind my ears.

The little boy had said, 'If it hurts, will you cry?'

'No,' I said.

He shifted on his heels and looked towards the far end of the playground.

'Are you crazy?' he said.

'No, just sometimes I feel better when I'm hurt.' I smiled up at the sky. It was drained of sun. 'And my boyfriend gets tired sometimes.'

'Oh, okay,' said the boy.

So I lay on the ground to make it easy for him. I could hear his feet slip in the mush of snow then his fist bounced into my face. The shock lifted my chest.

'Harder,' I said.

The boy's fists punched into my face. I breathed each time, and when I tasted too much blood I pushed him away.

He fell back and snarled.

I sat up and watched the world slide in and out of focus. I could hear the cars growl on the street beyond the park's wall. Someone yelled for someone, and I knew if it was Peter yelling for me then it would be too early. I needed the pain first.

'You okay?' the boy said. He danced on his feet.

I said nothing for seconds. The boy kicked about and glanced towards a group of adults at the far end of the play area. Then he shoved his fists into his coat pockets and looked at me.

'Where's my money?'

I took my purse from my coat pocket and handed him ten dollars. He rolled the note between his fingers.

'You'll have to hide it,' I warned.

He spat out phlegm. 'I have places Mom will never find.'

I gazed at my blood in the snow.

'Like candyfloss,' I said out loud to no one.

One of Those Stories

Anthony Glavin

THERE ARE STORIES YOU HEAR once in a blue moon if
you're lucky – lucky, I think, in that life can still stop
you in your tracks – though that's two clichés already,
and, whatever else, the stories I'm on about do not traffic
in cliché. Instead, something in their configuration – in
how they work themselves out – seems to speak, however briefly, to the heart of the matter. To stuff like loss,
longing, love, or mortality. But for this story, blue moon
is maybe okay, as there was actually one up there the
night I heard it.

Painting is my game, not narrative, but I remember thinking as I walked home that night how where
you hear certain stories – and from whom – invariably
becomes a part of them. And marks them out, I suppose, from stories you merely read, unless of course, like
Coleridge, you happen to fall asleep over one to dream
of something seeded by it – only for your mobile phone
to ring and leave you haunted by what you might otherwise have had: a story of your own. But the story I'm
talking about, the one I heard last week and haven't been

able to get out of my head since, I heard at a dinner party.

Or before the dinner party started, seeing that Fergal, our host and my solicitor, told it to me at the cooker where we had started on the first bottle of Rioja. As he added the butter beans to the paella, Noreen, our hostess, chatted with the first of the two couples to arrive, handing them the tomato and basil starter to place around the table. 'Please don't!' I had pleaded a few months earlier, after Fergal and Noreen had asked another single guest to dinner, a very pleasant journalist, Meredith, whom they thought I might like to meet. 'Or only if you'll otherwise end up some night with thirteen at table,' I lamely quipped, making Noreen, who had loved my Detta, wince and turn away.

Fergal had only heard the story himself that morning, from Seamus, a friend who has known him far longer than I, part of a circle he and Noreen used to drink with years ago, four or so couples who met up in Birchall's of a weekday night or the odd weekend afternoon, after a rugby match or some exhibit maybe. Not all of the gang were solicitors like Fergal and Noreen; Seamus works for a design agency, while Henry and Mary, whose story I suppose this really is, were a civil servant and clinical psychologist respectively.

I had that much from Fergal by the time the sliced red peppers went into the big paella pan and the remainder of the story before we all repaired to table and a third bottle of Rioja was shortly uncorked. How Mary had fallen in love some thirty years ago with an American anaesthetist practising here in Dublin, for whom she left both Henry and their two small children when her lover returned to his native Tennessee.

'She left the kids?' I said, only to hear Detta in my head, interrogating me in turn whether I'd have bothered asking that, had it been Henry who'd bailed out instead? I don't doubt Fergal's Noreen might have challenged me too, but seeing it was just we two at the cooker Fergal merely nodded, 'They were lovely kids, a girl seven and a boy a year or two younger.'

He and Noreen had seen something of the kids too, for Henry used to bring them into Birchall's the odd Saturday or Sunday, buy them a mineral and crisps, after which they would play with whatever other children in the circle had accompanied their parents there, including, on occasion, Fergal and Noreen's two young daughters, both married now with kids of their own.

But then, two years later, Mary had come over to Ireland for a visit and taken both children back with her to Nashville when she left. I didn't think to ask Fergal about custody, nor does it really matter, I think. What mattered at the time, however, was Henry's by now twice-broken heart and how heavily he had begun to drink. Already shaken by the dissolution of his and Mary's marriage, his friends now circled ever more protectively around Henry, mounting various interventions to get him to cut down on the drink: invitations to dinner, various out-ings or offers of cottages in Connemara and Kerry. But nothing they could do impacted in any real way on his decline, which sadly ended two years later when he died from a pernicious dose of viral pneumonia.

The talk at table, after the other couple had arrived and we all sat down to eat, was not surprisingly of lighter stuff, the usual blather about house prices or giving out about the government of the day, which threatens to become the government of yet another decade after being again returned to power in a dispiriting general election last month. But none of that truly matters to this story; nor do the names of the other guests, though, for the record, they were Maurice and Anne, a pair of academics, Trinity College sociology and University College Dublin geography I think, and Peter and Grainne, both in finance.

I doubt that kind of tandem vocational act would have worked for me and Detta, who undoubtedly felt one taciturn, moody painter under her roof was more than enough, thanks very much. Nor would I in a million years ever have the patience for her primary-school charges – though the fact I make most of my bread from teaching at the National College of Art and Design arguably made us a pair of pedagogues after all.

In any event, the dinner table chat was okay – nothing memorable, but certainly pleasant. Nobody asked me what kind of paintings I do, which invariably makes me want to reply, 'Acrylics, unless it's a good summer and oils will dry.' Mindful, I suppose, of what Matisse advised, 'If you want to make art, cut off your tongue,' though Edward Hopper once chanced saying how all he wanted to do was paint sunlight on the side of a house. Nor did I feel that evening too much like a spare among the company either – unpartnered, the odd man out. Or, for that matter, like I was once again seated in the Mexican Ambassador's chair. We'd had a good laugh about that, Detta and I, comparing conversational notes over a nightcap in our own kitchen after a dinner party thrown by somebody we hardly knew – a publisher for whom I had done some line drawings for a poetry book – and deducing how we had only been invited, more or less at the last minute, after the Ambassador, their neighbour, had rung the publisher to say his wife was not feeling well.

That was all on an early spring night two years ago, a couple of months before Detta herself took ill. Our laughter, before we took ourselves up to bed that night, suggests how much better we were doing that year, having decided the previous Christmas that we would not walk away from our marriage, not yet anyhow. Would give it and ourselves another chance instead. Would *work on our relationship* as a Yank might say, though I can see Detta making that gagging gesture she loved, forefinger thrust down her throat, at the very sound of such. We still fought plenty, but fact is we were on an upswing, even if all that were happening, or so it seemed afterwards, in a universe parallel to the one in which Detta went off to our GP that June to see about a mole on her neck. A small, scabby mole that would do for her before November was out. And while part of me knows that I'm blessed we were doing so much better before Detta died, another part still resents her for dying just as we'd maybe finally figured our way forward out – as if this time she had slipped out of the house altogether, not just disappeared behind our loudly slammed bedroom door as she sometimes would in the middle of a row, to put on Loudon Wainwright, whom she knew I couldn't abide, at full volume.

Anyhow, there was nothing strange or startling about last week's dinner party, no diplomats in absentia, nor hostess upending the entire contents of a cutlery drawer in an ear-splitting, silvery waterfall onto the hardwood dining-room floor, as the unfortunate wife of a department head at the art college, a sorry, secret drinker, had managed to do while rummaging for a cake slice some years ago. Nor had a lecherous guest chanced his arm, or hand rather, beneath the table, moving it slowly up the leg of the woman seated next to him, as happened once to Caroline, a friend of Detta's, who described with great glee her happy anticipation as your man's hand eventually encountered the strapping of her prosthesis, and then the successive expressions that flitted across his face, like a film on fast forward: befuddlement, horror, mortification.

What did happen, though, was a second recounting of the story Fergal had told me at the cooker, only undertaken this time by his Noreen as she parcelled out the fruit meringue and handed round a bowl of freshly whipped cream, on which, in the sorry, health-obsessed age we inhabit, half of the table passed. And here, too, I can imagine the spirited exchange Detta and I might have had, once home, had she been there to hear me shortly take over the story from Noreen. But I honestly don't think it was chauvinism that spurred me to take up the thread, unless it was possibly Fergal's own, seated there like a lump as Noreen handed round the coffees, plus a camomile tea for Grainne in finance, all the while trying to do her best with what she had heard from Fergal, who, to give him credit, had finally bestirred himself to fetch and uncork what I seriously hoped would prove the last bottle of Rioja.

In any event, after Noreen had interrupted herself yet again to fetch a mint tea for Maurice the sociologist, who had decided against coffee after all, I – whose table it was not, whose story it was not; I, who have never fathered a child, never mind a daughter – suddenly found myself now telling the end of it. Telling how Fergal and Noreen's old friend Seamus had heard a few weeks previously that Henry and Mary's now grown-up daughter – Claudia let's call her – was coming back to Ireland to give a talk at an international conference here. And so Seamus had gone along to the Burlington Hotel, and after Claudia had finished speaking, had gone up to her. 'You won't remember me,' he introduced himself, 'but I knew you as a child. And I want to say the only thing wrong with your wonderful talk tonight is that your father couldn't have been here to hear it.' To which Claudia had replied, 'Oh, hold me. Hold me, please!' which Seamus did, putting his arms around her as she laid her head on his shoulder and quietly sobbed her heart out in the crowded function room.

And then I told the final bit of it, just as Fergal had done earlier at the cooker, where he gave her name for the first time, revealed who the seven-year-old daughter, now thirty-nine-year-old woman, was. A name I knew – not Claudia, which I made up – but the name of somebody whom the others around the table now also recognised: not a film star, singer or so-called TV celebrity, but somebody in public affairs who had been briefly in the news earlier in the year. But suddenly realising, even as I gave it, that I wouldn't tell that part of it again, suddenly seeing how Claudia's real name makes it another story altogether, and one that by all rights belongs to her alone.

That part of it still makes sense, but I puzzled afterwards how my not having known any of the principals – Henry, Mary, Claudia, Seamus – had not appeared to particularly matter, and since I wasn't making a mess of it, and since Noreen was by now handing round the cheese platter, and Fergal refilling our wine glasses, the story apparently could be as easily finished off by me. I also have found myself wondering since what might have happened to Claudia's brother, or whether their mother stayed with her American lover. Or, for that matter, what Mary went through herself to pull up stakes like that, seeing as she does not get a chance to tell her side in any of this. But all of that is, as they say, another story.

Yet what struck me most, I guess, is the impact the story had on all of us around the table. I can only speak for myself of course, and admittedly not all that clearly. The fact that I lost my father around the same age as Claudia did hers is perhaps part of it, though mine scarcely drank himself towards death, but was rather knocked down by a car while walking back from a late evening stroll on our summer holidays in Connemara when I was twelve. Still, I don't think it's so simple as some kind of identification or transference either, given that, as I already mentioned, Detta and I never managed to have a child – daughter or son – a shortfall, as it were, which underlay a good deal of the unhappiness that ate into us. But whatever our various stories around the table that night, each of us seemed to feel that sudden surge of Claudia's grief upon hearing her father summoned forth out of the blue like that, nearly thirty years on; felt the palpable heartache that had me, too, wanting to hold her in that hotel function room, along with Seamus, only that way lies sentimentality, and this was harder, truer, more adamantine than that. Not sentiment so much as some class of cathartic, subterranean sorrow – what have you – as if words are ever of any use.

'Mind yourself, won't you?' Noreen said, kissing me good night on the cheek at their door, myself as always the last to leave. 'Are you sure you don't want us to call a taxi?' But I always walk home from their house, a forty-minute trek from their end of Ranelagh to Rialto, and last Saturday night was clear, the blue moon overhead floating like a white dinner plate on the canal waters where my mobile had beeped twice: a text wishing me *Safe home* from Noreen.

She's sound, Noreen is; no longer pushes anywhere

as hard about how am I doing as she did in the first months after Detta's death, though still very much to the fore of the handful of friends who circled round, same as she, Fergal, Seamus and others had minded Henry years before. As I left the canal behind, I thought of how she had called by that February to insist I accompany her over to the Northside for a walk in St Anne's Park. A day of bright sunshine, and mild enough for us to sit for a spell on some stone steps down where the park meets the Howth Road, a tiny waterfall at our backs, a small pond in front, and all of Dublin Bay stretched out beyond.

Noreen had remarked on all the water when we sat down and had spoken something about its correspondence with the emotions when we left, the kind of spiritual-speak stuff that I'm not keen on but have learned to let go by unremarked the odd time I encounter it. But I won't deny that I broke down entirely on those steps, after I had finished telling Noreen of the September weekend Detta and I had grabbed in Venice, between radium treatments, and before we knew which way her illness might be heading. Describing for her the small piazza across the Ponte di Rialto where we had sat for an hour on a bench by a narrow canal, watching the gondolas pass by at eye level, the pale yellow sunlight on the wall of an adjacent church like fresh paint on old stone.

Yet the tears only came as I began to recount for her the dream I'd had of Detta just the night before, the pair of us searching everywhere for something we had mislaid, emptying out the cupboard under the stairs and then the garden shed, all of it slightly skewed the way dreams are, but the two of us together again, as low-key and ordinary as if she'd never left. Noreen was great anyhow, didn't say much, mostly just listened as I tried and utterly failed to describe a loss that, when I finally lifted my head, seemed as if it were being stitched into the pale blue sky by three black chevrons of Brent geese passing overhead.

At least I'd stopped crying by the time this other couple comes along, Polish maybe, or Eastern European anyhow, in their early thirties. I like the way the new Irish inhabit Dublin, flocking to the parks or Dollymount Strand on the weekends, fishing in the canals and, better yet, or maybe worse, eating what they catch. Anyhow, the guy, a strapping bloke in a bright yellow sweatshirt, comes up and holds out a tiny mobile phone in his big mitt. 'You know to use this?'

'I do,' I agree, though I'm not entirely sure what he's asking.

'I want you take picture of wife and me please,' he points at a woman in a brown anorak with frizzy blonde hair, who smiles awkwardly back at us. So Noreen tells them to stand in front of the tiny waterfall, after which I hold the phone up and shoot them posing there, arms around each other.

'Who in God's name scripts this stuff?' I ask Noreen who just shakes her head as we walk back along the wooded path to her car. But I think maybe I've figured that much out by now. How we do that scripting bit ourselves, make our lives into stories as we stumble along. Not that we're anyways aware of that – the way I thought last week, standing at Fergal's cooker and later at the table, how that was Henry and Claudia's story, which it is, of course, but which has oddly since also come to feel in a way like my own. Perhaps that's the way certain stories work, the luck I mentioned at the start, reminding us that some, if not all, of what we've lost and found has been known by others, and in the telling or listening life can come to feel a bit less like a game of solitaire. But I hadn't that part of it until just now, certainly hadn't it the other night when, finally reaching our place, I managed, despite the Rioja and abetted by the moonlight, to get the key into the lock on the second go, after which I walked into the empty house.

Giant

Julia Kelly

DOT BROKE AWAY FROM THE rest of the group who were still loitering in the gift shop of the British Museum. She crossed the road at High Holborn, an untidy tourist, coat slung over arm, a plastic bag of souvenirs looped around and digging into her wrist, and hurried along Lincoln's Inn Fields, eyes to the ground, trusting neither the uneven pavement nor her own increasingly unreliable feet.

She joined the queue for the cloakroom at the Hunterian Museum, rooting in her bag for her reading glasses and crowding the person in front of her, the way the elderly do, impatient and anxious to be rid of her baggage, unable to stand back and wait her turn.

She climbed the marble staircase to the first floor and entered a hushed, carpeted room. Still a little out of breath from the stairs, she gave the security guard standing in an empty corner a cursory nod and was then immediately preoccupied by the exhibit she wanted to find.

The room was stuffed floor to ceiling with medical curiosities of a Victorian past: images of tuberous leprosy, a foldable and adjustable birthing chair made of walnut, phallic amulets worn as symbols of fertility, illustrations of syphilitic malformations of teeth, gangrene of the foot . . . warts and all. Her satisfaction at quickly and easily finding what she had come to see caused her to exclaim aloud. An art student sketching foetal abnormalities looked up, tired of being interrupted, then went back to her rendering, tongue in cheek with intent.

Tilting slightly back on her heels to take all eight foot, two inches of him in, Dot surveyed the extraordinary size of the skeleton. She took her glasses from their coffin-like case and stooped to read the information plaque near his metatarsal bones:

Charles Byrne (1761–1783) was one of a few famous 18th-century Irish giants who were among the group of human curiosities who had celebrity status in London theatres, making fortunes from people who would pay just to see them on stage. He is believed to be originally from Cork, but emigrated to London to earn a living. He was found dead in his apartment on Cockspur Street, Charing Cross at the age of just twenty-two following a bout of excessive drinking shortly after having his life savings stolen from him.

Dot stood there for a few seconds longer. She had read somewhere that the giant's dying wish had been to be buried at sea, as he did not want to become a specimen for anatomists or to remain an eternal freak show after death. Yet here he was, all his sadness contained behind glass, and here *she* was staring at him, now with an odd sense of remorse.

She felt for her wristwatch, calculated how long she could remain where she stood before she would need to get back to her group: a nomadic assortment of octogenarians, gay men and always the one unfathomable (no one was sure why she was there), all partaking in a frantic ticking off of antiquities and places and events, from the Mona Lisa to the tomb of Tutankhamen, that they felt were essential to a life fully lived.

Soft rainfall had left the air freshly wet that Sunday evening, petrichor, perfect running weather. Joe no longer felt that burn at the back of his throat – a sure sign that he was once again fit. He had drunk no alcohol for a month and was on a fruit-only diet for breakfast and lunch each day.

In the Liberties, at the top of Meath Street, where it intersects with Thomas Street, a red light had allowed him brief respite. He had stood, head bowed, hands on knees, catching his breath, and when he looked up again, he was met with a close-up of his own face on a billboard on a hoarding opposite. He appeared moodily handsome, as he had hoped he might, in profile in a black polo neck, intelligence in his eyes, just the right amount of stubble. It had been twenty years since he'd seen his face on a poster. The brief sensation of celebrity it had given him made him run further and faster than he was fit for. He reached that sweet spot, where running felt as effortless and as natural as walking. He could have pounded the pavements forever.

In the shower, suffused by the mild euphoria that follows exercise, he turned his face directly into the powerful stream of hot water, endorphins smothering the pain of a blister on his heel brought on by the five-mile run in new Nikes.

Two local radio stations had added his latest song to their playlists. Its lyrics had come to him, perfectly formed, in the bath, where all his best ideas were born. At their zenith, The Tribe could fill the National Stadium to capacity; Joe was a gifted songwriter and a natural front man: on stage he had been captivating. At the end of gigs he would stand, sweat-drenched and proud, beaming at the cheering audience and their rousing chants of 'More! More! More!'

They appeared on the nation's biggest chat shows, heard their songs played in record stores around the city. They could smell success, could very nearly touch it. They were where it was at. Then two things happened: creative differences in the band and a fickle change of fashion. The drummer wanted to be heard better, the bass player seen more. The ego that had brought them together was the same ego that broke them up.

Joe pulled over the shaving mirror, rubbed away some condensation and, holding his hand as still as possible, ran a kohl eyeliner pencil along his lower lids. He patted a little of his wife's concealer over the pronounced bags beneath them and, wincing, tried to force a stud earring into the long-neglected piercing in his left earlobe.

He stood on the scales: a happy ten pounds lighter than he'd been a month before. He had developed a solid, Easter-egg-shaped paunch that no amount of deprivation could dispel but that comfortably accommodated his guitar. All black would be best: T-shirt with witty maxim, black jeans and Day-Glo yellow trainers, giving him the look less of a rock star, more of a squat snorkeler, but no one was going to go there.

He looked over the guest list as he ate a light dinner – pasta with tomato and chilli. His stomach was churning, he was nervous, but ready to go. He saw the night ahead: the room busy with bodies, hushed and smiling or nodding as they identified with, or suddenly remembered, the brilliance of his lyrics, written in his head on runs, in the bath, in the staffroom between lessons, even sometimes during sex. A former female backing singer from The Tribe was going to join him on stage for two songs, to give him a bit of relief, in case his voice couldn't sustain him on his first night as a solo artist, his comeback gig.

Dot was home from London, at her dressing table, deliberating about what to wear. She hummed tunelessly as she rooted through a small china bowl containing hair clips, miscellaneous buttons, a torn theatre stub – all soft with dust – for a suitable pair of earrings. She provided her own soundtrack to whatever she was doing: when she ran her morning bath, threading fingers through water to check its temperature, on her way to answer the front door, to let whoever it was know that she had heard them and that all was as it should be, in the evenings as she waited for the milk in the saucepan to warm, practising what she'd learnt at ballroom dancing that week with her invisible partner, slippered feet moving lightly across the kitchen floor.

'Ah, Dot,' she quietly goaded herself when she spilt face powder on the bedroom carpet. She had talked to herself since her husband died fifteen years earlier and probably even while he was alive, in the room beside her, but not listening. He smiled at her now from a framed photograph near her hand, a memory in miniature, his angular glasses, paisley tie and side-parted hair existing for eternity in the past and so far away from his animated, life-sized wife.

It would be hot; it was always so hot in those places, so something light, and comfortable shoes because there might not be somewhere to sit. She had spread three possibilities on the bed behind her. She eyed them now, in their mirror image, as she cleansed, toned and moisturised her face, vaguely alarmed to see an elderly woman looking back at her. She wanted to wear something 'with it' but didn't know quite what with it could be. Perhaps the purple dress she bought in the little French shop on the high street? Or the flirty lemon-coloured skirt, that kicked out as she moved? She had worn it one evening in London but it travelled well – all her clothes were made from fabrics that were practical. But what top would be best with that? And what necklace? No, not a necklace. Maybe a scarf? She opened the drawer below her and felt around for an emery board.

The evening began late. The support act were delayed in traffic coming up from Limerick; there had been some trouble with the acoustics and the organisers wanted to wait until the venue was a bit fuller. It had seen better days – the small, sweaty room looked as jaded as some of the acts that had passed through it.

Finally, lights were dimmed, and there was a herd movement towards the stage. 'Ladies and Gentlemen, would you please welcome, after far too long in exile, Joooooe McCann!'

Joe took his place centre stage under the spotlight, a pint of Carlsberg by his feet, his guitar strapped round his shoulders. He opened the set with a few old favour- ites: feet began tapping, a hippy girl swayed, a Beaker-like man in glasses with not much hair nodded, eyes closed, to concentrate on the songwriter's words. There were a few bum notes, broken strings, false starts, but that was always a given. Joe gulped his pint between songs and told stories that made people smile.

Dot McCann's feet were tired, she couldn't make out the lyrics, couldn't see her son clearly from where she stood, beside some noisy girls who seemed to be quite tight. She wondered why they had bothered pay- ing in, standing there with their backs to the stage. She had arrived when the doors opened at eight o'clock, had chatted to a few of her son's pals, had had two mineral waters, and now she wanted to sit.

None of her friends could go with her that evening. They never told her straight, but the truth was they didn't enjoy her son's gigs. They were always too loud, too hot and too long, and Margo had been caught short in the Ladies' last time. Dot didn't mind, she was quite used to doing things on her own.

There were seats at the front – what better place to hear and watch her son perform? There was a good deal of getting organised, getting settled, and a lot of head-turning to see if she could locate Joe's wife, who was being deliberately low key, still in her coat and standing by the bar. Dot had saved a seat for her, her coat draped possessively over its plastic.

With her hands on top of one another, mid-chest, she lightly tapped her fingers and swayed her head from side to side, perfectly out of time. She felt immensely proud as she studied the CD that she'd bought at the door, even though she already had one in her car. She was flush to the stage, could feel the music reverberating against her knees. She watched Joe's every nuance, every move. They were so like one another, mother and son – he had adopted many of her gestures: he held his finger in the air, just as she did, when making a point, and closed his eyes, smiling, the way Dot did, as he tried to remember something he knew he shouldn't forget.

Cradling her drink in her lap, she bent to put it by her chair leg as each song came to an end, so that her hands would be free to applaud. She looked around her and saw other people, strangers, tapping their feet or mouthing the words of her son's songs, couples swaying, intertwined.

At the end of his set, while he waited stage side near the speakers, because there was no green room at the venue, people cheered, took to their feet, shouted out requests. After enough persuasion, Joe climbed back on stage, shaking his head, grinning, and as he adjusted his guitar he told his audience all about his new song, 'Giant', dedicated to an eight-foot freak of nature, forever encased behind glass.

Dot knew most of the words; Joe had played a recording of the song to her and his wife at Sunday lunch, for several Sundays, scrutinising their faces for reaction and drumming his fingertips against the kitchen counter, leaving greasy, temporary imprints on the Formica. 'It's very catchy,' Dot had said as she listened – all her son's songs were.

She began to quietly sing along. And that was when Joe became aware of her, his mother, too close, out of context. The mother he loved so entirely, so simply, the flowers he always remembered for her on Valentine's Day and on her birthday. The room seemed suddenly smaller; he lost a bit of his courage. He couldn't gyrate his hips as he had done in rehearsal, he'd have to mind his language, he felt the sex drain out of him, he was a little boy again, performing tricks for his parents. He knew that his mother would be there that night, but he wanted her somewhere in the shadowy darkness, not beside him, willing him on.

At the end of the night, Joe reappeared, sweat droplets across his forehead, towel around his neck like a post-fight pugilist. A girl wanted his autograph, the Beaker-like man wanted to talk about words. Joe scanned the room for his mother. She had hovered, wondering whether to offer him a lift home, then thought better of it. This was his place, not hers. She slipped away without saying goodbye, her left ear ringing and blocked.

Dot sat at her dressing table, tired, ready for sleep. She thought of the evening: the music, the words, the response. She thought back to London and the desperate vision of a soul too sad to live, wanting only obscurity. This song unearthed the dead: the dead giant who never wanted fame, the musician who wanted nothing more.

She rubbed at the inky, illegible smudge of the admission stamp on her hand. How incongruous it looked with the risen veins, liver spots and loose skin of age. She licked her finger and rubbed it again; no use. She would take a nailbrush to it in the morning.

Aisling

Colum McCann

I WOKE UP, OPENED THE CURTAINS, found my nightgown, made the bed, tightened the sheets, fluffed the pillows, donned my slippers, turned the tap, filled the kettle, hit the switch, boiled the water, brewed the tea, stirred the milk, climbed the stairs, woke the boys, combed their hair, straightened their curls, brushed their teeth, buttoned their buttons, zipped their zippers, checked their homework, poured their cornflakes, ladled the milk, toasted their toast, packed their lunches, checked their satchels, fixed their collars, tied their laces, wiped their noses, kissed their cheeks, unlocked the chain, crossed the threshold, tapped their bottoms, waved them off, ran the driveway, called their names, held their shoulders, kissed their foreheads, trudged on home, keyed the lock, climbed the stairs, brushed my teeth, washed my face, slipped on sandals, filled my clothes, ignored the mirror, jumped out the window and developed two huge wings on the way down. Of course I didn't.

★

I nuked the tea, blew it cool, sipped it down, junked the teabag, threw it out, made some toast, spread the marmalade, flicked the television, jumped the channels, killed the remote, dialled the radio, broke the static, heard the weather, turned it off, ached for rain, waited for sunshine, rinsed the cup, cleaned the plates, separated the forks, licked the knives, sliced my lip, bit the blood, loaded the dishwasher, hit the switch, heard it hum, boiled the kettle, made more tea, rifled the cupboards, found the gin, opened the freezer, broke the ice, shook a cocktail, drank it down, recalled my husband, mutilated him twice, fair is fair, what he deserves, wept an aria, made another drink, iced it up, held the sink, poured it down, heard it gurgle, guilt and grace, phoned my friend, forgot her number, ordered a private jet to bring me all the way up to Cornelscourt and flew along through Monaloe Park on the back of a very handsome nightingale. Well at least I tried.

I took off shopping, inserted a euro, got a trolley, pushed it along, patrolled the aisles, ignored the prices, passed the specials, squeezed some apples, filched a grape, shook the cereal, eyed the ham, flirted with watermelons, lingered at lemons, checked the calories, avoided all fats, filled my trolley, wandered the wine, grabbed the Bordeaux, queued at checkout, flicked the magazines, waited for hallelujahs, started to fret, checked my purse, berated the Lithuanian, felt briefly guilty, paid by credit, bagged the groceries, trawled on home, took the overpass, walked down Clonkeen, used the doormat, ate a pill, skipped the stairs, thought of visions, destroyed all trinities, had a love affair with a tar-dark Gypsy who rang the doorbell and afterwards, in the driveway, had a minor collision with fifteen hundred nuns from Loreto Foxrock, oh my darling you're a child of the Immaculate Mary and you don't have to kiss him until you're entirely ready. But I very well might.

I looked at photos, saw myself young, did my homework, ran to mass, wore brown smocks, hemmed them up, plucked my eyebrows, bared my ankles, skipped the Gaeltacht, hired a tutor, got into college, painted my toes, tattooed a butterfly, danced the Bar, went to Glastonbury, got some sense, filled the forms, cajoled a job, paid the taxman, queued at Lillie's, tipped the barmaid, ate at Trocadero, learned to lament, flew to Paris, swam a lake, lost my passport, bussed it home, kissed my parents, called them prodigals, hailed a taxi, erased the tattoo, moved to Ranelagh, leafed with lovebanks, developed an accent, bought some stocks, read *The Times*, commissioned a painting, found two bedrooms, thought it three, lost the run, forgot the poem, married the hard-working boy who came up from the country while the dead girl flew off in the shape of a question mark, thinking well you can eat around the bruised part, my dear, but the core is still altogether dark I fear.

★

I went to hospital, had the children, settled in Monaloe, painted the walls, planted the garden, weeded the lawn, bought some secateurs, clipped the begonia, fertilised the floribundas, plucked the weeds, changed the vasewater, ate small portions, loved the boys, learned about porridge, loved the boys, went Sunday driving, girls' night out, ironed the towels, shook out wrinkles, folded the underwear, whitened my teeth, lost the time, learned the lament, forgot my prayers, loved the boys, ignored the bills, begged the bank, loved the boys, remembered their birthdays, slept beside them, sent off faxes, played the exchange, mortgaged the mortgage, laid the table, ordered the china, saw Aidan shudder, watched him leave, opened the champagne, called my friends, remembered their numbers, loved the boys, hired a solicitor, had an affair, broke the fever, extended the line, wrote on pillowcases, filled my heart full of petrol and poured it out into a styrofoam cup.

I woke up alive, filled the kettle, boiled the water, recycled the teabag, defrosted the loaf, cut the crusts, corked the wine, emptied my mind, designed an escape, changed the plan. The fridge sang, the mice groaned, the radio fizzed, the clock droned, the grass grew, the birds flew, my bones hollowed, my head hurt. I fell in love with all the cereal boxes I hadn't yet arranged on the shelves. The dustbins keened, the postman knocked, the bills arrived, the cheques bounced, the creditors wept, the reaper wrote, the church collapsed, the child returned, the sky-woman fell through the roof. I thanked God for ceilings so I wouldn't have to hit the stars. I cleaned windows, watched the clock, got myself together, paced the hall, wore a pathway, awaited the boys, sang this ditty. *Be not sad, Roisín, for all that happened thee.* I watched the clock, saw it strike, heard no footsteps, thought of suicide but the beauty of just about everything else took my courage away.

A Gift for My Mother

Viv McDade

IN THE YEAR I TURNED TEN I picked my mother a bunch
of wild flowers in the bushveld behind our house, tiny
star-shaped flowers with white on the top and pink
underneath, daisies the colour of egg yolks and a sprig
from a lucky bean creeper.

'They're beautiful,' she said, turning the little bunch
to look at the shape and colour of each flower, the red
and black lucky beans snug in their dry brown pod. She
arranged the flowers in a jar of water and put them on
the windowsill beside the stove so she could see them
while she was cooking.

'I love a fresh flower in the house,' she said in her
dreamy voice. 'If I had my time over, Lucy, I'd have
everything just perfect, nothing but the best.' I knew she
was thinking about the houses on the other side of the
railway line, houses with hallways and moulded skirting
boards and neighbours who didn't go down to the shops
with chiffon scarves over their curlers. But that evening
they weren't on her mind long enough to make her
angry or sad and after a little while she moved the jar of

flowers along the windowsill into the last of the sunlight, and she was humming when she wiped down the sink.

I sat at the kitchen table doing my maths homework until I heard Dad's car and ran out to meet him. He opened the door and leaned out to kiss me. 'Hello, my precious.' My mother hates that. 'For God's sake, it's a wonder the child hasn't grown up thinking her name was *My Precious*.'

'I was the only one who could spell *illiterate*,' I tell him.

'Fantastic. You're the best speller I know.'

'I'm stuck with a maths problem. If eight men dig a ditch in two hours how many eight-hour days will it take two men to dig the same ditch?'

'We'll work it out when we put our minds to it.'

He's very good at explaining things and never makes you feel nervous or stupid. My mother thinks his job at the garage isn't much, but he's a far better teacher than Mrs Emmerson.

He wiped his shoes on the mat before we went into the kitchen. 'Hello,' he said, as if he was asking a question, and my mother's voice was tired and small when she answered him. He took a deep breath and slapped the little brown envelope of wages down on the table.

'How much is there this week?' asked my mother, and she gave a little laugh.

'As much as I've earned, that's how much.'

'What you've earned isn't enough for us to live on.'

'Then die on it,' he said, walking out of the kitchen, 'because it's all there is.'

My mother snatched a pot from the cupboard, banged it into the sink and opened the tap so wide the water ran over the top. After she switched off the tap she looked out the window for a long time.

It was getting dark outside when she told me to set the table. I switched on the light, and she pulled the curtains closed, leaving the jar of flowers in the darkness.

Next day after school I went around the back of the supermarket and searched for a box in the yard. Most were cardboard and too big or too deep but in the end I found a shallow wooden peach box that was perfect.

At home I put tins of water in the box, changed into old clothes and went out the back gate with the box and scissors from the kitchen. The paths that led through the bush over to the factories on the road to the airport were sharp and clear but I chose an overgrown path. The leaves of the msasa trees were shiny, and the sun made it look as if there were diamonds on the big granite boulders.

After a while my arms got tired holding the box so I sat on the edge of the path and watched a line of polished black ants follow each other into the long yellow grass and listened to birds calling *pttt pttt* from the trees. I left the box in the shade of a boulder. The ground felt hot through my sandals and the long dry grass scraped my legs. There were all kinds of daisies: tiny and white, and yellow and orange ones as big as my hand. I cut the stems as long as I could and took each handful back to the box to put them in water. I was reaching over a

clump of blackjacks to cut off their flowers and they'd
scattered their tiny black spikes on my T-shirt and shorts
when I spotted my first flame lily, its wavy swept-back
petals bright red at the top and yellow at the bottom
exactly as if it was on fire. Mrs Emmerson had shown
us a picture and told us it was illegal to pick them and
you were very lucky if you saw one. I longed to give my
mother something so beautiful and precious but shivered
at the thought of becoming a criminal. I was lucky to
find a big bush full of tiny white candle-shaped flowers
with yellow tips and trumpets of witch weed with black
spots in their hearts. A long creeper of wild spinach had
lots of flowers but their stems weren't long enough to go
in a bunch. In places where the leaves of the msasa trees
were starting to turn different colours I cut delicate gold
and red sprigs.

By the time I got home the long grass was making
shadows across the path and I'd worked out everything I
needed to do. I laid out the flowers and divided them into
ten bunches – some all one kind of flower, others different
flowers but shades of the same colour and others I mixed
up. I made daisy chains out of string and used them to tie
up the flowers before arranging the bunches in the tins of
water and putting my purse in the box beside them.

On the street I decided not to start with the du Toits or
the Thompsons because they lived beside us and might
tell my mother. Instead I walked five streets away and
went to the house at the end. It felt safer to start with
strangers.

There was a tricycle in the garden and a puddle of water around the sprinkler in the middle of the yellowy lawn. A safety chain held the front door slightly open and inside a voice on the radio was talking about a shop that had been burgled and a man who was helping the police with their investigations.

A woman's voice called out, 'I'm telling you for the last time, put those toys away.'

I knocked on the door, a soft knock at first and then louder. I was thinking about leaving and going next door when I heard flip-flops slapping to the door. A woman carrying a baby, so small its head had hardly any hair and its cheek was squashed against her shoulder, looked through the gap in the doorway.

'Good afternoon,' I said. 'Would you like to buy some flowers for sixpence a bunch?'

A telephone started ringing in the house, and she hesitated for a moment as if she might go to answer it, then changed her mind. 'Flowers?' she said. 'You must be joking!' She turned her head. 'I'm not going to say it again. Put those toys away this minute.' Then she looked at me again, took the chain off and opened the door.

'Does your mother know what you're doing, pet?'

'No,' I said. 'I'm going to surprise her.'

'Well, your flowers are beautiful. It cheers me up just looking at them.'

She took one of the mixed bunches into the house, and when she came back she gave me a sixpence and four toffees in waxy white paper with blue writing. 'You be careful crossing the road with that box,' she said.

On the way out I put down the box and closed the gate, then opened it again when I remembered that was how I'd found it.

In the garden two houses down a man was pruning a creamy rose bush beside his veranda, standing back a little to look at it and pinching his cheek slowly before he cut off each branch. He turned when he heard the click of the gate latch and put his head to one side as he walked down the drive to meet me.

'Those look nice,' he said.

'Do you think you might like some?'

'Of course I would like some,' he said. 'What are you charging?'

'Sixpence a bunch,' I said, and immediately wished I'd lowered my price.

'Bring them up here,' he said, going onto the veranda. 'I'll go in and get my wife so we can choose together.'

His wife was round and quick with a smile that took up her whole face. 'What will you do with the money you get from the flowers?'

'It's going to be a surprise.'

'That's nice,' said the man.

'For my mother,' I said.

His wife loved all the flowers but the little white daisies were her favourite because she said 'Definitely these' when her husband asked 'What'll we get?'

In the end they bought three bunches: daisies for the

kitchen and two mixed bunches for the lounge. The man fetched his wallet and gave me two shillings. 'There you go,' he said, 'and you can keep the change.' When I looked back from the gate he held up his thumb and called out, 'Good luck.'

I could feel the purse in my pocket and I knew the flowers were even more beautiful than I'd thought. People were friendly and interested to know my name and where I lived and if my mother was at home, and although the bunches with longer stems went first, nearly everyone found it hard to know which ones to choose.

At one house a boy with pimples and a black T-shirt that had 'So what?' in pink writing on the front, came to the door with a cigarette in his hand.

He looked at the two bunches I had left. 'So how much money have you made?'

'Four shillings and sixpence so far,' I said.

'Cool. Almost enough to buy yourself some wheels. Look here, my old lady's out at the moment but if she wasn't I reckon she'd buy.'

In less than an hour I'd sold the ten bunches and went home with the purse full of money. I emptied it onto the kitchen table and made a little tower of each kind of coin. Five and sixpence: five shillings for the flowers, and the extra sixpence from the people who'd bought three bunches.

I thought about boiling the kettle and setting out the cups. I'd make the tea when I heard the bus, and when we were settled at the table I'd casually show her the money. But I was too excited to stick to the plan so I washed my face and legs, changed into fresh shorts and my lace-collar blouse, ran down the road to the bus stop and sat on the verge, jiggling my leg against the fat purse in my pocket.

The bus pulled in and my mother was sitting right at the front. As soon as she got up from her seat she saw me and waved, and hugged me against her when she came down the steps. 'That blouse is lovely,' she said. 'You're a good girl to come down to the bus in it.' I took the shopping bag from her and saw there was milk and a packet of meat. 'Are we having chops?' I asked.

'Chops?' she said. 'Where would the money come from for chops?'

'I've got a present for you.'

'A present?' she said. 'Have you really?'

In the kitchen I opened the purse and emptied it onto the table. 'It's for you. It's the present.'

She looked at the money and then at me. 'Where did this money come from?'

'I got it from flowers, flowers like the ones I gave you.'

'What are you talking about, Lucy?'

I started to tell her about the peach box I'd found in the yard behind the supermarket, the daisy chains and the flowers, but before I could finish she slapped the table hard with both hands. 'Are you telling me, are you really telling me that you went around the neighbourhood selling bits of flowers you got from the bush?' She sat down like an old woman and put her elbows on the table and her head in her hands. A big sob came out of her, and when she looked up her face was twisted and wet. 'People will think I sent you, they'll think I dressed you up and sent you out to sell flowers from the bush.'

'I didn't dress up,' I said. 'I dressed up for you.'

'Look at you!' She pressed her fingers against her eyes and shook her head. 'I want you to go back. Go and give the money back. Tell them your mother won't let you keep it.'

'I don't want to keep it,' I said. 'It's for you.'

'Listen to what I am saying, Lucy. You are to say your mother will not allow you to keep the money. That's what you must say.'

I went back with my purse to each of the houses and told the people I had to give back the money. 'Well, if that's what your mother wants,' some said. Others asked why I had to give it back but I wasn't able to tell them. The man and his wife who had bought the three bunches weren't at home so I left the money on the mat in front of their door.

The last person I went to was the woman who'd bought the first bunch and given me the toffees. 'Look,' she said. 'I don't know what all this is about but you can tell your mother I will not give back the flowers. If she's not happy with that, she can come up here to me and we'll talk about it.' I walked home thinking about how everyone else had taken back their money as though it had nothing to do with the flowers.

'Well,' said my mother, 'What did they say? Did you tell them your mother wouldn't let you keep the money?'

I put the sixpence on the table. 'One woman wouldn't take it. She said you can go and see her about it.'

'What woman?'

'I don't know. She lives in the big yellow house near the shop.'

My mother reached across the table for her handbag. 'I have nothing to say to her, or to any of them,' she said. She put the coin in her purse and then went over to the sink. Her knife was sharp and fast against the potatoes, and the water splashed when she threw them into the pot.

Chicago Here We Come

Belinda McKeon

STANDING IN THE PLANE AISLE at O'Hare, elbows prodding her and shoulders jostling her and asses backing into her, Alice looked at the two words on her phone screen and wondered why she felt so sad. They were the words of a worried mother. Of an abandoned lover. Of a baby trapped at the bottom of a well, except that a baby trapped at the bottom of a well could never send a text message saying 'Please call', for reasons to do with infant intelligence and hand-to-eye coordination and phone network coverage below ground.

They were none of these things, Alice knew. They were the words of her Chicago relations – some of her Chicago relations, one of her Chicago relations, just looking at the number she could not tell which one – asking her to call when her flight landed. They were the words of someone who was polite, so they put the word 'please' in front of the word 'call'. That was all. But still they were words that made her feel wretched. She leaned forward and showed the message to Joe. He was standing in front of her, watching the long queue nudge its way towards the cabin door, holding the bulky black form of her laptop bag in his arms.

'Huh,' Joe nodded, as he read the message. 'That's interesting. That's the first time I've ever actually seen someone use one of those.'

Alice stared at the screen. 'One of what?' she said, more sharply than she had intended.

'One of those templates,' Joe said. 'For texts. There's a set of them already stored in your phone when you get it. You just send them off ready-made. They're for people who don't want to be bothered typing an actual message.' He shrugged. 'Or for people who can't.'

Joe shifted his hold on Alice's bag, moving it into the crook of his opposite arm. 'This thing weighs a bloody ton,' he said. 'Why d'you have to bring it everywhere with you? It's not like you're going to get any chance to use it here.'

'I didn't ask you to carry it for me,' Alice said, but a space had opened up in the aisle ahead of Joe, and he was gone quickly on.

With every phone call and every email from home, Alice's mother had pinned the idea of taking a trip to Chicago deeper and deeper into her mind, closer and closer to the raw stuff of conscience until finally, with a passing comment the previous month, it had found its grip. *While there's time*, an email had said, before moving on to a matter completely unrelated; *While there's time, it would be nice to do.*

It would be nice to do. Bill and Ellen: her mother's uncle and the Leitrim woman he had married within six months of arriving in Chicago. The wedding photograph had been the most precious of all the precious things in her grandmother's good sitting room. The heavy silver frame. The tint like a tea stain to the paper. The train of Ellen's satin dress pooled wide around her, the lace of her sleeves dipping low and close over her hands. Bill looked like Frank Sinatra, or Perry Como, or one of those guys: a face like a boy and dark hair side-parted into a bump, the flower on his dark suit pinned almost level with his narrow white bow tie. On their visits home, during a handful of the summers of Alice's childhood, they had been celebrities. New white paint and pebbledash on her grandmother's house, on her own house. New glass-fronted presses in the kitchen one year, a new leather suite with little squares of wood on the armrests. The squares of wood came up if you slid your fingers under them. You weren't meant to. You weren't meant, either, to eat any of the small salad sandwiches, or pick at the pieces of bacon on top of the quiche. That meant trouble.

One thing it enabled you to do, having the Americans home on holiday, was to go into the overstocked gift shop on Cashel Street without being chased off the premises by the owner. He only wanted Americans in his shop. He smiled at them and talked to them and stared at them. His shop sold Irish souvenirs, and you would never imagine it was possible to make so many Irish souvenirs, that it was possible for them to come in so many configurations, that there was a way to fill a shop with them in a town in the Irish midlands in the middle of the 1980s that got no tourists, but there was, and they did. Most of them seemed to be made from some kind of twisted, blackened branches glossed over with varnish. He sold toys, as well, but if you tried to go in there by yourself to look at the toys he would shout at you to get out. Everyone was a knacker to McGorty. Until you came in with your American great-aunt and great-uncle. Then he looked at you as though you were adorable. Then he laughed when you put on the gorilla mask and as you got a plastic egg out of the machine and opened it to find a tiny bundle of tiny parts to put together to make a tiny car. Maybe, if you didn't open your mouth, he thought you were also American. Maybe, for a while, you thought that too.

When Alice went to college, where, until the year when they all stopped coming, the American tourists piled in and lined up to see the Book of Kells, she realised that the sight of their white shoes was making her nostalgic. That she would see a tour bus full of American pensioners and want, suddenly, inexplicably, to be on it. It would be a crushing bore, she knew. They would talk the head off her. But still, she started to feel a pang of wishing, something, every time she saw a bus. It made no sense. Bill and Ellen had never taken a tour bus. Bill and Ellen had always hired a car.

As they waited for their baggage, Alice noticed again how

strange Joe's clothes looked, the way he had put them together. He only ever wore that shirt with jeans, but it was with a jumper now, a jumper he only ever wore over a T-shirt, and the trousers of his dark suit didn't look right without the jacket, and they needed to be pressed. She had not said anything to Joe, as they had packed that morning, about his trousers needing to be pressed. They had not said very much to one another at all. It was the morning after Thanksgiving, and on Thanksgiving there had been a dinner in Williamsburg, and after dinner there had been a bar, and between the cab home from the bar and the cab to JFK there had been maybe two hours. And Joe had remembered to wear his suit pants, and not to wear his Converse, and in the airport toilets he could have a shave, and that was good enough.

Where are you going to be, they wanted to know when she called the Chicago number. What exit are you going to come out at? Let us know, so that Mary can bring the car right up to the door and pick you up.

She thought they said Mary. Or maybe they said Maureen. Maureen was their daughter. No, the daughter's name was Maura, and Maureen was the neighbour who sometimes helped them out with things. She couldn't remember. She texted her mother in Ireland again to ask her about the daughters' names.

The photographs from her mother's trip to Chicago were all Polaroids, pasted into a fat album covered in what looked like velvet flock wallpaper. In them, her mother was thin and long-haired and twenty-three. She sunbathed in a garden with her American cousins and posed with Bill and Ellen in front of a fountain and up at the top of Sears Tower. The colours were bleached, as though everything had been left sitting in a window too long. Bill and Ellen and their children were tanned and her mother was big-eyed and pale. The houses in the photographs were wooden; they had porches. The cars were long and low and brown. Bill smoked a cigar and Ellen and her mother and the daughters wore paisley skirts that hit far above their knees. There was a boy, with thick dark hair, in flares. Alice and her sisters looked at the album over and over again. The first photograph was taken from inside the plane. It was of a plane window and of the grey air outside that plane window. Whatever else had been outside the plane window had not come out in the photo. CHICAGO HERE WE COME, her mother had written with a blue biro, in big slanted capital letters, on the inside of the album's front cover.

Her mother texted her straight back. She must have been waiting to hear something. Their names were Maura, and Alma, and Agnes, her mother texted her, and only Maura was unmarried, and Alice was to call as soon as she got the chance with news of how they were getting on.

Whichever of the daughters it was, she pulled up opposite the door in a black SUV and waved over to them. By the time they had crossed to her, Bill was out of the car too, standing very still by the open passenger door, watching. He was smiling; he lifted one hand high in greeting and began to walk towards them as they lifted their bags into the trunk.

'Daddy, it's freezing,' the daughter said, and he shook his head and laughed, and as he reached her he lifted his hand again, as if to hit her, and clasped her instead by the shoulder. Everyone laughed.

'She's always telling me what the weather is like,' Bill said, and he hugged Alice and shook Joe's hand. They all said some sentences to one another over and over, and then they got in the car, Bill wanting Joe to sit in the front, and Joe insisting that Bill sit there, and the daughter telling Bill to get into the car out of the cold, and then it turned out there was a child sitting in the back of the car, a girl of about eight, strapped in and smiling, and on the whole long drive home from the airport they were all able to keep talking to one another because the child was there, because nothing makes it easier to talk to other adults than the presence of a child. Send every word through the child, open every subject up through them. The child will smile and nod and say sweet, high-pitched things, and the adults will laugh and look each other in the eye and jump off from the springboard of the child into other, suddenly possible things.

When they reached the house, Ellen was in a state of distress. She was sitting on the staircase with another of the daughters standing beside her. Her head was in her hands. Bill went to her immediately and put his hands on her shoulders, facing her. She shook her head, and she was half laughing, half crying. She had called the police again, she said. It was something she kept doing, because the area code was so close to the number for the police. She had tried to cancel, but, the daughter explained, you couldn't cancel the police. They just came. They would think, said Ellen, that she was so foolish, so foolish. Ellen had always been very thin. She had a way of holding her shoulders, inside her chenille sweater, that made her look braced against the wind, even indoors, even sitting on the carpeted stairs of her home.

The police turned up. Two young men. Both tall and thick-bodied, with brown hair cut tight to the skull and eyes that immediately read the room. They were understanding. It happened all the time, they said; the numbers were too much alike. Bill walked them to the door.

'That was quick,' said Joe, as they left.

'Yeah, they're good around here,' said the daughter. 'Come on, Mom, it's not a big deal. You heard them. It happens all the time. It could happen to anyone.'

'I'm so stupid, so stupid,' said Ellen. She was still sitting on the first step of the staircase. When Bill came in from the porch she looked at him and shook her head. 'I'm so foolish, so foolish,' she said. She put her face in her hands again.

'They were very nice young men,' Bill said, and he held his hand out to Ellen to help her to her feet.

In the bedroom, Alice saw the photograph first, and she saw the neatness, and the sense of everything in the room being cared for, and being kept in just its right place, second. The black beads of a rosary hung over the mahogany frame. Someone had chosen that frame very carefully. Someone had decided against lesser frames, lighter frames, thinner frames and had taken just this one home. The photograph was on a bedside table, by a closed book, by a lamp with an angled arm. In the photograph, the son was still a boy. He had no baseball bat, no leather mitt, no oblong brown ball, none of the props American children always seemed to have in photographs. He was, maybe, eight. The camera had been pointed down at him from a height. His smile was a child's smile, two rows of teeth gleefully exposed, gleefully clenched; that they were perfectly white and straight, that was the American part. And the smooth brown skin, and the brightly printed T-shirt and the canvas runners like the children wore on *Sesame Street*; he was sitting on what looked like a park bench, and his knees were drawn up, and his arms were thrown wide.

'This is all right for you?' Bill was saying from behind her, and she heard Joe say that it certainly was. That it was a lovely room, a lovely size. When she turned around to say something similar to Bill – something about neatness, something about the many books in the room – she saw that he was only halfway into the room, that he was still standing in the doorway, and that he was reaching, once again, for her case. She shook her head. She had already tried, twice, to stop him carrying her case. It was too heavy. She had, as usual, overpacked. She had brought things like snow boots, even though the forecast had said only some snow, no accumulation, and anyway she had no intention of walking around in the snow, accumulated or otherwise. And Bill had insisted on carrying her case to the bedroom door, and now he was moving to lift it again, and bring it, she supposed, into the room for her, and she wanted to stop him. She went to him, quickly, and put her hand on the case, to let him know that she would take it, that she would bring it to wherever it would stand for the rest of the weekend; that she would take it from here. She did not say any of this but tried to communicate it with a smile and a slow shake of her head, with a pat on his hand as she lifted the case away from him and into the room. Bill looked at her a moment – strangely, she thought, sort of hesitantly, with an odd sort of slant – and then shrugged. He did not stop smiling, but the shape the smile put on his mouth had changed; the smile was pulling at his lips now, rather than pushing them. The smile was working out a way to stay.

'Well, there's another room in there if you want it,' he said, gesturing across the hall. 'I guess,' and he paused and looked to the door, 'which ever one you prefer. You can have my room, or you can have Ellen's.'

'This one is lovely, Bill,' Alice said, but as she spoke she felt Joe touching her on the arm. Not touching her, prodding her. She looked at him. His eyebrows were almost comically high. His eyes were saying something to her. They were going down to her case and sideways to Bill and back to her. They were telling her something urgent. In a moment or two, Alice knew, she would see that urgent thing and understand precisely what it was. She would act on it. She felt herself twitch, even, with the beginnings of that movement, with the first firings of that thing she would do. But she didn't have it yet. She was waiting for it to slide itself, the perfect, compact clarity of itself, into her mind. She stared at Joe, raising her eyebrows in imitation of his. Joe raised his own eyebrows still higher. Hers couldn't go that far.

'What?' she mouthed to him.

'I think Bill means, if *you'd* like to have the room across the hall,' Joe said.

She stared at him. 'If I'd like . . . ?' She looked to Bill, who shrugged again. 'Whatever you'd like, whichever suits you best,' he said.

'Okay,' Alice said in a voice that sounded to her like the voice of someone who was trapped under a fallen piece of furniture and who was trying to be sportsmanly about it, trying not, just yet, to give them any cause for undue concern.

'I'll take the other room, Bill,' said Joe.

Alice understood. In a panic, she looked at Joe, and Joe touched her on the arm as he passed, but he was already moving with his bag to the other room, and Bill was nodding and leading the way. How did she repair this? How did she come back from walking up to her eighty-three-year-old grand-uncle and practically slapping her case out of his grip as he tried to put her in a separate bedroom to her boyfriend? Obviously they would be sleeping separately. It didn't matter that they had been living together in Brooklyn for almost three years. They knew the score. They were unmarried, and they were staying with elderly relations – very, very Catholic elderly relations – and so they would be sleeping in separate rooms. It was fine. It was simple. And now the memory of the way Bill's gaze had slid sideways at her and away from her in that instant when she took the case from him was pulsing flushes up and down her entire skin.

'Jesus,' she said, and sat down on the bed. 'Jesus, Jesus, fuck.'

'We'll be in the kitchen,' Bill said, from where he was standing in the hall. He had shown Joe into the other bedroom. Maybe he hadn't heard her. Maybe she hadn't said it so loud. He gave her a wave, the same wave he had given her at the airport. A salute. The arm raised, frozen in the air a second, then dropped to the side with a half laugh. A shake of the head. 'See you in a while.'

'See you, Uncle Bill,' Alice said. She had never called him Uncle before. Now seemed like the right sort of time to start.

'You're overreacting,' Joe said, when she called in to him in the other bedroom. She had made a big thing of this, that she was calling in to him; she had knocked loudly on his door, hoping they could hear her from the sitting room, and she had called something like, 'All right for me to come in?' Shouted it, really. Joe had given her a look of weary bafflement when he opened the door.

'You're getting worked up over nothing, as usual,' he said, as he folded the clothes he had taken from his bag and laid them on a chair. The chair was white, and carved, and cushioned, like many other things in the room; it was a room swimming with soft surfaces, with pillows and shams and ottomans and lace-edged quilts and doilies hanging over dressing-table shelves. This was the room she had been meant to sleep in, no doubt about that. Joe looked like a burglar standing in the middle of it, nicely dressed though he might have been; he was too tall, and his hair was too wild, and he hadn't shaved in the airport bathroom after all. He looked as though he would move his hand any second and break the bedroom in half.

'He'll think I'm an assertive little bitch,' Alice said.

'No he won't. And you are assertive, anyway. And there's nothing wrong with being assertive.'

'Aggressive, then. He'll think I'm aggressive.'

Joe put his arms around her where she liked it – right where her arms became her shoulders, right where, according to every magazine she looked at, she was sup-posed to be hard and toned.

'You're second-guessing, like you always do,' he said. 'You can't go second-guessing your way through your whole life.'

This phrase came up often. Alice was growing to like it. It made what she was always doing – getting herself into a welter of paranoia about what other people thought of her – sound somehow cerebral, somehow considered.

Somehow more than the narcissistic pity party it simply was. Still, she couldn't just let him get away with that.

'You didn't shave that time, did you?' she said.

He got that look in his eye, which was the one she had been intending him to get, but which made her feel guilty, all the same. He was trying, the look said, he was doing a lot, but there was always something he would turn out not to have done, and Alice would always make damn certain to remind him. And it was always something small and stupid and utterly irrelevant in the larger scheme of things, the look also said, but Alice would still pounce on it like a cat chasing after every piece of crap that trails or floats or falls, and, in spite of everything, that was a disappointment, wasn't it, when it came to her, and, in spite of everything, wasn't it a pity that she had to be a nag like all the rest of them.

'We should go down to the sitting room,' he said.

In the sitting room, Bill and Ellen sat close together on the sofa. There was room beside them for one other person, and Alice intuited that she should be that person, being the actual relative, and Joe sat across from them in a leather armchair with a footrest that came up with the pull of a handle. He pulled the handle; Bill insisted on it. He might as well be as comfortable as he could, Ellen said by way of agreement. Alice looked at him, with his legs hoisted up, and his body thrust back, and thought, for some reason, of the hurricane.

They watched television – a lot of television. In

Brooklyn, they had no television. They watched *Will &*
Grace, *Ballykissangel* and a film on the Hallmark chan-
nel about the widow of a young firefighter who died
saving the life of a child. It seemed likely she would
marry again, but she was having a hard time giving
herself the permission to be happy.

'He's meant to be gay,' said Ellen, when she switched
over and found a documentary about a Hollywood actor.
Bill clasped Alice's wrist again, as if to apologise.

'All these programmes,' he said. 'Do you want to watch
anything?'

'We're happy,' said Alice. 'Don't worry about us.'

But they worried. Every time Ellen changed the chan-
nel, she looked for a moment afterwards at Alice, and
then at Joe, seeming to want to gauge from their reaction
whether this was the kind of thing they liked watching,
whether this was the way you made people of their age
feel at home these days.

'The grandchildren have their things they like to
watch when they come here,' she said after they had been
watching the Hallmark film for another while. 'I don't
know, I don't know if you'd like to do anything.' She
looked to Bill. He nodded.

'We'll go down to Mac's place for dinner soon,' he said.

And Bill worried; he had worried all afternoon. When
Joe had told him the names of some of the men that
his father knew in Sligo, Bill had realised that one of
the men had a brother living nearby, a brother who had

come to Chicago in the forties, too, and he had picked up the phone and called him, and after a few awkward words of greeting and of explanation, he had put him onto Joe. Joe, Alice could tell, was thinking of as many things to say as he possibly could. She felt bad about the shaving remark. He looked good with the stubble. And it was hardly true what she had thought, that Bill and Ellen would think him rough if he was unshaven. Bill and Ellen had had a son. They knew things weren't straightforward.

'That was a coincidence,' said Bill, when Joe handed him back the phone. 'I haven't talked to that man in maybe ten years.'

'Nine,' said Ellen. 'We talked to him nine years ago.' Her mouth drew in on itself, and she shook her head quickly, as if trying to remember something she had been about to say.

Bill stared at her, startled. 'That's right,' he said after a moment. 'Nine years.'

Alice remembered the day the call had come about their son. She had taken it. She had been on a weekend home from college, helping her mother to take the groceries from the boot of the car. Get that, will you, said her mother, when they heard the sound of the phone ringing in the hall, and Alice had run. And so, probably, she had been out of breath when she picked it up, probably, she had panted, gasped all down the phone. Bill's voice had been unmistakable, and what was in his

212

voice had been unmistakable, too. His son had been sick
for three months. Alice knew why he was calling, knew
why there was that stillness in his voice when he asked
for Alice's mother, but still she had to talk on at him and
say, this is Alice, and say, how are you, and say – though
she knew what the answer would be, why did she have to
ask it? – how is Jack, and when the answer came back as
the news, delivered with such dignity by Bill, explained
to her with such beautiful calm, she knew that she was
only, still, a child. Because she could not think of the
right thing to say back to him. She could not get into her
voice the right kind of tenderness, the right kind of love.
She said something, and Bill thanked her, and then she
turned with the phone to her mother who was framed
with her box of groceries in the doorway and who was
staring at Alice as though she had been the one to create
this news, to thrust it, in all its cruelty, onto this side of
the ocean, into this springtime Saturday.

After the film about the firefighter had ended with a
wedding in a shrub-filled summer garden, Alice took out
her laptop and showed them some of the photographs
from her last trip back to Ireland. Bill sat on one side of
her, and Ellen on the other, and in the armchair Joe put
his head to one side and fell asleep.

The photographs were just right, but there were too
many of them. She had a digital camera which allowed
her to take five hundred, six hundred photographs before
she had to erase some, to make room for more, and it

meant that she had no discipline when she took photographs, which she liked to do; it meant, for example, that
she pointed a camera at her grand-uncle, Bill's brother,
the one who lived in Sligo, and she held the shutter down
for ten, twenty, thirty photographs, that she followed him
around taking photographs until she noticed him looking at her strangely, looking at her with a little flint of
irritation in his eye, and she stopped. These were photographs from the agricultural show in Gurteen. She had
gone, out of boredom, with her parents, and had spent
the day trying to take arty photographs of bullocks and
pullets and prize-winning bales of straw, and of her
grand-uncle, who had come in his good clothes to walk
the fields and study the animals being paraded inside
each ring.

'He looks good,' Ellen said, leaning in to the computer
screen. 'He looks strong.'

'That's him again,' said Bill, very quietly, as Alice clicked
onto the next, identical photograph, of Bill's brother
standing with his back to the camera, standing with his
hands in his pockets by an open horsebox.

They had dinner in an Irish bar. One of the daughters
came along, and afterwards they posed for Alice's camera
in the lobby of the bar, where there were hung wooden
shields with the name of every county and a famine
monument depicting a man in shirtsleeves and with
a moustache standing over his exhausted, drooping
family, a ship with several sails and a thatched cottage
etched into the background. For the photographs,

everyone smiled in front of the monument, but what else could they do; they had to have something interesting to stand up against, as Ellen said.

'We have no horseboxes,' Bill said, and he was laughing.

'Wait, wait, don't take it yet,' Ellen said, and she reached up and took the baseball cap off Bill's head.

'What does it matter?' Bill said.

'Appearances,' said Ellen, glancing down at the buttons of her cardigan.

That night, long after they had all said goodnight and made their way to their separate beds, Alice got up to go downstairs for a glass of water. She stepped as quietly as she could; there were only two bedrooms upstairs, which meant that Bill and Ellen were sleeping in a room somewhere on the ground floor, and she did not want to wake them.

But as soon as she reached the bottom of the stairs she could see them clearly. The glow from the street-lights came through the sitting-room window, touching them – almost, you could deceive yourself, warming them. Bill lay on the armchair with the pop-up footrest, his head to one side just as Joe's had been earlier, his hands clasped, over a blanket, on his lap. The shape on the couch, under another blanket, was Ellen. They were sleeping. One of them breathed in slow, and the other exhaled quickly; one of them took in a breath like a gasp, and the other one sighed. Something seemed to shudder at the window, and Alice saw it, falling idly, falling in the yellow light. It would not accumulate, she told herself. It would not chill them, it would not reach them; it would not creep towards them across the sitting-room floor. The next night, she and Joe would take the couch and the chair, they would not take no for an answer, would not take their beds from them for another minute. They would insist on it.

Back in the bedroom, she could not bring herself to put out the light. The boy smiled up at her from somewhere, and she forced herself, for a moment, to look him in the eye.

Handmade Wings

Eoin McNamee

ALL THROUGH AUGUST CHERYL HAD SEEN THE LIGHT
outside the hangar buildings at night. Cheryl lived in
a mobile home in the caravan park at the edge of the
aerodrome and could see across the empty aprons and
deserted runways. Some Russians were running a coachworks from the hangar buildings. The runways were used
by autoclubs for racing and rallys and there was a need
for custom auto parts. The aerodrome had been built
during the war and used as a staging post for the D-Day
landings. It had closed in 1949 when the last Americans
went home.

The Russians had come in 2003 to work in the fish
factories in the town. They had been drawn to the aerodrome from the start.

'They have dreams of America,' Dieter said, 'here is
closest they will ever get to it. There are cities in Russia
that were left off the map during the Cold War,' he said,
'whole cities with millions of people hidden from the
outside world. What sort of country is that, do you think?'

Dieter came from Latvia. He cut his hair in jagged

futurist shapes. He wore studded belts and leather jackets embossed with runic symbols and read manga comics. Cheryl was tall and thin with straight blonde hair to her waist, and Dieter said she had the pallid beauty of the women who inhabit future cities, citizens of the mutant outworlds.

Cheryl shopped at a discount clothing outlet in the town. The Russian men brought their women there on Saturday morning. They followed their wives and girl-friends into the changing cubicles. They would hold negligees and other complex undergarments at arm's-length and comment on them. They issued curt instructions. They held dialogues on the fit of a basque.

'What kind of man is that?' Dieter said. 'I show them what a man is.' He said he had learned karate at a dank gymnasium in Latvia.

There was a seriousness to the way the underwear fittings were conducted that she had not noticed in couples before, or imagined necessary. She had no idea what was at stake in these transactions.

Cheryl worked in the aircraft factory, manufacturing cabin interiors for Boeing. She worked with epoxies and resins, strung wiring looms through ducting. One night she fell asleep on the sofa. When she woke up Dieter was crouched over her with his eyes closed. He said the door had been open. He said he was breathing in her work smells, inhaling the scent of advanced aero lubricants.

In winter Cheryl would drive home to the mobile home at dusk in November, crossing the empty runways.

Sand blown up from the shore would blow across the apron. It was as if the place had its own weather system. You could see the lights of container ships coming up the lough.

Cheryl went to the gym in the town. One day she saw one of the Russians watching her through the glass that separated the gym from the rest of the complex. She was on a running machine which made her move in a lop-sided, gangling way. The Russian was in his mid-thirties. A large man with hair sprouting from the cuffs of his boilersuit. He told her that his name was Sasha and that he owned the coachworks. He smelt of blood feuds. Of wolf-prowled outlands. Cheryl thought of a fabled man-beast from an old book of hours, a folkloric terror.

'You work late,' she said, 'I see your light.'

'That's not work,' Sasha said, 'come and see.'

She looked at him carefully. She wasn't afraid of him but there were complex nostalgias at work out on the aerodrome, and not everyone was capable of grasping them.

She drove to the coachworks that night. As she did she thought about a photograph of her grandfather at home. He was sitting among other men who had worked on the construction of the runways in the early years of the war. They were looking across the aerodrome with troubled expressions as though the building of it had uncovered a desolation in the landscape that no one had been aware of up until then.

Sasha had set up a video projector outside and was

showing films against the wall of the coachworks. A group of older Russian men made up the audience. They were watching Nascar races from Daytona beach. It was old footage and driver fatalities were not uncommon. The Russians watched the drivers as they were hoisted shoulder high, placed onto podiums where they stood looking out over the crowd, sombre garlanded figures.

'They have big talent,' Sasha said, 'everybody has big talent for something.'

'I don't know what mine is,' Cheryl said. One of the older men said something to Sasha in Russian.

'He wants me to put on another film,' Sasha said, 'we are learning about America.'

When she got back to the caravan Dieter was sitting on her sofa, drinking cider and watching bootleg porn videos on her television.

'Greetings, earthling. How does it go with red menace?' Dieter said.

She started to go over to the coachworks in the evening. Sasha repaired vintage racing cars, Porsches and RS2000s, for the autoclubs who used the aerodrome at the weekends. Business was good. Sasha took her to the discount outlet on Saturday mornings and followed her into the cubicle. He brought basques to her, high-cut underwear. He touched her lightly on her stomach and bare thighs to show how things fit, the elements you had to pay attention to. He liked things that were glove-tight with American names like Gore-Tex. She liked being dressed in newly invented materials, clothes that were svelte and snugly contoured. It made her feel part of a higher purpose.

A week later he rang her, and she went over to the hangar. They climbed a metal staircase to a loft above the workshop.

'No one has touched it since the war,' Sasha said. 'Pilots were billeted here. Americans. Yankees.'

There was a dartboard drawn in pencil on one wall. Beside it, on the rafters, the pilots had written their names and home places. Brooklyn, Des Moines. Places that sounded like lost townships.

Sasha bent down and pulled an old cigarette pack from the space between the joists.

'Look,' he said, 'Camel cigarettes.' He put his hand on her arm. He smelt of aerosol paint and solvent.

Cheryl painted a sign for the side of the coachworks. Sasha gave her the words. Custom Spoilers, Car Body Kits, Handmade Wings. She took a long time over it, using tins of metallic paint that she took from the aircraft factory. Underneath it she painted a pair of wings, each one about six feet long and painted in black and bronze. They looked as if they belonged to a dire angel.

'I didn't mean that kind of wing,' he said, pointing to the damaged front wing of a vintage Porsche. Then he told her to turn her back to him. He lifted her sweater and undid the strap of her bra. He touched her twice, just below her shoulderblades.

'But I make you wings,' he said, 'I put them there.'

All that summer blue exhaust fumes hung in the air

above the concrete. The young Russians gathered at the perimeter to watch the races, drinking vodka and high-alcohol beers, watchful, remote figures. Sasha bought a video camera. After they had slept together for the first time he filmed her lying on his bed. She regarded this as an aspect of his melancholy inner life.

One evening in September Sasha called Cheryl outside. He had found a reel of 16mm film in the loft upstairs. He had transferred it to videotape. There was footage of bomber crews being addressed by a man in a general's uniform in the winter before D-Day. They are wearing flying jackets and looking in the General's direction. Behind him you can see a squall, coming up the lough. The runway lights are reflected off the dark clouds, and the airmen are watching this uneasily. There were many shadows on the film and no sound. There was snow on the ground.

'That's Patton, General George Patton,' Sasha said, 'standing right here in this place. Before D-Day.'

Cheryl went home. She woke during the night and saw that the projector was on. She thought of Sasha left with his lonely heroes. She put on a dressing gown and walked across the aerodrome, the mast lights of container ships moored outside the bar showing her the way. As she approached the coachworks she saw a giant elongated figure projected onto the wall of the hangar building. She saw that Sasha had been joined by the other older Russians. She stood outside the circle of light. She barely recognised herself on the screen. She wasn't sure if it was betrayal or something even worse. She looked like some-one from one of the ghostly cities that Dieter had talked about, one of their pale citizenry. She walked into the circle of light.

'You have a talent all right,' she said, 'you Russian bastard.'

She walked back across the aerodrome. She took off her dressing gown and got into bed and tried to sleep but could not. She lay awake, dressed in garments whose purposes she no longer understood.

She got up and went to work the next day, but every-thing seemed very far away and the words coming out of her mouth did not seem to belong to her. She felt like a character from one of Dieter's counterfeit porn movies. Flickering, badly dubbed.

She went to the gym on her way home. She looked up and saw Sasha watching her through the glass. Caught in the cathode-ray reflection of the television set, the death glow. She felt like something in danger, injured, hunted through the forest. He knew that she was wounded. He was drawn to her damaged lope.

At eleven o'clock that night there was a knock on her door. When she opened it, one of Dieter's friends was standing there. He pointed across the aerodrome at the hangar buildings.

'Dieter heard about the film. He's gone to get Sasha,' he said, 'Sasha was Spetsnaz, Russian special forces. He fight in Chechnya.' Chechnya. Spetsnaz. There would be ruined villages. There would be barren and wintry scenes of loss, children and dogs wandering in the ruins. As she drove across the aerodrome towards the hangar buildings she thought about Dieter. He wouldn't know about Spetsnaz. He would adopt some doomed martial-arts stance in the face of seasoned veterans. He would rely on complex honour codes. He would defend her extraterrestrial beauty.

When she got there, the men were sitting quietly watching scenes from the collapse of the World Trade Center. Dieter was leaning against the hangar wall. There was blood on his mouth. The film showed figures jumping from the windows and the roof.

The people on the screen fell silently as though overcome by transcendence in flight. Dieter was looking at it open-mouthed, as though Heaven had collapsed and angels, the actual agents of divinity, were falling from the sky. The Russian men were watching it steadily. They were soldiers. They had an appetite for atrocity. Dieter was different. She wanted to tell him to close his eyes. That you looked away from God's work, good or bad. You did not gaze openly on it.

Sasha looked at her, and she felt the two spots above her shoulderblades where he had touched her prickling and knew what he was thinking.

She got Dieter into the back seat of the car and drove back to the mobile home. For people like him, it was about getting through things, getting off the ground in a small way from time to time. It was different for Sasha. War and cruelty had left him with epic needs. He could never be sated.

When Dieter was asleep she looked out at the aerodrome. There was a glow of light from the hangar buildings. She thought about the Russians sitting there, watching their death films, and how much they reminded her of the pilots listening to General George Patton. She felt a desire to see the footage of Patton at the aerodrome one more time. The navigation lights of their bombers flashing on the snow-dusted apron and the lights of the aerodrome complex giving an orange glow to the underside of the clouds above, the storm clouds, the thunderheads borne in across the tumultuous waters of the lough, knowing that they would soon be aloft, storm-borne.

She Came to Me

Rebecca Miller

DRIVING UP THE HELIX-SHAPED CAR PARK, Ciaran Fox
crept through floor after darkened floor, searching for a
vacancy. Looking for a parking space in Dublin during
working hours was just like trying to come up with a
new idea for a novel, he thought as he turned the taut,
leather steering wheel of his Mercedes gently, rounding
the concrete curve and accelerating up yet another ramp:
every time you thought you might have found one, it
turned out to be taken by someone else. Sweet Jesus, why
was it so fucking hard to find a space to wedge his god-
damn, shitting car into? Seven floors of gleaming steel,
SUVs parked hip to hip like cows eating out of their
troughs. It was the women, he thought, clotting up the
place with their absurdly unnecessary off-road vehicles.
Did any of them actually need to drive today? Carbon
footprints as big as bathtubs, and for what? To shop, in all
probability.

Ciaran emerged at the vivid sky. The final floor. And
there it was. His space. A nasty, inconvenient little gap between two gleaming monsters. Ciaran detested parking.

His wife was, he had to admit, far cooler when it came
to backing into tight spaces. Maeve. He imagined her
watching him as he reversed and moved forward, reversed
and moved forward, tugging at the steering wheel furiously, left, then right, then left, then right, like a desperate
sea captain trying to right a ship in a battering storm. At
last, he turned off the engine, his heart hammering. His
face felt coated in sweat. The car was parked so close to
the SUV on his side that he could only open his door an
inch. He had to clamber over the seats and squeeze out
on the passenger's side.

He walked down Dame Street, hands in his pockets,
head down. Like a man pawing the grass for a lost contact lens, he was searching his mind desperately for an
idea, a memory, a notion, a headline. What if he never
wrote another book? He hadn't written well in eight
months, and it was two years since his last novel was finished. Every morning he thudded down in front of the
computer and wrote words down, but they were dry and
tasteless as old raisins. No juice, he had no juice in him
anymore. He had mined his childhood, his first marriage,
every love affair before Maeve. He had tried to write
historical fiction, yet he couldn't make it real for himself.
He wasn't that kind of writer. What if he had used himself up? He was beginning to panic.

Finding himself staring into the great glass wall of
Hodges Figgis bookshop, he glimpsed his own reflection
in the glass: grey, thinning hair fanning up from his head
in the breeze, bags under his eyes, his gangly, lumbering

body hunched against the cold, hands in the pockets of his shapeless down jacket. Dispirited, he stalked into the bookstore and automatically made his way to the fiction area, scanning the shelves for his own work. They had a single copy of three of his novels. He reached down and pulled one of the books out – his first real success. A novella, it seemed shamefully flimsy to him now, the scant pages flopping over in his thick fingers like a limp wrist. He took the book in both his hands, stiffening it, and peered at the author photo. A slender, thirty-year-old man in a tweed jacket looked out at him with a bemused expression: shoulder-length hair, hands in his pockets, nostrils slightly flared – there was something questioning and arrogant in his gaze. Ciaran felt no sense of connection with that young writer; what's more, he reckoned if he met him, he wouldn't like him too much.

Ciaran knew that he was digging himself into a good old fug. Not just a bad mood, but a trench he would be inhabiting for a long time. He felt a sour, familiar comfort as he moled his way into this darkness. There was something almost reassuring about the descent – down, down, down – to a place where no one could reach him, where he loved no one, and no one loved him. There was pleasure – yes, he confessed it, knew it: there was onanistic pleasure in his sadness and he didn't even feel guilty about it. At least it was honest. He had had enough of impersonating happiness, of his wife's faintly accusatory, percussive kisses on his head at breakfast, his daughters' wily attempts to make him laugh, his own brittle resolve to make it to the next book without getting depressed again. He didn't know how many more of these bouts Maeve could take. One day he feared he'd wake up and she'd be gone. A woman like that, a humorous, sensual, hard-headed woman, was a queen who stayed until she left. Eighteen years so far, but she was capable – the most loyal woman on earth, salt of it – was capable, he knew, of leaving. Like a feral cat, tamed for a time, she'd slip away with her kittens. He mustn't take her for granted. And yet he felt himself drifting away from her and everything incandescent in his life, like a man succumbing to a dream at the wheel, eyes fluttering shut, his car careening across the dual carriageway.

He replaced his book on the shelf and walked out onto the street again. So many bodies – why weren't they at work? Who were these people? Tourists, students, suits on lunch breaks, mothers killing time till the next school run. Stories in each of them, infuriatingly locked away from him. He peered into their faces for clues. This was what he needed, he thought: he needed to get out more, to be among strangers. He craved new encounters. He had been holed up with his little family for so long, he had run out of things to say. He couldn't write about his marriage, it would be a violation. His conjugal happiness had tied his writer's hands. He would come into town more; he would write in cafés. Volunteer in a homeless shelter. He needed a pee. The old pub on the corner was glossy black as liquid tar, with gilt lettering. He hadn't been there in years. Maybe he would stop for a pint. It was time to break some patterns.

The place was empty, save one young woman sitting at the bar. Late twenties perhaps, a little pudgy, with black-rimmed eyes and a delicate, pointy nose, she reminded Ciaran of a raccoon. The many silver bracelets on her wrists made a tinkling sound as she raised the glass to her lips, sampling the Guinness and putting it down again after a swallow. She was probably a tourist, Ciaran mused as he walked towards the Gents'. Dublin girls came out at night. Maybe she was Eastern European. As he walked back into the bar, he observed her. She had pale skin that glowed against the dark walls of the pub. Her lank hair was brown, cut in a bob, with a hard-edged, short fringe. There was something sleek and mysterious about her, even though she was plain. On the street you wouldn't look at her twice, most likely. But here in this dim pub at one o'clock in the afternoon, drinking by herself, she seemed damn interesting. He sat down at the bar, ordered a ham sandwich and a pint, snatched a handful of peanuts from a dish at the bar, then slid the dish over to the young woman.

'I just read you can get hepatitis from that,' she said in a flat voice. American. Ciaran winced. He found American English as alluring as a cold fried egg.

'From what?' Ciaran asked, already walking down the street in his mind.

'Communal nuts,' she said. He looked at her to check if she knew that was funny. She did.

'Where in the States are you from?' he asked.

'I wish I could master a fake accent,' the woman said, flattening her mouth in a little grimace. He glanced at her body; she was all in black — loose sweater, leggings and ballet shoes. She had big, shapely legs that tapered abruptly to delicate ankles and small feet. She looked at him from the side of her painted, raccoon eyes and asked, 'Are you from Dublin?'

'Yes,' he answered.

'Lucky,' she said.

'You like it here?'

She thought it through for a moment. 'Yeah.'

'How long are you here for?' he asked.

'We leave tomorrow,' she said. 'I'm here with my parents and my brother.'

'Did you drive around the countryside?' he asked.

'No, we just stayed in Dublin. It's a sort of rest cure.'

'For who?'

'For me,' she said.

'Oh,' he said.

'I'm sort of getting better . . .' she said. There was a long pause. Suddenly, Ciaran needed to find out who this person was.

'Would you like to . . . take a walk?' he asked. She hesitated.

'Just a few blocks', he added. In broad daylight. To see the city.'

'Sure,' she said.

He paid her bill and his own, and they walked out of the dim pub, into the glare.

They walked along a canal, the water shivering, silvery.

'What do you do?' she asked.

'I'm a novelist,' he said.

'Wow,' she said.

'You?'

'I work at a pet store in Cincinatti,' she sneered. He looked over at her again, imagining her with a hamster curled on her chest. Suddenly, he had her placed, he knew her American type: nerdy, angry, compulsively wise-cracking, often Goth girls who are inevitably chubby and look perfect behind the counters in pet stores, record stores, clothing stores – any service job suits them. They are intelligent but without self-confidence. All interest fled him as he pigeon-holed her.

'My daughter has a turtle,' he said. 'I bought it in a pet store. I found the place a little depressing, to be honest.'

'There are very few people who actually love animals,' she said. 'Most people turn animals into people, little people they can control, who won't hurt them because they depend on them for food. It's pathetic.' Her darkly painted mouth, Ciaran noticed, was defined by two sharp points, a cupid's bow.

'So I won't be buying you any pets,' he said. She looked at him sharply, as if he had said something startling.

'No,' she whispered, a slow smile creeping across her face.

They walked along the docks and looked out at the big boats.

'Where's your family now?' he asked.

'They're at the National Museum,' she said. 'They think I'm getting a facial.'

'And why aren't you getting a facial?' Ciaran asked.

'I don't believe in them,' she said.

He smiled and looked over at her. Her hair was whipping around her full, starkly made-up face. You couldn't say she was pretty, but she had something.

As they walked back, she paused at a narrow, white, Georgian house. A sign outside read 'Bed and Breakfast'.

'I have a room in there,' she said. They both stopped to look at the place. 'Do you want to see it?'

'I don't feel up to meeting the whole family,' he said.

'Oh, no,' she said. 'We're all staying at Jury's.' He was about to ask what she meant when she hurried up the walk and paused on the bottom step, waiting. He saw her in her totality then: thick, muscular legs in black leggings, little feet, erect posture, big black tent of a sweater masking her body, those blackened eyes. His curiosity coagulated again.

'You want to?' she asked.

The room was furnished with a bony double bed and a tilted painting of a foxhunt hung curiously close to the ceiling. Maroon drapes were pulled adamantly shut. The girl lit a candle by the bed. It gave off a strong scent of vanilla.

'If your family is staying at Jury's,' Ciaran ventured, 'Why are you . . .'

'I rented this place just for myself. They don't know. I'm sleeping at the hotel with them.'

'What do you use this place for?'

'It's my nest,' she said, falling down on the bed straight as a pin and looking up at him. He sat on the edge of the bed beside her.

'Why do you need a nest?' he asked.

'I always need my own space,' she said, sliding off her bracelets and placing them under her pillow.

'And what', he said, feeling acutely alert, 'is it that you are recovering from?'

'I'm addicted to romance,' she said. He chuckled.

'Isn't everybody?'

'It's a recognised syndrome,' she said seriously, folding her hands on her chest.

'And what are the symptoms of your malady?' he asked, looking down at her.

'If I see a romantic movie,' she said, 'I can fall in love with the man in it. It's pretty bad. I've been arrested for stalking. I'm not allowed to tell you who it was, though.' Ciaran nodded his head in sober agreement. 'So I can't go to romantic movies any more.'

'What else?'

'Well, I'm not supposed to do this. Renting a room like this is a real no-no but – I couldn't help myself.'

'You mean to say you rented this room secretly so you could –'

'Meet people,' she said.

'And have you?' he asked.

'I met you,' she said, removing her bulky sweater and revealing a creamy silk camisole. Her breasts were small and pert, a girl's breasts. She was sitting up now, staring across the bed at him with such frankness. A black widow, he thought, waiting in her web to catch unwitting male flies. He must leave. He was absolutely leaving.

She leaned forward and reached between his legs, her hand not quite touching, as if she were warming her hand over a stove, or casting a spell. He felt helpless, leaden, and faintly sick. She had a box of condoms under the bed.

Her sex was stripped hairless as a child's. Nipples pink as tea roses. Her belly was fleshy, springy. She mewed when he touched her, eyes closed like a new kitten. He felt repelled by his desire for her. He wished he could spread the condom over his head, his whole body, to shield himself from this experience. Yet he was having it, oh, he was having it! Faithful for eighteen years, he was gobbling up a disturbed American pet-store clerk at two in the afternoon, and he was doing it fervently, desperately, hungrily. He, Ciaran Fox, and no one else on earth, was doing this!

Afterward, he lay there, staring at the ceiling in blank disbelief.

'Will you come visit me in America?' she asked, her voice higher now than he remembered it. An icy feeling of panic washed over him. He sat up and thrust his hands deep into the bedding, his fingers scrabbling for his briefs.

'No,' he said, seizing them at last, 'I won't.' She was sitting naked on the bed, her firm, plump belly creased at the waist, big legs flung out at odd angles, as if she were the doll of a giant. Her round face was getting blotchy, a film of tears dulling her raccoon eyes.

He was hopping on one foot, pulling on his rumpled woollen trousers. 'I'm sorry but – that is unrealistic. If you're going to get better,' he said, reaching absurdly for a therapeutic tone, 'you need to learn to see things as they are.'

'Why did you say that, then?' she asked petulantly.

'Say what?' he said.

'About how you wouldn't be getting me a pet.'

'What are you – '

'I said most people turn pets into little people they can control, and *you* said, "I won't be getting you a pet, in that case."' She was angry now, and tugged her leggings on forcefully.

'I was joking! I was flirting!'

'I wouldn't have slept with you if you hadn't implied we had a future!'

'That's –' *crazy* he began to say, then stopped himself.

'You know how you feel about me,' she said, dressed now, and calmer. Her voice had gone soft and assured. 'You just can't admit it to yourself.' She was smiling slightly, gazing at him with tenderness and – was that pity?

'Oh my God,' he said. 'I am so sorry.'

And then he fled. He ran – truly ran – all the way back to Clarendon Street, taking the most higgledy-piggledy route he could think of, so he could be sure to lose her. A grown man, acclaimed novelist, sprinting through the

streets of Dublin like a purse-snatcher. When he reached
the parking lot he had to stop and catch his breath,
doubled over, the heels of his hands pressed into his eyes,
as if to erase the memory of the naked girl. He felt as
though he might faint. Fingers trembling, he tried to
coax a dirty twenty euro note into the slot of the pay
kiosk, but the bill kept reversing back out at him like a
mocking blue tongue. Once in his car, he raced down
the ramps of the lot, brakes squealing, and sped home to
Dalkey.

Maeve was in the kitchen making tea when he walked
in. He stood in the doorway for a moment to take her
in. Her long, black hair was threaded through with silver
strands; the lines of her body were coltish, athletic. Her
little paunch seemed a joyful imperfection, a reminder of
three girls whom he adored. The fact of his wife made
him euphoric, nearly tearful with relief, as though he had
woken from a nightmare to the smell of toast. Hearing
him, Maeve turned and checked him warily, as if to gauge
his mood, to predict the scene ahead. He wanted to rush
straight over to her and take her in his arms, but, afraid
that the scent of the girl was on him, he walked over to
the couch by the window and beamed at her. He felt so
grateful.

'How was the meeting?' she asked.

'What – oh shit!' He had completely forgotten the
lunch with the film producer. That was why he had
driven to the centre of town! 'I forgot all about it.'

'But you *drove* there to –'

237

'I – I was thinking,' he said. 'I just – I was thinking, and I lost all sense of where I was supposed to be.'

Maeve shook her head and smiled, the thin skin around her eyes crinkling into a fan of wrinkles. 'Thinking about what?' she asked.

'I might have a book in me,' he said, realising at that moment it was true. 'A character. She came to me today, in town.'

'That's wonderful,' she said.

Boom

Mary Morrissy

'DEE-DAW.'

'Did you hear that?' Patrick Shaw has just come into the kitchen. It is a late summer's evening after rain, drenched and lambent. He is in shirtsleeves, tie loosened, elasticated braces like forked leather tongues. 'He said Daddy!'

Rosemary, rubber-gloved in suds, turns around to look down at her toddler son. Little Timmy is sitting in the play-pen on an upholstered bottom, clenched fist aloft in salute.

'Dee-daw.'

The child seems rapt at something going on at calf level – the tanned denier of his mother's stockings, her pert kitten-heeled slippers, the pink feathery rosette on her instep that he always wants to eat.

'He said Daddy!'

'No, he didn't!' Rosemary lifts a glass in her muffled paw and holds it up to the golden light.

'I tell you, he said Daddy.'

Timmy's father stoops down, a big urgent face leering through the bars. 'Say it, Tim, say it again.'

Dee-daw.

'Oh Pat, you're hearing things.' Rosemary tamps down something on her eyelid with the back of her pink gauntlet.

'Say it, Tim, Da-dee. Da-dee.'

'Dee-daw!' the child brays. 'Dee-daw!'

Today you have been to see the Man with the Quiet Voice who smells of tobacco and wet tweed and isn't called The Doctor. The Doctor has an office full of sneezes, a torch with a blazing light and a finger made of sandpaper that he puts on your tongue. Not like the Man with the Quiet Voice who sits on a wet park bench with his hands hiding in his pockets while the rain drips from the hood of the go-car down onto your knees. Your mother in her clear plastic raincoat so that you can see her dress and her cardy and everything underneath, opens her mouth and the Man with the Quiet Voice looks inside.

And how's my little man, he says, gripping your nose in a fleshy vice between his big fingers.

Say hello, your mother says, sweet and secretful. Say hello to the nice man, Tim.

Tim! Ti . . . m?

His name has always sounded emaciated to him. Timid, timorous, a thin-lipped emaciated hum. When the strangeness of waking up calling out his own name passes, he thinks it might have been Reggie calling him. Maybe she's left a message and it's her subliminal voice that has woken him. But no, when he checks, the red light is steadfast.

'You still have a machine!' Reggie marvelled.

Voicemail and texts and disembodiment, that is Reggie. Now, there's a name! He loves the two-syllable strength of it, the juicy rich double consonant of the diminutive.

'Yeah, well, you can imagine what convent girls made of Regina,' she'd said. 'They pronounced it with an I!'

Tim was lost.

'Rhymes with?' She'd cocked a saucy eyebrow. Tim had to think hard. Sometimes Reggie made him feel quite maidenly.

Now that he's up he goes to the window and stares out over the water. His is a docklands flat. Regenerated. The water below is a hemmed-in canal basin. At the other side is a large flour mill. A pair of monolithic towers of bleached concrete rise up looking like they've been lightly dusted with confectionary sugar, a six-storey warehouse of blistered stone with cataracted windows stares back at him. As Tim watches, a door opens in the lowest floor at water level and a man steps out onto a metal platform. He lights up. His cigarette tip glows against the inky water and the glower of a wakening sky. In his white baker's coat and paper hat he looks like a clownish doctor, a refugee from a Marx Brothers fancy-dress party, stepping out of a portal of the last century. Tim inches the sash window open a fraction and the spell is broken. The rattle of a candy-coloured commuter train leaving the depot at the far end of the basin animates the silent scene. Its empty windows are ablaze, a glow-worm on the move, its clatter at a distance like industrial knitting. There it is, Tim thinks, the world is officially awake now.

Paris is an hour ahead but even so Tim does not dare to ring Reggie at this hour. She would be livid. Their life is like this – careful calculation and fearful discretion. One weekend in three they spend together. Here, there or somewhere in between. The rest of the time airline schedules keep them apart. To anyone looking in from the outside, they are a boom-time couple. What is the sound of boom? The rush and seethe of cappuccino makers, Tim would say, the bloated heartbeat of car stereos. But these were only the signature tunes of prosperity. What of the boom itself? Was it the low, threatening rumble of thunder, the zip and whistle of fireworks or the flat thud of explosion? The abstract sound of boom.

'Oh God, Tim,' Reggie would say when he would speculate like this, 'get a life!'

But Tim is old enough to remember what everyone calls the bad old days. Dole queues and hunger strikes, explosions on the streets, when everything seemed in short supply, except chronic damage.

The first time the Man with the Quiet Voice comes to your house he brings a comic. You sprawl on the kitchen floor as the colours leap out at you in great muscled arms – Zap! – and fiery explosions. Boom! He and Mum sit at the kitchen table. There are a lot of silences between them just like when you and

Mum are together, Mum doing the ironing, the smooth sway-ing motion of her hand, the small slap of the iron's flex hitting against the legs of the board. It creaks when she puts her weight behind something tricky — the collars and cuffs of Dad's shirts. She hums along to a tune playing on the radio, catching a word here and there. Hello darkness, my old friend. Dah, dah dah dah again . . . Except today she's not ironing; she's saying small soft things to the Man with the Quiet Voice and then laughing in a silvery way. You can see the Man is holding her hand, exam-ining her fingers like the Doctor checking for warts. You know what's going to happen next. She's going to open her mouth and say Aaaaah.

'Aw, Rosemary!'

It's Dad, voice vivid with complaint.

'What?' Mum turns around, hand on hip.

'How many times have I told you? I don't want Timmy reading comics.'

Dad stands, arms crossed, bulging biceps, cape flying.

'Sure he can't read yet, isn't he just looking at the pic-tures?' Mum says.

'I just don't want this kind of rubbish in the house.' Dad leans down and whips the comic away. *Whoosh!*

He rips it in two.

Wa-a-h! Hot tears of injustice.

'Perfect!' Mum bangs the iron down. 'Just perfect!'

He likes the disruption that is Reggie Mundy. Her flights away, her lavish returns. He's in love, or at least in thrall, and he has never felt so helpless. He is dazzled by her and dazed by the distance between them. She's only twenty-four. Then there's her job. A trolley-dolly with Plein Air, that's how she described herself.

'We're there to distract their attention from what they're not getting,' she explained. He finds Reggie's sardonic tone, this light contempt, disconcerting. (Is this how she talks about him behind his back?) Tim loves his work; it's a calling. If he ever got to the point of regarding it as lightly as Reggie does hers, he'd have to jack it in.

He took her on a tour of the studio one night when P45 was recording. She was coolly impressed.

'P45,' she breathed, 'that makes you a legend!'

Or did she mean a has-been, Tim wondered. When other teenagers were buying rock albums, he was buying LPs of sound effects. Most people could detect that boy in him, until, that is, he saved some coked-up boy band from mediocre oblivion. *Then*, he was a wizard.

'My God, Tim, it's dark down here,' she said. 'Don't you feel buried alive?' In comparison to Reggie's world of harshly over-lit terminals, the studio must have seemed sunk in a scriptorium gloom.

He did his best work in the graveyard hours. There was a sanctity about the studio then as if it were a cathedral of sound, though sometimes that idea was hard to sustain watching wasted musicians sitting around smoking their brains out. He was the organist, the sound channelled through his hands and transformed. He wanted to mix music so that each constituent part – the woozy reverb of a bass, the crystalline ting of a high hat, even the grating dry rub of a palp along a string – would detach itself and cry out, so that the listener might think he was stoned. He loved the absolute clarity of those moments himself, the certainty of singular sensations. That's what he wanted to reproduce, *that* purity. But he couldn't possibly explain that to Reggie. Purity? Reggie?

Once you meet the Man with the Quiet Voice in the church. You have to sit at the end of the last pew on the aisle that leads to brazen glory while he and Mum go off to light candles.

You say your prayers, Timmy, there's a good boy, Mum says.

She seems flustered; she storms up the aisle. She seems always to be running away.

Pray for your mother's intentions, Sonny, the Man with the Quiet Voice says as he follows her, coat-tails flying. Their voices came back to you, solemn and jilted, from the side aisle where the shrine to the Blue Our Lady is.

What's that man's name, you ask when Mum comes back.

What man, she replies crossly.

They had met in Paris. It sounded romantic in the telling. What they neglected to say was that it was not in the Luxembourg Gardens or Montmartre, but in a launderette near the Rue Mouffetard on a Sunday afternoon. Tim restless in the desolate idleness of a foreign city; the band was sleeping it off at the hotel. There were museums he could have gone to but Tim was not up to the solemn, wearying silences of art. He was drawn into the launderette by the sound of it.

'How sad is that!' Reggie said.

No sadder than doing your laundry amidst the splendours of Paris, Tim thought. It was one of those automated places. A voice from a tall headstone of stainless steel barked the machine number, the programme required, the length of the wash. It was a flat voice, Daleky, robotic. Tim liked the effect of it and the absurdity of the disembodied voice like a muezzin calling for prayer, issuing instructions to the unwashed. When he stepped inside the small glassy shop he was met with the bland owlish glare of stacked washers and dryers. Reggie was standing in front of the talking plinth, coins in one palm, the other hand raised in expansive helplessness while she howled at the flinty dial. 'But how much do I put in?'

'Can I help?'

She turned swiftly. He got an impression of blonde exasperation.

The Quiet Man appears out of the bathroom wearing Dad's dressing gown. You are laying in wait outside for the game you and Dad play. You hide in the well of the stairs and when you hear the bathroom door open, you leap out with a tiger growl – Grrr! – and Dad grabs you and tickles you until you cry for mercy. You pounce.

Jesus Christ, the Man swears.

Denis!, Mum cries and puts her hand over her mouth.

Then she yanks you up roughly by the arm from the top

step and propels you down the landing. Go to your room, this instant, and not another word!

Dee-daw, dee-Daw, dee-daw, dee-daw . . .

Tim turns on the TV and slumps in front of it with the sound down. The breakfast news comes on. The newscaster, dressed like a sober schoolboy, sits casually on the side of the desk, feigning informality. Suddenly there is live coverage. Footage of panic, a fluorescent street strewn with wrecked cars, the glare and dim of pocking fire engines. Stretchers bearing shrouded forms being humped inexpertly along; the walking wounded lean and limp. Northern Ireland, Tim thinks dully, an old response, but no, he corrects himself, aren't we living in a time of peace? The Middle East, then. He catches a glimpse of the wrought intaglio of a Metro sign. Jesus, this is Paris! Where Reggie is. She might be lying under debris, mangled, mutilated. Her fiery head crushed, her hair smeared with blood. He imagines phoning her and her mobile ringing out. Before he can locate the remote, the carnage has disappeared and it's back to the newscaster with a tickertape of shares running along the bottom of the screen. Has he dreamed it up?

Bleary-eyed, he makes for the kitchen, checking the clock over the cooker hood before starting to make coffee. It is 7 a.m. The clock makes a silent digital calculation. He still expects it to declare itself. He remembers the magnified announcements of the wall clock in his grandmother's parlour, which measured the hours with a grinding wheeze and the minutes with a disapproving tick, as if every moment mattered. And every moment did – there was a time for the kettle to be boiled, for the cake of bread to be taken out of the oven, for incantation of the Angelus.

The Angel of the Lord declared unto Mary . . .

'You'll love it,' his father had said in that tone of false encouragement. Like when he wanted Tim to play foot-ball. *Thwack!*

'Will Denis be there?'

'Who?' Dad barked.

Mum glared at him and left without saying goodbye.

The two weeks they were away – a package holiday to the sun; well, they'd sent men to the moon, hadn't they? – seemed endless. He listened to the mournful bellowing of cows, the slap of their full fat udders swinging rudely from side to side, the splattery skeetering of hooves in the mud, the hup-hup of the boy who drove them. There was the racket of the tractor and the baler passing by the gate, the melancholy ripple of birdsong when he was put to bed even though it was still light outside.

'Time for bye-byes,' Gran would say. She still used baby talk though he was nearly seven.

But mostly he was listening out for the scrunch of wheels on gravel and for Mum to come home.

To his shame he is persistently and sickeningly jealous. He has fantasies of throttling anybody who looks crooked at

Reggie. He would use his bare hands, blacken eyes if needs be. *Ker-pow!* He has logged away all of the stray names she mentions – Jason, the steward who's emphatically not gay; Ted, the divorced pilot; Marco, the great guy on the ground at Fiumicino – so that when she's delayed he visualises her being with one of them simply because he knows their names. He has pressed her gently for details.

'This guy, Jason, have I met him?'

Reggie would shake her glorious hair. 'No, he lives in Paris, with Kate,' she would say evenly.

'And Ted?'

'We met him at check-in once, remember? Tall guy with epaulettes? Drives a plane.'

'I'm only asking,' he would say.

'You're not only asking, Tim, you're checking up on me – there's a big difference. Don't you trust me?'

No, no, no. He could see how clichéd it was, the jealous older man making inventories of possible betrayal. Even after a year with Reggie, he still felt like he was handling unstable explosives, except he was the one ready to go off at any moment.

The last time you see the Man with the Quiet Voice is in Bradley's. You remember the cold clammy feel of the gauge as the shop lady measures your bare feet for sandals and your mother kneading her fingers on the top of the clover pattern in the leather to make sure you have enough room to grow. Suddenly, he is upon you.

This fella's going to be big as a house, eh Timmy, me boy, he says loudly. He grips you on the shoulder and does a trick with his hand so that a florin suddenly appears at his fingertips.

Denis, Mum hisses.

Jesus, Rosemary . . .

The two of them go off and huddle in a corner of the shop. And Mum says please, please. And the shop lady says Would Sir like to . . . ? You flex your feet in the new sandals with the blonde soles. You don't want him here. You want it to be just you and Mum and the shop lady marvelling at what a big boy you are as she puts your old shoes in the cardboard box that is like a coffin for a hamster. And when the shop lady attaches the balloon that comes free with each purchase to your finger, you want that moment just for yourself too. And you want to wave to the lady and to reach up for Mum's cool hand. You don't want her saying don't and please and not in front of the child or the shop lady saying is everything all right, Madam? or the man saying Jesus Christ and you can't and please, please. Or Mum suddenly catching you and dragging you out of the shop so roughly that . . . Bang! It is all over.

He burst my balloon, you yell.

You are out on the street, and Mum is crying. And the Man with the Quiet Voice is standing in the doorway with his hands up as if he's done something wrong.

No, no, it was just an accident, Mum says, we'll get you another one.

Her tears keep coming. The string is still attached to your forefinger. It trails on the pavement behind you with the torn red scrap that was your balloon at the end of it.

That man . . . you begin again.

And she turns, your mother, and strikes you – Wham! – across the face.

There is no man, she says. Do you hear me? There is no man.

To this day he cannot bear to be in a room full of balloons; too much imminence.

'A sound man?' Dad is incredulous.

His mother presses START. It is Maeve's birthday, and she is baking a cake so their conversation is punctuated by the aggravated whirr of the Magimix.

'He'd be an engineer, though,' Mum counters, 'a sound engineer. That's what they call it.'

'He'll be gofer in a studio, more like. Making the tea.'

'We all had to begin somewhere, Pat.'

Patrick Shaw, self-made man, scrap-metal merchant, bristles. He is clutching his son's exam results; Tim is sixteen and wants to leave school. He's eavesdropping at the kitchen door, egging his mother on silently.

'No son of mine . . .,' his father starts. STOP.

The no son of mine speech is well rehearsed. Tim can recite it by heart. His mother interrupts. 'Your son has always answered the call of a different drum.'

She is scraping the bottom of the bowl. Tim can hear the impatient slap of the rubber spatula.

'You've always been a fool about that boy, Rosemary.

Needs a good kick up the arse, if you ask me. Look at this – an F even in Geography!'

'What does any of it matter, once he's happy?'

'Oh well, excuse me pardon! Once he's happy! There's a recession on out there, in case you hadn't noticed.'

Rush of the tap as his mother fills the mixing bowl and sets it aside to steep.

'He'll be turning his back on everything I've built up.'

'For God's sake, Pat, isn't it obvious he's never going to follow you into the business?'

'Not to me,' Dad says, and for the first time Tim feels sorry for him.

Dad used to take him along to the scrapyard on Saturday mornings. It was a hellish place even though his father sat in an elevated Portakabin high above it, doing business over the phone, looking down on the hillocks of twisted metal, the mountains of toothed machine parts, the crushed fangs of cars. Dad didn't seem to register the sudden, calamitous vomiting of scrap from the buckets of the diggers, the hollow volcanic thud of empty skips being hoisted and dropped, the shattering waterfall of shards rushing down the chutes into huge containers. How could he bear all that deafening medieval clangour and still have appetite for battle when he got home? When he was little, Tim would put his hands to his ears to shut out their rows – his mother's shrill defiance, his father's querulous misapprehensions. Later, he used headphones. Heavy metal was best.

Mum opens the oven door. The unoiled hinges protest.

'Ah Pat, can you really see it?' his mother says, all tempered reason. 'Our Tim!'

Our Tim. He can't work out her tone.

His father harrumphs.

'Anyway, if it doesn't work out, sure doesn't he have the business to fall back on?'

'Oh yes, good old dependable Pat, always good to fall back on.'

'Don't be like that, Pat,' he hears Mum say.

There is silence then. Is that a prelude to agreement, Tim wonders. His mother makes some move. Tim imagines her stroking his father's temple with a floury hand.

'Do it for me,' his mother wheedles, 'for my sake.'

Tim can hear her desperation now – not for him but for herself and for fear of the memory of the man with the quiet voice whose name cannot be spoken. His father is silent; somehow, she has bought his acquiescence.

'Reggie?'

'Tim,' she says.

Oh relief. Thank God! He imagines her corpse reassembling itself into just-woken Reggie, like a roll of film rewound. As if his call has brought her back from the dead. There is a sound in the background. Like the movement of sheets, like a companion disengaging. His heart tightens with a familiar constriction. Dread giving way to something meaner and entirely more personal. Gone now the images of carnage, the blood-spattered pavement, the public calamity.

'Are you all right?'

'Yeah . . .' she says uncertainly. He imagines her blurred by sleep, hair comically askew, leaning on a plump elbow. Post-coital.

'I just saw it on the TV, the bomb.'

'Bomb – what bomb?'

'You didn't hear it? In a night-club, some kind of explosion.'

'I was fast asleep. What time is it?' She is waking now, coming into focus.

'I was worried – I thought you might have been caught up in it.'

She rises, he can hear her. He imagines her, mobile in hand, with the sheets draped around her, stumbling towards the window, parting the nets and looking out onto a Parisian street, narrow, cobbled, slimed with rain. He hears her opening a window. He imagines her sticking her blowsy head and goose-pimpled shoulders out over the sill.

'Ugh, wet!'

A siren wails.

'What's that?' he asks as he hears the latch closing.

'Nothing,' she says.

'There's someone else there, isn't there?'

'Oh Tim, don't start . . .'

An ambulance, Tim guesses, listening to the Doppler effect, the off-tune coming and going of it. Maybe one he has seen earlier on the TV? Maybe on its way back from the scene? The immediacy of connection startles him – images he has just seen translated to a bowl of sound at his ear.

Dah, dee-da-da-dah, dee-da-da-dah, Dah, dee-da-da-dah, dee-da-da-dah.

Each city had its own tonic sol-fa and Tim recognised them all. He'd never told Reggie; it seemed too anoraky even for him, or maybe it was something he was keeping in reserve. For a moment just like this . . .

Dah, dee-da-da-dah, dee-da-da-dah . . .

That wasn't Paris; that was Rome.

'You're lying, Reggie,' he says simply.

There is silence at the other end of the phone.

'How do you know?' Her voice has lost its penny-bright insistence.

Pooof! All over.

Like someone letting the air out of a balloon.

You'd had to walk all the way home, your feet hurting in the new sandals. You'd reached the Green when you heard the first explosion. All you remember is the funny smell, a strange silence as Mum halts and listens as if to some soft aftershock. Then the banshee wails begin as fire engines pass blaring importantly, ambulances cluck and pock. It is a symphony of distress as if the world has been agitated by your private tempest. That day of all days, no one takes any notice of a pregnant woman trailing along the street weeping silently and a boy still smarting with hurt, holding onto his fury by a string and blaming the Man with the Quiet Voice for all of it.

Dad is frantic.

Jesus Ro, where have you been, I've rung every hospital in the city.

He catches you by the lapels and examines you like the doctor in a temper. He pauses at your reddened cheek.

Haven't you heard? Three bombs, all at the same time, I was out of my mind with worry. In your condition! What were you doing in town, anyway?

Shoes, Mum says dully.

You often think of him afterwards, Denis, imagine him blundering down Nassau Street straight into the fiery red maw of it . . .

He goes to his parents for Sunday lunch, roast beef with all the trimmings. Something else Reggie sneered at. Tied to your parents' apron strings, she would say. But she was at an age where she was still rebelling against hers; he has gone beyond that. Age has chastened his mother, or is it the longevity of her deception? His father has mellowed, too; a bad hip has softened his cough. His sister Maeve – conceived on that holiday in Majorca, Tim supposes, which his mother bashfully referred to afterwards as their second honeymoon – has taken over the family business, rebranding Dad's scrap metal as architectural salvage.

'Where's Reggie?' Mum asks as she clatters round the kitchen tidying up after lunch.

'In Paris,' he says.

No, he corrects himself silently, Rome. In Rome with bloody Marco.

'How do you keep up with her?' Mum says as she

scrapes the gravied remains of the plates into the bin. 'All that gadding about! Wasn't like that in our day. You put up and shut up.'

This is for his father's benefit, like much of what she says these days.

Over coffee, his parents fall into musing about the past. When Reggie was around, they retold all of Tim's baby stories, but he realises they don't need an audience to retreat into reminiscence.

'Remember when Tim said his first word?' his father starts.

'He was slow to talk,' Mum chips in with that old reflex of contradiction.

'I was absolutely convinced you'd said Daddy,' his father goes on. 'I heard you say it. Clear as a bell. But would your mother believe me? And would you say it again? On demand?'

'Curse of the firstborn. Poor Tim wasn't allowed child-ish babble,' Mum says ruefully. 'Every sound had to have a meaning.'

Tim enjoys these archival squabbles. It gives his parents a chance to be softer with one another which they weren't in the original versions of these stories. And he hasn't the heart to correct them. His first word was not for either of them. Even then it was the song of the sirens he heard.

The Blacklight Ballroom

Peter Murphy

NEARLY A YEAR INTO THE civil war that no one cared to declare a civil war, they grew tired of hatching their fires and waiting to die in their dressing gowns, and blitz spirit drove the first ones out like animals after hibernation to smell the air and test the inclination of the wind.

Then, as if privy to the twitchings of antennae or some hive-mind transmission, somebody got word from somebody who heard of a place to congregate on Saturday night – the Blacklight Ballroom in the basement of the old Bailey Hotel. That was three years ago. If not for the weekly militia tribute, those black armband boys might have shut it down on the grounds of illegal assembly or breach of curfew or whatever. But come fetor or freeze, snipers or shelling, the show goes on. It's been postponed only once, on account of August's epizootic.

From all over the county they come, huddled like wet-backs or cattle in the trailers of tarped artics, in four-wheel drives and SUVs, in dented Zetors canopied with asbestos and three-inch Plexiglas, in pocked or perforated coaches customised with great plates of tin or aluminium nail-gunned to the panels.

Some come singly and some in fleet. Headlights streak like tracer fire all down the N11. When the hotel's desk clerk sees the convoy reach Three Mile Lane he flips a switch that triggers automatic gates ivied with barbed wire coils. Wheels bump over cattle-grids. Diesel engines roar towards a courtyard swept by searchlights. There they dock in ad-hoc formation under a bullet-proof dome and discharge their human freight in ones and twos, in dozens and in scores, like squads of stiff-backed astronauts set down upon a shanty moon.

No one tarries in the parking dock, just the odd 'G'mora' or mutter about the night's bombardment. Shotguns and side arms, picks and pikes, hatchets and slash-hooks – all surrendered at the sentry booth, tagged and bagged and stored in barrels called the Blood Buckets. They'll get them back when the show is over.

Some shower they are, cursing in the dark as they pick their steps across panes of frost like the crocked fearing a slip or sprain – except on sniper nights, that is, when they hide beneath corrugated-iron shields and hell-for-leather it towards the hotel's double doors.

Every soul among their number has lost a loved one or a limb. There's Mary Ellen Cash, a beauty in her day, cheeks now drawn from long hours' labours in those polytunnel silos down the Ballo road. Naeem Hammoud, stocious with grief, a photo of his late wife Rita pinned to the lapel of his greatcoat. Susannah Codd, cute as

you like in her flak jacket and para boots, that gloved
prosthetic like a circus bird-girl's claw: two years ago a
Salamander landmine mixed her fingers with the turnip
crop.

And here comes Long John Donegan, still scatty from
nerve-gas shock, lips blistered after a week of sucking fuel
from Hummers junked or sunk in mud. And, of course,
the legendary Evelyn Brown, five foot four in her boots:
Christmas Eve she heard a thief at her peacocks, tore out
there and took skull and all off his shoulders with a forty-
pound Steel War sledge.

Here they come then, them and the other regulars,
bearing their woes like full pails of water, sorrows individual and sorrows common. Up the steps and through
the lobby, past the check-in desk into the basement lift.
A succession of metal detectors, then an airlock, then the
decontamination chamber where they tug off gloves and
coveralls and rubber boots and hobnail boots and dump
them in plastic fruit trays to be hosed and sprayed with
anti-pathogen.

Quickly they hit the showers and submit to the jets,
and when the live grime is blasted from scalp and pelt
they're brighter-eyed and more inclined to chatter. Now
they towel off and from assigned drawers take embroi-
dered shirts, gaudy western suits, tuxedo jackets, satin
elbow gloves, high-heeled shoes and strappy little numbers, and they fix their hair and snap on costume jewel-
lery and preen a bit and praise God this night is Saturday.

The ballroom's walls, three feet of concrete, seem to

swell from the sound contained within. The door's pulled back: a surge of music, a riot of light. The cones of those old Bose speakers throb like small black hearts, and overhead the silver mirrorball spins and shimmers. Long John Donegan, gagging for porter and meat, charges the bar like he's a centaur. Steel shutters go up, and here it is, your cash-free society: transactions conducted by tokens indexed to the barter system (you mind my childer for the night, I'll lag your tank). Homebrew can be got for very little. Once in a blue moon there's black-market harder stuff, but who here has the tokens for it?

Some dance, some prefer to watch. Some pair off and pull their partners close, and if you've credit there are rooms to let in the upstairs wing, discretion guaranteed, no nudge or wink. Everyone knows the score: it could all be over in the time it takes to squeeze a trigger or thumb a detonation code, so steal a little sweetness when you can – right now it's Saturday night and hold that thought. Hold that thought.

Here is where they set it down, the weight they've borne, the penance done, where they array their woes together like tributes at a grotto, or offerings to be burnt. That weight too great to be carried is a cosmic sadness, faith, a lament for all that has been and gone. Vast, ineffable, that big sky sadness that speaks to living things of all things lost, of histories cancelled out, of what a wonderful world, the late great Planet Earth, Groucho Marx and Penny Lane and the Wizard of Oz and poor old Superman, and you won't be seeing rainbows anymore, it's over, over for Mary Ellen Cash and Naeem Hammoud and Susannah Codd and Long John Donegan and Evelyn Brown, and over for you and I.

But not just yet.

The hour draws near, and they gather at the bandstand, not just to witness but to imprint on their minds the memory of what's before them and so to later tell others of their witnessing.

'Will he come?'

'He always do.'

'But what if he don't?'

House lights dim. Drapes draw back. A beam flickers and takes form.

And when tonight's final song is sung and the rite's complete, when that mirrorball stops spinning and those house lights flicker on, the assembly will drain their drinks and say 'G'mora' and goodnight and at last disperse to suit up and boot up and scatter back into a night barely lit by the fading moon, where a day will come with a pitiless sun, or maybe no sun, and the fields might bake and the roads might bubble like soup and quakes rend the hills and split the rocks and the wind howl like trumpets in a crazy woman's dream, and objects become detached from their names, rivers lose their riverality, earth its earthliness, symbols sunder from the things they signify – no matter what awaits, these people will bear these airs and melodies with them, sustain themselves with songs akin to ghostly echoes of some revival or requiem mass or chain-gang holler or death fugue, the widow's cry for her lost at sea, the prayers of buried miners, scraps of words and melodies fluttering in their souls like fireflies lost on the river, I'll never get out of this world alive, I'm so lonesome I could cry.

And so yes, here he is at last, the vision made incarnate in his fine white suit and his shining white boots and great white hat, a white guitar strapped across his chest. The room is *filled* with his pick and strum. So hark now: hear this voice so high and wild and lonesome. Hear the angel sing.

And if you should weep, well, that's all right, that's all right. You weep because you're mended. And if what you see here makes no sense, then ask yourselves, would you really want the mystery undone, to hear it's a trick of the light, a lantern shadow show, a hologram or hallucination or electro-magnetic anomaly or an apparition or visitation or even to hear it's a miracle?

He is among you, faith. That is all that matters. You can look into those two blue eyes that bear the light of one close to death, the contours of a face so gaunt it's just bones pushing out skin like tentpoles under tarpaulin. You can watch his bony fingers twang the strings and hear the truth of his heart and the raw song in his mouth like the call of a wounded old wolf. You can mend.

And if only for this hour are you consoled and mended, then this hour only it must be.

The Fuck Monkeys

Philip O'Ceallaigh

I'D BEEN WALKING ALL AFTERNOON in the sun. I reached the house and knelt under the pump and let the cold water pour like a river over my head. I drank until sated then sat there dizzy in the dirt as the cicadas shook their rattle at the cooling evening. Then I got up and walked across the yard to the hammock, strung between two bent pines, and kicked off my boots and pulled the cork on a bottle of rakia. Settling back and drinking, I stared up at the branches, needled green against the blue. I closed my hot eyes. The swollen heavy sun sank into the waves.

I was woken by the scraping of their claws on the flag-stones, and saw them there in the dusky light, as though through smoke, these little creatures that wouldn't have come up as high as your knee – copulating. I remained absolutely still. If I moved they could take fright, scarper back into the undergrowth, back into the falling night. They were some kind of animal, some kind of monkey, with long tails. Yet they had curiously beautiful, almost human, faces. Their eyes were impossibly big, hers long-lashed, with high arching eyebrows. She reached behind, gripped him, danced him into herself, glancing over her shoulder, making tiny panting noises, something between a sigh and a squeak – she was on all fours then, but there was nothing submissive about her. She danced and sang it, grinding him, grinding her teeth, grinding out the fuck. He was on his knees, spine arched and head thrown back, arms limp pendulums grazing his ankles, the rest of his body strained taut towards where he was hooked.

They might have been tiny humans, if you forgave the tails.

He began to twitch, dry branch about to snap, and she disengaged and spun fluidly to face him, and gripped his cock – huge, in proportion to the rest of him – and licked at him with her pointed tongue. She worked on him, devouring him, gathering rhythm as the waves in the background began to fizz and roar.

She released it from her mouth, and with the final shakes of her little fist he became a fountain of seed, shooting high through the air. She caught the next shots on the face and in her open mouth. He pumped until it dripped from her. Just when it had to be all over, she gave his balls a little tickle and he arched his back and shot the last of it.

He stood up, tottered a few steps – she was rubbing it on herself and convulsing with what I took for laughter – and toppled over on his side, chest heaving, tail twitching. She leapt to her feet and danced little circles around his body, hopping from one foot to the other, arms in the air. She finished it off with a tap dance, slapping her soles violently on the flagstones right before his face, then back-somersaulted so fast into the darkness and the vines that she left a faint blur hanging in the air after her, like dissipating smoke.

He lay facing away from me, as though asleep, but I supposed he was listening to the tremor of the waves on the rocks, coming up through the rock of the earth, purified on the cut stone where his skull rested. Slowly, slowly, he raised himself on his little elbow and gazed towards where she had disappeared. His tail twitched, shot through with electricity, like a sleeping cat hit in its dreams by the shadow of a bird passing overhead. He got to his feet and limped away, to disappear among the vines.

I lay very still. The pounding of the waves was a dull echo in my ears, like far-off thunder.

Then I moved too, slowly, recalling my body, recovering my nerves and muscles from paralysis.

The hammock lurched as I reached for the bottle. I raised it to my eyes; it was almost full.

The yard before my house, lit now only by a candle burning in a lamp hanging on a nail on the gable wall, swayed and settled as I lay back, cradling the bottle. I could not recall having lit the candle. It had still been bright when I had lain down. A bat swooped and flitted and was gone again into the darkness. I took a pull from the bottle, and it burned down into my gut, into my blood.

Then, far away, from across the waves of the bay, over

the headland, the breeze carried the sound of the church bells. The wind was blowing from the town. I counted them off, and then it was just me again, and the sea.

I had arrived about a month before the thing with the monkeys occurred.

The old man met me where the ferry docked, on the side of the island facing the mainland. I boarded his skiff. People were milling upon the docks, disembarking, and we were already heading out to sea again, rounding a headland, leaving it behind. I watched bays and inlets and long stretches of cliff go by, and seen this way the island was bigger than I had expected. The limestone ridges of the hillsides were pale jutting bones in the evening light. Scrub and small pines clung where they could on the heights. When the sun, which had been hanging over the island when we had docked, was over the sea, I knew we had reached the far side of the island and were approaching our destination. We rounded a point and entered a small rocky cove. He cut the engine, and we glided silently the last distance. Cigarette pinched in the corner of his mouth, he planted his hand on the wooden post of the jetty and leapt with unexpected litheness. He secured the boat, and I rose, stiff from sitting crouched, unsteady as the boat shifted under my weight. He extended an arm strong as a dry old branch and hauled me onto the jetty. I stood there, dizzy at the swaying world, staring out at the dazzling waves. When I turned around I was blind. The world was bleached of detail. All I could discern was the form of the old man, walking away. I took my pack from the boat and followed him.

We ascended the rough track. I struggled to keep up. Warm breaths of pine and sage and rosemary rose from the baked earth. The land levelled out and a squat house of neatly cut stone came into view. A high narrow stone chimney rose from its roof of rough tiles. Heavy flagstones paved the yard in the front of the house. Woody shrubs had taken root in the cracks between the stones and some of them had grown large. All around were neglected fruit trees and vines, the grapes in dense unripe clusters.

He turned a key in the cracked wooden door and forced it open with his shoulder. He handed me the key and I followed him inside. He moved through the cool gloom, opening windows and shutters, letting in light, revealing a single large room with a narrow iron-frame bed set against the far wall. From a wooden trunk he extracted a pile of blankets and dumped them on the bed. He indicated a metal tub and a lump of brownish soap. The stove was set with papers and kindling, and he put a match to it, and we watched the flames for a moment. Logs were stacked on the floor. He opened a dresser and showed me old pots and plates. He indicated my provisions: a large jar of cloudy olive oil, a big sack of rice, smaller sacks of cornmeal and beans, a large dusty demijohn of red wine and several bottles of rakia. He wiped a couple of cups with his sleeve, uncorked the wine and poured. He handed me a cup, clanked his own against it and downed it. I drank too, thirstily. He put his cup on the shelf, and I followed him outside.

The pump stood in the yard in front of the house. He worked the handle. It looked too loose, broken, then it resisted and gushed brown water. When it ran clear he had me work the handle while he threw water over his face.

He stood upright, shaking water from his hands.

We gazed down the slope, past the vines that had run wild, through the trees, to where the sun hung low over the expanse of open water. The bay had sunk into shadow but further out the water still caught the light in a wild and brilliant sparkling, a trembling so intense you knew it could not possibly endure for long. And against this, towards the horizon, was a remoter, smaller island, monochrome and two-dimensional, like a paper cut-out. The old man raised his arms from his sides, palms outward, and let them fall, as if asking what more I could want. I felt he was mocking me. I took out my wallet and gave him the money. He counted out the notes, nodded, folded the wad and put it in his back pocket. He took his cigarettes from his shirt pocket. He offered one, and I accepted. It was the first friendly gesture I had felt from him. Soon I would be alone in this place, with my sacks of rice and cornmeal and beans and my jug of wine, and it would be dark. We smoked for a moment, looking at the sea. This is what people do, I thought. They look upon open spaces, where light falls. Then he turned and pointed, to a place to the right of the house from where we stood, where a hammock hung between two pines, and spoke one word.

I shook my head, uncomprehending. Then, having barely lifted his hand in farewell, he was descending the path. I continued smoking in the gloom, until he was gone from view.

I tossed the butt. It hissed briefly where the water from the pump had pooled in the dirt.

I stood about for a long time then went into the dark house and put a log on the stove to keep it going. And then I remembered the hammock, and the wine. I poured myself a glass. I emptied it and poured another. I brought out the demijohn and arranged a big log as a table beside the hammock and settled in. One by one the stars came out, and I befriended them all, smothering my hunger in wine.

On the first morning, I ripped the wild growth from between the cracks in the flagstones. In the afternoon I assessed the land, striding about, bareheaded in the sunshine, anticipating the labour to come. Late in the afternoon I went down to the cove. In the clear water among the rocks I could see fish swimming.

The following day I set to work. Ripe apricots and figs burst in dark stains on the dry ground where they fell and I ate what I wanted from the branches. I spent the morning clearing the vegetation choking the vines and breaking the hard earth between the rows with a hoe. I pruned back the vines until it was too hot to work. Then I sat in the shade and admired my tidy patch of cultivated land, the dug soil with the tinge of moisture showing darker against the pale baked earth around. Even as I watched it was drying to the same dusty colour. It was rocky land, mostly, all around. Evidence of the struggle to subdue it was all about. Great mounds of rock were stacked on the hillsides and ran along the slopes in long lines. Where the gradient was gentle enough, these deposits of rock narrowed and became the walls of terraces, giving the land a sculpted look. At one time it must have been a garden. It had been won over generations. But the terraces were overgrown now, and collapsing. Working alone, at most I could hope to subdue the flat area around the house.

In the evening, when the sun had cooled, I went down to my cove. I experimented with baits – bits of sea anemone, cockles, little seasnails – and cast out with the hand reel. No fish bit. All I could reel in were crabs, hanging stupidly in the air, dripping water in molten beads, clamped obstinately to their prey even as they became prey themselves. The fish ignored me, but the crabs kept coming. In the end I kept three; back at the house I boiled them with rice, smashed the claws and extracted the scraps of flesh.

The good man is a tree that grows beside a stream, tall and straight, and bears fruit at the chosen moment. But time was out of joint even before the fuck monkeys came.

I had lost track of the days, but always counted off the bells from the church when I could hear them. Soon they were irregular. They would toll two and the next time four. Or toll the same number of times on two consecutive hours – I presume they were hours – and I did not know if the second occasion was a mistake or the rectification of a previous error. Errors in the stone tower of the church? The sun climbed the sky and fell, and did not care for hours. In the middle of the day I was junked out on sun and untroubled, even when I observed the shadows nudging across the yard stop and slowly draw back again, for what might have been an hour. What did I care, if the sun rolled backwards? What did I care about the giant spider spinning between the trees? All you want is one day, beneath the sun, like a butterfly.

My glass would refill when I was busy meditating on the insects in the grass, and at first I supposed I had lost the capacity to judge the true sequence of events. But this happened many times; I'd drain the strong red wine, enter my house to look for a knife perhaps, or a piece of string, and when I returned, my glass, which I'd left drained on the stump by the hammock, was brimming so full I'd have to lean down and slurp at it ungracefully.

I decided to test it, one day. I drained the glass, took a good hard look at it, said, I'm watching you. I gutted some fish. When I went back, it was still empty. Because it only refilled when my mind was elsewhere.

But as long as the monkeys, or whatever it was, were refilling my glass, giving me more hours not less, I was happy to go along with it all. My work was coming along. I had a stretch of well-tended vines and the grapes were swelling and filling with their syrup, and in the rows between I had the beginning of corn, tomatoes, beans and peppers, and my fishing was improving. Each morning I woke early, splashed water on my face, then worked among my plants. I had made mistakes in the past, on the mainland. The why of things had not been revealed for me. And so I was patient in the new place.

Then, dozing in my sling, the bottle nearby, I would hear the scratching of their claws on the flagstones, and I would half open my eyes. The monkeys began to come like this regularly, and always when my mind was elsewhere. Sometimes they fucked with tenderness, sometimes anger, but always afterwards he was alone, and it seemed he remembered what it was he went there to forget. He would fall and lie with his skull against the flagstones and his little ribcage – rabbit ribs, fishbones – would stand out with each laboured breath. He'd limp away into the tunnel of darkness between the vines and I'd reach for my bottle and take a slug.

And I recalled the old man, that first day, pointing at the courtyard, saying one word. I couldn't be sure, I might have remembered wrong, or misheard, but I know it had three syllables and I remembered the initial letter clearly.

I had turned away from the cities of the mainland, where they love what is worthless and worship that which is false. That part of my life was done with. But I grew curious to see what was over the promontory, to see the town from where the sound of the bells came when the wind blew from the east. Eventually I would have to go there. I was not yet producing enough to eat.

And I had nothing left to drink, even with the refills.

I set off, empty bottles rattling in my pack. The spiders had been spinning in the cool of morning. The webs between the branches of the trees and the bushes were strung with tiny pearls of moisture, and I slashed ahead of me with a stick to clear the way. The path climbed gently, following the seaward stab of the promontory, and as the sun gathered strength the dew burned off and the smell of the pine and rosemary rose on the warm breeze. The sea became bigger and brighter with each step upwards, the light breaking and scattering on the wavetops, and when I looked back I could see my home, and the evidence of my work and striving: a tiny patch of order suspended in the infinite wild universe of earth and wave and sky. And each time I looked back it was smaller, and dearer to me. Then it was gone, and I was high above the world and cresting the promontory, keen to see what was on the other side.

The track reached its highest point, and the vista of an immense bay opened on the other side. And straight ahead, in the distance, where the steep hills met the water, was the town, with its harbour and fort and the steeple that rang the distant bells that came to me on the wind. I caught my breath and gazed.

I removed my pack and sat on the rock. It would be one of those Venetian towns of clean-hewn stone, built to face the sea. A point on the trade with Ragusa and

Constantinople. Perhaps it had seen Turks and Crusaders in its time, before settling into the era of peace. I could imagine the gardens in the outskirts, tame fig and lemon trees, bees bumbling in the lavender and oleander. I could imagine the narrow alleys of the centre, the high windows and heavy doors of the houses of merchants. There would be wide quays, fishing boats swaying in a forest of masts, men conversing in the cafés. At one point I rose and put on my pack and continued along the track, the town glittering ahead of me. But then I stopped and turned back and sat again upon a rock, my head in my hands, undecided. I stood up and my bottles clanked again and I felt foolish and cowardly. I had to buy provisions.

I set off again towards my destination, but I was soon stopped again, this time by the sight of a small boat in the bay. I could not be sure at first, but then it appeared to me to be the old man, on course to round the promontory. I turned and hurried back, running at times, to arrive at the bay, or at least the house, before he could.

I reached the house, sweating, breathing hard, and unloaded the bottles from the pack. I did not wish him to know what I had been about to do. I found him down at the cove, unloading supplies onto the jetty. He laughed when he saw me – my beard was now as long as his. He seemed better disposed to me than the first time. And I was glad to see him. I had seen nobody since I had come to the island. He had brought wine and rakia, rice and flour and oil, matches and candles, and jars of various delicacies – olives and capers and honey. With a stubby pencil he scratched out a sum on the wooden boards of the jetty, listing each item. It meant the end of my money, almost. We carried the supplies together up towards the house.

He looked at my improvements with grudging admiration. Some of the grapes were ripe already, and we cut a load, which I bartered against the price of the rice.

I fetched two cups and we sat on logs on the veranda and drank.

I pointed to the hammock and spoke the word he had said that day. He shook his head. I repeated it, trying variants, putting the stress on different places in the three-syllable word. His face hardened, and he shook his head. I was sure this was an act, he knew perfectly well what I was referring to. I tried to speak his language. You say. Word. House. Night. Word. Night. And I repeated again the word he had said, pointing to the hammock and the place near the vines where the monkeys would appear from.

He shook his head and rose. I rose also, tossing the last drops of rakia from my cup onto the ground. There was nothing I could do if he would not talk. We carried the grapes down to the jetty, not speaking. I went back up to the house and began to drink the wine.

The weeks passed in work, and my grapes were swelling and becoming sweet and were particularly abundant in the area close to the house, where I had worked hardest. But I did not know how I would manage. I had no way to transport the ripe grapes. I had no boat, and going by foot over the headland would be too laborious. The solution was to make wine at the house, but I had no barrels. And no experience making wine. A small mistake would ruin everything.

At some point I would need help, and that meant dealing with the town. In the meantime, I carried on working.

I'd drink the wine, the moon would rise, and I'd fall asleep in the hammock and dream intricate pieces of theatre where the actors swapped masks and voices. Impossible cities, tunnels and trains and staircases and corridors. Money that disintegrated when you went to pay for the ticket. Broken phones. Guards that demanded the password that you had on a scrap of rag, ink washed out with the rain. Maps that grew and shifted beneath your eyes. The key dropping through the bars of the drain in the crowded street. The impossibility of ever getting home, of ever coming to rest; only the endless trials of the endless road, the purpose of the journey misconceived from the outset. Dreams where your teeth crumbled in your mouth and your hair fell out. Dreams that resembled life. One night I woke in the hammock from my troubled visions, my mouth dry from wine, to the scratching of their claws on the stones. I opened my eyes and saw the stars as a spray of luminous dust, as it appears only in parched and blacked-out lands where you are utterly alone.

I turned my head, and saw that they were three. The new one, I knew, was trouble. He was heavy, thick-necked and brutish, short wiry hair over most of his body. He slouched insolently. The first male was tugging at the arm of the female, entreating her, as she glanced towards the brute. This went on for some time, the brute lying on the ground on his side, leaning on one elbow, picking at his teeth with a twig, watching some point in the distance. Once he turned to look at the lovers, and spat. The first male tried to embrace the female, to kiss her shoulder and neck, but she was writhing away from him. She broke free of his grip and hissed in his face, baring her teeth, and he struck her face with an open-handed blow that made her totter to the side, clutching her face, whining in pain and anger. The male stood over her, fists bunched, ready to do it again. She glanced at the brute, who was now paying attention. He tossed away the twig and slowly, heavily, got to his feet and lumbered over to the smaller male. It looked choreographed and inevitable. There was no contest, but the smaller male was obliged to see the scene through. The blow – a swift uppercut to the chin – sent him sailing back through the air. His head hit the flagstones with a crack and he lay sprawled, out cold, legs splayed, arms in the crucifixion position, ribcage heaving. The brute turned to the female. Her resistance was token. He forced her down and got her legs apart. It seemed to cause her some distress at first, but then she got the hang of it. It was a different kind of mating to what she'd entered into with the little fellow, each thrust from the brute pushing her back across the ground. The muscles across the brute's back tensed. He grunted and his body slumped, pinning her beneath him. He disengaged and got to his feet, while she lay there, looking soft and bruised. He picked her up, threw her over his shoulder and walked away, disappearing in the leafy darkness beneath the vines.

Slowly, the little monkey managed to raise himself to a sitting position. His tail twitched uncontrollably. He climbed to his feet and, looking all the time at the ground, hobbled in the direction the others had gone.

When I could no longer see him and it was again entirely still, I reached for my glass, on the treestump beside my hammock. It was full to the brim, though I could not remember having filled it.

The work continued, and I became troubled. I was concerned about the grapes, that all I had laboured for should fall to the dust and rot, when it might become good wine, something to store and to savour. Yes, it was the wine pulling me back to the world, the swelling grapes demanding to be picked and pressed, me wandering the rows, knowing I would have to soon go back over the promontory and ask for help. I could tell the summer was at its peak and already foresaw the grey days of winter, the falling of cold rain, gusting in from the sea, me shivering by the stove in the house. I was thinking about the future again.

The sun went down on our world of trouble, and the moon rose red, and I sipped the dark wine, and my eyes rolled back in my head. When they opened again the stars were singing, and there was sound on the wind like the tinkling of bicycle bells, windchimes. The stars blurred and swam about the sky like little silver fish. I turned my head, and there he was, the brute, riding a little red open-top motor car, one hand on the wheel, elbow of the free arm resting on the door, the female in the passenger seat. It was an old model, big round headlights, all curves, and he was making circles and figures of eight in this toy-town machine. Beyond, towards the vines, a party was going on, the creatures – monkeys, little people, I no longer knew – were swarming in and out of the shadows of the plants. It was pretty lively around the bar, the males trying to attract the interest of the females, a lot of fooling around, tugging and shoving, strutting and dancing. One little fellow was doing magic tricks, finding coins behind the ears of a female. I spotted the male I know from before, the one who took the beating, and he was on the hard stuff, propping up the bar, while behind him a bartender was mixing cocktails, throwing bottles in the air and catching them behind his back with his tail, that kind of thing. And over the buzzing of the little car's motor the tinkling and ringing was getting louder, mixing with other sounds, becoming music, and a swing band was braiding through the vines in procession, the horn notes punching through the night, the tails of the players swaying to the beat. Finally, all these little creatures were through – the bass cellist, struggling to keep up, was last in position. The car screeched to a stop, and the brute and his monkey-bitch jumped out and started jiving. The monkeys at the bar were all shaking it, the whole joint jumping to the rhythm, I felt the ground itself shaking to the beat. The barman was showing off, dancing about with a cocktail shaker in his hand like a maraca. The little drunken monkey remained alone at the bar. He tried clicking his fingers, but his rhythm was long gone, and his foot slipped from the footrest, and he nearly toppled over. The tune ended, the brass section dipped their instruments, and an accordionist and a fiddle player stepped forward and struck up a tango. The dancefloor turned serious, even the brute straightened up and threw his head back, took his partner's hand and pranced her across the floor. They leaned towards each other, appearing to support each other, moving as a single being, her doing little decorative sidesteps and drawing little circles and half-circles and *ochos* in his orbit. The sad monkey drank and watched. When the end of the melody came, the crowd cheered the brute and his bitch, and he leapt into the driver's seat, over the door, and flicked hers open. She got in, and they did a final circuit of the assembly, her waving as they cheered, then accelerated into the night. The party began disintegrating after that. Monkeys were getting more evident in their lasciviousness, pairing off, there were some nasty little scuffles, mean but brief, while it was established who got who. The bar was shutting up, and the musicians were moving off in a line, playing 'When the Saints Go Marching In'. They twined in and out of the grapevines until they were lost to sight, the sounds becoming smaller and smaller, the tinkling windchimes of the stars ringing again in my ears with the chatter of the cicadas in the still hot air of the summer night – and I could remember the words from somewhere:

> Some say this world of trouble
> Is the only one we need
> But I'm waiting for that morning
> When the new world is revealed
> Oh when the saints . . .

All that was left of the party finally was the wounded little monkey, lying on his side, tail limp and lifeless with drunkenness. I reached for my brimming glass and drained it, spilling half over myself, then I rolled out of the hammock and hit the ground. Don't worry, monkey, I said, as the stars waltzed round my head, I'll save you. But I appeared unable to rise. I was glued to the ground. I lifted my arm but the gravitational force of the earth was more than usually strong and my arm slapped back down. My legs and my head had no better luck.

I awoke and the earth was shaking. The stars were blown out, and I could hear the vines and trees whipping and tossing like they feared to be torn apart in the wind and the rain. The clay beneath my face had turned to mud. My bare feet splashed through puddles as I stumbled to the house. Inside was pitch darkness. I felt my way to the cot in a dream and collapsed there.

Dead things are heavier. You sense when you pick up a living creature in your hands how little it weighs. A cat weighs nothing at all when alive, you feel when you hold its warm springy body that this is a creature that darts up trees, flies across rooftops. A dog too, even a big one, if standing, can be scooped up easily and will seem quite light. It's different when life has fled from the flesh. And so it was the next morning when I picked this tiny creature up from where he lay beneath an awning of vineleaves, on the damp earth. Even though he weighed almost nothing, the surprise was that he weighed anything at all. How is it, I wondered, that he had become real, finally, being dead? And again this life seemed to me a dream, all light and movement, only exposed for what it was by the weight of the dead flesh.

His bones – his ribs and shoulders, the little knots of his joints – protruded terribly. His skin was cold and clammy to the touch, and his eyes, like the eyes of any dead creature, be it fish or man, were duller than the stones on the ground. I lifted his corpse in my cupped hands and carried it towards the house and laid him on the flagstones. I went and got an old sack that had contained beans, and I ripped the cloth apart and wrapped him inside this shroud. I had to bury him so that the remains would not be attacked by birds and rodents. I fetched my mattock and carried that in one hand and held the bundle to my body with my other arm, and I ascended the path up the hill, high up, past the last of the crumbling abandoned terraces. The storm had blown itself out, and yet there was still a lot of dirty cloud scooting about, and a breeze was blowing the tops off the waves on the choppy darkened sea. Where my feet kicked the gravel of the path the soil beneath was dark with moisture. Yes, when the sun shone again the earth would put out its greenest shoots, the buds would sense their moment and burst into leaf and bloom. It would happen all over again – growth, pollination, the bringing forth of fruit, and its sure decay.

I reached a patch of flat open ground with a pleasant outlook over the terraces below. Higher up, vague mounds and lines of rocks indicated long abandoned terraces. Lower down, and abandoned more recently, they gained definition. They became finely wrought geometric shapes just above my house, where I had lovingly cleared the land and tended the soil. The house itself was set in the middle of a swathe of level ground where long straight rows of vines flourished. It looked rich down there. It was my season's work, though I had no idea if I could save it. Perhaps this view was my only reward: my land, and my little bay, and the sea beyond beneath the vast curving sky. I laid the shroud on the ground and began to dig. I hacked and chipped, and I levered out stones and rocks until the hole was deep enough, then I laid the bundle inside and began to cover it up, beginning gently with the finer soil and sand, then with the smaller stones, and then with the larger ones, which I tamped down with my foot. Finally, I searched the area for large clean rocks, and when I had enough I began to pile them up. I started with the largest flattest rocks and built up until I was using the smaller stones. I lost track of time, caught up in my work, and when I stepped back at last the grave was a beautiful thing, a gently curved cairn that rose from the land as if part of it, set in that natural clearing, overlooking the world. I had the satisfaction at least that I had acted fittingly. I wiped my dirty hands on my trousers, picked up the mattock by the shaft and went back down towards the house.

As I descended, the clouds broke, and the sun shone upon the land, transforming it again. By the time I reached the house the fever was overtaking me. I was cold in the sunshine and sweating. I took the bucket and fetched water. By now every movement was costing me great effort, my limbs were heavy and my mind torpid. With the bucket of water and a ladle by the cot, I lay down and covered myself with all the clothing and blankets I had, and still it was not enough, I sweated and I trembled. And yet it was strangely pleasureful as it progressed, to be drifting back and forth through sleep and wakefulness, detached from the world, opening my eyes again and seeing that it was still bright day through the door, and it seemed the longest day ever. In my indifference to time and its passage, I might have been awakening to a succession of days, more or less the same. It was unimportant, because all I wished for was to be allowed to lie there and do nothing. I would be drifting into unconsciousness, and I would wake myself with little yelps or shouts that seemed to have no source in anything I could remember imagining or dreaming but reminded me of a dog when it is disturbed in its dreams. And I recall thinking every creature is tortured in its dreams, the lowest and the highest, always running, pursued by phantoms, even when stretched out unconscious on the ground. But at last the evening did draw in, very slowly, and the night too was one of sleeping and waking, and all my heavy flesh wished for was to wish for nothing, to lie there, kissed by nothingness.

By morning it had mostly passed. I rose and went outside in the growing light and beheld my gardens, my land, the house where I had laboured, and it was all changed. I was free of it. I looked at the full vines and now it meant nothing. It was not my problem.

I had come to the island to hear only the sounds the earth made, the sea and the wind and the animals, to sustain myself in its grace, to eat what it yielded me; I had gone there to shrug off the nagging frightened flesh, its memory and craving, believing thereby my journey was at an end. But I had understood nothing. The journey never ends. I looked at the vines and saw in the swollen berries the problem I had wrapped myself around and which had tied me there, a dream – like that of the woman and the man in their perfection, each striving towards the other, both towards release, and then falling, knowing it is to begin all over again from the start – and now it mattered no more that the grapes would lie where they fell. There was nothing to be saved. There was always too much fruit, and it rotted where it fell. How had I forgotten that?

The sun rose over the sea, and I went to the pump and washed the sweat off myself. The fever had not entirely passed but it was pleasant, the cold water. Then I dressed in clean clothes and put a few things in my sack. I did this without thinking, naturally, because going to the town was what I wanted, in that moment. I'd had all the solitude a soul could take. I wasn't going anywhere for any reason. I wasn't setting out on a journey. I was just going for a walk.

I picked a bunch of ripe grapes to eat while I walked. I climbed the path along the hillside, eating them, spitting seeds as I went.

Goose

Joseph O'Neill

IN LATE SEPTEMBER, ROBERT DALY flies New York–Milan.
He travels alone: his wife Martha, six months' pregnant
with their first child, is holed up at her mother's place
upstate, in Columbia County. Robert is going to the
wedding of Mark Walters, a Dartmouth roommate who
for years has lived in London and is marrying an English
girl with a thrilling name – Electra. Electra's mother is
Italian, hence the Italian wedding. Although he has been
to Europe a number of times, Robert has never visited
Italy. Italy, New York friends tell him, is the most beautiful country in the world.

Robert is happy to find himself in the most beautiful
country in the world. He needed a pick-me-up. Life at
the bank has been downright difficult. His solitude is
also a cause of happiness because being alone, these days,
is a harmless form of freedom. However, driving out of
Malpensa Airport in his tiny, chariot-like rental car, gripping a shift stick for the first time in years, Robert is frustrated. Every time he turns onto a road he believes will
lead him south, he winds up heading in the direction of

the Alps, snow-capped even at this time of year and altogether astounding in their abrupt and fearsome immen-
sity. Eventually he makes his way onto the *autostrada*.
There, cruising at what he believes to be a fast speed of
120 kilometres per hour, he is repeatedly menaced by
light-flashing cars – with mysterious invariability, silver
cars – and, finally, by a racing pack of motorcyclists cos-
tumed in chequered leather outfits. Robert makes way
for the zooming harlequins. His place is in the slow lane,
between gigantic trucks that almost frighten him.

He is bound for Siena, and at Bologna he goes west-
ward. He plans to spend the night in what may well be,
in the further assertion of his New York informants, the
world's most beautiful city. The road takes him through a
mountain range he cannot name. On the far side of the
mountains, at dusk, in a vista of almost ridiculous painti-
ness, Florence presents itself. Robert takes in the bright
low rays, the pretty mist, the shining agglomeration of
domes and rooftops, the gloriousness, and thinks, Okay,
I get it. The temptation pushes at him to skip Florence,
to keep going, but he resists. Down he drives, into the
legendary city.

Once there, he is foiled. He passes a full two hours
trapped in powerful but sluggish flows of traffic: twice
the Duomo comes into view, and twice he is helplessly
borne away in slow motion to a district of muddy apartment buildings to which all roads lead and which must
be, a grim Robert surmises, Rome. When at long last he
penetrates the city's historic section, he stops at the first

hotel he sees because it comes with a courtyard where he can park and to find parking is to find peace of mind. The receptionist shows him a mini room with a mini TV and a mini bath. No mini bar, however. Robert takes the room, just as he takes the receptionist's plainly careless recommendation of a restaurant a few blocks away. The wine he orders warily and gloomily: in the past year he has barely tasted anything as a result of a sinus affliction that took him at the age of thirty-eight and, inhalants and nasal sprays notwithstanding, has left him in an all-but-odourless world. The affliction does not touch him most keenly in the matter of food. He can no longer smell his wife. He can no longer detect those scents that, as a husband, are his alone to detect.

Dinner over, he wanders in a warm night. It is past ten o'clock. He sees only tourists. He winds up following a sign to the Ponte Vecchio – the name definitely rings a bell – where an Italian guitar player is singing Simon and Garfunkel. Robert thinks, You come all this way, you come to the world's most beautiful city, and you end up with Simon and Garfunkel. Actually, Robert acknowledges that he would rather listen to a terrible version of 'Bridge over Troubled Water' than visit a museum or a church. He knows what the latter would involve: an hour or more of waiting in line with chattering art-aficionado-mimickers in order to be confronted with a vaguely familiar Michelangelo or Botticelli or what-have-you that's no better than its postcard reproduction. He leans on the edge of the bridge. Surrounding him are American retirees and irritatingly self-contained German girls with small bears hanging from their back-packs. Robert gazes at the river, the Arno: it is moonlit and atmospheric and so forth. He gets the river.

At midnight he walks back to the hotel.

In the morning, he takes a scenic route. Robert clocks the scenery: hills, hill towns, and sloping fields evidently cultivated for millennia. So this is Tuscany. It feels to Robert like one of those counties around Santa Barbara. Then, Siena. His hotel is in the old city, and the old city, as per the wedding instructions, is an intricate medi-eval arrangement of alleys and squares set on a steep hill. Robert finds parking outside the old city and walks to his hotel. Now what? He tries to eat lunch but cannot: the restaurants are all closed for the afternoon. So for half an hour he strolls. He has nothing to do until the evening, when an eve-of-wedding reception will be held. Back in his hotel room, he phones home – Everything is fine, just fine, reports Martha, hanging up before Robert is quite ready for it. He browses through a hotel leaflet about Siena's history. Once upon a time, he reads, Siena was a great banking centre. Robert muses on how invest-ment banking might have been structured in what was, he presumes, a pre-corporate age, and who the bond-holders might have been, and whether their crises were like the one that's happening now. Robert assumes so. Then the leaflet reveals that a plague struck Siena and the city lost its power. He flips to the next page but there's nothing more.

Plague, loss of power, period. Robert is taken aback by this.

He decides to shave for the party. This takes care of five minutes. When Robert heads out he steps into an internet café and logs on. His intention is to look at his email. Instead he gets distracted by a headline on the AOL home page.

5,000-YEAR-OLD SKELETONS LOCKED IN ETERNAL EMBRACE

By coincidence, the story comes out of Italy. In the north of the country, archaeologists have discovered the remains of a man and woman buried for five thousand to six thousand years. The intactness of the teeth indicates that these were young persons. It is apparently a remarkable find, even for professionals who spend their lives finding things of this kind. A Neolithic double burial is very rare, and what's more the man and woman are hugging: It's unmistakable, states the archaeologist, who says she is very moved. There is a photograph. The youngsters' skeletons lie face to face. Each has its arms wrapped around the other skeleton. Undoubtedly the skeletons appear to be a pair.

The question in Robert's mind is whether the couple arranged themselves in this way, or whether their bodies were arranged in this way by others.

There's a second question, asked by the article: *Is there someone you'd like to spend 5,000 years buried with?* There's a Yes tab and a No tab.

Robert floats the cursor toward the tabs and clicks the

Yes tab. It has not been discussed, but it is logical that Martha and he will lie together, or at least near each other, for the next five thousand years, give or take the few decades of their joint lives.

The welcome party is being held at a splendid old building down the hill, and Robert walks there, shoes echoing. He wears no socks. His loafers are brand new. The last thing Martha did before driving upstate was drag Robert into a shoe store on Madison Avenue. Now you're respectable, she said, handing him the shoebox. The purchase was a weight off her mind, Robert saw, a loose end tied. With the baby just three months away, Martha has been spotting loose ends everywhere: the need for a paint job in the baby's room, the dangerousness of the electricity sockets, the inadequacy of the freezer compartment. Martha is on a tear. In recent weeks she has carried around a checklist and a marker pen that makes a fat, satisfactory stripe when a to-do is done. Robert recently picked up the list and read it with awe. A one-word item earned his closest, most amused, most mystified attention. The word, which had a line drawn through it, was his name.

Arriving at the reception, Robert wonders who from the old Dartmouth days will have made the trip. The answer, he discovers, is himself. Either Mark has lost interest in the Dartmouth crowd or vice versa or both. The last possibility is the most likely, mutual loss of interest. After all, Mark has been abroad for a long time. Moreover, a year after his first marriage came to an end, Mark quit

his London job – as a boutique picker of Russian invest-
ments, an undertaking whose huge success truly regis-
tered with Robert only when he heard that Mark was in
the habit of rollerblading from his Mayfair flat to his St
James office – quit his job in order to work in Africa in
an opaque help-the-needy capacity. Consequently Mark
himself became a little opaque, at least to his American
circle. Robert guesses that his status as the only present
Dartmouthian may be referable to the $2,000 cheque he
once wrote in favour of Mark's African cause – and in
secret, because Martha would have thought it excessive,
particularly given the recipient's reputation as a Mayfair
rollerblader.

Whatever: the Dartmouth crowd has not made it over.
Pretty much everyone is from London. Robert recog-
nises that he will need to drink heavily. He has some
experience of being the lone American at a gathering of
English people.

A couple of vodkas later, Mark appears with his fiancée – his wife, in the eyes of the law, since they submitted
to an Italian civil marriage that afternoon. Mark is happy
to see him and in fact hugs Robert, which has never happened before, and introduces him to Electra. Electra falls
into the beauty category, with long red hair and legs that
move in almost supernaturally small steps and bring to
Robert's mind, for the first and possibly the last time in
his life, he thinks, the word *elfin*. He remembers how, in
one of their few transatlantic communications, Mark had
mentioned meeting a redhead. I need to move fast, lock

this down, Mark said. Well, he's done it, Robert thinks. He is glad for his friend and glad to accept another vodka.

You've got to give the English this much, Robert thinks: they know how to throw a wedding. The Saturday afternoon is a sunlit one, and as he sits in the chartered bus he knows already that the proceedings will be a marvel of invention and organisation and poetry.

The venue for the marriage blessing is a manor house on a hilltop ten miles outside Siena. There is a garden with views of five valleys and, for the ceremony, an arbour. Robert is the first to take a seat among the chairs artfully scattered on the lawn. He puts on his sunglasses and stretches out his legs. He is no longer hung over. He feels, for the first time on this trip, relaxed; and his thoughts run with more freedom.

What he thinks is that he may very possibly be the only person here, Walters family excepted, who attended Mark's first wedding, to Jane. It was held on a dark afternoon, nine years ago, at a church on the Upper East Side veiled in a black net. Inside, statues of saints and benefactors hovered in little nooks, to grotesque effect. The father of the bride, dying of cancer, was held up by his only daughter as they walked up the aisle. He died the following week, and two years later Jane died, very courageously, of cancer. Jane was small and dark-haired, altogether different from Electra. Robert remembers the homily at Jane and Mark's wedding, a homily memorable because Mark was pretty much the first of their crowd to get married (Shit, how old was everybody – twenty-eight? twenty-nine?) and because the homily itself was such a downer. It concerned what the minister termed *the will to love*. The will to love: Robert remembers how he'd felt under assault from this sombre, slippery theme. He'd even taken offence on behalf of the happy couple. Even today, when of course he is able to take a pretty good guess at where that minister was coming from, he's hoping he won't hear any admonitions or life lessons, which nobody believes make any difference to anything and which certainly are way too cloudy for a wedding. Give people a break for one fucking day of their lives.

The seats begin to fill up – how middle-aged everybody looks, Robert thinks, even Electra's crowd, in their early thirties – and a young Scottish clergyman wears an expectant, official expression. Mark, a handsome straw hat covering his bald head, nervously makes conversation. Robert limits his greetings to a double thumbs-up. Then Electra makes her entrance, in white, escorted by her father. The blessing ceremony begins. Robert is not really listening. He is dwelling again on Mark's first wedding.

After the marriage, Mark and Jane led everybody to a nearby restaurant. At dinner – dessert was being served – Robert checked his phone and saw that he'd received three missed calls, all from the same unknown number. Sneaking out, Robert returned the calls. It turned out they were from the animal hospital where his cat – Buster, formerly the cat of his sister, whose travels made it impossible for her to keep a pet – was undergoing surgery on a blocked intestine. Buster had a history of such blockages. There'd been a fur ball, then a piece of leather, then another fur ball. He'd needed three operations. There was fur-ball medication, of course, but either he or his sister had neglected to give it to Buster or the medication didn't do the job. Now there was this new fur ball and this fourth operation.

Robert, a finger plugged into his free ear, spoke to the veterinarian surgeon. He knew this woman from the day before and didn't like her. When examining the cat, she'd remarked that Buster had fleas and had been all sniffy about it. Buster himself had jumped off the examining table and taken an interest in the room. Then he was taken away.

Through New York's roaring, Robert heard this vet quite animatedly telling him that the operation had gone well, only then mentioning that Buster had reacted badly to the anaesthetic and was – Robert had to extract the words from her – in a coma. It was a case of a brief but serious deprivation of oxygen to the brain. Robert found himself unable to speak. He went inside to Martha – a brand-new girlfriend back then. The two left the wedding immediately and took a short taxi ride to the animal hospital on York Avenue. They were shown into a room. Robert saw a creature stretched out on a table with its eyeballs turned into its head and its mouth stretched open by a tube. Its four legs, strapped to the table, were splayed out in a way that made no sense. The cat looked nothing like Buster. It didn't even look like a cat. The vet offered some clearly dishonest and meaningless statistics about the thing's chances of recovery. Also she mentioned the expense of keeping it alive. Martha held Robert's hand as he listened to all of this. When she understood that Robert still could not speak, she took it upon herself to ask the vet the necessary questions. When the vet again said, The operation was a complete success, Martha said, You know what? We'd appreciate it if you stopped saying that.

The next morning, nothing had changed. The plug was pulled on Buster. There were various options with regard to the remains. Robert decided on the gratis option, namely the garbage. Buster was garbage at this point. Over the next few days, handwritten condolence cards arrived from vets. Bills, too.

On the other hand, this was when Martha had revealed herself to be a rock, and that turned out to be a big deal.

Suddenly everybody stands for a hymn, and Robert can barely get to his feet.

Under God, Mark and Electra make their vows. When the service comes to a close, Robert locates the small packet of rice he noticed earlier under his seat. He empties the packet into his hand and tosses the grains on Mark and Electra.

Dinner is in the manor house. The names on the place cards are anagrams, and Robert Daly takes the seat set aside for LADY T. BORER. He finds himself between a

Colombian and an Indian: evidently, this is the foreigners' table. Robert spends the first part of dinner pretending to take an interest in the Indian man's bizarrely forceful opinions about the future of the dollar and the euro and the yen. (The Indian man calls Robert Roger. Robert begins to correct him, meaning to point out that his anagram name has no *g* in it, but abandons the correction. Roger, Robert, whatever.) The second part of dinner is devoted to the Colombian woman. They talk about kidnapping insurance, which it seems is a necessity in Colombia. These conversations are disturbed from time to time with talk of the goose. Apparently there is a goose present at the wedding. The goose lives at the villa and is very socially sophisticated. Everybody at Robert's table seems to have a story about the goose.

The speeches start. They are all funny and pointed and confident and moving, and Robert, who has witnessed this national facility time and again, wonders whether making after-dinner remarks is somehow part of the British educational curriculum. Mark's speech mentions him for having come all the way from New York. None of the speakers mentions Mark's first wife. It is Electra's day.

Night falls. A dance floor has been designated on the flagstones of the terrace, and dancing begins. Here the wedding's weakness shows itself: the disc jockey is an Italian, and the one flaw in the Italian race – Robert knows this because of his failed attempts, when driving down from Milan, to find a not-shit radio station – is its tin ear for pop music. The dancers must struggle with a weird mix of lesser eighties hits and hyperbolic Italian ballads. But everybody has fun. The clergyman twirls in a kilt. Robert, who is not much of a dancer, is happy to hold a constantly replenished drink and look on. Mark joins him and puts an arm on his shoulder. Robert tells Mark how good he's looking. Bob, I feel good, Mark replies. Man, I feel good. Then he bounds onto the dance floor and shimmies up to his wife. The new Mrs Mark Walters, Robert sees, is a quite remarkable mover. That bodes well, he theorises, for the bedroom. How did Jane dance? He tries to remember but cannot. He didn't really get to know Jane. She parachuted into Mark's life and then disappeared with him to England and then never came back, because she was buried there, in England, even though her family was back in Massachusetts.

On his way to the bar, Robert trips and almost falls. The Indian currency expert approaches him like the oldest of friends and refines a point he made earlier about the euro versus the dollar. Roger/Robert nods and nods. Then, interrupting, he says, *Cambio*. This draws a silence from his interlocutor. Italian for *change*, Robert says. Maybe it's Spanish, too. Anyhow – *cambio*. Remember that word. And *bureau de change*. Very useful. Fully obnoxious, he pats the expert on the back and goes toward the action. Now he will dance.

Robert dances.

When he is done, he picks up a chair and drags it one-handed beyond some bushes until he comes to the edge of the hilltop. He accomplishes this barefoot. He has kicked off his painful new loafers, which lie somewhere on the lawn behind him. He crashes down on the chair and drinks from a beer bottle. An incline is detectable a few feet away, and beyond that is some kind of drop. Further out there's a single road curving between hills. Every other place is free of human activity and thus free of human lighting. The hills are very black. There's the matter of the moon, however. The moon is big, circular, ablaze. Robert thinks, This wedding is a masterpiece. They've roped in the fucking moon.

He turns to see if he can catch a glimpse of the newly-weds through the bushes. There is no sign of them, indeed almost no sign of the wedding: it seems to have drifted away. He is conscious of the grass under his feet, and he shuffles his feet to feel the grass more intensely. His tactile faculty, at least, is fully operational, so much so that he becomes aware of the bones in his right foot and, phantasmally, of the foot-thumb his most distant ancestors possessed but which vast ages have gradually amputated. He stamps his foot to get rid of the sensation, which is not a new one to him. He thinks, Jane was buried in England, far from home, because she expected that Mark would be buried with her.

He has company. It is the goose. The goose is white, with an orange beak. Robert catches the goose's eye and the goose looks right back. He is all set to dislike the goose but finds he cannot. Actually, he takes a shine to the goose. Hey there, buddy, he says. The goose is still looking at him. The name's Roger.

Robert looks out in the direction of the hills, the valleys, whatever out there has blackened. Well, old buddy, Robert says to the goose.

He looks at the goose. The goose is purely there. Back at dinner, somebody said that the goose thinks it's a dog. No it doesn't. It doesn't think it's a dog. The goose doesn't think. The goose just is. And what the goose is is goose. But goose is not goose, Robert dizzily thinks. The goose isn't goose.

Robert cannot look at the goose any more. The goose is nauseating. He looks away from the goose but he finds he cannot look at anything without thinking that it is all goose, that he is goose, everything is a burying ground of goose out of which nothing can ever be unburied, he was born buried, the air is just a material of burial, the universe is itself buried, his child is buried in Martha and will come out buried.

Presently the goose is gone.

The wedding has been coming to an end. A while ago the bus started ferrying people back to Siena; now somebody is laughing and shouting, Last bus, everybody, last bus. Robert stands up. For a few seconds, he goes nowhere. Then he walks toward the laughter and the shouts. Somewhere up there are his shoes.

Footnote

Glenn Patterson

BACK IN THE DAYS WHEN that was the sort of thing that did happen, Maurice McStay passed on details of his neighbour's car to another man he knew as a result of which the neighbour wound up dead. No one ever suspected Maurice. He had gone to the funeral with the rest of the street. He had puts his arms around his neighbour's wife, shaken the children's awkwardly offered hands. The youngest boy looked Maurice in the eye. I wish it had been you and not my daddy, he said. The boy's mother was appalled, forgetting for the moment in her rush to apologise her own grief. God forgive you, she said, and to Maurice, he doesn't understand what any of it means. Maurice was nursing the hand he had with difficulty wrested back. There's no need to apologise, he said. The boy had buried his face in his mother's skirts. She tried to get him to turn round. Really, Maurice said, no need.

The afters was in a hotel on the road into town from the cemetery. Maurice left as soon as was decent and stopped in at a bar he knew for a drink. When he reached out for the glass his hand shook so badly he had to pull it back below the counter out of sight. He tried another two or three times, but it was no use. I know how you feel, the barman said as Maurice got up to go, his drink still untouched. Maurice's neighbour had used to drink in the bar the odd time too. Once the two of them had gone in together on their way from a match. They had been at opposite ends of the ground and had laughed about it. Here . . ., the barman wanted to give Maurice his money back. Maurice didn't trust his hand out of his pocket. Put it in the charity box, he said. The hand carried on shaking for a week after that. Then it stopped. Maurice went over again the claims made by the man who had asked him for the details of his neighbour's car. Kill or be killed was what it came down to. Nobody ever said these weren't tough times.

Later that year the neighbour's wife and her children moved away. The boy who had wished Maurice dead at the funeral waved as the car pulled away from the kerb for the last time. He had grown about six inches in as many months. You would hardly have recognised him as the same wee boy at all.

The new people only stayed in the house a year, the people after them eighteen months, after which it lay empty for a time. A landlord bought the house and broke it up into flats. The woman, Jane, who moved into the bottom one was divorced. She had two teenage children, a boy and a girl, who had her heart broke, effing and blinding, staying out to all hours, getting up to God knows what. She took to calling at Maurice's door in the evenings the worse for drink. He would stand there and listen to the day's litany while she wiped at her eyes, spreading the sorrow. I'm sorry, she said every time, I've nobody else. One night in winter Maurice just said to her come in ahead out of the cold and that was it. Jane kept the flat next door – she didn't want Maurice thinking he had to take on responsibility for the children too – but she was there when he closed his eyes at night and there when he opened them again in the morning.

He helped her to stop drinking. He had never taken that much himself so it was no hardship for him to stop with her. The teenage children straightened up and in time moved out. Jane tried to persuade Maurice to sell his house and move next door. Prices in that part of town had been rocketing since the ceasefires and it wasn't as if they needed the room. But, no, Maurice said, he wasn't ready for a flat yet. Maybe when he was seventy-two, not fifty-two. Admit it, Jane said, you're too comfortable where you are. Maurice said nothing, which for Jane was admission enough. I knew it, she said. I just knew it.

Jane had been in catering before she met her husband and had her life almost ruined. It had been her dream then to have a place of her own. Now that she was sober and the children were away she started looking around for a little café she could run. She and Maurice drove all over the city viewing properties. In the end it came down to a choice of two: a Copper Kettle in the east and the well-named Nothing Fancy at the back of the university. They sat at the dining-room table over cups of camomile tea discussing the pros and cons. The east was up and coming; the east was still the east. You would be hard pressed not to make money within a mile of the university in term time; you would be standing looking out the window the other half of the year wondering where the next customer was coming from.

The Copper Kettle shaded it. Jane signed the lease on her forty-eighth birthday and started in the day after that with the redecorating. A week before she was due to open a police car pulled up in front of Maurice's work. He knew before the peelers inside had finished adjusting their hats that they had come for him, but still when one of them started talking about the Copper Kettle and some sort of fall he looked at them uncomprehending. Jane? was all he could say. He rode to the hospital in the back of the patrol car asking the questions he had not had the presence of mind to ask back at work. Hadn't anyone been holding the stepladder steady? How high up had Jane been when it collapsed? What way had she landed? Only when the car drove past A&E did he realise his questions were all academic.

The ladder had tipped backwards while she was stretching to reach a ceiling rose. The wee girl who had been lending her a hand had tried to describe for the police the sound of her head striking the tiled floor. It was like, I don't know, you just knew that was her, you know? Jane, the doctors told Maurice, would not have felt another thing until she was pronounced dead five minutes before he was ushered into intensive care. He sat beside her for three-quarters of an hour holding her hand until the mortuary attendants arrived. She still had on the twisted scarf she had used to tie up her hair that morning. A look on her face like whatever it was was calling her she hadn't quite heard it the first time. The police had already contacted the son – he was in England now, doing well – and the daughter, who was driving up from down south with her boyfriend.

Later that night they sat, all four, in Maurice's front room, strangers, unable to speak. Jane had been failed somehow, alone at the top of that ladder. To have said more would have been to apportion blame.

Some time after nine Jane's ex-husband arrived with his second wife, who waited in the car until he had gone in to check that she would be welcome. Maurice had only met the man once before, the new wife never at all. He felt seeing her for the first time something of Jane's affront, often rehearsed in those drink-sodden laments on Maurice's doorstep, that her husband could have chosen this sharp-nosed little creature over her, over his own children. But her arrival prevented the evening from descending still further into grief and unspoken recrimination. She had the knack of starting a conversation then, when she was confident it could carry on without her, withdrawing, disappearing from the room altogether. By the end of the night the children were in a clinch with their father while his wife rinsed glasses at the kitchen sink and the boyfriend dried. Maurice went out to stand on the front step. There was music coming from the bottom flat next door, folkish. He could not have told you any more who was living there, the tenants came and went that fast. He could hardly have told you who was living in any of the other houses. The street was changing. People didn't bother the same way. He was aware that there was something perverse in this line of thought, but he felt it nevertheless to be true. They just didn't bother.

Five Entries from a Fictional Diary

Angela Power

THE WILDFLOWERS AROUND HERE ARE flourishing. I have four chickens from herself, and the lack of pleasure in their conception doesn't seem to inhibit her as a mother. She bustles around full of importance and seems to look down on the others who have done none of the lying down and fussing that she did.

Is Mrs M the grandmother of my lovely little fluffy ones? If so, God help them. They don't take after her (well, maybe a little around the beak). The old tom is not impressed, he looks at them as if he remembers somewhere in his head that he is supposed to chase little fluffy things with two legs but by the time his legs get the message, his head has forgotten, and he flops back down again.

Mrs M'll have a bit of a wait for the spuds as they're only about a foot tall and no sign of a flower. I suppose that'll be another black mark for me.

The tinkers called today. I think they called to see what the new Mrs Mel was like. I don't know if I passed the test. Old Mr H spent a long time staring at the clock over the fire, and, when I didn't take the hint, he told me the eyesight was bad and could I ever read the time for him. This is a fine clock, one of Mel's bargains from an auction in one of the big houses near here, so I don't think it was Paddy's sight that was the problem. I never wanted Mel to buy that clock in the first place. I'm a bit scared of its history. It is balanced very high over my head, and it is watchful. The dust that gathers on it does not seem to be my dust.

The tinkers are used to being treated with great respect around here and don't spare the name of those who do them down. I hope they go and say that the new missus isn't too bad. I bought a few mothballs and managed not to laugh when Mrs H produced the 'last of the cracked Holy Marys'. For some reason Mel laughed till he cried about this and kept repeating it under his breath for the evening and going off into fits like a small boy. It is lovely to see him laugh and to see the strain in his face just flow away.

I think I am getting the hang of the delicate social relationships around here. A good day, thank God.

There was a funeral in the old graveyard today. The sound of the 'Last Post' and the gun salutes clung to the air like the touches of frost to the turnip pile in the yard. I didn't really expect that. They were paying homage to an Old IRA man gone to God from the safety of his armchair.

I hated him.

He went off to fight with his passion for the land and forgot the woman on her knees by the fire, shivering with every footfall and brush of a branch on her window. He did his duty by his country and climbed over his children to get there. I'm tired and cold, and my face hurts from smiling and agreeing with everyone that he was a good man I had been unfortunate not to meet.

I never want to meet his like.

The sound of empty chatter and gunshots will never persuade me that he was a hero. Heroes don't die of old age. It was past midnight when the last person left. I stayed to do the washing up, alone.

I don't think words can paint a picture of today, but it deserves to be recorded anyway. The tabby had four kittens yesterday, four tiny, blind little scraps. How like big mice they are when they are born! Mother Cat looked up at me with a mixture of pride and delight. I felt as if I was looking at tiny little miracles. The little ones sucked away with the fury of staying alive. You should see the nest they were in, an old barrel with hay and a meal sack in it. I thought she chose it to protect the little ones from rats. I was wrong. The enemy was much nearer home.

When I told Mel, he said the kittens would have to go. We would be overrun otherwise. I thought of the proud, content little mother, snuggled in her warm bed after a night of exertion, and I pleaded, but to no avail.

Mel went out, picked up the tiny, warm little parcels and thrust them into the cold, rain barrel by the shed.

I held the mother, who had murderous intent in every sinew of her body. The little ones never even cried out, and the little balls of wet fur were cast under the bushes where the mother spent a futile, frantic few hours trying to lick them back to life. Her cries, coupled with coaxing purrs, tore at something in me. Is it because I am female? Is it because I am unable to cope with the dark side of this bloody awful business of farming? Maybe it is because I know the primitive pain of being a female deprived of the object of her love. I think Mel was shaken by the whole thing too even though he kept saying that I couldn't afford to be sentimental about cats. He went off for a walk by himself and didn't eat any supper. He was quiet all night and went to bed early without reading. The cat is still howling pitifully around the yard, and I am sick to my soul.

April 10th

A dress in the wardrobe. Red with white polka dots. Did I wear it? The perfume of that evening still sticks to it as the memory does to my mind. No amount of washing will wipe them away. Vera Lynn on the radio and a clear polished floor to dance on. He was home on two days' leave. We never slept. Sleep was for the unloved and the alone. We had nowhere to go. Nowhere open after dark and a red dress that had to be seen. It was, briefly. No air-raid shelter for us. The thud of bombs jumping 'The White Cliffs of Dover' on the gramophone. Vera repeating herself, over and over. Impossible, desperate love by the light of a gas fire and flickering, faraway buildings. Now the dress hangs in a country wardrobe on a bright spring morning only a shadow of its greatest hour when it lay crumpled on a Hammersmith floor.

The Old Regime

Kevin Power

1

LET ME TELL YOU HOW I BEGAN my career as a fixer. It happened in college, as these things do. I can give you the exact moment, if you like. It was a February morning, very early, eight or nine. The campus was quiet, like an airport at dawn. The concourse was deserted. Dew glittered in the shadowy grass. And Francis Mulligan came over to me and asked me for a favour.

But wait – wait. This is the end of the story, more or less, and I haven't even told you the beginning.

2

It was spring 2006: election season. The windows of the Library looked molten in the light of lengthening evenings. That was where I was spending most of my time, back then: in the Library. I wasn't a fixer, at that stage. I wasn't even a hack. I was just a student – and an interested observer.

I suppose the real beginning of the story is Chris Cooper and his inaugural encounter with the Swizzies.

But you'll need some background, in order to understand why Coop's first drink with Alan Harper was viewed by so many of us as a troubling development, and why Coop himself was seen as such a crucial figure. (I've changed everybody's name, by the way – but you already knew that.)

Our Students' Union elections are held in February every year. The Union constitution mandates that five sabbatical officers – so-called because they take a paid sabbatical in order to fulfil their duties – be elected every spring, to serve during the next academic year. The five positions are President, Deputy President, Welfare Officer, Entertainments Officer and Education Officer. But the only sabbatical position anyone gave a fuck about was President.

The Union, like all of our student societies, had evolved into a kind of permeable clique. You didn't need to have been elected, or even to have worked on a campaign, to hang around the Union building and to act like one of the gang. We had a name for hangers-on like this, though: we called them hacks.

Most of the hacks felt justified in spending their free time in the Union offices because they were affiliated with a political party. Each of the national parties had its campus branch: Labour, Fine Gael, the Greens. And our elections tended to follow the national pattern, which meant that the same campus party had controlled the President's office for the last five years. This party was Fianna Fáil.

In February 2006, the President of the Students' Union was a stocky, red-haired politics student named Barry O'Neill. Barry was also the chair of the Kevin Barry Cumann, the university branch of Fianna Fáil. You tended to find that most of the hacks who hung around the Union corridor were members of the KBC. I once asked Barry O'Neill about this. He said, 'It's just the natural order, like. Who runs the show? We run the show.'

Barry's triumphalism was one of the things that had got him elected. The other thing was Francis Mulligan, who had been Barry's campaign manager during the 2005 sabbatical elections.

Francis Mulligan had been a student for so long that no one remembered what he was supposed to be studying. Every year people would say, 'Mulligan *must* have graduated by now.' But every year, there he was, striding past the sunlit oaks with an armful of freshly bought textbooks, patting the top of his head as if to make sure his thinning hair was still in place.

Despite the books, no one ever saw Mulligan at a lecture. He had made the Union and the study of the Union the central business of his college life. For this achievement he was widely hated. Once, I asked him how he felt about this. 'Sure it's all the same to me,' he said. 'What matters is the job.'

The smallest political party on campus was the Student Socialist Workers' Party. Grandly, they called themselves the SSWS. Everybody else called them the Swizzies.

The Swizzies hadn't had a party member in the

President's chair for five years. Their last viable candidate, Mark Callaghan, had been arrested in the middle of his 2005 campaign when a city-centre bin-tax protest turned violent.

(The Swizzies were always getting arrested. They saw it as a mark of their commitment to socialist ideals. Their opponents saw it as a mark of the Swizzies' basic estrangement from the political consensus – this, at least, is how Francis Mulligan would have put it.)

In February 2006, the Chairman of the Swizzies was a fair-haired sociology student named Alan Harper. Alan had attended the same South Dublin private school as Francis Mulligan, where Francis played rugby and Alan did not. But Alan never mentioned where he had gone to school. Instead, he told you about his father the trade unionist. He told you about *The Eighteenth Brumaire of Louis Bonaparte* and *The Condition of the Working Class in England*.

Under Alan Harper, the Swizzies had managed to attract a record active membership of ten. To put this in perspective, in 2006 the KBC had an active membership of over three hundred. Alan Harper was not discouraged by these statistics, even though most of the Swizzies who claimed active membership were loafing idealists, content to lounge around their Baggot Street bedsits rolling spliffs on the cover of *The Communist Manifesto*.

Alan knew that there was only one point to a political party, no matter how small. And that was to be in power.

But neither Mulligan nor the Swizzies are where

things really began. If you ask me, things really began with Coop, the man that everybody liked.

3

Chris 'Coop' Cooper was from Illinois – not so much a mark of distinction as he might have hoped, in a university that turned out to be overrun with visiting Americans doing their Junior Year Abroad. But it was not in Coop's nature to feel overwhelmed. The university housing department put him in a hot, stuffy room in the off-campus residences in Blackrock. Everyone who lived in the rooms around him was American. But Coop hadn't come to Ireland to hang around with Americans. In his first month, he set out to meet some Irish people. And, very quickly, he succeeded.

Nobody ever found out a whole lot about Coop's background. We knew he wasn't rich. When people asked him why he had come to Dublin, he said, 'Because all the other European colleges are, like, *way* too expensive, man.'

If you had asked us, in September 2005, what would happen to Coop during his year in Dublin, we would have told you: nothing much. Coop was all set to spend his year as one of those Americans who visits our college, makes a few stray friends (charity hikes, the folk group), and goes home with his GPA intact.

But Coop was different.

He might not have been rich, but when Coop arrived he dressed in a style we called *preppie*. He wore slacks, white loafers and short-sleeved shirts with crocodiles on the breast. But less than a month after term began he showed up in the Arts Café one morning wearing Hollister sweatpants, a Ben Sherman shirt and a pair of docksider shoes with the laces untied.

In other words, Coop now dressed like one of us. And everyone accepted it. Within a couple of weeks, it began to seem that Coop had lived here all his life. And although the more alert among us surely sensed how strange it was that this American had somehow earned our love, we had our reasons. Coop got us, for one thing. He got our jokes. People even started quoting *Coop's* jokes, the surest measure, we felt, of the guy's likeability and charm.

I suppose I'm making it sound as though Coop was suppressing his true nature in order to belong. But that wasn't it. Coop *liked* the Hollister sweatpants and the Ben Sherman shirts. He admired the people who wore them. He wasn't pretending to be Irish. He spoke about Chicago all the time, as if to remind us that his home was somewhere else. But for the duration of his year abroad, Coop was one of us. And everyone loved him for it.

Well, I should amend this. In the first few months, everyone loved Coop except the Union hacks, who refused to wear Ben Sherman shirts out of principle and who were regarded by the rest of the students as dowdy, resentful weirdos who had inexplicably conned the university administration into giving them a whole building to themselves.

So, you see, it wasn't inevitable that Coop would end

up becoming a hack. And that's why people were amazed when it actually happened.

Coop's ascent to the peak of popularity was a glorious thing to behold: effortless, unhindered, like the swift, sure flight of some migrating bird. Coop made friends as if making friends were simply a knack he had been born with, like the gift of divining for water. By Christmas, he was practically living in the bar. And everyone who walked in recognised him.

The point is this. By the second week of February 2006, when the Swizzies blanketed the campus with posters saying COOP FOR PRESIDENT – VOTE SSWS!, nobody needed to be told who Coop was.

Everyone already knew.

4

All through that year, as I walked through the Arts Block, I saw the same piece of graffiti, written in neat black letters on the wall beside the library tunnel. It said, 'If you die in college, do you die in real life?'

5

The Swizzies drank at the Bachelor's Inn, a decaying workman's pub on the north quays. They liked it because of its stained oak panelling and its settled fug of Woodbine smoke. It was here that Coop met Alan Harper for the first time. The reason, of course, was a girl.

It was January 2006. Coop had by now acquired his first steady Irish girlfriend, a second-year law student named

Aisling Moore. People have wondered what Coop saw in Aisling. But to me the thing made sense. The highest compliment Coop could offer was to say that you were 'real'. 'He's *real*, man, you know? No bullshit.' And Coop would shake his head in wonder.

Thinking about this now, it occurs to me that there was no other way in which Coop seemed so profoundly American.

Aisling Moore suited Coop just fine. She wanted to be a human-rights attorney. She wasn't one of those law-yers-in-training who trawled the bars wearing a T-shirt that said 'I Can Get You Off'. She preferred to sit in the Library and read up on Japanese whaling activities or the rights of Muslim prisoners in Guantánamo Bay.

The general response to Coop's relationship with Aisling Moore was one of semi-tolerant bemusement (the girls) and dissimulated envy (the boys). Dozens of Abercrombied rugger-huggers sniped at one another about how 'boring' Aisling was and how Coop could totally have done, like, so much better. The boys, most of whom had wanted to fuck Aisling Moore for years, understood Coop's interest in her – or thought they did.

What matters at this point in the story is that Aisling Moore had been the secondary-school girlfriend of Alan Harper – a union that was widely held to have made total sense, given Alan's predilection for earnestly hectoring the student body about Noam Chomsky and Howard Zinn and Aisling's interest in what Barry O'Neill once described as 'hippy-dippy pinko-liberal bullshit'.

They were still friends, Aisling and Alan, which explains why Aisling took Coop to the Bachelor's Inn one night in January 2006 and how Alan and Coop had that fateful first pint together.

6

Alan Harper's father worked as a fitter for the railways. He had served, Alan said, for thirty years as shop steward for the transport union. When Alan was a child, his father would take him every now and then into the Works in Inchicore to see the big refit sheds where he worked. The sheds were cold and full of the clanging sound of heavy machinery. Men in overalls with sooty faces, perennially unoccupied, stood around like striking miners. Alan's father assured him that these men were indispensable to the continued running of the national railway service. 'Good union men,' his father said. Outside the sheds, in the maintenance sidings, dormant rolling stock waited, the battered carriages uncoupled from their engines and seemingly rusted in place on the tracks.

Later, Alan's father was promoted out of the refit sheds and began to work in an office located on the top floor of a small cottage that stood on a weedy patch of ground between two warehouses. 'This,' Alan's father told him, 'is the real nerve centre of the operation.' In the cottage people sat at desks and pecked at computer keyboards. To Alan it seemed much less interesting than the refit sheds. But his father, after he moved into the administrative cottage, began to hum with a new and contented energy, as though he had finally worked his way to the secret heart of things.

What Alan liked best about the cottage were the maps on the walls. The largest showed the Irish railway network as it had existed in 1952: the green teddy bear, with its pencilled veinwork of iron causeways. It gave Alan a sense of power to stand in front of this map and to broodingly survey the country's train routes. He felt like a general, pondering the ground over which he would dispatch his infantry. But what excited him most about this map was the sense of connectedness it gave. The map showed that every town in Ireland, no matter how small, was connected to every other town. And even if you started from the most insignificant place you could still get anywhere in the country you wanted to go.

7

In the foyer of the Students' Union building was a large wooden plaque on which were printed in gold leaf the names of every president the Union had ever had. The most recent name, of course, was Barry O'Neill's.

It was generally agreed that Barry was a pretty okay president. He welcomed invited speakers with flattering introductory rambles. He chaired the weekly Union meetings with bluff efficiency. He gave statements to the university newspaper about the Islamic Society's right to free expression. And these, by and large, were the only duties that Barry, or any Students' Union president, would ever be expected to perform.

That the presidency of the Union was a sinecure was our university's best-kept open secret. What made the job worthwhile was not what you did while you held it – any Union president who wanted to effect real change quickly found himself stuck in an administrative dead end, tied up with memos and protocol. No, what made the job worthwhile were the things it could do for your career, especially if you were Fianna Fáil. Union presidents who were also KBC loyalists were looked upon with interest and encouragement by the national party. They were seen as rising stars. 'It looks good on your CV,' was Barry's stated reason for his presidential run. 'It's all about building the CV, man. Know what I mean?'

This, more than anything else, was why President was the only sabbatical office anyone gave a fuck about. It would do more for you than any number of diplomas or degrees, and, in return, all you had to do was get yourself elected.

And everyone understood this to be true.

8

Coop kicked at a frayed corner of the ancient, foul-smelling carpet of the Bachelor's Inn and revealed that one of the reasons he had come to Ireland was his disillusionment with America's right-wing corporate world view. He wanted to see how things were done in Europe.

'You guys have, like, socialised medicine and shit,' Coop said.

'That is so not true you don't even know how not true that is,' Alan said.

'But you know what I mean, right?' Coop said. 'Back home, it's all like, "Fuck you." But here, you have this system that actually, like, looks out for people.'

Alan thought about this and then said, 'I know what you mean.'

If I reveal at this point in the story that Coop was a socialist, you might not believe me. And you'd be right, in a way: Coop didn't become a socialist proper until the next day, when Alan Harper signed him up as a member of the Swizzies. It seems clear that, by the time this happened, Alan had already convinced Coop to run for Union President on a Swizzie ticket. The way Alan achieved this was to make it sound like fun.

'Think about it, man,' Alan said to Coop. 'You love it here, right? This way, you get to stay another year. And they *pay* you to stay.'

'Okay,' Coop said, and smiled his heartbreaking smile. 'It'll be a riot.'

We were, all of us, stunned by this development.

'What the fucking hell,' people wondered aloud, 'is Coop doing hanging out with the Swizzies? They're such unbelievable *losers*.'

And other people murmured things like 'It's Aisling's influence, obvs,' and moved uneasily on to some new topic.

I think that Coop's decision to join the Swizzies had less to do with his own desire for some kind of authentic political engagement and more to do with Alan Harper's ability to read people, to divine, in a single conversation, their true political nature. Like most people who hold deep political beliefs, Alan had a keen eye for ideological positioning. And he immediately pinned Coop as a fellow traveller.

There was also the fact that it was almost election season, and the Swizzies had no presidential candidate. Alan had even considered running himself. But he wasn't thrilled at the idea of being beaten by whatever candidate Francis Mulligan was managing. Alan needed a candidate who was already popular. He needed a candidate who might actually win.

Coop was the solution to Alan Harper's problems. And so Alan presented himself as the solution to Coop's.

When the barman called last orders in the Bachelor's Inn, Alan went over to Aisling Moore and said, 'Have you slept with Coop yet?'

'Not yet,' Aisling said.

'You should,' Alan said.

9

Francis Mulligan called a crisis meeting in a sushi bar on Dame Street. The KBCers gathered round a long table and looked out at Dublin Castle and City Hall. Barry O'Neill sat at one end of the table in silence, glumly eating a bowl of wasabi peas. He didn't like sushi.

Mulligan made a short speech during which he did not mention Coop. Then he said, 'We're running Barry for a second term.'

This decision did not meet with universal approval.

'Can we really run Barry against Coop?' someone asked. People began to murmur things about Coop and how popular Coop was.

Francis Mulligan leafed through pages in a ring binder. 'You're never stronger than when you have incumbency on your side,' he said. 'If George W. Bush can get re-elected, then so can Barry.'

Barry looked up from his bowl of wasabi peas. No one met his eye.

One of the freshers spoke. 'What I can't understand,' he said, 'is how come Coop isn't running for us. Not for President, obviously' – he nodded at Barry – 'but for, like, Ents or something.'

People agreed that Coop would be a natural candidate for Entertainments Officer. 'He's so popular, like,' someone observed.

Francis Mulligan ignored this and began to hand out photocopies. 'Now,' he said. 'Here's the plan. The return-ing officer will have his team of observers keeping an eye on every little thing. So we have to win it through a fair fight. We're going to need everyone campaigning at full strength going forward. Get your friends involved. Use your society connections.' He peered down at his notes. 'We're actually going to try to let Barry off the leash as little as possible this time around. The last thing we need – with all due respect, Baz – is you going around shout-ing about how you run the show.'

Barry asked the waitress for another bowl of wasabi peas.

'We'll also need girls,' Francis Mulligan said. 'Get them standing around in their string tops and their little pink shorts, handing out fliers.'

'It's February,' someone pointed out.

'They won't mind.' Mulligan knocked back his thimbleful of sake. 'I'm also setting up a task force.'

'For what?'

'Watching the Swizzies like a fucking hawk. I want to know if they break a rule. Anything that could get them reported. Posters in the wrong place. Graffiti. Financial irregularities. Anything at all.'

Mulligan looked at Barry. 'I've booked you a weekend course with a public-speaking instructor, Baz. You need to exercise the old rhetorical skills a bit.'

Barry looked out at Dublin Castle, the old seat of power, with its wainscoting of municipal light. He had finished his third bowl of wasabi peas.

10

You have to remember that Francis Mulligan had been around a lot longer than the rest of us, and that he had thought more deeply and more pointedly than anyone else in the Union about how the Union worked and what it was for. When people asked him why he had never run for office himself, he would say, 'Ah sure, who'd vote for the likes of me?' But the truth was that Francis Mulligan had no interest in that kind of power. He was after something deeper.

Francis Mulligan's paternal grandfather had been

a Fianna Fáil TD representing a rural constituency for thirty-one years. When Francis was twelve, his grandfather died, very slowly, in Blanchardstown Hospital. Francis's parents brought him into the ward half a dozen times, but it was the final visit, the visit before the funeral, that Francis remembered most clearly.

In the sunlit hospital room Francis's aunts and uncles sat around on stiff school chairs, wearing plastic gloves and filmy aprons that tied at the back. His grandfather lay in the wheeled bed, curled up like a child, looking up at nothing. Francis stood with his hands clasped in front of him, wishing he could take off the clammy plastic gloves. He looked at his grandfather's tiny body: the half-closed and glistening eyes, the efforful but regular breaths. There were gauze patches on his grandfather's head, covering little cancerous tumours that there was no longer any point in treating. The room overlooked a car park and a busy bypass beyond.

Francis's mother said, 'The lavender is blooming, all along the roads.' She smiled down at the man in the bed. 'He'd be thrilled.'

His father stirred and went to the window, his hands in his pockets. 'That man never looked at a lavender bush in his life,' he said. 'If it wasn't party politics, it didn't exist, as far as he was concerned.'

Francis thought about this statement for a long time afterwards. He wondered if it was something that would become true about him, when he was older.

II

Before we knew it, the election had begun. The Union, prompted by its own peculiar calendar, emerged, blinking, into the light of popular scrutiny. It was like watching a flower that blooms only at night suddenly open its petals to the glare of afternoon.

Francis and Barry had briefly entertained the doomed hope that Coop's campaign would fail to muster the two hundred signatures necessary to secure a nomination. But Coop, wearing a tuxedo the colour of vanilla ice cream paid for out of Swizzie funds, took the entry forms with him to the Arts Ball and emerged from the Burlington Hotel with over three hundred names drunkenly scribbled on the dotted lines. Alan Harper filed for nomination, and the Swizzies, with unprecedented haste, began to print posters, pamphlets and fliers. The posters showed a smiling Coop, in stonewashed jeans and a Che Guevara T-shirt, leaning against a bare brick wall, gazing intently out of frame.

If you looked closely at Coop's campaign literature, you saw a small SWSS logo in the top right-hand corner, just above Coop's stylishly raised aviator shades. But almost no one outside the Union noticed this logo, or seemed to care what it meant.

The Returning Officer, Richard Lyons, was one of those academically ungifted middle-aged men who cannot bring themselves to leave university. He worked in an office in the Union Building, surrounded by female students who processed Union paperwork part-time for minimum wage.

Early in the campaign, Francis Mulligan went to Richard Lyons and proposed that the party logo on the Swizzies' posters was small enough to be in violation of an obscure rule governing the design of campaign materials. Mulligan also tried to interest the campus paper in this theory. But nobody was buying.

We arrived on Monday morning to find the concourse commandeered by roving hacks. Overnight, buildings and noticeboards and lecture theatres had been plastered with campaign bumf. From a thousand glossily monochrome posters, Coop and Barry looked down at you, soliciting your love.

Barry's posters featured the Fianna Fáil logo, prominently displayed. Francis Mulligan had also convinced Barry to wear a three-piece suit for his campaign photos and public appearances. It was a very expensive tweed suit, with a gold watch-fob dangling beneath the crisp lapels.

Sabbatical candidates were given two weeks to campaign. Their teams set up tables in the faculty buildings. They wore gaudy T-shirts emblazoned with their candidate's name and picture. Lecturers were importuned to delay their classes while the candidates unfurled their rousing spiel.

From adjoining tables in the Arts Block, Alan Harper and Francis Mulligan plotted their campaigns. Although they worked within ten feet of each other every day for a fortnight, they seldom found a reason to speak.

Three days into the campaign, it became clear that Coop would be our next Union President. Because the campus paper appeared too infrequently to conduct useful polls, the campaign managers organised their own. Hacks conducted vox-pop interviews with students on their way to class. Francis Mulligan and Alan Harper urged their party's class reps to find out, informally, which way their friends were planning to vote.

'Be subtle,' Francis Mulligan said. 'Just bring up the election casually in conversation and see what people say.'

'Tell people to vote for Coop,' Alan Harper said, 'and see what they say.'

By these imperfect methods, Alan and Francis became aware, more or less simultaneously, of what Francis called 'the state of play'. The students who planned to vote were planning, overwhelmingly, to vote for Coop.

Alan began giving Coop some books to read. He gave him *American Power and the New Mandarins* and *The Autobiography of Malcolm X*.

Francis bought Barry a new suit.

Both parties engaged in what some people referred to as dirty tricks. Francis Mulligan directed his task force to request an audit of Swizzie finances. (The Swizzies had no finances to speak of, since society funds were allocated on the basis of membership size. Alan had practically bankrupted the party when he bought Coop the ice-cream tuxedo.) Mulligan also instructed teams of KBC hacks to raid the campus at night and tear down Coop's posters.

In retaliation, the Swizzies collected Barry's fliers and dumped them in the Secret Lake, a small pond hidden behind the Agriculture Building.

But it was the Hustings Debate, held at the beginning of the election's second week, that convinced us Coop was headed for a landslide. Under the lecture-theatre lights, Barry sweated in his suit and blunderingly deployed the Mister-Speaker orotundities he had picked up at debating camp. And Coop – well, Coop fired off zinger after zinger, to the raucous approval of the crowd.

'How much longer,' he demanded, 'do we have to put up with a president who once referred to Temple Bar as "the West Bank of Dublin"? I mean, come on guys,' he said, flattening his palms on the lectern. 'I'm American. I *know* what it's like to have a moron for President. I feel your pain. And I'm here to tell you that *you can do better!*'

'It's a no-brainer,' Alan Harper said when the Hustings was over and Coop was hugging Aisling Moore in the centre of a stage filled with fallen streamers. 'This thing is down.'

Barry O'Neill sloped over to Francis Mulligan. 'How do you think it went?' he asked.

'Fine, Barry,' Mulligan said. 'It went fine.'

On the Tuesday morning that followed the Hustings, Alan Harper walked up to the Union Building to talk to Richard Lyons. His ostensible purpose was to collect documents for Coop that explained the duties of the President of the Union. In fact, Alan was interested in discovering the limits of whatever authority was about to

accrue to his party. He told himself he was doing something no Swizzie had ever done before: he was preparing
to seize power.

Outside the office of the Student Executive Forum, he
ran into Francis Mulligan.

'Hey Francis,' Alan said.

'Morning, Alan,' Francis said. He paused. Then he said,
'I meant to ask you something. You know on the nomination form, right? Where it says, *The candidate must be a
recognised student of the college in good standing?*'

'Yeah.'

'You lads ticked that, right? You had to tick it.'

'I ticked it,' Alan said.

'All right so,' Francis said. 'Sure I'll see you on Friday.'

Friday was Election Day.

Alan lingered outside Richard Lyons's office for a
moment. Then he went inside.

Francis Mulligan went home early that afternoon,
leaving Barry's campaign in the hands of the KBC hacks.
Rumours spread that Barry's manager had abandoned
him, that his campaign was, in the words of a rival staffer,
'holed below the waterline'.

At Coop's table in the Arts Building, someone opened
a bottle of champagne, which was immediately confis-
cated by campus services. At four o'clock, Coop went
to the bar to meet Aisling Moore. He was greeted at the
door by a round of applause.

★

334

12

And now it is time for me to enter the story, at this late, last minute, when everyone knows the state of play and our ending is all but a foregone conclusion. I can give you the exact moment, if you like. It was a February morning, very early, eight or nine. The campus was quiet, like an airport at dawn. The concourse was deserted. Dew glittered in the shadowy grass. And Francis Mulligan came over to me and asked me for a favour.

'We need you to call your dad,' he said.

And I knew exactly what he meant.

13

On the eve of the election, Richard Lyons called Alan Harper into his office and said, 'We have a problem.'

Alan sat in the chair in front of Richard's desk. It was eleven o'clock in the morning.

'What's up?' Alan said.

'Coop's not Irish,' Richard Lyons said.

Alan was prepared for this. 'There's nothing in the Constitution that says you have to be Irish to be a sabbat,' he said.

'This is true,' Richard said. 'But the university administration feels that Chris Cooper doesn't reflect the student body as a whole. In the sense that he's a visiting student on an exchange programme.'

Alan was silent.

'It came to their attention,' Richard Lyons said, 'that a Junior Year Abroad student was running for President of the Union. They consulted with Chris's home university in the states, and it was agreed that . . .' Richard looked at the floor. 'Coop's own college isn't happy with him running for a non-academic office in another institution. The administrations of both colleges feel that if Coop wants to run for a sabbatical position here he should register with us as a full-time degree student.'

'But there isn't a rule,' Alan said. 'It's within the guidelines.'

'The administration is framing new guidelines.'

Alan thought about this. 'The Union will have to vote to approve any new guidelines.'

Richard turned down the corners of his mouth. 'You know that's just a formality, Alan,' he said softly.

'The election is tomorrow,' Alan said.

'We're having new ballots printed. Coop's name will be replaced with RON.'

RON stood for Re-Open Nominations.

Alan knew what he had to do. He had to get everyone who had been planning to vote for Coop to vote for RON instead. He left Richard's office and raced down to the campaign table in the Arts Block. But even as he ran he knew he would be too late.

14

The decisions that affect our lives most deeply are so often taken by other people, in contexts that seem, at first, to be quite distant from our own experience. So it was with me, at least.

He was an old friend of mine, Francis Mulligan. We were in school together. 'We need you to call your dad,' he said, and in those words I discovered something new about myself, a sense of purpose, a sudden clear awareness of the course my life would take.

So I did what he asked. I called my dad, and he called some friends, and they called some friends, and the outcome of our university's 2006 election for Student Union President was decided by people who had nothing whatsoever to do with it.

Late on Friday evening the Returning Officer declared that Barry O'Neill had been elected to a second term by a comfortable margin, ensuring that the Presidency of the Union remained in the hands of the KBC for another year. It wasn't a landslide victory, by any means, since voters abandoned the polling booths in large numbers when they found they could no longer vote for Coop. All in all, five hundred and ten people voted for Barry, and a further two hundred voted for RON. Of the more than twenty thousand students in our college, that's how many voted, in the end: seven hundred and ten.

15

A few months after he graduated from college, Alan Harper found a job at an American investment bank that had its European headquarters in the Dublin docklands. He worked there, short-selling stocks and bonds, for two years, until the bank went under during the financial crisis and was bought out by a competitor. He was then hired as some kind of consultant by the Department of Community, Rural, and Gaeltacht Affairs.

Aisling Moore broke up with Chris Cooper just before Coop flew home to Chicago at the end of May 2006. She and Coop spent their last three months together helping each other study in Coop's overheated Blackrock dorm room. Nowadays, according to the last report I heard, Aisling works in Japan, teaching English to salarymen on weekends.

Barry O'Neill became a Dublin City councillor in the local election of 2009. I run into him occasionally, now that we work in the same field. He tends to have the harried, unkempt air of a man who is afraid he will miss his flight and cannot stop to talk.

Coop went back to Chicago. In his final year of university there he formed a band that attempted to fuse hip-hop with grunge-metal. They came close to a record deal, or so I was told. He kept in touch with Aisling for a while. She was supposed to go and visit him, as we are all supposed to visit the long-distance lovers we meet and lose in college. But I heard she never did.

As for what Coop is up to these days, I have no idea. He has fallen out of the range of my interests, and I am content to leave him there. But I'm grateful to him, nonetheless. We should always be grateful to the people who help to make us what we are.

Francis Mulligan studied law for a year at King's Inns and then became a policy adviser for the Fianna Fáil parliamentary party. I see a lot of him, too, in various offices

and corridors, at racetrack meets and committee break-
fasts. He's getting fat, these days, and his hair is thinning
out and turning the colour of old straw. His manner has
grown bluff and reminds you of the old-boy bonhomie
that used to distinguish Barry O'Neill – the very quality,
some would say, that had gotten Barry elected President
in the first place.

Occasionally, as in his Union days, someone asks
Francis Mulligan if he has ever considered running for
office himself.

'Ah sure,' he says, 'who'd vote for the likes of me?'

And he laughs, and slaps you on the back, and
moves on.

The News from Dublin

Colm Tóibín

THE CHILDREN HAD GONE UPSTAIRS so they had a few minutes together as Maurice ate his breakfast.

'You woke at four,' Nora said. 'You know that.'

Maurice did not look up from the table.

'I asked you to wake me,' he said. 'That's all I asked.'

'And you tossed and turned for about half an hour,' Nora continued, 'but even when you stopped moving I knew you were still awake.'

'Forget about it,' he said. 'You don't have to worry about it.'

'You just can't go down there, that's all. I asked Dr Cudigan, and he says it's highly infectious. The others have probably become immune, but if you are not used to being in the house with him . . .'

Maurice glanced up at her. He needed to change the subject.

'All the teachers will have ashes on their foreheads and most of the boys.'

'When I saw you sleeping soundly, I didn't want to disturb you.'

'It wasn't your decision to make, it was mine.'

He put his hand over the cup when she offered him more tea. Once the children had come back downstairs, she went to the kitchen and returned with porridge for them. They seemed preoccupied and subdued. Maurice knew how much they hated getting up in the morning. He had been the same, he remembered, when he was that age. He realised that if he did not say something now he would find himself in bad humour throughout the day.

'I don't have ashes on my forehead, and the rest of the school will. The rest of the school will have been to eight o'clock mass.'

He noticed her moving to the fireplace but did not think anything of it and so was looking away as she placed black soot from the chimney with her thumb on his forehead.

'Now, there,' she said. 'You have ashes. And nothing to worry about.'

He stood up as the children gazed at him in astonishment.

'You can't do that!'

'I just did.'

He went to the mirror. The black smudge on his forehead looked exactly as though he had received ashes at the altar rail in the cathedral. He almost laughed.

'No one will ever know the difference,' Nora said.

The children glanced from one to the other and then went back to eating their breakfast.

'Neither of you is to say anything about this,' Nora warned.

'If anyone found out . . .' Maurice began.

'You go to school,' Nora said.

A few times that morning in the staffroom and in various classrooms he had the impression that the ashes on his forehead were being studied carefully by colleagues or by students. But in the bathroom during a break when he looked at them himself again he could see no difference between the colour and texture of the soot on his forehead and the holy ashes which most of the others wore. The idea of it put him in good humour until later in the morning when he grew tired and felt desperately in need of sleep, having to suppress yawn after yawn in the classroom, and then he felt that what Nora had done was wrong and disrespectful. He was almost angry at the thought that she would not listen to him if he came home at lunchtime or at the end of the day and began to complain about it.

Later, as he sat in the staffroom during a period when he had no class, and Christian Brothers wearing ashes on their forehead came in and out of the room, he smiled to himself. How little they knew, these Brothers, he thought, about the secret life of the teachers, the things which married men had to tolerate! He had to concentrate hard on the copybooks he was correcting to stop himself laughing.

At the end of the day's teaching as he was walking from one of the classrooms which were in a building away from the main building, he saw his brother Tom waiting for him. Since it was Wednesday and the *Enniscorthy Echo* where Tom worked had gone to press, Tom would have time on his hands. But Maurice knew by the way he was standing that this was more than a social call, more than a casual way of meeting so they could go for a drink or two in Mylie Kehoe's before Maurice went home.

Maurice made a signal to Tom that he would be with him in a moment, and then he dropped some copybooks back in the staffroom. By the serious way Tom had nodded to him, he knew that this visit was about Stephen, their younger brother who had TB. Something must have happened. He lingered in the staffroom, arranging the copybooks and then rearranging them, and checking if there was anything else to do, because he dreaded going back out to the school yard and finding Tom waiting in the shadows. When he went to the bathroom, he barely glanced in the mirror; suddenly the ashes and their origin had ceased to be of any interest.

'Is there something wrong?' he asked Tom when he found him outside.

'He's been bad over the last few days.'

He noticed the ashes on Tom's forehead and realised that Tom must have been at eight o'clock mass and must have looked for him there. He wished now that he did not have the smudge on his forehead; it would be hard to explain how it got there. They walked silently together over the railway bridge towards the bottom of Slaney Street.

'I can't go down. Nora is terrified about the children. She went and asked Dr Cudigan,' Maurice said.

'That's all right. They understand that. No one blames Nora for that. I had to call into Uncle George, King George, this morning after mass. Someone told me that he has a coffin at the back of the workshop and it has some flaw in it and that he said to someone that it would do for Stephen when the time came. He's one big ignorant gobshite.'

'What did you say to him?'

'I told him that there'd be no coffin for him when I was finished with him, but we'd sew him into a sack and send him wriggling down the river. I told him if he thought we had disbanded and gone all political, then he might be right, but we'd make an exception for him. And I'd know the boys to pick. I wouldn't have to ask them even. I'd just make a sign, and he'd be gone down the river and he'd be found washed up in Edermine.'

'Did you really?'

'I did. I did all right.'

'He denied the whole thing and then he said that he wouldn't do it again. He is a big eejit.'

'Did Stephen hear about it?'

'No, none of them heard about it.'

They walked along Slaney Place.

'But Stephen heard about something else and so did Mammy. There's a drug, it's been discovered, and it does the trick. I have the name of it written down.'.

'A cure?'

'I suppose.'

'Who told him?'

'It was in the *Irish Times*. Freddie Sutton brought it to the door. And it's on Stephen's mind now that this drug can be got.'

'Where?'

'It's not available to everyone yet, but it will be, or it might be. I don't know when. But some people can get it. They're trying it out on some people and it's working.'

'What's it called?'

'I have it written down.'

Once they were sitting at the bar in Mylie Kehoe's and had ordered two pints of ale, Tom showed him a slip of paper with the word 'streptomycin' on it.

'Sounds like something you would use for cattle,' Maurice said.

When their drinks came they sat at the bar for a while without saying anything.

'So?' Maurice asked eventually.

Tom sighed.

'So Daddy was in Frongoch with Jim Ryan, and you introduced him on the platform in the Market Square, and you must have met him a few times. I know he's only a month or so as Minister for Health but he must know about this drug. It'd have to be a priority.'

'There were hundreds in Frongoch.'

'Daddy says they took Irish lessons together and they were in a punishment cell together. Or maybe it was the same thing.'

'Don't insult Irish lessons. I have just spent the day with them.'

'Don't insult punishment cells, you mean,' Tom said. 'The one thing I could never do was learn the first national. It's hard enough to talk English.'

'Was that the time in Frongoch when Daddy shouted "Is liomsa é" when the guard asked whose bed it was, and the guard said "Lumps or no lumps, you get into it, mate",' Maurice asked.

'Yeah,' Tom said, 'it was that time all right. And Jim Ryan was there too, and now he's Minister for Health.'

'You know, I just introduced him once, and I met him another time, but we've never actually talked,' Maurice said.

'They want you to go up to Dublin and ask him.'

'When?'

'Soon.'

'But I said I don't know him.'

'Daddy is going to contact Sean Flood, and he will decide what would be the best day. He's going to do the introductions.'

'But he's just a backbencher.'

'They're in the same constituency, and they know each other. Anyway, we're waiting to hear back from Sean. Can you get a day off?'

Maurice nodded in assent.

'A day off for good behaviour,' Tom said. 'Speaking of which, I didn't see you at mass this morning.'

'I slipped off as soon as it was over.'

346

'Where were you sitting?'

'I was at the back.'

'Funny now,' Tom said, 'I didn't see you going up to get the ashes.'

Maurice sipped his drink.

'And you slipped off before it was over?' Tom continued. 'That's a bad example for a teacher to be giving.'

'That's not what I said. I didn't slip off before it was over,' Maurice said and smiled. 'I waited until it was over, and then I slipped off. Journalists should listen.'

Tom looked at the ashes on Maurice's forehead.

'You slipped off anyway. I'll say that for you.'

When Maurice arrived home, Nora was in the kitchen. She turned when she saw him.

'Ash Wednesday, that's a nice day to go drinking,' she said in mock anger.

'How did you know I went drinking?'

'They can smell you in Ballon.'

She laughed and moved towards him.

'I don't know what this house is coming to,' she said. 'No religion and falling home from the pub at closing time.'

'It's not closing time. It's only six o'clock.'

She laughed again and put her arms around him.

'And your ashes are a work of art. Did anyone admire them?'

'The whole town,' he said.

Later, he told her what Tom had asked him to do.

'I saw the article in the *Irish Times* too,' she said. 'Vera

Irwin showed it to me. But the drug won't be available for a year or more.'

'Yes, but it must exist.'

'That's what Fianna Fáil is for,' she said.

'It's for more than that.'

'Well, you're in the party. If you weren't in it, it would be different.'

'I have never asked them for anything before.'

'Well, this is important. What else could be more important? It's worth trying. I mean, you can't even go in the door of the house where you were born.'

He glanced away from her.

'You didn't go down, did you?' she asked.

'No.'

'You don't even have to touch the person, that's what Cudigan said. You don't even have to touch them. It's in the air. It's the most frightening thing.'

That Friday during a break between classes he found Brother O'Hara in the staffroom and asked him if he could take the following Wednesday off.

'Of course you can,' Brother O'Hara said. 'As long as you're back on Thursday.'

'Just one day,' he said.

He wished that he could seem as nonchalant and relaxed as Brother O'Hara whose face darkened now as he noticed that there was a problem.

'Is there something wrong?' he asked.

'Ah no, just I have to go to Dublin. But I'll give the boys work to do so they won't make a nuisance.'

348

'You've never taken a day off in all my time here.'

'So it's all right then?'

'Are you sure there's nothing wrong?'

'Ah no, nothing.'

Suddenly, Brother O'Hara moved towards the door and shut it and moved closer to him and spoke in a hushed voice.

'Are you all right?' he asked.

Maurice was alert immediately to what the Brother meant.

'I'm absolutely fine.'

'If there's anything I can do?' the Brother asked.

'No,' Maurice said as he held his gaze.

Since he knew that everyone in the town was aware that Stephen was sick, it was clear to him that Brother O'Hara wanted to ask him about it but felt that he could not, or should not.

'That's fine, so,' the Brother said. 'We'll see you on Monday and Tuesday and then on Thursday and Friday. I might take a few of your classes myself on Wednesday. I might learn something.'

The following Wednesday he got out of the train at Westland Row and walked to Kildare Street where he asked at the porter's desk, as he had been told to do by Tom, for Sean Flood.

'He's expecting me,' he said.

'Are you another yellow belly,' the porter asked.

'I am,' Maurice replied. 'I'm from Enniscorthy.'

'Oh Enniscorthy's in flames,' the porter replied as

he dialled a number, 'and old Wexford is won and the Barrow tomorrow we cross.'

There was, it seemed, no reply from the number he had dialled. He checked through a book of numbers and tried another.

'He doesn't seem to be there,' the porter said. 'Would you like to leave a message?'

'He's expecting me.'

'Well, there might be a vote soon, so if you take a seat I'll try again in a while.'

He had visited the Dáil before as part of a delegation from the town. He remembered how nervous the others were as they waited to be taken beyond the porter's box and how strange it was to see figures, ministers and prominent opposition politicians, whom they knew only from photographs and whom they read about regularly in the newspapers, walking the corridors. He remembered being led in to see the Minister for Local Government and the sense of occasion as each of them was introduced. They were taken by Sean Flood afterwards to the public bar where other TDs were buying drinks for constituents.

He did not know what Sean Flood had arranged, whether he would meet the Minister in his private office, or in the bar or the restaurant. Now that news had been published about the drug, he wondered if others had come asking as well. Surely, he thought, Sean Flood would have advised him not to make the journey if he had believed that his request was likely to be dismissed or handled brusquely. It struck him for a moment that maybe he would actually have to say very little to the Minister, that he might be told that the drug was available, given the name of a doctor or dispensary to contact, and there would be nothing else to discuss. But he knew also that Stephen was bad, that the drug would have to come soon, or maybe it might even be too late. He resolved that he would make clear to the Minister that it was urgent. It might be better, he thought then, not to say too much about his own work for Fianna Fáil in case the Minister thought that he was involved in the party only for what it might give him in return but emphasise his father's time in Frongoch, maybe even Tom's time in the Curragh, although it might be best not to dwell too much on the Civil War.

When he caught the porter's eye, the porter made a gesture indicating that he had not forgotten about him, and then he checked a list of numbers and dialled again. This time there was a reply, and he spoke for a moment before putting the phone down.

'He'll be right with you,' he said. 'He didn't even want to know your name. He's expecting you.'

As soon as Sean Flood appeared and shook his hand, Maurice regretted the many jokes which he and Tom had made about him over the years, about how long and repetitive his speeches to the local cumann were but how in the Dáil he had only ever spoken to ask them to open the window a bit. Or how he was the only GAA official who didn't know the difference between a hurley stick and a shovel. He seemed friendly now as he explained that it was one of those days when there could be a vote at any time, when most of the ministers were in the house, but it would be impossible to pin any one of them down about a precise time for a meeting. He was going to leave Maurice in the visitors' gallery, and he would signal to him from the Dáil Chamber itself if he should leave, if the time had come when they could get the Minister's full attention in between votes, or if it seemed that a debate or an extended question time was going to hold business up. The opposition had grown long-winded, Sean said, they smelled an election, especially the Labour Party, and it was always hard to know what they would do.

Maurice had presumed that an appointment had been made with the Minister, or at least he had been told why Maurice wanted to see him, but it seemed now, as Sean Flood ushered him into the visitors' gallery and disappeared, that nothing had been arranged in advance and that it was maybe not even certain that he would meet the Minister face to face.

The debate was about agriculture, and someone on the opposition benches whom he did not recognise was speaking passionately against the export of live cattle. The two or three men sitting close to the speaker seemed busy with paperwork. The Minister for Agriculture was on the government front bench with another minister. There were four or five deputies scattered in the seats behind them. There was no sign of Sean Flood or Jim Ryan.

As he looked around him on the gallery he saw that there were a number of men following the speech with fierce concentration. One of them was taking notes. He wished that Sean Flood had given him an agenda for the day's work in the Dáil, or some idea how long this debate might go on and what might follow it. He was hungry and regretted that he had not had a sandwich in one of the hotels near the Dáil. He had been too eager to get here, he thought, and now he was trapped waiting for Sean Flood to appear in the chamber and make a sign to him.

He studied the speaker, supposing him to be from Fine Gael, and then he looked over at the government benches. The Fine Gael people were different, he thought, they wore better suits and seemed more prosperous. The Fianna Fáil backbenchers, on the other hand, had a look that he recognised and liked, less arrogant than the Fine Gael deputies – they were softer in some way, like men who would be easier to approach, men who would send their sons to the local Christian Brothers school and be satisfied with that and whose sons would respect the teachers and the Brothers and do their best.

Slowly the chamber was filling up. One of the Fianna Fáil deputies began to heckle the speaker and was told to sit down and obey the rules of the house by the Ceann Comhairle. Instead, he stood up and left the chamber, laughing and exchanging quick bantering remarks with those entering.

Maurice turned to watch as the men who had been following the debate on agriculture beside him on the gallery stood up to leave. He noticed two or three people coming to sit in their places. When he looked back down into the Dáil chamber there were a number of figures who had recently placed themselves in the front row of the government benches. Among them was the Minister for Health Jim Ryan who was busy whispering to the minister beside him as order was called and an announcement came that a vote was to be taken on this stage of the Bill and that all those in favour were to line up, and all those against were to line up also. Since no one paid the announcement any attention, the Ceann Comhairle pressed the bell on his desk and called for order, but still he was ignored as deputies milled around each other at random, some taking their seats, others standing on the stairs.

Suddenly, Maurice saw that a way was being cleared on one of the central stairways as the figure of de Valera was being helped down the steps. He felt the tears coming to his eyes at the sight. De Valera was as tall as he remembered him when he had seen him speaking in Enniscorthy, but he seemed even more dignified now, almost solemn, as he moved slowly down towards his seat. He looked straight ahead of him, not allowing his failing sight to affect the serenity with which he moved; his steely distance from things was further emphasised by the bustle around him. As deputies made space for him, they moved away slightly. No one, other than the younger man in a suit who held him at the elbow, came close to him. No one put a hand or an arm out to assist him. He was utterly in command, the set of the jaw stubborn and unafraid. Once he was seated, he lifted his head but did not look around him or move. Were he to appear in a classroom, Maurice knew, he would cause an awed silence to descend.

One of the visitors who had arrived at the gallery a while earlier tapped him on the shoulder and pointed down into the Dáil chamber where Sean Flood was gesticulating to him. Maurice had been so wrapped up in watching de Valera that he had not noticed him. Once Sean Flood saw that he had Maurice's attention, he indicated to him that he should leave the visitors' gallery and come out into the corridor that led to the chamber. When he checked to see where the Minister was, he saw that he was still in his seat on the front bench, busily talking to a colleague.

'I told him I have a constituent who wants a few minutes with him,' Sean Flood said when they met. 'So what we do is we wait here, and we'll either go to the bar or to his office when he appears. It's a busy day but he knows we are here.'

Maurice was about to ask if the Minister knew why he had come but he understood from what Sean Flood had said that the Minister did not. In the way Sean Flood had said 'constituent' he realised that he would have to tell the Minister from scratch who he was and who his father was before telling him why he wanted to see him. He hoped that he would not have to do this with other people milling around.

As they waited, deputies from all the parties began to spill out from the chamber into the corridors. Maurice knew how much Tom and his father would be interested in them, and was surprised at how friendly they all seemed with each other, no matter what party they belonged to. They all greeted Sean Flood pleasantly. He wished that he were just here on a visit with no purpose and would have loved coming home with the account of how he saw de Valera, and which ministers he had seen, and how men his father and Tom hated seemed friendly and ordinary as they came into the corridor and stopped for a second to speak to Sean Flood. Even though deputies from all the parties stopped, Maurice was amused at the fact that he was only introduced to the deputies from Fianna Fáil. The deputies from Fine Gael and Labour were not introduced by name.

When the Minister appeared he was joined by a man whom Maurice later learned was his private secretary. It took Sean Flood a minute to move towards him, having signalled to Maurice to stay where he was. He spoke quietly to the Minister as the private secretary stood by impatiently. Maurice noticed the Minister's shoes, which were of soft black leather, and his grey suit, white shirt and dark-red tie. As he listened to Sean, the Minister's face remained impassive, his expression thoughtful; he was concentrating. Eventually, he nodded but did not speak as Sean turned and gestured to Maurice to approach.

The Minister shook his hand. And then, Maurice saw, he looked around him, the expression on his face suddenly severe and distant. He was, it seemed to Maurice, alert to his own dignity and wanted to see who was watching him and wanted to be sure that it was apparent that he stood apart from Sean Flood and his private secretary and Maurice. As he led them down a number of corridors, he did not speak. He walked slowly, deliberately, like a man with much on his mind. If de Valera were to retire, Maurice thought, the Minister would be among those who could easily replace him. Even though he was not as tall nor as imposing a figure, he had his own dignity and a sense that he could not easily be crossed and that he would take a calm and astute view of any problem that arose.

When they reached the bar the Minister's private secretary found them a corner table and placed himself opposite the Minister and Maurice, with his back to the door. He had a file in his hands which he opened and studied while Sean Flood went to the bar, having been told by the Minister and Maurice that they each wanted tea.

'My father,' Maurice said to the Minister, 'isn't well at the moment, and he asked me to come. He is Patrick Webster, and he sends you all his best regards. He says that you might remember him from Frongoch.'

'Frongoch,' the Minister repeated, smiling faintly as though it was a place of which he had fond memories.

'And I am the secretary of the local cumann, Sean

might have told you. I introduced you when you came to Enniscorthy, the time you spoke in the Market Square.'

'That's right,' the Minister said vaguely.

'Sean might have mentioned that my brother is sick,' Maurice said.

'He did,' the Minister replied and, looking away, moved close to Maurice so that Maurice would not have to raise his voice.

'At home they saw a report in the paper that there was a new drug for TB . . .' he began.

'Is your brother in the sanatorium?' the Minister interrupted.

'No, he's at home.'

'He might be better in the sanatorium.'

He looked at Maurice sharply.

'There are coffins coming out of there every day,' Maurice said. 'And they are not letting visitors into the wards themselves. You have to shout things out from the door for everyone to hear.'

The Minister knitted his brow and did not reply. Maurice was worried in case his seemed like a criticism of the health service.

'Well, it's infectious, you know,' the Minister said.

Sean Flood came back with a tray and put it down on the table and sat opposite them.

'We read about the new drug,' Maurice said, addressing the Minister only, 'and we were wondering when it might be available.'

The Minister nodded his head and moved forward and

358

began to pour tea for himself and Maurice, putting milk and sugar into his own cup and then taking the cup and saucer in his hand.

'It'll be a while,' he said.

'Do you mean a few months?'

'It might be longer. It's still being tested.'

'We read that some people are getting it as part of a trial.'

The Minister sipped his tea.

'They are all being done in England and on the Continent. I wish the *Irish Times* hadn't reported it. It's irresponsible of them.'

'So there's nothing here?'

'He would be better in the sanatorium. If anything comes in, it will be through the sanatorium.'

'And will they have the drug?'

'In the course of time, I hope.'

Maurice put milk into his tea and lifted the cup and took a sip.

'We thought that because of my father . . . I mean that you might have some way of helping us.'

'It's a bad business, TB,' the Minister said.

'They asked me at home to come up and see you anyway.'

'We're doing the best we can,' the Minister said.

'Oh, I know that.'

'Sean says that you are a teacher?'

'That's right.'

'Secondary or primary?'

359

'Secondary. I'm with the Christian Brothers.'

They were silent for a while. The Minister looked around him as Sean Flood sat quietly opposite them and the private secretary continued reading the file.

'There's not much we can do at the moment,' the Minister said eventually. 'But they have to worry about infection. If you need any help to get him into the sanatorium, let me know.'

'Ah no, it's all right.'

The Minister turned and looked at him.

'I hope I see you the next time I'm in Enniscorthy.'

He stood up.

'Did you say your father isn't well?'

'He has a bad heart.'

'Will you give him my best wishes? From one Frongoch veteran to another.'

'I'll do that,' Maurice said.

As Sean Flood saw him out to the front gate of the Dáil Maurice made no effort to break the silence. Even as they parted, he said nothing, merely walked away curtly. He would see Sean Flood in Enniscorthy, but he hoped it would not be for a while.

He had missed the train that left Westland Row in the early afternoon and would have to wait, he realised, until six o'clock for the last train. It was hard to think what to do. For a second, he began to imagine that he was a student again and he could walk from Kildare Street to Earlsfort Terrace, and he quickly realised that he would have given anything to be back in Dublin then with only exams to face, with long days to himself, with the welcoming smiles of his landlady Mrs Ruth and her sister when he came home every evening in Terenure, how they had soda bread or currant bread and butter and jam waiting for him, the table set as though for someone important. At the beginning, when he went home to teach in Enniscorthy, he had sent them Christmas cards each year and then one year had forgotten and had lost touch with them. Mrs Ruth must have been seventy when he last saw her, he thought, and her sister older, and he calculated then that that was fourteen years ago, so maybe they were dead now, or too old to have lodgers.

In Dawson Street he walked into Hodges Figgis, smiling to himself when he saw the same sales assistant at the cash register, the one he had always remembered. She had not changed. Once she would have known him by sight, but she must have forgotten him now. Years ago, she was on the lookout for students like him who would spend hours in the shop reading a book and taking notes as though the place was a library. She would come over and stand silently behind him, he remembered, blocking his light, glowering at him when he looked up and then accompanying him to the door with a look of grim satisfaction on her face.

He perused the section on history and saw a few books that he might have bought had this been a different day. He would buy nothing now, nor even look at any volume for too long. He had to keep his mind busy, let himself think of things, anything to keep himself from wondering how he was going to face them at home, what he might say. They would, he knew, expect him to walk over from the train station to their house before he went to his own house, if there were any sort of news. He could imagine Stephen sitting by the fire, with a book maybe in his hand, or playing chess with his father, his cheeks red from the heat of the flames. He could imagine his mother moving in and out of the room. They would expect him to knock the door and then walk back along the path to the gate before it was answered. His mother, he knew, might blame Nora for his not coming into the house, but Tom would understand. And it would probably be Tom who would answer the door and come to the gate to hear the news.

He had nothing to tell them. He knew that they would, once the train whistle had been heard, wait in silence for his arrival at the door. He wondered now, as he went and looked at the shelves of books in Irish, if it would be worse to come with the news, which was no news, or if it would be better to leave it, go home to Nora. And let them realise as time passed that he had not come to them because he had no reason to come. The clock over the mantelpiece would tick and then chime gently on the hour. By nine, they would know he was late; by ten, they would be certain that he was not coming.

Out on Dawson Street again he could not think what to do. Even though he was now no longer hungry, he thought that he might go to Bewley's on Grafton Street and have soup and brown bread, or maybe a sandwich. He bought an evening newspaper in Duke Street. He liked the crowds in the streets as he walked along and began to wonder if he should have looked for a job in Dublin once he got married, if Nora and he would be happier in a house, say, in Terenure or Stillorgan, where they would know only some of their neighbours, where they could go to the shops, or into the city centre, without meeting anyone they knew at all and not have to stop and talk to anyone. He realised as he reached Grafton Street that he had just fooled himself into thinking that if he lived in Dublin none of this would be happening. He sighed at the thought that everyone would, in fact, be just the same, the scene in the house where he was brought up, the house where his younger brother was now in slow decline, would be just as tense and watchful and would later be just as forlorn as each of them went to bed knowing that there was no news from Dublin and that there was nothing that could be done.

It was when he came to Bewley's that he noticed the lane which led to Clarendon Street Church. He decided to walk down towards the church. He would not pray, he thought; he would not ask for anything which would not be granted. There had been enough prayers said, and they had made no difference. He was not sure, despite what others believed, that God interfered in small matters. But this was not a small matter for Stephen, he thought; it was only a small matter for those who did not know him. No one on this street knew anything about him. They were all themselves, living in their own minds, just as Stephen now was living in his and dreading its own extinction, the great change which was beyond imagining, which nobody knew about for sure, no matter how strong their faith was, no matter how hard they prayed.

He sat at the back of the church and let the minutes go by. There was a time, even when he was a student, that he would come into this church for mass, or on Saturday evening for confession. He had no knowledge then what a desolate place this church would be at a time in the future that was now. He could not think of anywhere more desolate. He stood up and genuflected and quietly left, realising that he was tracing steps in the city which he would never be able to retrace without remembering this, the day when he had been to the Dáil and seen the Minister.

He knew that Tom would be waiting for him after school the next day, and as he walked up Grafton Street towards the Green, he pictured Tom's face when Tom realised for certain that Maurice's not coming the previous evening had been deliberate, that he had nothing to tell them except that his journey to Dublin had been in vain. They would walk over the railway bridge together, past the bottom of Slaney Street, and they would walk past the Cotton Tree and into Slaney Place past Kelly's Pharmacy and then up Castle Hill. They would stop and face each other at the door of Mylie Kehoe's, and Maurice would shake his head, and then Tom would nod to him blankly, and they would turn away from one another in silence. They would not go into the pub. Tom would go home. And Maurice would walk on his own along Friary Place and then up Friary Hill to Court Street and John Street, feeling with each step he took that he was leaving a ghost trailing behind him, hovering in the darkening air, a solitary figure asking him if there was any news, if there was any hope. He would, he knew, make his way home then without looking back for a single moment.

The Crippled Man

William Trevor

'WELL, THERE'S THAT IF YOU'D WANT IT,' the crippled man said. 'It's a long time waiting for attention. You'd need tend the mortar.'

The two men who had come to the farmhouse consulted one another, not saying anything, only nodding and gesturing. Then they gave a price for painting the outside walls of the house and the crippled man said it was too much. He quoted a lesser figure, saying that had been the cost the last time. The men who had come looking for work said nothing. The tall one hitched up his trousers.

'We'll split the difference if that's the way of it,' the crippled man said.

Still not speaking, the two men shook their heads.

'Be off with you in that case,' the crippled man said.

They didn't go, as if they hadn't understood. It was a ploy of theirs to pretend not to understand, to frown and simulate confusion because, in any conversation, it was convenient sometimes to appear to be at a loss.

'Two coats we're talking about?' the crippled man enquired.

The tall man said they were. He was older than his companion, grey coming into his hair, but that was premature: both were still young, in their twenties.

'Will we split the difference?' the crippled man suggested again. 'Two coats and we'll split it?'

The younger of the men, who had a round, moon face and wire-rimmed glasses, offered another figure. He stared down at the grey, badly cracked flags of the kitchen floor, waiting for a response. The tall man, whose arms hung loosely and were lanky, like his body, sucked at his teeth, which was a way he had. If it was nineteen years since the house had been painted, he said, the price would have been less than would be worthwhile for them now. Nineteen years was what they had been told.

'Are ye Polish?' the crippled man asked.

They said they were. Sometimes they said that, sometimes they didn't, depending on what they had previously ascertained about the presence of other Polish people in a locality. They were brothers, although they didn't look like brothers. They were not Polish.

A black cat crept about the kitchen, looking for insects or mice. Occasionally it would pounce on a piece of bark that had fallen off the firewood, or a shadow. Fourteen days the painting would take, the young man said, and they'd work on a Sunday; then the cost of the work surfaced again. A price was agreed.

'Notes,' the tall man said, rubbing a thumb and forefinger together. 'Cash.'

And that was agreed also.

★

Martina drove slowly, as she always did driving back from Carragh. More than once on this journey the old Dodge had stopped and she had had to walk to Kirkpatrick's Garage to get assistance. Each time the same mechanic told her the car belonged to the antique brigade and should have been off the road for the past thirty years at the very least. But the ancient Dodge was part of Martina's circumstances, to be tolerated because it was necessary. And, driven slowly, more often than not it got you there.

Costigan had slipped in a couple of streaky instead of back rashers, making up the half pound, he'd said, although he'd charged for back. She hadn't said anything; she never did with Costigan. 'Come out to the shed till we'll see,' he used to say, and she'd go with him to pick out a frozen pork steak or drumsticks she liked the look of in the shed where the deep freeze was, his hands all over her. He no longer invited her to accompany him to the deep freeze, but the days when he used to were always there between them, and she never ate pork steak or chicken legs without being reminded of how afterwards he used to push the money back to her when she paid and how in the farmhouse she hid it in the Gold Flake tin.

She drove past the tinkers at the Cross, the children in their rags running about, feet bare, heads cropped. The woman whom the noise of the Dodge always brought out stared stonily, continuing to stand there when the car went on, a still image in the driving mirror. 'We'd do it for four and a half,' the man in Finnally's had offered when she'd asked the price of the electric cooker that was still in the window. Not a chance, she'd thought.

About to be fifty and putting on more weight than pleased her, Martina had once known what she wanted, but she wasn't so sure about that any more. Earlier in her life, a careless marriage had fallen apart, leaving her homeless. There had been no children although she had wanted them, and often since she had thought that in spite of having to support them she might have done better if children had been there to make a centre for her life.

She drove through the turf bogs, a Bord na Móna machine drawn up at the cuttings, an uncoupled trailer clamped so that it would stay where it was. Nothing was going on, nothing had changed at the cuttings for maybe as long as nine months. The lack of activity was lowering, she considered every time she saw, yet again, the place as it had been the last time.

She turned at Laughil, the road darkened by the trees that overhung it. She couldn't remember when it was that she'd last met another car on this journey. She didn't try to. It didn't matter.

The two men drove away, pleased that they'd found work, talking about the man who'd called out and said come in when they'd knocked on the door. All the time they were there he had remained in his chair by the fire of the range, and when the price was agreed he'd said go to the scullery and get the whiskey bottle. He had gestured impatiently when they didn't understand, lifting his fist to his mouth, tossing back his head, the fist going with it, until they knew he meant drinking. He was convivial then; and they were quick, he said, to see the glasses on the dresser and put three on the table. They were uncertain only for a moment, then unscrewed the cap on the bottle.

'We know about Poland,' he'd said. 'A Catholic people, like ourselves. We'll drink to the work, will we?'

They poured more whiskey for him when he held out the glass. They had more themselves before they left.

'Who was here?'

She put the bag of groceries on the table as she spoke. The whiskey bottle was there, out of his reach, two empty glasses beside it, his own, empty now also, in his hand. He held it out, his way of asking her to pour him more. He wouldn't stop now, she thought; he'd go on until that bottle was empty, and then he'd ask if there was one unopened, and she'd say no, although there was.

'A blue van,' she said, giving him more drink, since there was no point in not.

'I wouldn't know what colour it was.'

'A blue van was in the boreen.'

'Did you get the listful?'

'I did.'

He'd had visitors, he said, as if this subject was a new one. 'Good boys, Martina.'

370

'Who?' she asked again.

He wanted the list back, and the receipt. With his stub of a pencil, kept specially for the purpose, he crossed off the items she took from the bags they were in. In the days when Costigan had been more lively she had enjoyed these moments of deception, the exact change put down on the table, what she had saved still secreted in her clothes until she could get upstairs to the Gold Flake tin.

'Polish lads,' he said. 'They'll paint the outside for us.' Two coats, he said, a fortnight it would take.

'Are you mad?'

'Good Catholic boys. We had a drink.'

She asked where the money was coming from, and he asked, in turn, what money was she talking about. That was a way he had, and a way of hers to question the money's source, although she knew there was enough; the subject, once raised, had a tendency to linger.

'What'd they take off you?'

With feigned patience, he explained he'd paid for the materials only. If the work was satisfactory he would pay what was owing when the job was finished. Martina didn't comment on that. Angrily, she pulled open one of the dresser's two drawers, felt at the back of it and brought out a bundle of euro notes, fives and tens in separate rubber bands, twenties, fifties, a single hundred. She knew at once how much he had paid. She knew he would have asked the painters to reach in for the money since he couldn't himself. She knew they would have seen the amount that was left there.

'Why would they paint a house when all they have to do is walk in and help themselves?'

He shook his head. He said again the painters were fine Catholic boys. With patience still empathic in his tone, he repeated that the work would be completed within a fortnight. It was the talk of the country, he said, the skills young Polish boys brought to Ireland. An act of God, he said. She wouldn't notice them about the place.

They bought the paint in Carragh, asking what would be best for the walls of a house. 'Masonry,' the man said, pointing at the word on a tin. 'Outside work, go for the Masonry.'

They understood. They explained that they'd been given money in advance for materials, and they paid the sum that was written down for them.

'Polish, are you?' the man asked.

Their history was unusual. Born into a community of stateless survivors in the mountains of what had once been Carinthia, their natural language a dialect enlivened by words from a dozen others, they were regarded often now as Gypsies. They remembered a wandering child-hood of nameless places, an existence in tents and silent night-time crossing of borders, the unceasing search for somewhere better. They had separated from their fam-ily without regret when they were, they thought, thir-teen and fourteen. Since then their lives were what they had become: knowing what to do, how best to do it, acquiring what had to be acquired, managing. Wherever they were, they circumvented what they did not call the system, for it was not a word they knew, but they knew what it meant and knew that straying into it, or their acceptance of it, however temporarily, would deprive them of their freedom. Surviving as they were was their immediate purpose, their hope that there might somewhere be a life that was more than they yet knew.

They bought brushes as well as the paint, and white spirit because the man said they'd need it, and a filler because they'd been told the mortar required attention: they had never painted a house before, they didn't know what mortar was.

Their van was battered, pale blue patched up a bit with a darker shade, without tax or insurance although there was the usual evidence of both on the windscreen. They slept in it, among contents that they kept tidy, knowing that they must: tools of one kind or another they had come by, their mugs, their plates, a basin, saucepan, frying pan, food.

In the dialect that was their language the older brother asked if they would spare the petrol to go to the ruins where they were engaged in making themselves a dwelling. The younger brother, driving, nodded, and they went there.

In her bedroom Martina closed the lid of the Gold Flake tin and secured it with its rubber band. She stood back from the wardrobe looking-glass and critically surveyed herself, ashamed of how she'd let herself go, her bulk not quite obese but almost now, her pale blue eyes – once her most telling feature – half lost in folds of flesh. She had been still in her thirties when she'd come to the farmhouse, still particular about how she looked and dressed. She wiped away the lipstick that had been smudged by Costigan's rough embracing when for a few minutes they had been alone in the shop. She settled her underclothes where he had disturbed them. The smell of the shop – a medley of rashers and fly spray and the chickens Costigan roasted on a spit – had passed from his clothes to hers, as it always did. 'Oh, just the shop,' she used to say when she was asked about it in the kitchen, but she wasn't any more.

They were distantly related, had been together in the farmhouse since his mother died twelve years ago and his father the following winter. Another distant relative had suggested the union, since Martina was on her own and only occasionally employed. Her cousin – for they had agreed that they were cousins of a kind – would have otherwise had to be taken into a home; and she herself had little to lose by coming to the farm. The grazing was parcelled out, rent received annually and now and again another field sold. Her crippled cousin, who since birth had been confined as he was now, had for Martina the attraction of a legal stipulation: in time she would inherit what was left.

Often people assumed that he had died, never saying a word, but you could tell. In Carragh they did, and people from round about who never came to the farmhouse did; talking to them, you could feel it. She didn't mention him herself except when the subject was brought up – there was nothing to say because there was nothing that was different, nothing she could remark on.

He was asleep after the whiskey when she went downstairs, and he slept until he was roused by the clatter of dishes and the frying of their six o'clock meal. She liked to keep to time, to do what it told her to do. She kept the alarm clock on the dresser wound, and accurate to the minute by the wireless morning and evening. She collected, first thing every morning, what eggs had been laid in the night. She got him to the kitchen from the back room as soon as she'd set the breakfast table. She made the two beds when he had his breakfast in him and she had washed up the dishes. On a day she went to Carragh she left the house at a quarter past two; she'd got into the way of that. Usually he was asleep by the range then, as most of the time he was unless he'd begun to argue. If he had, that could go on all day.

'They'll be a nuisance about the place.' She had to raise her voice because the liver on the pan was spitting. The slightest sound – of dishes or cooking, the lid of the kettle rattling – and he said he couldn't hear her when she spoke. But she knew he could.

He said he couldn't now, and she ignored him. He said he'd have another drink, and she ignored that too.

'They're never a nuisance,' he said. 'Lads like that.'

He said they were clean, you'd look at them and know. He said they'd be company for her.

'One month to the next you hardly see another face, Martina. Sure, I'm aware of that, girl. Don't I know it the whole time.'

She cracked the first egg into the pool of fat she made by tilting the pan. She could crack open an egg and empty it with one hand. Two each they had.

'It needs the paint,' he said.

She didn't comment on that. She didn't say he couldn't know; how could he, since she didn't manage to get him out to the yard any more? She hadn't managed to for years.

'It does me good,' he said. 'The old drop of whiskey.'

She turned the wireless on, and there was old-time music playing.

'That's terrible stuff,' he said.

Martina didn't comment on that either. When the slices of liver were black she scooped them off the pan and put them on their plates with the eggs. She got him to the table. He'd had whiskey enough, she said, when he asked for more, and nothing further was said in the kitchen.

When they had eaten she got him to his bed, but an hour later he was shouting, and she went to him. She thought it was a dream, but he said it was his legs. She gave him aspirins, and whiskey because when he had both the pains would go. 'Come in and keep me warm,' he whispered, and she said no. She often wondered if the pain had maddened him, if his brain had been attacked, as so much else in his body was.

'Why'd they call you Martina?' he asked, still whispering. A man's name, he said; why would they?

'I told you.'

'You'd tell me many a thing.'

'Go to sleep now.'

'Are the grass rents in?'

'Go back to sleep.'

The painting commenced on a Tuesday because on the Monday there was ceaseless rain. The Tuesday was fine, full of sunshine, with a soft, drying breeze. The painters hired two ladders in Carragh and spent that day filling in the stucco surface where it had broken away.

The woman of the house, whom they assumed to be the crippled man's wife, brought out soda scones and tea in the middle of the morning, and when she asked them what time was best for this – morning and afternoon – they pointed at eleven o'clock and half past three on the older brother's watch. She brought them biscuits with the tea at exactly half past three. She stayed talking to them, telling them where they could buy what they wanted in Carragh, asking them about themselves. Her smile was tired, but she was patient with them when they didn't understand. She watched them while they worked, and when they asked her what she thought she said they were as good as anyone. By the evening the repairs to the stucco had been completed.

Heavy rain was forecast for the Wednesday, and it came in the middle of the afternoon, blown in from the west by an intimidating storm. The work could not be continued, and the painters sat in their van, hoping for an improvement. Earlier, while they were working, there had been raised voices in the house, an altercation that occasionally gave way to silence before beginning again. The older painter, whose English was better than his brother's, reported that it had to do with money and the condition of the land. 'The pension is what I'm good for,' the crippled man repeatedly insisted. 'Amn't I here for the few bob I bring in?' The pension became the heart of what was so crossly talked about, how it was spent in ways it shouldn't be, how the crippled man didn't have it for himself. The painters lost interest, but the voices went on and could still be heard when one or other of them left the van to look at the sky.

Late in the afternoon they gave up waiting and drove into Carragh. They asked in the paint shop how long the bad weather would last and were advised that the outlook for several days was not good. They returned the ladders, reluctant to pay for their hire while they were unable to make use of them. It was a setback, but they were used to setbacks, and, enquiring again in the paint shop, they learned that a builder who'd been let down was taking on replacement labour at the conversion of a disused mill – an indoor site a few miles away. He agreed to employ them on a day-to-day basis.

The rain affected him. When it rained he wouldn't stop, since she was confined herself, and when they had worn out the subject of the pension he would begin again about the saint she was named after. 'Tell me,' he would repeat his most regular request, and if it was the evening and he was fuddled with drink, she wouldn't answer, but in the daytime he would wheedle and every minute would drag more sluggishly than minutes had before.

He did so on the morning the painters took down their ladders and went away. She was shaking the clinker out of the range so that the fire would glow. She was kneeling down in front of him, and she could feel him examining her the way he often did. You'd be the better for it, he said, when she'd tell him about her saint, you'd feel the consolation of a holiness. 'Tell me,' he said.

She took the ash pan out to the yard, not saying anything before she went. The rain soaked her shoulders and dribbled over her face and neck, drenched the grey-black material of her dress, her arms, ran down between her breasts. When she returned to the kitchen she did as he wished, telling him what she knew: that holy milk, not blood, had flowed in the body of Saint Martina of Rome, that Pope Urban had built a church in her honour and had composed the hymns used in her office in the Roman Breviary, that she perished by the sword.

He complimented her when she finished speaking, while she still stood behind him, not wanting to look at him. The rain she had brought in with her dripped through her clothes on to the broken flags of the floor.

★

The painters worked at the mill conversion for longer than they might have, even though the finer weather had come. The money was better, and there was talk of more employment in the future: in all, nine days passed before they returned to the farmhouse.

They arrived early, keeping their voices down and working quickly to make up for lost time, nervous in case there was a complaint about their not returning sooner. By eight o'clock the undercoat was on most of the front wall.

The place was quiet and remained so, but wisps of smoke were coming from one of the chimneys, which the painters remembered from the day and a half they'd spent here before. The car was there, its length too much for the shed it was in, its rear protruding, and they remembered that too. Still working at the front of the house, they listened for footsteps in the yard, expecting the tea that had come before in the morning, but no tea came. In the afternoon, when the older brother went to the van for a change of brushes, the tea tray was on the bonnet, and he carried it to where the ladders were.

In the days that followed this became a pattern. The stillness the place had acquired was not broken by the sound of a radio playing or voices. The tea came without additions and at varying times, as if the arrangement about eleven o'clock and half past three had been forgotten.

The Crippled Man

When the ladders were moved into the yard the tray was left on the step of a door at the side of the house.

Sometimes, not often, glancing into the house, the painters caught a glimpse of the woman whom they assumed to be the wife of the crippled man they had drunk whiskey with, who had shaken hands with both of them when the agreement about the painting was made. At first they wondered if the woman they saw was someone else, even though she was similarly dressed. They talked about that, bewildered by the strangeness they had returned to, wondering if in this country so abrupt a transformation was ordinary and usual and was often to be found.

Once, through the grimy panes of an upstairs window, the younger brother saw the woman crouched over a dressing-table, her head on her arms as if she slept, or wept. She looked up while he watched, his curiosity beyond restraint, and her eyes stared back at him, but she did not avert her gaze.

That same day, just before the painters finished for the day, while they were scraping the last of the old paint from the kitchen window-frames, they saw that the crippled man was not in his chair by the range and realised that since they had returned after the rain they had not heard his voice.

She washed up their two cups and saucers, teaspoons with a residue of sugar on them because they'd been dipped into the bowl when they were wet with tea. She wiped the tray and dried it, and hung the damp tea towel on the line in the scullery. She didn't want to think, even to know that they were there, that they had come. She didn't want to see them, as all day yesterday she managed not to. She hung the cups up and put the saucers with the others, the sugar bowl in the cupboard under the sink.

The ladders clattered in the yard, pulled out of sight for the night in case they'd be a temptation for the tinkers. She couldn't hear talking and doubted that there was any. A few evenings ago, when they were leaving, they had knocked on the back door and she hadn't answered.

She listened for footsteps coming to the door again but none came. She heard the van being driven off. She heard the geese flying over, coming from the water at Dole: this was their time. Once the van had returned when something had been left behind and she'd been collecting the evening eggs, and she had gone into the fields until it was driven off again. In the kitchen she waited for another quarter of an hour, watching the hands of the dresser clock. Then she let the air into the house, the front door and the back door open, the kitchen windows.

The dwelling they had made for themselves at the ruins was complete. They had used the fallen stones and the few timber beams that were in good condition, a doorframe that had survived. They'd bought sheets of old galvanised iron for the roof and found girders on a tip. It wasn't bad, they said to one another; in other places they'd known worse.

In the dark of the evening they talked about the crippled man, concerned – and worried as their conversation advanced – since the understanding about payment for the painting had been made with him and it could easily be that when the work was finished the woman would say she knew nothing about what had been agreed, that the sum they claimed as due to them was excessive. They wondered if the crippled man had been taken from the house, if he was in a home. They wondered why the woman still wasn't as she'd been at first.

She backed the Dodge into the middle of the yard, opened the right-hand back door and left the engine running while she carried out the egg trays from the house and settled them one on top of another on the floor, all this as it always was on a Thursday. Hurrying because she wanted to leave before the men came, she locked the house and banged the car door she'd left open. But the engine, idling nicely, stopped before she got into the driver's seat. And then the blue van was there.

They came towards her at once, the one with glasses making gestures she didn't understand at first and then saw what he was on about. A rear tyre had lost some air; he appeared to be saying he would pump it up for her. She knew, she said; it would be all right. She dreaded what would happen now: the Dodge would let her down. But when she turned off the ignition and turned it on again, and tried the starter with the choke out, the engine fired at once.

'Good morning.' The older man had to bend at the car window, being so tall. 'Good morning,' he said again when she wound the window down although she hadn't wanted to. She could hear the ladders going up. 'Excuse me,' the man who was delaying her said, and she let the car creep on, even though he was leaning on it.

'He's in another room,' she said. 'A room that's better for him.'

She didn't say she had eggs to deliver because they wouldn't understand. She didn't say when you got this old car going you didn't take chances with it because they wouldn't understand that either.

'He's quiet there,' she said.

She drove slowly out of the yard and she stalled the engine again.

The painters waited until they could no longer hear the car. Then they moved the ladders, from one upstairs window to the next until they'd gone all the way round the house. They didn't speak, only glancing at one another now and again, conversing in that way. When they had finished they lit cigarettes. Almost three-quarters of the work was done: they talked about that, and calculated how much paint was left unused and how much they would receive back on it. They did no work yet.

The younger brother left the yard, passing through a gateway in which a gate was propped open by its own weight where a hinge had given way. The older man remained, looking about, opening shed doors and closing them again, listening in case the Dodge returned. He leaned against one of the ladders, finishing his cigarette.

Cloudy to begin with, the sky had cleared. Bright sunlight caught the younger brother's spectacles as he came round the side of the house, causing him to take them off and wipe them clean as he passed back through the gateway. His reconnoitre had led him, through a vegetable patch given up to weeds, into what had been a garden, its single remaining flowerbed marked with seed packets that told what its several rows contained. Returning to the yard, he had kept as close to the walls of the house as he could, pressing himself against the stucco surface each time he came to a window, more cautious than he guessed he had to be. The downstairs rooms revealed no more than those above them had, and when he listened he heard nothing. No dogs were kept. Cats watched him without interest.

In the yard he shook his head, dismissing his fruitless efforts. There was a paddock with sun on it, he said, and they sat there munching their stale sandwiches and drinking a tin of Pepsi Cola each.

'The crippled man is dead.' The older brother spoke softly and in English, nodding an affirmation of each word, as if to make his meaning clear in case it was not.

'The woman is frightened.' He nodded that into place also.

These conjectures were neither contradicted nor commented upon. In silence the two remained in the sun, and then they walked through the fields that neglect had impoverished, and in the garden. They looked down at the solitary flowerbed, at the brightly coloured seed packets marking the empty rows, each packet pierced with a stick. They did not say this was grave, or remark on how the rank grass, in a wide straight path from the gate, had been crushed and had recovered. They did not draw a finger through the earth in search of seeds where seeds should be, where flowers were promised.

'She wears no ring.' The older brother shrugged away that detail, depriving it of any interest it might have had, irrelevant now.

Again they listened for the chug of the car's unreliable engine, but it did not come. Since the painting had made it necessary for the windows to be eased in their sashes, any one of them now permitted entry to the house. This was not taken advantage of, as yesterday it would have been, this morning too. Instead, without discussion, the painting began again.

Undisturbed, they worked until the light went. 'She will be here tomorrow,' the older brother said. 'She will have found the courage, and know we are no threat.'

In the van on their way to their dwelling they talked again about the woman who was not as she had been, and the man who was not there. They guessed and wondered, supposed, surmised. They cooked their food and ate it in uncomfortable confinement, the shreds and crumbs of unreality giving the evening shape. At last impatient, anger had not allowed a woman who had waited too long to wait, again, until she was alone: they sensed enough of truth in that. They smoked slow cigarettes, instinct directing thought. The woman's history was not theirs to know, even though they now were part of it themselves. Their circumstances made them that, as hers made her what she'd become. She held the whip hand because it was there for her to seize, she'd see to it that still the pension came. No one would miss the crippled man, no one went to a lonely place. Tomorrow she would pay for the painting of the house. Tomorrow they would travel on.

Midnight Blue

Elaine Walsh

CON LOCKS THE DOOR AND turns the brass sign. With a damp cloth he wipes around the thick, raised letters, their edges worn with the years. He had paid a pound and six pence for that sign in Hayes' Hardware Shop on Capel Street not long after his father died. He recalls the joyless relief he felt taking down the old wooden sign that had hung on the door all through his father's life and part of his own – the name 'Slattery & Sons, Tailors' engraved deep into the varnished oak. Con had the shop front repainted too with what little his father had left him. Ever since, it was just called 'Slattery's Tailors'. That was the summer Senator Kennedy was shot and Con had turned twenty-eight. At the time, he had thought about walking up to the Dáil to sign the book of condolences but he never did.

He lowers himself into the corner chair. September is closing in but today was fine; cold and crisp with a bright sun and there's still some stretch in the evening. As he shifts the chair nearer the window, stripes of weak sun creep in through the gaps in the Venetian blind and line his navy pants. A few late-night Thursday shoppers pass up Talbot Street carrying paper bags from Clery's and Boyers and shops the names of which Con doesn't recognise. The street is quieter of late – people hanging onto their cash with all the talk of doom and gloom. He has seen the ups and the downs before and is still here after all these years looking out at the world from the same corner. As a boy, he had used this very chair as a table, kneeling on the floor to do his homework. Underneath, he kept a neat stack of green and orange copybooks, one for each subject and a special one for maths with squares to put the numbers in. He had a knack for the sums back then, wearing pencils down to a stub from all the long divisions. It drove his father mad but that didn't stop him bragging to all and sundry about it.

'Do you see this young whippersnapper here?' his father would ask one of his customers or GAA pals who dropped in for a chat. 'He has all the makings of a top-class tailor if you could only keep him away from the sums for a solitary minute. He'd have your heart broken with the books.'

Con looks across at the counter. The big, round-shouldered figure of his father stooping over it never really left. There he is snipping away at a length of cloth, turning it this way and that, shaping arms and legs and torsos.

'He got that from his mother, may the Lord have mercy on her poor soul,' his father would continue. 'Wants to be a maths teacher no less! My poor shop isn't good enough for our young professor!'

Con pulls his chequered jacket over his shoulders. The shop feels colder, empty of the things that had made it a shop for so many years. Most of it he has sold or packed away except for a roll of wool-worsted cloth left out in case he has to make any adjustment to Barney Keogh's suit when he calls in for his final fitting tomorrow. Whatever bits and bobs remain he'll try to shift in tomorrow's clearance.

A loud knock on the window stirs him. Con peers through the blind at a face peering back. His jacket slips off his shoulders as he rises to unlock the door. It opens to the low, mingled noise of the street and Paul, a lanky courier with a hungry look, who's been making deliveries for him for years.

'Sorry about the delay, Mr Slattery. The traffic on the quays was brutal.'

He looks at Paul's pushbike and knows that traffic couldn't have slowed him. It doesn't matter.

'Not to worry, Paul son. I was here anyway.'

His right knee cracks when he bends down and reaches under the counter for a parcel containing two white shirts for Mr Higgins SC. He had pressed and folded them in purple tissue paper earlier and put them under the counter out of the way. As he pulls out the parcel, the back of his hand meets something cold and hard. Con picks it up. It's his father's black-handled steel shears. He had been looking for it recently, and now his heart drops at the sight of the large, heavy tool. 'My old, reliable friend,' his father liked to call it. It had been a present to him from his own parents on his marriage to Con's mother.

Con returns to the door, the shears in one hand, shirts in the other.

'Big day for you tomorrow, Mr Slattery,' says Paul, stuffing the brown paper parcel into his satchel.

Con wants to tell him not to crush it like that, that it contains two shirts that have been pressed, but he says nothing.

'You'll have all the time in the world to spend that money of yours!'

Paul puts his hand on Con's shoulder. Con feels the cold fingers through his shirt and tenses.

'Ah, I'm only having you on, Mr Slattery.' He takes his hand away. 'Best of luck with it anyhow and sure, we might see you around.'

'Thanks very much for everything Paul,' says Con, and awkwardly hands him a tenner.

Con follows the black and yellow lycra-clad figure zip up Talbot Street towards the Spire and turn left onto O'Connell Street. He stands a while against the door watching the last of the evening crowd pass. The steel warms in his hand as he holds it. Black fellas, white fellas, yellow fellas. How times have changed. He bends down and rubs his right knee. The racket that had earlier been blaring from the music shop opposite is silent now, and a young girl sporting an earful of metal piercing is on her hunkers locking the shutters. Her companion stands above her, pulling cockily from a cigarette, white belly flesh falling loosely out over low-cut jeans. They move in Con's direction. He turns away.

'Nice evening, Con,' says Nancy Murphy, walking towards him from Nolan's bakery where she has served behind the counter for almost as long Con has in the shop.

'It is, thank God, Nancy.'

Three loaves of white bread jut out of the gingham bag she carries. There had been talk long ago that she had her sights set on Con. There was a time right enough when she dropped into him – almost every evening when his father got sick and after he passed away too. Once, she told Con that his father had terrified her – pounding the shop floor with his metal-toe shoes, swinging his scissors and ordering Con about in a loud, deep voice. The thing with Nancy all came to nothing in the end, thank God, and soon after she married Jimmy O'Brien from Pearse Street. She stopped calling after that, but Jimmy was dead now, and she sometimes dropped by again with some leftover bread from Nolan's or a corner of tea brack. A nice woman, thinks Con, but he is relieved to see her march by. He doesn't feel up to a long chat this evening.

'Important day tomorrow, Con!' shouts Billy O'Connor from the electrical shop up the way. 'I'll drop in when things are quiet.'

'Grand so, Billy. Thanks,' says Con and steps back inside.

The shop is darker now. Con turns on the light switch and rests the shears on the counter. A few scraps of navy cloth from Barney Keogh's suit lie scattered on the floor around it. He sweeps them up with a dustpan and brush. Standing up he regards the suit hanging lonely on a rail behind the counter, covered in plastic. It is made from the finest blend of wool – midnight blue Super 180 – a strong seller, imported from Thailand and good quality too, no matter what his father might say. His father had no time for anything foreign unless he wanted it himself – then he found plenty of excuses for having it. It's difficult to believe looking at the suit, cut in the low, wide shape of Barney, that it is Con's last. The process is so familiar, such a part of Con, that he doesn't think himself so much director of it as him and his fingers just another element of it. The methodology and repetition of it calms him, not unlike the sums long ago – taking the first measurements with white tape, rolling and smoothing out the fresh material, chalking out a pattern, patiently stitching, fusing, steaming, pressing, but most of all the soft, hollow sound of the shears cutting through cloth.

Con tips the dirt into the bin and puts the pan and brush away. The electric light bounces off the big shears and catches Con's eye. He is tired now, and his knee is at him. He forgot to take his tablets again. He goes into the darkness of the back room.

The back room was small, and the top of the boy's head knocked against the skirting board with the force of each thrust. It was faster and harder now, and the boy's eyeballs felt like they were going to pop out of their sockets

393

and smash against the wall with the pain. It was over when his da let out a big shivery sigh like someone had thrown a bucket of cold water over his head. And then his da flopped down on top of him like a dead elephant squashing him into the floorboards. As he gulped, the boy tried to think of Dastardly Dan being flattened like a pancake by a big roller truck in Tommy O'Connor's cartoon book.

Afterwards, the boy lay still while his da fixed himself. When the front door slammed, the boy got up and wiped the white stuff off his leg with some old newspapers he kept hidden behind the broom cupboard. He zipped up his pants and walked into the front shop. There he snooped with only the lamplight from the street, opening and closing drawers and presses. He found a spool of brown thread and slipped it into his pocket to show Tommy. Then he took hold of his da's huge scissors and tried to cut a straight line down the roll of material standing against the back wall. Outside, a man shouted 'Up the Republic. Out with the Brits at last!' The boy wasn't scared. He was learning about the new republic in school. A woman laughed, and a bottle rattled across the pavement.

Con pours two capfuls of Jameson into a glass and tops it up with musty tap water. He pulls the string on the overhead light and goes back out front carrying the glass and the bottle with him. He puts the bottle down on the counter beside the shears and sits back down into the chair and takes a sip. The sharp taste of whiskey tingles in his mouth. It runs through him, heating his chest.

'Agh, that's better.'

He rests the glass on his thigh with one hand and makes a gap in the blind with the other. The weather has turned, and there's a light drizzle over the lamp heads. A few souls hurry by in the yellow light of the wet street. He releases the blind and sits back. His father had never said it out straight to him, but he always knew when Con had been snooping about. He'd say, 'There must be a very large mouse in my shop because this looks remarkably crooked to me,' holding out a roll of cloth to one of his pals, or, 'They're some people around here who have no worries about the cost of things to those that feed them,' or, when they were alone and he had a few drinks, he'd call him a useless robbing thief just like his trollop of a mother. But still he'd never accuse him directly. That would be to admit to the other thing. Con takes a drink from the glass.

The thing in the back room stopped just after Con's thirteenth birthday. Father Murphy from Henrietta Street called one day and asked his father to teach tailoring to disadvantaged boys twice a week. On those days, Con took a half day from school to look after the shop. There wasn't much time for sums. By seventeen, he was more or less keeping the place going although his father always began each new suit which Con would then take over, with his father stepping in again at the last to check his work and complete the finishing touches. And it was his father who mostly dealt with the customers, right up to when he got too sick. Sometimes, the two of them would eat together in the small kitchen his father had built onto the rear. Con would make a pot of tea and lay out ham salad sandwiches from Byrne's Grocers across the way. There'd be a bit of chat about the world outside – the latest GAA scores, Bank of Ireland's new Prize Bonds, Dev's return to power – but mostly they carried on in difficult silence.

First it was the heart, then the liver. In his final year, his father could do nothing for himself. The doctor occasionally called around, a community nurse once a month, but mostly Con nursed him through days and nights of feeding, medicine, bedpans, washing, changing. And Con watched as the strength of the man deserted the still broad body first and only towards the end the mind. Once, as he was fixing him up in bed, his father grabbed his wrist and looked at him straight. It had been years since he had met those grey eyes. Con pulled his arm away.

The business was in trouble by then. His father ranted to his priest friends about the 'hood-nosed foreigners in Clanbrassil Street sweating him out of it with their cheap suits'. But Con knew times were changing – Nancy Murphy's best friend's boyfriend who worked in the Bank told her it was no longer the thing to have your suits made when you could buy them off the hanger in one of those fancy new shops on Henry Street. In that last year of his father's life, Con had half-baked notions of selling up and finding work as a bookkeeper. He would have liked that – left alone with his numbers where no one would bother him much. But when it came to it, he could never bring himself to let go of the place, to allow it to become someone else's. Too much had happened here.

Con's glass is empty. He gets up and walks to the counter where he has left the bottle of Jameson. The shears are once more cold in his hand when he picks them up. Back in the chair with his glass full, Con runs his thumb gently down the blade edge. Still sharp. His eyes are heavy now. Tomorrow, he thinks. The day after tomorrow. The day after that. He finishes the whiskey and puts the glass down beside the leg of the chair. His head drops, lifts, drops. The shears fall from his lap and slide onto the floor.

Notes on the Authors

Kevin Barry is the author of the story collection *There Are Little Kingdoms*, which won the Rooney Prize for Irish Literature, and the novel *City of Bohane*. His stories have appeared in the *New Yorker*, *Best European Fiction*, *Phoenix Best Irish Stories* and many other journals. He also writes plays and screenplays. He lives in County Sligo.

Dermot Bolger is a novelist, poet and publisher, whose ten novels include *The Family on Paradise Pier* (the story in this anthology is based on the later life of its central character), *The Journey Home*, *The Woman's Daughter* and *A Second Life*. His plays include *The Parting Glass* (2010) and his recently published *Ballymun Trilogy*.

Aifric Campbell is the author of two novels, *The Semantics of Murder* and *The Loss Adjustor*. She was born in Dublin, studied in Sweden and now lives in the UK. Her forthcoming novel, *Dead Cat Bounce*, is inspired by her former career in investment banking.

EMMA DONOGHUE was born in Dublin. Her books include the novels *Stir Fry*, *Slammerkin*, *The Sealed Letter* and *Room*, which was shortlisted for the 2010 Booker Prize and became an international best-seller. She has also written literary history and has edited collections of fiction. She lives in Canada with her family.

GERARD DONOVAN's novels are *Schopenhauer's Telescope* (2003), winner of the Kerry Group Irish Fiction Award, *Doctor Salt* (2004) and *Julius Winsome* (2006). A story collection, *Country of the Grand*, followed in 2008. He is a lecturer at the University of Plymouth in Devon, England. 'Festus' is from a novel-in-progress.

RODDY DOYLE is the author of nine novels, including *The Commitments*, *Paddy Clarke Ha Ha Ha*, which won the Booker Prize, and *The Dead Republic*. He has written several books for children as well as pieces for stage, screen and television. His most recent book is *Bullfighting*, a collection of stories.

CHRISTINE DWYER HICKEY has published five novels, the latest of which is *Last Train from Liguria*. She has twice won the Listowel Writers' Week short-story competition and has also been a winner in the Observer/Penguin competition. Her stories have appeared in numerous anthologies. Her first collection is due to be published in 2011.

RICHARD FORD was born in Jackson, Mississippi, in 1944, of Irish grandparents (Gibsons, Parkers and Carrolls), who emigrated from County Cavan to America in the 1890s. His fiction includes the novels *A Piece of My Heart*, *The Ultimate Good Luck*, *The Sportswriter* and *Independence Day* and three collections of stories: *Rock Springs*, *Women With Men* and *A Multitude of Sins*. He is Adjunct Professor at the Oscar Wilde Centre, Trinity College, Dublin.

ÓRFHLAITH FOYLE was born in Nigeria to Irish parents and is currently based in Galway. Her first novel, *Belios*, and a collection of her short fiction and poetry, *Revenge*, were both published in 2005. Her first full collection, *Red Riding Hood's Dilemma*, was published in 2009. She is working on her second novel.

ANTHONY GLAVIN is the author of *Nighthawk Alley*, a novel, and two short-story collections, *One for Sorrow* and *The Draughtsman and the Unicorn*. He served as editor of 'New Irish Writing' in the *Irish Press* from 1986 to 1988 and is a commissioning editor for New Island Books.

JULIA KELLY's debut novel *With My Lazy Eye* won the Newcomer of the Year Award at the 2008 Irish Book Awards. She lives in Bray, County Wicklow, where she is completing her second novel.

COLUM MCCANN is the author of two collections of short stories and five novels, including *Dancer* and *Zoli* and the 2009 US National Book Award winner *Let the Great World Spin*. He lives in New York with his wife and three children and teaches in the Hunter College MFA programme.

Viv McDade was born in Belfast, grew up in Africa and now lives in Dublin. She is an English literature and psychology graduate, with an M.Phil. in Creative Writing from Trinity College, Dublin. She has worked in education and commerce. Her stories have appeared in literary magazines and anthologies and have been read on radio.

Belinda McKeon was born in County Longford in 1979. She is an arts journalist with the *Irish Times* and also a playwright. Her debut novel, *Solace*, will be published in 2011.

Eoin McNamee was born in County Down. His first book, *The Last of Deeds*, was shortlisted for the 1989 Irish Times/Aer Lingus Award. He was awarded the Macaulay Fellowship of the Irish Arts Council in 1990. *Resurrection Man* (1994) was adapted by Eoin for film, while *The Blue Tango* was longlisted for the Booker Prize. Eoin's other novels include *The Ultras* and *12:23*. His latest novel, *Orchid Blue*, was published in 2010.

Rebecca Miller is the author of the short-story collection *Personal Velocity*, the novel *The Private Lives of Pippa*

Lee, and the films *Personal Velocity*, *Angela* and *The Ballad of Jack and Rose*. She is working on a novel.

MARY MORRISSY is the author of a collection of short stories, *A Lazy Eye*, and two novels, *Mother of Pearl* and *The Pretender*. She has been a Lannan Literary Award winner, and her novels have been shortlisted for the Whitbread (now Costa) Award and the Kerry Group Irish Fiction Award. She is currently at work on a second collection of stories.

PETER MURPHY's first novel *John the Revelator* was short-listed for the 2009 Costa Book Awards. He is a member of the spoken-word/music ensemble the Revelator Orchestra, whose debut album *The Sounds of John the Revelator* has been described as 'a neat piece of work that somehow combines the weirdness of Poe with the coolness of the Beats over a soundtrack that might've been created by the Velvet Underground . . . if they'd had Irish accents.'

PHILIP O'CEALLAIGH's collections, *Notes from a Turkish Whorehouse* (2006) and *The Pleasant Light of Day* (2009), were shortlisted for the Frank O'Connor International Short Story Prize. He edited *Sharp Sticks, Driven Nails* (2010) and has been a recipient of the Rooney Prize. His screenplay adaptation of his story, *A Very Unsettled Summer*, is to be filmed.

The Netherlands and lives in New York City. He is the author of three novels, most recently *Netherland*, which received the Kerry Group Irish Fiction Award and the PEN/Faulkner Award for Fiction, and of a family history, *Blood-Dark Track*.

GLENN PATTERSON is from Belfast. He is the author of seven novels and two works of non-fiction. A new novel, *The Mill for Grinding Old People Young*, will be published soon. Among his awards have been the Rooney Prize and the Betty Trask Award.

ANGELA POWER was born near Killeagh, County Cork, and lives in Dublin. Her work, until now, has only been read by family, close friends and the People's College Creative Writing class of 2009–10. 'Five Entries from a Fictional Diary', part of a work in progress, is written through the voice of a newly married woman whose first husband was killed in the Second World War and who has returned from London to live in the rural Ireland of the 1940s.

KEVIN POWER was born in Dublin in 1981. He is the recipient of a Hennessy Award for Emerging Fiction and the Rooney Prize for Irish Literature 2009. His first novel, *Bad Day in Blackrock*, is published by Pocket Books.

COLM TÓIBÍN was born in County Wexford in 1955. He is the author of six novels, including *The Master* and

Brooklyn, and two collections of stories, *Mothers and Sons* and *The Empty Family*. He is Leonard Milberg Lecturer in Irish Letters at Princeton University.

WILLIAM TREVOR was born in Mitchelstown, County Cork, in 1928. He has won the Whitbread Prize three times and the Hawthornden Award once and has been nominated five times for the Booker Prize, most recently for his novel *Love and Summer* (2009). His *Collected Stories*, volumes 1 and 2, were published in 2009.

ELAINE WALSH was born in Carlow and is a graduate of Trinity College, Dublin. She lives in Dublin, where she works as a lawyer. She began writing short stories after attending a creative-writing workshop with Claire Keegan. This is her first published work of fiction. She is currently working on new short stories.